KEEPING HOUSE

A MADAME PRESIDENT MYSTERY

Book 1 of the House Mystery Series

by

Denise Tucker

International Standard Book Number 13: 978-1-60452-025-5
International Standard Book Number 10: 1-60452-025-6

Library of Congress Control Number: 2008943446

BluewaterPress LLC
2220 CR 210 W Ste 108 #132
Jacksonville, FL 32559
http://bluewaterpress.com

This book may be purchased online at -

http://bluewaterpress.com/keepinghouse
or through
amazon.com

Table of Contents

This book is dedicated to my friends and colleagues

Dr. Gary Jacobson

and

Dr. Craig Newman

Thank you for listening to my stories.

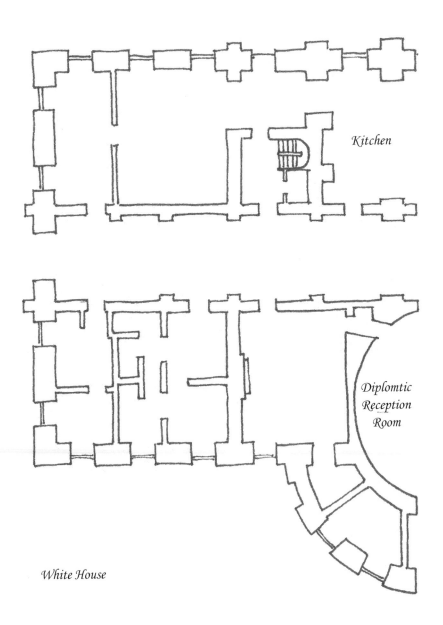

Kitchen

Diplomtic
Reception
Room

White House

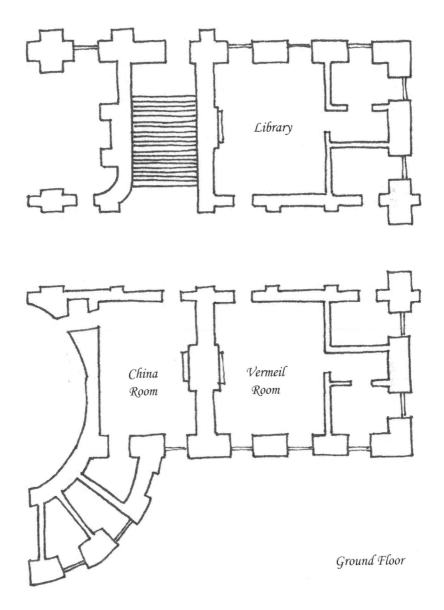

Library

China
Room

Vermeil
Room

Ground Floor

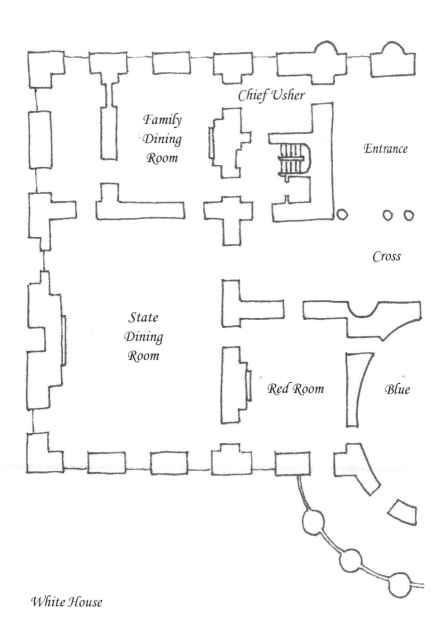

Chief Usher

Family
Dining
Room

Entrance

State
Dining
Room

Cross

Red Room

Blue

White House

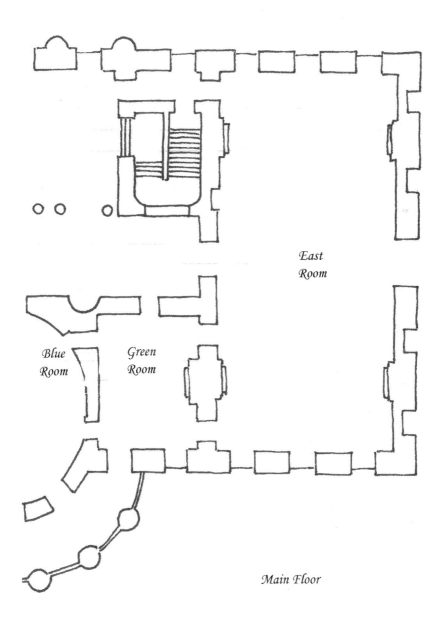

East
Room

Blue
Room

Green
Room

Main Floor

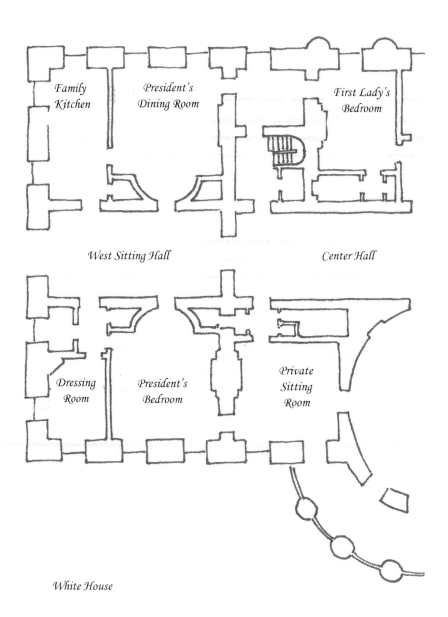

Family
Kitchen

President's
Dining Room

First Lady's
Bedroom

West Sitting Hall

Center Hall

Dressing
Room

President's
Bedroom

Private
Sitting
Room

White House

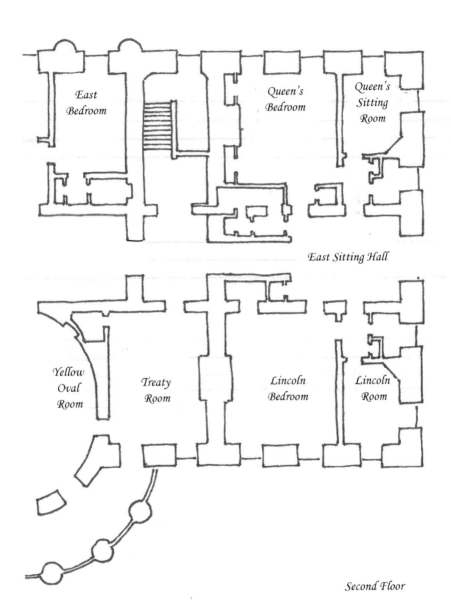

East
Bedroom

Queen's
Bedroom

Queen's
Sitting
Room

East Sitting Hall

Yellow
Oval
Room

Treaty
Room

Lincoln
Bedroom

Lincoln
Room

Second Floor

Prologue

October 19, 1820

I t was almost sunset when a horse-drawn carriage slowly turned off the main road and entered the dirt driveway leading into a beautiful Virginia Piedmont plantation. The road was long, going straight up to an octagonal-shaped mansion. Directly in front of the house was a circular carriage turn-around with rose bushes planted in the center. The shrubs were heavy with sprays of crimson fall flowers. Surrounding the outside of the entire property was another circular road lined with handsome paper mulberry trees. An elderly gentleman, well into his seventies, leaned out of the window of the carriage and called to the driver to stop. The old man got out.

"What is it, Grandfather?" asked one of two well-dressed young ladies sitting inside the carriage.

"Nothing to fret about, Ellen," said the man calmly while carefully closing the door to the carriage. "It's a beautiful evening, and this old farmer wants to take a leisurely walk about his property."

The other girl looked anxiously at her sister and leaned forward towards the carriage window. "Are you quite sure, Grandfather? It's right cold outside, and your knee has been bothering you so. We promised Mother . . ."

"To spy on me in her absence. Your mother dotes over me more than her own mother did, Cornelia, which," said the old man with a glimmer in his eye, "I enjoy immensely. Now you two go on ahead while I have a good look at my trees before the sun goes down. And see that Hannah has got supper ready. After two days on the road, I'm starved."

With a loving smile to his granddaughters, the old gentleman cheerfully patted the side of the carriage and instructed the driver to move on. The carriage slowly pulled away, leaving the old man alone to begin his steady walk towards the main house.

At the intersection of the carriage drive and the circular road that surrounded the plantation, he paused to gaze up at the tulip poplar trees. They were old friends to him, rustling their welcome home in the autumn wind. They had been planted there a few years before his wife inherited the farm. Seeing them always reminded him of her. It had been almost forty years since her passing. How he missed her still! Tonight, surrounded by her dear poplars, he could clearly recall her every feature, imagine her light step along the wooded path. He could almost hear her sweet voice amid the evening sounds in these old woods.

The man walked over and tenderly put his gloved hand out to touch the bark of one of the trees. He took a deep breath and looked up into the thick branches overhead. Life and country had demanded so much of him, far beyond anything he might have imagined as a young, idealistic student in Williamsburg. With a smile, he remembered the long hours of study with Dr. Small and the hot afternoons listening intently to debates at the doorway of the House of Burgesses. Those were heady days. He leaned up against the poplar tree, much like he had leaned against that doorway long ago.

Those were historic times not to be forgotten, days of great importance to him and to his newly-established country. It was then that he had met his sweetheart — she a young widow and he a lonely lawyer. Martha had been with him in the early days of the Revolution, along with his energetic friends Dabney, John, and Patrick. But she had left him too early. If only she could have shared his hectic days in Washington and Paris. Oh, how Martha would have loved Paris!

The man gazed solemnly at the darkening forest surrounding him. Soon, perhaps, he would join her. The crisp autumn air reminded him that life was quickly drawing to a close. And he had no regrets. He had done his duty in service to his young country, offering the best of his intellect, his leadership, and his pen. Now, after years of public service, he was content to spend his final days with his granddaughters, his beloved books, and his well-tended gardens.

Another breeze of chilly night air and growing hunger pains forced him to stir from his happy reverie and compelled him to continue walking. As he briskly strode towards the house, he saw the front door open and a short, plump black woman standing in the doorway, holding a lighted lantern out for him.

"Evenin' sir," she said pleasantly, holding up the light in greeting.

"Evening, Hannah," said the gentlemen stepping up onto the entrance of the north portico. "The girls are getting settled in, I trust?"

"Yes, sir. Miss Ellen and Miss Cornelia are in the east bedroom, washing up and changing their clothes for supper. They are looking mighty tired after being on the road so long, but a bowl of my beef stew will fix them up in a jiffy."

The man smiled broadly. "A bowl of your beef stew wouldn't do me any harm either. The trip seems longer this year. And what's this? Do I smell apple cobbler?"

The black woman nodded proudly. "Made from apples picked just this mornin'. It's been a mighty good year for apples, if I do says so myself. You'll have plenty to take back to the mountain with you for Thanksgiving. Now come on inside and warm up by the fire."

The man paused. ""It's good to be back, Hannah."

Hannah raised the light up higher and looked at him.

"Yes, sir. It's always good to be home, but sometimes I wonder if you miss being back up there in Washington."

The man smiled modestly.

"Happily, I have retired to my family, my books, and my farms. Never did a prisoner, released from his chains, feel such relief as I did shaking off the shackles of power. Nature intended me for the tranquil pursuits of science, by rendering them my supreme delight. But the enormities of the times in which I have lived, have forced me, Hannah, to take a part in resisting them, and to commit myself to the boisterous ocean of political passions. I thank God for the opportunity of retiring from them without censure, and carrying with me the most consoling proofs of public approbation." *

Hannah shook her head. "I don't know much about boisterous oceans, sir, but I do know you did much for the cause of liberty."

The man's eyes opened wide. "Ah, this ball of liberty is now so well in motion that it will roll 'round the globe, I think. It is our glory that we first put it into motion. And I will be pleased to sit back and watch it roll on from the mountaintop of Monticello." *

Hannah nodded her head in sound agreement.

The man turned and looked out one more time at the dark red roses and rustling trees of Poplar Forest plantation in the fading twilight.

"You do a mighty fine job running this place, Hannah."

The old woman blushed. "How you talk! You're one who did the building, Mr. Jefferson. You build fine buildings, and come to think of it, you did a mighty fine job building this country, too!"

Thomas Jefferson, architect, master gardener, author of the Declaration of Independence, founder of the University of Virginia, and third president of the United States, took off his gloves and handed them humbly to his trusted housekeeper.

"I suppose you're right, Hannah. I guess you could say that I take keen pleasure in *keeping house*."

Chapter 1

The Campaign Rally

Tuesday, October 10, 2000

It was a sparkling day.

Gary Craig lowered his camera and looked out across the lake, having just taken a picture of a group of mallard ducks swimming peacefully by. It was mid-autumn in central North Carolina, the air was crisp, the sky was a deep penetrating blue, and the sun shone brightly overhead. It was a season full of rich color, a time to slow down, a time to rest.

If only he could.

Gary Craig, age 40, was currently working full-time on the presidential campaign of Virginia's Senator Stan Taylor. That meant long grueling days and even longer nights at rallies, on buses, on planes, on phones, and at receptions. Gary had spent the last nine months of his life putting in seventy-plus hours a week on the campaign trail, and now there were only four weeks left to go. Gratefully, all the hard work and lack of sleep appeared to be paying off, for Taylor was ahead in the polls.

All that hard work meant that Gary was physically and emotionally wiped out. So it was a bit of good luck that he was sent down to his hometown of Greensboro, North Carolina, on special assignment. At the end of the week, Senator Taylor was scheduled for his third and final national debate at Wake Forest University. Gary's boss, Ned Baldwin, had assigned Gary and his work associate, Blaze Phillips, the job of squaring away last-minute details for the debate and setting up an additional daytime rally at the University of North Carolina at Greensboro campus.

By getting their business done early, Gary and Blaze were able to squeeze in a rare morning off. They spent it with Harriet Simmons, Gary's landlady, and Mildred Long, Harriet's sister-in-law and upstairs tenant. The four friends took a morning tour of the historic Guilford Battleground Park, a Revolutionary War site where long ago the forces of Lord Cornwallis clashed with the armies of General Nathaniel Greene. After the tour, Gary and his friends enjoyed a picnic lunch underneath a shelter at Greensboro's County Park. Gary consumed a rather large lunch, enjoying Harriet's homemade southern cooking, a feast of crisply fried chicken (cooked the old-fashioned way in a black iron skillet), German potato salad, spicy baked beans, and light as air, made-from-scratch buttermilk biscuits. God bless Harriet! For dessert, she had made two of his favorites: strawberry red velvet cake and banana pudding. While Blaze was having seconds of everything and the ladies chattered, Gary took out his camera and stood apart taking pictures, giving his stomach and his frazzled nerves a much-needed pause before attacking dessert.

During the past year, Gary had been a workaholic. But in all honesty, this behavior wasn't solely due to his commitment to Senator Taylor. The truth was he hurt. Behind the frazzled nerves was a broken heart. Gary stood still and gazed out across the water, his thoughts turning inward. Deep emotions rose to the surface in still moments like this. And today was particularly difficult. It was one year ago today that his divorce was final.

He had fallen madly in love with the daughter of a North Carolina textiles tycoon. She was an attractive redhead with striking blue eyes, sharp intellect, quick wit, and oodles of charm. Gary fell for her hard, and they were married after completing respective graduate schools, hers being business, his being law. Then Gary and Janet settled down in Greensboro, with Gary working for Janet and her father in the family mill business, which made fabrics for the nearby world-wide furniture industry in High Point.

The first five years together were happy ones.

But over time it became apparent that Janet Marie Benson-Craig wasn't much interested in starting a family. Gary wanted kids. Janet did not. No, Janet wanted to help Daddy build the business and to build her own portfolio instead. It took a while for reality to hit, but being an extremely stubborn male, Gary refused to call it quits. He decided to use his creative side to improve things at home. He had always loved gardening and cooking, so for the next ten years he passionately labored to make their home a haven. He took gourmet cooking classes. He cooked. He cleaned. He landscaped. He faux painted. He overdosed daily on television home and garden shows. He did all this, hoping it would save their marriage.

It did not. When Daddy Benson keeled over and died (suffering a stroke while putting on the third green at Pinehurst), leaving his daughter with the family mills and his amassed fortune, Janet decided it was time "to cut bait" (a favorite expression among North Carolina bass fishermen). She packed her bags and dropped the divorce papers and a pink slip on top of Gary's plate of homemade waffles one morning as she left for the office. Gary lost his job and his marriage in one fell swoop.

During the messy divorce, Gary took refuge in Harriet's quiet garden cottage, found employment in a local law practice, and retreated into his backyard garden. Then last December, Ned Baldwin, an old friend from law school, called Gary up out of the clear blue and invited him to join the Taylor campaign for president. Gary instantly said yes. The grueling work had been a panacea for Gary. He threw himself into the campaign and did his best to ignore the news stories about his ex-wife dating the up and coming junior senator from South Carolina.

Gary shook off his painful thoughts and refocused his attention into his camera lens. He wanted to get a few shots of the foliage — leaves of varying shades of red, orange, and yellow surrounded the lake waters, which sparkled serenely underneath the cerulean sky. Gary took some pictures of trees. Then he scanned his camera down the hillside to the lake's edge near a playground and a large wooden dock. Moored at the dock were several brightly-colored paddleboats for rent. He smiled as he grabbed a shot of a young girl in pigtails, wearing an oversized blue sweater, skating near the dock.

It was there Gary spotted them.

On the dock were two young men dressed in black denim jeans, black T-shirts, and black cowboy boots. Each man wore a strange red armband tied tightly around his right forearm. Their heads were completely shaved. On the back of their T-shirts there was a white lightening bolt. The two stood on the edge of the paddleboat dock, talking and smoking cigarettes. Gary recognized them instantly, and a cold feeling of alarm ran down his back.

"Blaze, bring me my other telephoto lens," Gary called out sharply, lowering his camera.

Blaze, a tall slender man with an endless appetite, looked up from his plate piled high with seconds. "Let me guess. You spied a wild rose bush growing by the water." Blaze turned to Harriet and grinned. "He's totally nuts about roses, you know. I think he dragged me through every rose garden between California and New York City!"

"Mr. Craig is an expert on roses," said Harriet authoritatively while slicing up cake. Harriet Simmons, a divorced woman in her mid sixties, was short, plump, talkative, and overly maternal. She handed Blaze a ridiculously huge slice.

"Gary planted the rose garden in our backyard, right beside my greenhouse," added Mildred smiling pleasantly. "You must come see my greenhouse while you're in town, Mr. Phillips." Mildred Long was sitting at the edge of the picnic table. She was in her early sixties, lean, elegant, and a widow of ten years. Mildred was Harriet's other tenant. She lived in an upstairs apartment in Harriet's enormous Victorian house, while Gary rented the small cottage in the backyard.

"Blaze, hurry up," Gary insisted. He glanced nervously back towards the docks. Good! The men were still there talking.

"Hold your horses! I'm coming," said Blaze as he put down his fork and stood up. Blaze didn't want to be parted from his cake, but he obeyed and went over to Gary's duffel bag lying nearby on the ground and unzipped it.

"Do you grow roses, Mrs. Long?" asked Blaze as he pulled the long telephoto lens from the bag.

"Oh, no," said Mildred modestly. "I only grow orchids. It's a hobby I picked up when living in Hawaii with my late husband, Harriet's brother. He was stationed there in the military many years ago."

"Milly hybridizes orchids and judges them at international shows. Last year, she traveled to London, Sydney, and Cairo!" added Harriet proudly. "She sells her plants on the internet, too. It's so amazing! She has a huge computer in the greenhouse just to handle the orchid sales and e-mail!"

"Come on, Blaze!" ordered Gary urgently. "You can gossip later."

Blaze walked over to Gary and handed him the lens.

"Here. What's the problem?"

Gary quickly changed lenses, raised his camera, focused, and rapidly began shooting pictures.

"You remember when we were down in Houston last April and all that hoopla surrounding the primary race for mayor?"

"You mean what happened to that Dickson fellow? He was supposed to be a shoo-in for the Republican ticket. Then some weird demonstration happened at one of the town hall meetings. A bunch of hoodlums showed up and protested Dickson's candidacy. It was well organized and turned real ugly. They burned things, and they exposed . . ." Blaze abruptly stopped, remembering he was in the presence of mixed company. "Well, they exposed things. And they said things, too. Most of it trash, but you know the press. The media loves a scandal. They grabbed hold of the story and ran with it for weeks. The protestors' claims were hashed and rehashed in the news, as if they were truth. Total horse hockey, of course, but Dickson had to spend a lot of time and a lot of cash on damage control, and it ended up sinking the poor guy's campaign."

"Right," said Gary, still clicking away with his camera.

By this time, Harriet and Mildred had walked over to join the men standing at the edge of the shelter.

"Who were they?" asked Harriet with alarm in her voice.

"Terrorists?" asked Mildred inquisitively.

"Sort of. Domestic, not foreign," continued Blaze. "They are a militant environmental group living somewhere in the middle of West Texas. I know, it sounds crazy. Normally you think of environmental groups as being peace loving. Not this bunch. They like to demonstrate literally with flare. The press loves a good show, and these nuts certainly can deliver."

Harriet stepped closer to Gary and anxiously placed her hand on his arm. "What are they called?" she asked in a hushed voice.

Gary stopped taking pictures and looked at his landlady.

"They call themselves, 'Stand Out.'"

"What a funny name! What does it mean?" asked Harriet.

"They're coming out and taking one," replied Gary dryly.

"Oh, dear," said Harriet, bringing her hand cautiously up to her throat.

Blaze looked at Gary uneasily. "Okay. So why are you asking about Stand Out?"

"Because," said Gary as he turned around and pointed at the dock. "Two members of Stand Out are standing out there right now by the paddleboats. They're here, Blaze, in Greensboro, three days before Taylor has his final presidential debate on national television."

☆ ☆ ☆

Gary's anxiety level quickly overcame his profound level of exhaustion, and he went into crisis mode and began barking out orders.

"Mildred, Harriet, start packing up the food. Blaze, get the ladies and the picnic baskets up to the car and stay put till I get back. If anything goes wrong, drive like a bat out of hell and get them out of here fast. Make sure Ned gets the information."

Blaze stared at his friend apprehensively. "And what are you going to do?"

Gary replied, "I'm going for a walk."

Before Blaze had a chance to argue, Gary turned and quickly started walking down the steep hillside towards the walking path that led to the docks. He clutched his camera close to his chest as he walked along the gravel path, crossing tree roots, jagged rocks, and gravel on his way down. His heart was pounding as he rapidly descended a short set of cement steps at the bottom of the hill which opened onto a paved walkway. He was completely out of his mind to do this, but pictures really weren't enough. If Stand Out were here to sabotage Taylor's election bid, Gary needed to give the Secret Service and FBI as much detailed information as possible. He just hoped he could deliver the goods.

Gary cautiously walked out onto the wide black asphalt pavement. Two female joggers ran past, each wearing a headset with earplugs. Great, thought Gary. If something goes wrong, they won't hear a thing. A grey-haired man riding a bicycle whizzed by. Gary stood still and waited until the man disappeared over a hill. Now, the only other human in close proximity was the girl with pigtails, skating about forty yards away, and she was headed in the opposite direction, away from them. Good. Gary didn't want anything to happen to her. He took a deep breath and continued walking towards the paddleboat dock.

The two men in black were facing the lake, their backs turned. Gary stopped and leaned forward trying to hear, but he couldn't quite make out what they were saying. Damn. He would have to actually get up on the dock. Gary took a few steps forward and then carefully stepped up. So far so good. They didn't turn around. Encouraged, he took another three steps onto the dock and slowly raised his camera. His hands were trembling as he tried to focus the shot. He silently prayed as his finger ever so gently hit the button. "Please don't make a noise, please don't make a noise." The camera obeyed and whirred quietly. The men didn't hear the picture being taken. Okay, he told himself, just a few inches closer. Gary lowered the camera and inched his way forward. He was close enough to hear them now . . .

"How was it?

"Perfect."

"Damn right, it's perfect. Too perfect, if you ask me. The stairs are right in front of the place where Taylor's going to have his rally, and the building sits on the corner of a major intersection leading straight into the campus. Everyone will be able to freaking see."

"Yes," said a very pleased voice. "Everyone."

"Yeah, we don't want nobody missing the fireworks. We've got the signs and torches ready. And Billy has the effigy of Taylor ready to burn. That should be fun. Want to start the party any earlier? The press is already there setting up."

"No. I told you before. We are to stick with the schedule. We start at 10:00 sharp on Friday morning. Timing is important. We start when Taylor arrives because —" There was a loud noise.

Gary turned around in horror! The girl in pigtails had stepped up onto the dock with a metallic clang and was skating towards him!

Gary quickly glanced back at the men. Two shaved heads had turned around. They stared sharply first at the girl and then over at Gary, who was standing behind them with his camera. From the look on their faces, Gary knew he was in big trouble.

"Holy shit," exclaimed one of the men. "Where did he come from? Do you think he could hear us?"

The other one stared at Gary, his eyes narrowing.

Clearly he thought so.

"We'll find out. Grab the girl first," he said angrily.

"No!" shouted Gary reaching madly for the girl.

The girl screamed.

As one of the men lunged at the skater, Gary reacted, taking his camera and slinging it at the man's head. It crushed the side of his exposed temple. Blood appeared. The girl screamed again. The man collapsed unconscious at Gary's feet.

"Go," shouted Gary to the girl as the other man raced forward and grabbed Gary from behind. The camera clattered to the ground as the girl escaped. Wincing, Gary was dragged backwards towards the end of the dock. The man from Stand Out held both of Gary's arms tightly as they stood close to the water's edge. Gary swallowed hard. He couldn't swim.

"Now, now, that wasn't very nice," said the man in a menacing voice. "You knocked out poor Davy before we had a chance to be properly introduced. And I thought folks here in North Carolina were hospitable."

"Sorry," muttered Gary eying the murky lake water nervously.

"Water's cold, I'm afraid. Want to go for a dip?" the man growled, sensing Gary's anxiety of the water.

"Not really," said Gary hoarsely.

"Alright, then tell me what you heard and what's on that camera?"

"Nothing," Gary lied. "I didn't hear anything. I was just taking pictures of the ducks."

The man laughed an ugly laugh and pulled Gary's arms tighter. "Why don't I believe you," he said with a sneer. He pulled Gary's arms even more tightly together, and Gary winced in pain. He could hardly breathe.

"Let's try again, shall we? Tell me who you are and exactly what you overheard —"

Whack! The attacker was hit squarely in the face with the remains of red velvet cake? Gary had heard of shock and awe. This was shock and icing. Blinded, the angry youth released Gary and turned rapidly to his left. A pointed toe of an old lady's black boot landed directly into the young's man denim crotch. He screamed and doubled over. Then a black leather purse, bulging at the sides, connected with the man's shoulders, successfully knocking the fellow over the edge and into the lake. Gary stared at his rescuer in disbelief.

"Mildred?"

The lady grabbed his hand firmly.

"Let's get out of here! And don't forget your camera!"

Gary gazed down at Mildred's handbag. "How did you do that? What's in there?"

Mildred looked at Gary and smiled sheepishly. "Rocks."

Gary held on to Mildred's hand tightly as they raced up the hillside towards the car. The young girl, having pulled off her skates, ran up the hill ahead of them in her bare feet and disappeared into the Natural Science Center as they reached the others. They found Harriet clinging to Blaze's arm, a nervous wreck, having watched the entire incident from the hillside above. Mildred took over and quickly got a blubbering Harriet into the back seat. Blaze tossed Gary the keys, and they jumped in the front seat. Gary slammed his door, gunned the engine, and sped out of the parking lot. He nervously glanced up into the rear view mirror. There was no sign of Stand Out anywhere.

"Oh, my God!" cried Blaze. "I can't believe it! I can't believe what just happened down there! I thought you were going to be killed!"

"So did I!" said Gary thickly. He took a deep breath and gripped the wheel tightly, hoping that would help his hands to stop shaking.

"What the hell happened? What did you hear?" asked Blaze insistently.

"It's bad. Stand Out is planning to demonstrate Friday morning at the UNCG rally."

"Holy crap!" Blaze cried. He pulled out his cell phone and madly started dialing. "I'm calling Ned!!"

"No," ordered Gary sharply. "Don't call Ned yet! We need to get Harriet and Mildred home first and make sure they are safe. And I want some time to think."

"Think?" shouted Blaze. "There's no thinking here. We gotta call this in *now*."

"Don't argue with me, Blaze! Just do what I say!" Gary yelled back.

Blaze looked at Gary fuming, but he closed his cell phone. Gary looked up gratefully into his rear view mirror at Mildred.

"That was some pretty fast thinking back there, missy. You saved my life!"

Mildred had her arm securely around Harriet's shoulder. She gazed back at Gary steadily, her face surprisingly clear and composed.

"I was a general's wife for many years, Gary," she said softly. "My husband taught me how to handle a crisis. I don't think the general would have expected anything less from me."

"I don't think he would have been disappointed," Gary replied honestly. "Thanks."

It was a relatively short ride back to Harriet's house in Fisher Park, and everyone fell silent for the remainder of the trip. Upon entering the house, Blaze and Mildred took Harriet into the living room, a cozy pink-colored parlor, to sit down and rest. Harriet looked anxiously out the bay window. Gary assured his landlady that no one had followed them and that they were safe. Gary told Blaze to keep an eye on the ladies while he headed to the kitchen to brew up some hot tea.

Gary felt at home in this kitchen. It helped to settle his own nerves to pull out the kettle, heat up the water, and hunt through Harriet's crowded pantry for teabags. He took out blue willow china cups and saucers from the cabinet, cut lemon slices, and made the tea. Soon, the four of them were sipping their hot brew and nibbling on Moravian gingerbread cookies that Gary had made the night before. Blaze had pulled out his cell phone again and placed it on the coffee table, ready to speed dial his boss's number the minute Gary gave the word.

Harriet was sitting upright on an oversized burgundy floral sofa. She was still looking somewhat frazzled. Mildred, on the other hand, sat stoically beside her sister-in-law, unruffled. Gary marveled at Mildred's continued composure. Life with the general had indeed made her strong. While they sipped their tea, Gary relayed to them exactly what he had overheard.

Blaze whistled. "Wow, when Baldwin hears about this, he's going to absolutely freak."

Gary sternly shook his head. "No, Ned will be fine. It's Hooper that will go nuts."

"Who is Hooper?" asked Mildred.

"Donald Hooper. He's a deputy assistant in the Taylor campaign. He'll be counsel to the president if Taylor wins the election. Donald worries about everything." Gary took a sip of hot tea and chuckled. "Course, if you are going to be the president's personal lawyer, it pays to be somewhat paranoid."

"The poor man," said Harriet, perking up. A good bit of gossip was just the thing to revive her.

"Well, I don't worry too much about Donald. He has Ken Friedman looking out for him. Ken is Donald's assistant counsel and is the most organized guy in the universe. He's a walking encyclopedia — a very smart and very competent guy."

"Yeah, Donald is lucky. He gets Ken and we get Jim Myers." Blaze rolled his eyes while reaching for the cookie plate.

"What's wrong with this Mr. Myers?" questioned Mildred.

"Let's see. He's young, single, handsome, richer than God, smart, and successful," said Gary sarcastically. "And he knows it. He'll be Taylor's chief of staff and our boss in the West Wing. Jim won't like this Stand Out situation. He doesn't like messes. He likes things under control."

Blaze agreed. "McKay will be the only one who keeps his head."

Mildred's eyes suddenly widened in surprise. "McKay? Not General Charles McKay?"

"That's right? Do you know the general?" asked Gary in astonishment.

Mildred smiled with pleasure. "Indeed I do. General McKay and my husband served together in the army years ago. The army is such a small world really. We were both stationed in England and later on together at Washington D.C. I was a good friend to the general's wife, Isabelle. Such a talented woman!" Mildred paused to sigh. "So sad about Isabelle. She died of cancer about nine years ago, one year after Harrison passed away. McKay is a fine man."

"He's the rock in the Taylor campaign," Gary observed candidly. "The general is a quiet guy with nerves of steel. He doesn't say much, but when he talks, we all stop and listen. No nonsense with him! He'll be national security advisor in the Taylor White House."

"I couldn't think of a better person," said Mildred whole-heartedly.

"Okay," said Blaze picking up his cell phone again and standing up. "We got the extra information you wanted. Now it's really time to call this in. We need to notify the Secret Service pronto."

"Do you think they'll cancel the rally at UNCG before the debate?" asked Harriet worriedly. "Canceling would be such a disappointment. I was so looking forward to attending. All the members of my Methodist Women's Circle were going to be there."

"They might not cancel," ventured Mildred hopefully. "All they need to do is double the security and get more local police or FBI agents covering the event."

Mildred's remark struck a nerve. Gary held up his hand for Blaze to wait. "You know, that's the problem, isn't it? If they increase security now, which they will, Stand Out can simply set up their demonstration somewhere else. Believe me, there are plenty of excellent public locations that would suffice before the debate — Taylor's hotel, the restaurant where Taylor and one of the local congressmen are having dinner that night, or at the Wake Forest campus where the debate is going to be held. And if the networks get to witness a full Stand Out demonstration, we're gonna be in big fat trouble."

Blaze suddenly looked hopeful. "Yeah, but Stand Out might not show up now that they attacked you. They'll expect either you or the girl to go to the police and file a report and that the FBI will be looking for them!"

Gary bit his lip. "I don't think so, Blaze. Listen, they don't know what I heard or that I'm connected with the Taylor campaign. I mean, my face is *never* on camera. Plus they don't know *we know* who they are."

"What about the girl?" Blaze asked.

"She didn't hear anything, I'm pretty sure of that. She was scared to death but not injured. So, if her parents do file a complaint, it will be against two unnamed youth at the park. Did anyone see her parents?"

"I did," said Mildred. "The girl came with her mother and two younger children. When we were unpacking lunch, I saw the girl go down the hill by herself to skate while the mom took the little kids into the Science Center."

"So, the girl should be safe. We'll have to watch the local news to see if the mom reports this to the local authorities. But I bet Stand Out will go ahead with their plans. If they've come this far, surely they won't let this stop them."

Blaze looked horrified. "You want them to appear?" He stood by, holding the cell phone in his hand, watching Gary and waiting for an explanation.

Something caught Gary's attention. He got up and walked across the room to the fireplace mantel, his eyes resting on a photograph of Harriet and Mildred. They were dressed up in Colonial attire. He picked up the framed picture and studied it carefully.

"What's this?" asked Gary.

"What? Oh, that!" said Harriet bemused. "That was taken in the spring at the re-enactment of the Revolutionary War Battle of Guilford Courthouse at Battleground Park. Our sewing circle dressed up and did a display on quilts."

"Right!" said Blaze. "That's the place we saw this morning. General Greene lost the big battle with the British right here in Greensboro."

"He lost the battle, true," interjected Mildred sagely, "but because of the major losses sustained in that battle, the British troops were significantly weakened, which proved deadly for Cornwallis and his men later on when they met up with General Washington."

Gary stared at the picture and then slowly a smile crossed his face. He put down the picture and spoke. "This morning the tour guide talked about how the British advanced and took their positions in the forest and how General Greene engaged them there. She said, 'In battle, it's an advantage not to just know *who* your enemy is but *where* your enemy is.' It is a good principle to remember when engaging the enemy, don't you think?"

Blaze's eyebrows rose with alarm. "What are you suggesting?"

"I'm suggesting that Stand Out appear Friday as planned. Hand me the cell phone."

"You're flipping crazy," said Blaze warily handing the phone over.

Mildred put down her teacup and eagerly leaned forward. "How can we help?"

Gary started talking rapidly.

"Blaze, how much money do we have left in the discretionary spending account?"

"Oh, not much," replied Blaze dryly. "Just six or seven million or so."

"Great! Get ready to spend some cold hard cash fast. Harriet, does that friend of yours still work at the big costume place downtown, the one that does the university and town theatre?"

"Betty at Eastern Carolina Costume? Why, yes, she does."

"Super. Get me her number. We're going to need white powdered wigs and red coats and muskets. And go get the phone numbers of your sewing circle friends. They can help, too. We're going to need every sewing machine they've got. And don't you belong to that senior citizens church group, the Shepherd's Center? I want the phone directory of that group right away. Didn't you tell me there were a number of veterans in that group? They'll be perfect. It will be your job to call them. Mildred, I'll need you to get hold of our Gourmet Cooking Club members. They've got three days to put together a rip roaring Colonial feast. Oh, and Mildred, get out my recipe card file."

Blaze stared at his friend in utter disbelief.

"Are you out of your cotton-picking mind?" Blaze yelled. "You've just been attacked by an extremist group plotting a demonstration against our candidate, the future president of the United States. When the Secret Service hears about it, they are going to go absolutely bananas! You know the drill, man. They go in a week before the candidate's appearance, make a security plan, seal off and search the area, and create the security bubble. With this information, they'll triple the protection and nobody is going to get fifty feet near Taylor! They'll never let you break that bubble, Gary, not if there is the slightest chance of Taylor getting gunned down."

"But Taylor isn't in danger of guns or bombs. Stand Out doesn't use those kinds of weapons. Until now, they haven't been known for blatant physical violence. And I'm pretty sure what I overheard was a plan only for verbal and visual disruption. Taylor's physical life isn't in danger. It's his political life that's in jeopardy."

Blaze crossed his arms and stared at his friend hotly. "And your solution to this situation is what exactly? Plan a party?"

"No," said Gary as he began speed dialing Baldwin's private cell number. "We're going to start a revolution."

Chapter 2

The Rally

Mid-Morning on Friday, October 15

*L**ive news broadcast on CNN:*
      "Good morning. This is Helen King on a special early edition of Inside Politics. *Less than a month remains before voters go to the polls, and presidential candidates Mike Harris and Stan Taylor were busy on the campaign trail today, getting ready for Saturday's final debate at Wake Forest University. New Mexico's Governor, Mike Harris, spent the day crisscrossing the Sunshine State of Florida in a last-minute bit of campaigning, all in an effort to shore up support and to gain what would decidedly be an upset victory in a state full of key electoral votes. Later on in our program, we'll go live to Brad Jacobs covering Governor Harris's campaign. But first, we turn now to North Carolina, where Senator Stan Taylor of Virginia is scheduled to hold an old-fashioned campaign rally this morning with a surprising twist to his "Back to Basics" theme. Covering Senator Taylor's campaign is our own political reporter, Jack Parish. Jack, what's happening?"*

      CNN cameras focus in on the network's new star political reporter, Jack Parish. Parish is a journalist in his forties and a Washington D.C. native with great looks to boot. His striking steel blue eyes are set off on camera by his naturally premature white hair and his sparkling, yet not so naturally, whitened teeth.

      "Helen, Senator Taylor is scheduled to speak late this morning at a rally on the campus of the University of North Carolina at Greensboro. This event was originally slated to be a standard campaign rally, like so many others we've covered over the past few months. But when Taylor and his group arrived here at ten o'clock, just moments ago, they were greeted by something altogether different."

CNN video news footage begins. Television viewers see an imposing red brick building, the Aycock Auditorium on the UNCG campus. The picture pans back, revealing the two major streets surrounding the structure. Tate Street on the eastern side and Spring Garden Street on the south side are shut down to regular traffic. In the front of the auditorium, a band of men — young and old alike — are dressed up as American Revolutionary War soldiers. They stand alongside the steps of Aycock Auditorium armed with Colonial guns and bayonets. Groups of soldiers are also camped out along the streets in small battle-ready tents. Additionally, the streets are lined with long tables full of food. Women of retirement age in quaint Colonial dress are standing beside the tables, serving up an old-fashioned brunch — plates of southern barbecue, corn bread, biscuits, and baked mini fruit pies — to hungry reporters and enthusiastic voters.

As cameras scan over the festive sight, Parish's voice continues. "The Taylor campaign went all out today with their 'Back to Basics' message, putting on a lively patriotic re-enactment of the famous Battle of Guilford Courthouse. This historic fight took place here over 200 years ago during the American Revolution. Colonial soldiers marched up and down the campus streets just before Senator Taylor arrived, engaging enemy soldiers in fierce mock battle." TV footage breaks away and shows clips of two soldiers confronting a British soldier with guns and then shows three more Colonial soldiers grabbing and subduing two more modern-looking enemies — a pair of young men all dressed in black with red ties on their forearms. Additional footage shows American soldiers capturing a group of Cornwallis' British troops pushing an old cannon down the street and then another group of younger American soldiers capturing several more men dressed in black who are carrying flaming torches. Firecrackers go off with each capture, and onlookers cheer on the sidelines, while eating barbeque and drinking punch, jubilant with each American victory.

The Parish report continues. "UNCG is known for its outstanding music, dance, and theatre programs, and the Taylor campaign put all of these to work this morning, highlighting the talents of American youth."

Film clips show a number of traditional Scottish bagpipers and Irish fiddlers on the steps of the Auditorium with a group of eighteenth century dancers performing in the streets. The music is quite loud, making it difficult to hear exactly what the soldiers and the youthful mock enemies with shaved heads are saying. The dancers also put on quite a show, pulling the spectators into the swaying circle. In some cases, with much laughter and good fun, the dancers pull the dreaded British troopers and those strange-looking men in black out of the streets and back into the thick hedges behind the campus buildings. Parish wraps up his speech with a winning smile. "For all the history buffs out there, you know that America technically lost the Battle of Guilford Courthouse, but today the Colonial troops were completely victorious, clearing the streets and leading the charge as Senator Taylor arrived to give his speech." CNN footage shows the presidential candidate and his party arriving moments earlier, waving and smiling at the cheering crowd as Revolutionary War soldiers young and old stand and salute as he walks up the steps of the auditorium.

Helen King looks quite amused. "Jack, is this the Taylor campaign's way of predicting victory in a few weeks?"

Parish grins and holds up a hot sandwich. "If so, I hope whoever made this barbecue will be in charge of the Inauguration Dinner."

Helen shakes her head and laughs. "Jack, you get all the good assignments."

Jack takes a big bite of barbeque and grins. "Yes, I do, Helen," he says happily. "I most certainly do."

✯ ✯ ✯

Beside a table stacked with baked fruit pies and nut breads, Gary and Blaze stood watching carefully as Taylor artfully worked the cameras and the crowds. Blaze was dressed normally, but Gary had on one of the Colonial costumes. As they watched, another man — short, bald, and heavyset — came and stood next to them. He reached down and picked up a slice of banana nut bread.

"Morning, gentlemen," he said crunching while casually scanning the crowded street scene.

"Hello, Ned," said Gary. Blaze silently nodded in greeting.

"Quite a little party you put together, Gary," observed Ned with an approving smile. "Press happy?"

"Extremely," said Gary. "All well fed, entertained, and distracted."

"That's nice. We like a happy press corps. Wish the Secret Service were as cheerful. Do you know what it took to get those boys out of their three-piece suits and into those Scottish kilts? The unit agent in charge had to learn to dance a jig to boot, and he's been complaining about his aching feet to me all morning long. I think you've given him an ulcer, worrying over this crazy plan of yours. Remind me to send him a thank you note, some Rolaids, and a copy of the Chieftains' latest CD."

"I'll make a note of it," replied Gary smiling broadly.

"Anyone recognize you?" asked Ned with concern.

"No one," assured Gary. "I think the one who tried dumping me into the lake was rounded up by the dancers a little while ago. With this hat, he never saw me." Gary tipped his hat to Ned.

Ned nodded and continued. "Good! The area FBI chief seemed to rather enjoy all this hoopla. He suited himself up in a British uniform and gleefully took over one of the cannons." Ned looked at Gary with satisfaction. "Well done, Mr. Craig. Senator Taylor and I are most impressed with your ingenuity and — how shall I say it — party planning? Such skills will not go unrecognized by our party. Per your request, we kept this whole thing rather hush hush, although we had to let McKay in on it, of course. Besides Charles, only you and I, Taylor, and Mr. Phillips know about the undercover operation inside the campaign. The rest of the staff just thinks this was a whole lot of fun. Let's keep it that way, shall we?"

Gary and Blaze immediately agreed to the superior's order.

"What about the girl?" asked Gary anxiously.

Ned smiled. "The director of the Science Center got the name and number of the mother and the child. The family has been protected this entire week, and the child has been given everything medically and emotionally she needed, at Taylor's own personal expense. The family is very grateful and is willing to keep it out of the press."

"Glad to hear it, "said Gary, much pleased. He had worried a lot about that little girl. When he and Janet were together, he secretly longed for a daughter, more than anything else.

"Well then, Taylor suggests — and I agree — that you should be made my deputy assistant once we win the White House." Baldwin reached down for a mini apple tart before leaving. "Ah, I see the university chancellor and Congressman Coble have just arrived. Better go shake a few hands and make nice. Keep up the good work, gentlemen."

With that, Baldwin quickly walked away into the crowd of well wishers and reporters. Immediately Blaze and two ladies standing nearby in old-fashioned dresses gather around Gary with their praises.

"Oh, Gary, how wonderful," gushed Harriet excitedly, wiping her hands on her white apron. "You're going to get a promotion!"

"Congratulations, Gary," offered Mildred sincerely while adjusting her wide-rimmed white bonnet. Her hat was designed to keep her face concealed as well. "Everything went according to your plan. You must be so pleased."

"Relieved," admitted Gary honestly. "I've not had much sleep the last two days."

"None of us has," added Blaze yawning. "And I thought this was supposed to be a vacation!"

"Don't you worry, Mr. Phillips," said Harriet, immediately handing Blaze an apple tart. "You and Gary will come to the house for dinner tonight, and I'll make you a homemade meal of meatloaf and country fried potatoes and onions."

"Be still my heart," murmured Blaze.

Gary laughed and was about to make a smart remark about Blaze's hyperactive metabolism when a firm hand was placed on Gary's shoulder.

"Mr. Craig?"

Gary turned and immediately came face to face with CNN's reporter Jack Parish. Gary had never met the man, but he had seen Parish many times at various rallies and photo ops along the campaign trail. Parish flashed him a very white smile.

"Yes?"

"I was wondering if I might have a word with you, Mr. Craig?" asked Mr. Parish softly. "In private?"

Gary stepped back cautiously. "Me? Uh, if you want an interview about Senator Taylor, Mr. Parish, I'll be happy to get you one through Mr. Baldwin. He handles —"

Parish stopped Gary mid sentence. "Oh no, Mr. Craig, I don't want Baldwin. I want to talk to the person who organized this little extravaganza. I've been asking around, and all fingers seem to be pointing squarely in your direction."

Gary stared at the reporter dumbfounded. He had never been asked to give an interview before. He looked around nervously. Given what happened, he didn't want to be on camera today of all days.

Parish flashed another camera ready smile. "Don't worry. It will be off the record. Look. My cameraman is over there across the street, trying to secure a phone number from a very attractive nursing student. Now, if you don't mind, why don't we walk over to the art gallery where we can be alone and talk? I promise to get you back before Taylor begins his speech."

Gary didn't like the prospect of having a talk alone with one of the nation's leading television reporters, but he didn't appear to have much choice. Reluctantly he quickly walked with Parish across the street and into the large building on the corner opposite Aycock Auditorium. The Weatherspoon Art Gallery had been closed that day to patrons, but Gary flashed his credentials to the security guards posted at the door, and they were immediately let inside.

Gary and Jack slipped into the first floor gallery, which was currently featuring a rare European exhibit of Pre-Raphaelite paintings that was touring the country. Harriet had told him about the exhibit. The Weatherspoon normally only featured works of modern art, but a very wealthy North Carolina patron with a big donation towards construction of a new extension for the museum insisted they take the exhibit. Jack stopped to admire a painting of John William Waterhouse, a lady in a red dress holding a crystal ball.

Gary waited anxiously. He didn't like this long pause.

"Well?" Gary finally asked. "What did you want to talk about?"

Jack smiled, gazing at the colorful painting, folding his hands up underneath his chin, almost like he was in prayer.

"That was some show you guys put on today. Quite *Out Standing.*"

Parish said those last two words slowly and distinctly. Gary felt his insides twist immediately into a knot. He shouldn't be doing this, not without Ned.

Parish casually turned and faced Gary with an amused look on his face. "Know what my favorite part was?"

"No," said Gary in a less than confident voice.

"It's a toss-up really. It was either seeing those ever-loving FBI boys wearing eighteenth-century powdered wigs stretched over their funny little ear pieces or it was watching the Secret Service agents showing their bare kneecaps mid-morning while dancing in plaid kilts."

Parish knew! This was not good. This was not good at all. Gary swallowed hard. Parish could blow the lid off the entire operation, and all their efforts and Gary's future employment would be shot to pieces. Time for some serious damage control.

Look shocked and deny everything.

"I'm shocked, Mr. Parish," said Gary emphatically, "and I'm afraid I don't know what in the world you are referring to . . ."

"Oh, really?" said Parish in an incredulous voice. "And I suppose you know nothing whatsoever about where the dancing Secret Service agents went off to, dragging the poor little Texas terrorists behind them?"

Gary froze. He could talk to Jack Parish no longer. Time to get out of there and fast!

"I'm afraid I can't continue this discussion," said Gary curtly, trying to walk away. "If you have any more questions, you'll need to speak with Ned Baldwin directly."

Parish quickly stepped ahead of Gary and blocked the doorway.

"Hey, you don't have to get all defensive with me, Mack. Listen, did I blow the whistle on your little hoedown out there? No, I did not. Did I mention that terrorists — pro-environmental terrorists — were on the scene? No, I did not. Did I show any of those hoodlums getting cuffed and carted downtown to the poky? No, I did not. No, I bellied up to the bar — in this case, the buffet table — and gave the members of our adoring public exactly what you guys wanted, a flowery report showing a patriotic parade and a mouth-watering picnic along the streets of sweet little old Greensboro. It was so clean it could have aired on The Disney Channel."

Gary silently stared at the reporter, suddenly now curious. Why had he done that? The story would have been a huge scoop. He must want something. But what? Whatever it was, this savvy reporter wasn't going to let Gary go till he got what he wanted.

"Okay. What do you want?" asked Gary coolly.

Jack stepped back a bit and smiled. "Now, now. No need to hurry or get in a huff. We'll get to what I want in a minute. I thought you'd be more interested first in how I figured it all out."

Gary finally gave in. "Okay. How?"

Jack motioned for Gary to take a little stroll around the exhibit as they talked. They walked down a corridor displaying a number of colorful paintings of Rosetti, Dicksee, and Burne-Jones. "Experience and luck. The experience comes from years living in Washington. You see, I'm a D.C. boy from birth. Born and raised inside the Beltway. My Dad was a G-man. Heck, most of my neighborhood worked for the government. I had plenty of high school friends with dads who were in some sort of intelligence work. On any given day, we never knew where in the world our fathers were or what they were doing. So, I was raised around cloak and dagger. Trust me, Mr. Craig; I can spot a federal agent a mile away, even one wearing a skirt. How in the world did you get them to do it?"

Gary looked at Mr. Parish steadily. "With lots of friendly persuasion and promised promotions. Okay, that takes care of the experience part. What about the luck?"

Parish chuckled and shrugged his shoulders. "I've got a wild and woolly Aunt Dorothy living down in Texas. She's a smart old gal, always sending me newspaper clippings, especially about things dealing with politics or the Dallas Cowboys."

"You like the Cowboys?"

Parish gave Gary a look of disdain. "Are you kidding? The Redskins are my team, son, which is why Auntie dearest sends me all the Cowboys crap. She likes to rattle my cage. Anyway, Auntie Dotty sent me some clippings about your precious little Stand Out crowd, detailing their antics in the state. Nasty little buggers. I sincerely hope your FBI drum and bugle corps threw the lot of them in jail."

"I think I can assure you, off the record of course, that Stand Out will have no worries finding accommodations for the weekend," said Gary dryly. "Obviously, Mr. Baldwin and I would like you to keep this entire matter quiet. So, what do *you* want, Mr. Parish? Let me guess. An inside track on the campaign in its final days?"

Jack Parish's bright blue eyes sparkled as he shook his head. "No, not at all. I'll tag along and beg for scraps of information like the rest of my pitiful comrades. And once your boy in is office, I'll sit around in the boring White House pressroom for hours on end, willing to wait for breaking news like the rest of the poor hacks." Parish then pulled out his business card and handed it to Gary. "Consider this day an investment, Mr. Craig. A down payment of good will. We both know that barring an act of God, your man is headed straight for the White House."

"We still have four weeks to go," argued Gary cautiously, feeling a bit more relaxed with this crazy reporter. Now that he knew Parish wasn't going to blow the whistle on the story, he found himself actually liking the fellow a bit.

Parish continued. "Listen, Governor Harris doesn't have a snowball's chance in hell of winning this election. Don't get me wrong. He is a really nice guy, but he is totally stiff — on and off camera. I mean, he makes Jimmy Carter look hyperactive, and I didn't think that was possible. If Harris got elected, he'd put his entire cabinet into a coma the first week."

Gary laughed. "That is true!"

"You bet it's true! God, some of my Democrat friends are going to vote for your guy on the sly. Taylor has done what Clinton did. He found a real middle ground, which is a real accomplishment for a Republican. Now, listen, there'll be plenty of important stories to report during the next four years — foreign and domestic. But I'm willing to bet that one day something major is going to happen, something big. I mean BIG in capital letters. It will be a situation where you might, you just might, need a careful reporter, like myself, to help break that story from behind the scenes. And when that day comes, I want that reporter to be me!"

Gary stared at Parish, marveling at the reporter's request. Then Gary looked down at the business card. It had a bunch of phone numbers on it: office phone, home phone, cell phone, car phone, and pager number.

"How many phone numbers do you have?" asked Gary.

"More than God," said Parish. "We got a deal?"

Gary took the card and put it in his shirt pocket, then extended his hand out to the reporter.

"Deal."

"Great!" said Parish shaking hands with Gary fervently. "Now, I've got one more question before you go."

Gary sighed. "Now what?"

Parish leaned close and whispered. "Who made the barbecue?"

Gary grinned. "I did."

Parish stared back at him astonished. "No kidding! You made that? Man, it was great. Seriously, that's the best damn sandwich I've ever eaten. Can I have the recipe?"

"I'm sorry. I'm afraid that information is classified."

Parish laughed out loud and punched Gary playfully in the arm. He was still begging Gary for the recipe when his cell phone abruptly rang. "Hang on, Fred," Jack said to Gary, putting the cell phone up to his ear. "Yeah, Parish here."

The voice on the phone started squawking immediately. Parish's face suddenly went pale.

"Oh, God, no! When?"

The voice on the phone continued loudly with the details.

"Okay, okay. I'm on it already. I'll get over to the auditorium, find my cameraman, and get the reaction from the Taylor camp ASAP. Will call you back in a few." Parish hung up and looked at Gary with wide horrified eyes.

Now Gary's own cell phone started ringing. He ignored it. "What is it? What did he say?"

"Crap." For a rare moment, Jack Parish was speechless. He bit his lip and finally spoke.

"Hey, I'm really sorry, man. I really am." Jack Parish shook his head and angrily pushed his thick white hair back with his hands to his head. "That was our news desk in Atlanta calling. There's breaking news out of Southern California. Senator Taylor's running mate, Congressman Eric Peters, had a heart attack a little while ago, at 7:00 A.M. California time. I hate to tell you this, but Congressman Peters is dead."

Chapter 3

Election Day

Tuesday, November 7

The shocking news of Eric Peters' death changed everything. The final debate in Winston-Salem was cancelled, the staff went into a state of mourning, and Senator Taylor's campaign got triple press. Taylor and his wife, Barbara, flew out to California to console Peters' widow. Three weeks before the election, they held the funeral and buried their dear friend, with the whole world watching. The remaining weeks of the campaign were intense but somber, and voters poured out in record number to express their support and deepest sympathy.

On Election Day, a group of animated reporters gathered around Ned Baldwin who was standing beside the life-size statue of Thomas Jefferson located in the upper entrance hall of the Rotunda, an imposing building in the center of the University of Virginia campus. Baldwin was holding his final press conference of the campaign. It was Election Day, and Senator Taylor would await the election results from his home state at his historic alma mater. Television crews were busy setting up inside the large building and outside on the front steps, where it appeared Taylor would be giving his victory speech before the night was out. Baldwin was in his element, and Gary and Blaze stood by listening in admiration.

"As you know, yesterday Senator Taylor made final campaign stops in several major cities. He began in Los Angeles and San Diego. Then he made stops in Chicago, Detroit, and finally a late-night stop in Philadelphia. He returned here about two o'clock this morning."

Fox News reporter Justin Arrington, speaking into his microphone asked, "What's Senator Taylor's schedule today?"

"Sleep," answered Baldwin smiling. The reporters laughed with empathy. Boy, could they relate.

"Actually, he was up early this morning thanks to his greyhound Gandalf's insistence on a morning walk around the old farm!" More laughter. Reporters who had been on the campaign trail with Taylor had made friends with Gandalf.

"What else is on his schedule?" asked Dan Grubbs of NBC News with a bit of edge in his voice.

"Nothing," said Baldwin firmly. "Mr. Taylor plans to enjoy a quiet day with his family until about four o'clock this afternoon."

All the reporters leaned in and held their microphones closer.

"What happens at four?" asked Grubbs on follow-up.

Baldwin grinned. "He plans to vote."

There was more laughter from the press, all of them making note to be at Taylor's polling station at that time. It would be an essential photo-op. Senior reporter Walter Irvin of CBS News asked the next question. "What time will Senator Taylor and his family be arriving at the Rotunda this evening and who has been invited to the reception?"

Baldwin pulled out a brown leather-bound notepad and checked his notes. "The Taylor family will be arriving here about nine o'clock. The reception will be held in the Dome Room on the top floor of the Rotunda. If you've been up there, you can see that space is limited, so our guest list is rather small."

"And exclusive," added Blaze in a whisper to Gary's ear.

"Shhh," ordered Gary, leaning back against the wall not wanting to miss Baldwin in action. He loved to watch Baldwin take the reporters head on. Gary couldn't wait to see Baldwin at work in the White House Press Room, fielding tough questions and dodging partisan complaints.

"Anyone we know?" prompted Bob Layton of ABC News.

"Yes, Bob, I believe there will be a few familiar faces. Governor Coffey and Senator Warner will be in attendance as will several local congressmen."

"Never mind them!" said Jack Parish with a smirk. "What about the local celebrities. Plenty of those are here in Charlottesville! Any of them expected to show up?"

"Besides you?" quipped Baldwin right back. The other reporters barked with laughter. Parish immediately flashed his famous wide smile back at them. "Uh, yes, Jack, a few Hollywood folks will be there. Sissy Spacek and her family are planning to attend, as are Sam Shephard and Jessica Lange. And I believe we just got a call from John Grisham. He's invited as long as he doesn't turn the night's activities into a plot for his next thriller."

Justin Arrington stepped forward and asked, "Will Taylor's new running mate be present?"

There was a long pause, a very long pause indeed. This was, of course, *the question* on everyone's mind. Baldwin slowly folded his arms and took his time in responding. "Nice try, Mr. Arrington. As you all know, the loss of Mr. Peters was a deep blow to Senator Taylor. Eric Peters and Stan Taylor were more than political allies. They were life-long friends. They grew up together in Lexington, Virginia, a small town just south of here. They went to law school together at UVA and served side by side in Congress for many years. And they ran this campaign together from the beginning. We buried Eric in Lexington a few weeks ago. I know there has been much speculation by the press concerning Senator Taylor's choice for his vice president. But he and his advisors both think such a decision is much too important and honestly too painful to be made right now."

"But does the Taylor campaign worry that people won't vote for Taylor without knowing who his vice president will be?" asked Arrington earnestly in follow-up.

"Well," said Baldwin with confidence, "I guess we'll find that out tonight, won't we?" Baldwin folded up his notes and added, "There is one decision that has been made, however."

The reporters stood frozen, pens ready for the next bit of information to be tossed their way. To Gary's surprise, Baldwin pointed his index finger right at him. "We have decided what will be served for dinner. And I believe you all know my able assistant, Mr. Gary Craig. He is in charge of tonight's menu and entertainment. Perhaps you'd like to direct a few final questions to him."

Suddenly, for the first time, all the lights, cameras, and microphones of the national media focused directly on Gary. Ned had thrust him into the spotlight, and nimbly Blaze stepped sideways out of the picture. Gary felt like a deer caught in headlights and looked to Baldwin for support. Baldwin looked back at him amused. Jack Parish looked ecstatic. Gary coughed to clear his throat and tried to sound more confident than he really felt.

"Ah, yes, well, tonight, as Mr. Baldwin alluded to earlier, we will be hosting a small number of guests here in the Rotunda while watching the votes come in. Many people from the community will be gathering outside of the Rotunda on the Lawn as well, and we're providing outdoor refreshments and music for them. For the Rotunda group, we'll have a seafood buffet dinner, featuring boiled fresh shrimp, Maryland crab cakes, and Maine lobster skewers with lemon and garlic butter. Additionally, we'll be having hot seasoned artichoke dip, a medley of fire-roasted vegetables, and strawberry-asparagus salad. For dessert, petite Boston cream pies, mini southern pecan crisps, and Swiss white chocolate cheesecake with raspberry sauce. The Monticello Trio, an internationally acclaimed UVA ensemble, will provide music for the evening. That's it. Uh, any questions?"

"Yeah," said Layton delightedly. "Do you do weddings?"

There was a roar of laughter, and the press conference ended. Most of the reporters went off in separate directions to pursue other interests. Blaze stepped aside to speak with Ned. However, Jack Parish and two other newspaper reporters remained close by. Jack, with a wicked glimmer in his eye, kept the camera rolling and tightly held his microphone.

Parish quizzed Gary. "Mr. Craig, I understand that besides having a talent for organizing events like this one, you are also a gifted gardener. You specialize in roses, I believe." Parish paused while one of the newspaper reporters, seeing the topic was turning to flowers, yawned and abruptly walked away.

Parish smiled and continued. "Seeing that Thomas Jefferson was a renowned botanist, I was wondering if you would like to show our viewers around Jefferson's gardens here at the university? I understand Mr. Jefferson brought a number of plants to America from France."

With that request, the other newspaper reporter lost interest, shut his notebook, and went off in search of a nearby place to eat. Parish then signaled his own cameraman to take ten, and he quickly took Gary by the arm to lead him outside and through one of the columned walkways on the Lawn.

"The Lawn," Jefferson's original academic village, is a large rectangle-shaped area of land at the center of the modern UVA campus. The Rotunda sits on the northern edge of that rectangle. Along the east and west sides of the Lawn run a series of impressive red brick mansions, called Pavilions, with five of them on the east lawn and five on the west lawn. Behind the ten Pavilions are ten Jeffersonian gardens, each with it own unique layout. As they hurriedly walked down a graveled path lined with s-shaped curved brick walls called "Serpentine Walls," Gary was pretty certain of one thing — Jack wasn't going to be asking him about shrubbery.

Inside Pavilion Garden VI, there was an oval gravel pathway with two white wooden benches on each end. In the center of the grassy circle was a large stone obelisk, the Merton Spire from Oxford's Merton College. The garden was empty, and Gary and Jack entered quietly and walked over and stood by the stone pillar.

Gary had other things to do and wanted to get this over with fast, so he took the lead in the conversation. "Alright, Mr. Parish, let's not beat around the bush, or in this case, around the spire. I know why you wanted this meeting."

Mr. Parish eyes widened. "Is that so? Do me a favor, and call me Jack."

"Okay, Jack," said Gary cautiously, taking out his wallet and pulling out Jack's business card. "You want to cash in your deposit with me for a lead story." Gary held the card out to Jack. "You want to know who Taylor's has chosen for VP."

Jack laughed heartily and pushed Gary's hand and his own business card away from his face. "Wrong. That I already know." Jack casually turned and walked over to one of the white benches, sat down with a plop, and pulled out a cigarette and lit up.

Curious, Gary followed Jack over to the benches and stood in front of him. "Oh, really? And just who would that be?"

Jack Parish took a long drag of his cigarette and confidently blew out smoke. "Nobody, that's who."

Gary eyed Parish closely. Jack was dead right, but he didn't want him to know that for sure.

"Are you sure?"

Parish laughed again. "Oh, yes, Mr. Craig, I am quite sure."

Gary huffed and sat down beside Jack. "Make it Gary. And just how do you know that?"

Parish smiled and offered Gary a cigarette but Gary passed.

"No, thanks," he said. "I quit last year after my divorce, and honestly I'm still not sure which experience was harder. I've switched to these." Gary pulled out a couple rolls of Lifesavers from his pocket. He chose a wintergreen and popped it into his mouth. He liked chewing on wintergreen ones when he had to concentrate.

Jack looked at Gary skeptically and then continued. "I know because if your guys had picked Taylor a running mate, you'd be falling all over yourselves to leak it to the press. Believe me, you'd be smiling and winking and dropping pieces of paper with the running mate's name written all over it. Nope, Baldwin was actually telling the truth up there. Taylor hasn't picked his VP yet. And besides," added Jack as he leaned back and airily blew out another puff of smoke. "I wouldn't waste my 'deposit' on that little transient piece of information."

Gary looked at Jack with frustration and grimaced. "Okay, so why the garden tour? What do you want from me?"

Jack quickly looked around for a moment and then answered in a serious, hushed tone of voice. "You got it wrong, pal. I didn't drag you down here to pump information out of you. I brought you here to give you information, on the QT of course."

Gary was taken aback. "You want to give me information?"

Jack finished his cigarette and threw it down. He ground it out firmly with the heel of his shoe and then leaned forward. "I got an interesting e-mail from my Aunt Dorothy in Texas. You remember me telling you about her?"

Gary nodded and listened intently.

"First of all, let me tell you a bit about the lady. Aunt Dotty is the social queen of Fort Worth, Texas. She's a widow now, but she was married to money — big oil money — and trust me when I say money opens a lot of doors down south. I'm convinced she's on a first-name basis with half of Fort Worth, and the other half is on her payroll. Anyway, Aunt D writes me about two weeks ago, filling me in on the latest scandals of the Lone Star State. She included something strange that got her attention. Caught my attention, too."

Jack paused to light up another cigarette. He got up and started pacing in front of Gary as he continued. "Auntie plays cards with a bunch of rich broads with heavy-duty investments in West Texas. If it has anything to do with oil, gas, or helium, they own it. They get together every week and whoop it up over bridge, champagne, and hors d'oeuvres. I live in mortal fear they'll advance one day to beer and strip poker. Dotty is very good at poker, by the way. Anyway, two weeks ago they gather for their weekly game of cards and dirty gossip. Sally Jo, one of Auntie's best friends — currently married to husband number five I think, a high-powered Dallas real estate lawyer — speaks up. Sally Jo tells the gals about a weird bunch of clients who recently showed up at her husband's office. Her husband said they looked scary. The young men came in and wanted to buy an office space in downtown Dallas. They opened a suitcase and laid down a cool two million — in cash — on his desk. It was a scene just like in the movies. Sally Jo's husband has been in business a long time, but he swears he's never had that much green stuff littered on top of his desk. Needless to say, it made him skittish."

Jack paused and waited for Gary to respond. Gary stared at him puzzled.

"Did Sally Jo's husband call the police?" asked Gary.

"Nope. Aunt Dotty said he was too frightened."

"Can't say I blame him," observed Gary truthfully.

"You don't get it, do you?" said Jack, puffing hard on his cigarette.

"No. Should I?" responded Gary impatiently, looking down at his watch, aware of the time and his pressing calendar for the day. "I don't see what this has to do with me."

"Oh, it has everything to do with you, Clyde!" Jack threw down his half-smoked cigarette, stamped it out, and sat back down beside Gary. "The guys with the suitcase were your two-stepping friends in Stand Out."

The mention of that name made Gary inwardly freeze, and he stared at Jack Parish in alarm. Had the guy in Stand Out figured out Gary was part of the Taylor team and the reason their attempt to demonstrate at the UNCG rally failed? Oh God! Gary had just given an on-camera interview! His face was on national television. If Stand Out didn't know Gary's connection before, they would now. Gary felt sick.

Gary asked, "Are they here?"

Jack eyed Gary narrowly. "You don't look so good."

"Well, if they find out I'm here, I'll look worse," muttered Gary.

"You personally? Why is that?"

"Um, I bashed one of them in the head." Gary then told Jack what happened down at the lake in Greensboro.

"Alrighty then," said Jack enlightened. "So Stand Out had a personal vendetta against you already. Interesting."

"Are they going to demonstrate against Taylor tonight?"

Jack threw his hands up in exasperation. "God! Do I have to connect all the dots for you? No, they aren't showing up tonight. Focus on the big picture, Sam. Focus on the money! You know the Watergate rule, follow the money. Stand Out is not supported by anyone on the Hill, Hollywood, or New York City. True, those folks love environment causes, but this bunch is certifiably crazy, and nobody likes them, and nobody gives them cash. So, the question is, how in the hell did they come up with two freaking million dollars?"

Gary gazed uneasily at Jack Parish, who continued speaking in a fervent whisper. "Still don't get it? Think, man! Your dancing demonstrators just didn't show up in North Carolina to crash your party last month because they had a beef with Taylor. What awful sin did Senator Taylor ever do to the environmentalist cause? They're not that mobile, they're not that smart, and they are not that patriotic. Nor did they suddenly appear out of a deep desire to star on national television. They showed up in Greensboro because somebody paid them to be there. Somebody hired them."

Hired them. The impact of those words hit Gary full force, and it suddenly all made sense. Now it was his turn to stand up and start pacing. He took out a roll of peppermint Lifesavers and popped two into his mouth. Peppermint was good for stress.

"But two million dollars? Why would somebody pay them that much money? Their plans fell through."

"Easy," said Jack coolly, carefully picking off a piece of lint from his pant legs. "They were paid half the cash up front. Which means you, my friend," he said emphatically pointing to Gary, "truly are in deep doo-doo, not for bashing one in the head. He probably gets bashed in the head on a weekly basis or should. Might knock some sense into him! No, the fact is that it was your tasty Colonial barbeque that cost them the rest of the loot, at least another two million is my guess."

Gary stopped pacing and faced Parish, who was eyeing him closely. Gary felt his mouth go dry.

"You think I'm a target now, you think I'm in danger?" he asked weakly.

"From Stand Out? Actually, no." said Jack plainly. "While they are annoying, loud, and volatile and while you did give one of them a nasty headache, they are strictly small potatoes, my friend. I seriously doubt they have either the brains or the means to give you or Taylor any further difficulties. Your first worry isn't about them."

"Who do we have to worry about?"

Parish looked at his watch and abruptly stood up. "You have to worry about whoever bankrolled the pre-empted show down in North Carolina, the real brains and dollars behind the operation. Somebody bad is out there, buddy boy, and is probably mad as hell. So, pay attention and watch your back!"

Gary took a deep breath and nodded his head in understanding. He extended his hand out to the reporter in gratitude.

"Thanks, Jack. Guess I owe you two stories now."

Jack gave Gary one of his awarding-winning smiles. "No problem. Just quietly pass the information along to your boss Baldwin and that large behemoth that works for you. What's his name?"

"McKay."

"Right, the ex-general. I feel like saluting every time he walks by. Anyway, tell them the skinny, and they can pass the intel along to whichever super secret agency handles that sort of thing. Taylor is going to become future president of the United States in a few hours, and all of you will soon be stepping into the crazy life inside the Washington Beltway. Take a word of advice from a homegrown D.C. boy: Trust no one."

Gary grinned. "Except for reporters?"

Jack laughed heartily as they started out of the garden.

"Especially reporters. Don't forget that. I'm the only one you can trust. Now, I need to run. I have a few incoming congressmen to harass and to hound."

Gary followed Jack to the white gate and down the three stone steps. "Sounds like fun. I've got an appointment, too, to deliver a personal invitation from Taylor to a local resident for tonight's party."

Jack instantly slowed his step and raised a curious eyebrow. "That's interesting. Anyone I should know about?"

Gary shook his head negatively. "Hardly. It's a her, and she's a widow with three kids."

Jack cheerfully put his arm around Gary's shoulder. "Not so fast. I happen to like women of all varieties."

They walked to the end of the gravel lane and re-entered the grassy Lawn.

"Trust me, Parish. You wouldn't like this one."

Parish feigned offense. "What makes you think that?"

"She's smart."

"How smart?"

"Real smart. She's the Dean of the UVA Law School."

Parish made a sour face.

"Sounds awful! Does she live in one of these mansion things?" Jack waved his hand around flippantly towards the brick Pavilions.

"She could have, but Ned told me she turned it down and lives in her own home somewhere in town"

Parish shuddered. "Smart and independent! What a lovely combination in a woman. I think I'll pass."

Gary laughed out loud.

Jack put his hands out in the air as if he were framing a picture. "I can see her now. She's about your height, thin, prematurely gray hair pulled back in a tight knot at the back of her neck, no makeup on whatsoever, bifocal glasses, faded wool cardigan (also gray), black sensible shoes (flats, no heels!), and disposition of a snake. How I wish I could go with you and meet this dream of womankind."

"Right," said Gary dryly. "Thanks a lot."

"Does this ravishing creature have a name?"

"Yes, wait a minute." Gary fished a small piece of paper out his coat pocket.

"Johnson. That's her name. Dr. Martha Dameron Johnson."

Cell phone call from Charlottesville that afternoon . . .

"The press conference just ended and everything is set for tonight. Too bad that nobody Craig went and wrecked all our plans. . . . I agree. It would have worked beautifully. Stand Out would have appeared on the sidelines, threatening to make a scene, and I would have stepped in and averted the crisis. Taylor would have been so appreciative of my leadership and negotiation skills that he would have turned to me for advice on selecting his new VP. Now that part of the plan is shot to hell. I hope taking out Peters doesn't prove to be a waste of time and money. Speaking of wasted, I understand there's news from Dallas. . . . So our protestors are protesting too much? Demanding the rest of their money? Well, maybe it's time for them to run into some trouble with the law, something like Waco perhaps?. . . Yes, I thought you would like that. Explosives should tie up that loose end quite nicely, and we can always blame the current attorney general's office later on if the need arises. . . . Right, I'll sit tight while you make the necessary arrangements. . . . No, no word yet on exactly when we'll hold the VP meeting with Taylor. But rest assured I will be there and will see to it our man is chosen. Then we can proceed as originally planned. . . ."

Chapter 4

The Invitation

Afternoon, Tuesday, November 7

With Jack Parish's vision firmly implanted in Gary's mind, Gary decided not to go it alone. With multiple promises of stopping at a nearby bagel place called Bodos, known for its rich garlic humus and aromatic Caesar salads, Gary talked Blaze into coming along with him to the Johnson's home to hand deliver the invitation. Fortunately, the address of the house was not far away from the UVA campus, so the trip wouldn't take long. Begrudgingly, they set off in their rental car.

The Johnson family lived a mile north from the Rotunda, in a densely-wooded subdivision located directly off Rugby Road. Blaze slowly drove the car around the neighborhood while Gary read the written directions given to them by Ned Baldwin. Turning down Field Road, they finally found the address at the end of the lane.

The Johnson home was a charming three-story white frame house. A wide porch with turned railings stretched across the front and a widow's walk extended above on the second floor. Stain-glass filled a third story round window. The shutters were painted black, and a red brick chimney rose above the roof. It was a quaint house with lots of old-fashioned charm.

Gary parked the car on the street and, feeling stressed, paused to get out another peppermint Lifesaver. He was sure he was going to go through this entire pack before the day was through. Better pick up some more before heading back to the Rotunda. Together the two men walked up the driveway where they ran into a boy, who looked to be about eleven years old, busy shooting hoops at a basketball net attached over the door of the free-standing garage. Gary and Blaze stopped and watched him attempting to shoot from free throw distance. He missed.

"Nice try," said Gary as he stepped over to retrieve the basketball that had just bounced back in his direction.

"I'm not very good," declared the boy looking dejected as Gary handed the ball to him. "Hard to practice when you only have girls around." The way he said the word, one would think girls were worse than measles, mumps, or cooked spinach. That opinion should change in a few years, thought Gary merrily. But, come to think of it, communicable diseases and bitter green vegetables were excellent analogies of life with the former Mrs. Craig. Such are the traumas of growing up. The boy extended his hand. "I'm Josh," he said eagerly. "Do you play basketball?"

"I'm Gary. No, trust me, I'm not the one you want," he conceded. He then pointed in Blaze's direction. "It's him you want, the tall one. He played college ball. Maryland."

Josh's eyes opened wide.

"No kidding? Cool!"

"Second string," added Blaze modestly. "Although I did get to play in two NCAA Tournaments. We beat the crap out of Duke!"

"You were on television?" The boy was clearly impressed. At his age, a television sports appearance would be the peak experience of anyone's life.

"A couple of times. And listen, you really aren't that bad. Your free throw just needs a bit of fine-tuning and some practice. How's your jump shot?"

Josh sighed. "Worse."

"Tell you what," said Gary to Blaze. "I think I can handle 'the girls' inside by myself. Why don't you stay out here with Josh and shoot a few while I go deliver the invitation."

Blaze looked at Gary with pleasure. "You don't mind, seriously?"

"No problem. If 'the girls' get out of hand, I'll yell for help." Gary paused, hoping that Jack Parish's dire prediction wouldn't be waiting for him inside. "By the way, Josh, how many girls live here?"

"Um, four, not including the cats. They're all girls, too," added Josh with disgust.

"Good luck," said Blaze cheerfully as he took the ball from Josh and began to dribble down the drive.

"And watch out for Sheba," called out Josh as he dove after the ball.

Sheba?

Was Sheba a kid or a cat?

Whichever it was, it did not sound promising. Gary went for another Lifesaver, and then turned and resolutely walked up to the front porch. With mixed feelings, he knocked on the front door.

The door quickly opened. A young lady stood there. She was lovely. She was stunning. She was a fairytale princess.

It was Snow White.

Okay, okay, okay, the chronic lack of sleep was obviously catching up with him. This was *not* a fairytale. This was Charlottesville. Focus. He shook his head, concentrated, and managed to say hello. Still, the image of Snow White lingered. The teenage girl before him had fair skin, long straight raven black hair down to her shoulders, and the biggest blue eyes he'd ever seen. And like most normal teenagers, she was holding a phone in her hand. She flashed Gary a brilliant smile and asked her caller to hold the line.

"Hello," said Snow White pleasantly. "Can I help you?"

Gary cleared his throat. "Yes, my name is Gary Craig and I'm with the Stan Taylor campaign for president. I believe my boss Ned Baldwin called earlier? I have an invitation to deliver personally to Dr. Martha Johnson." Gary held up the paper invitation for her to see.

"Oh, right. They said you would be coming by. Just a minute." Snow White motioned for Gary to come inside the front entryway while she finished her phone conversation. Gary stepped inside the house and immediately admired the décor. The entry was an open area with pale yellow walls and navy blue oriental rugs. A large pine grandfather clock stood by the door. Gary could see what seemed to be an office or library to his left and a large living room to his right. The kitchen must be located down the hall, as Gary could smell the inviting aroma of something wonderful baking in the air.

"I've got to go, Patty. Somebody's here at the door. Now don't do a thing till I call you back. Promise? . . . Good! I mean it. I want to be there when you go over and talk to David. He's being a total jerk, just like Christopher. You've got to make him listen. . . . Great! It's a deal. I'll help you blast David, and then you can help me straighten Mr. Chris out. Okay. Bye"

The young lady promptly hung up the phone and introduced herself.

"I'm Eliza Johnson. Sorry about that," she said nodding to her phone. "Everybody's breaking up. My girlfriend and her boyfriend had a huge fight last weekend. And my boyfriend and I had a big blowout last night!"

This was an unusual opening conversation. Gary tilted his head with interest. "I'm sorry to hear that, Eliza. Have you talked to him yet?"

"No," said Eliza rolling her eyes. "He's not talking. I've called three times, but he's not answering his cell. And Patty's boyfriend isn't speaking either. So we've decided to take matters into our own hands and go over and make them talk!"

Gary bit his lip. Here he was, out of the blue, a total stranger, and this was none of his business. But he felt compelled to give the girl a, well, male viewpoint. After all, as observed by Josh earlier, male viewpoints in this house were severely under-represented.

"This is none of my business, but having been a jerky guy myself in the past, might I offer a small word of counsel?"

Eliza's brilliant blue eyes sparkled. "Oh, please do!" She pointed to the living room indicating that Gary should go in there to talk. They walked through an arched doorway into the formal room. The walls were painted a deep cherry red, which was offset by white crown molding around the ceilings and an impressive white marble fireplace mantle. Gas logs were on inside the fireplace, flickering peacefully. Over the mantle was a golden-framed impressionist portrait of a man with red hair and fair skin. He was standing in the midst of a vast flower garden holding the hand of a young girl. The garden was full of colored blossoms, and Gary recognized the Palace of Versailles in the background. Two large overstuffed sofas covered in a navy, red and white floral pattern flanked the fireplace. One sofa was positioned directly underneath the front window, which sofa Gary promptly sat down on. Eliza Johnson sat down on the other sofa, near French doors that led into the dining room.

Gary cleared his throat. "I know this sounds simplistic, but men aren't like women. Always remember that. Men are totally different creatures, aliens from a different world. There's a great book written all about it, *Men are from Mars, Women are from Venus*. It's great! I'll send you a copy. So, for example, when you have a problem, what do you do?"

Eliza tilted her head back slightly and gazed upward towards the ceiling for a moment in contemplation. "Well, I guess I talk about it to my mom or my friends."

"Exactly," said Gary without hesitation. "Women talk about it. They talk about it and talk about it and talk about it. The more they talk about it, the better they feel, right?"

Eliza giggled. "Right."

"Men on the other hand," said Gary solemnly, "they don't need to talk. They need to think about it. And think about it and think about it and think about it. They need to process inside their thick little skulls alone." Gary took a moment to take his fist and knock his own head for demonstration purposes. Eliza laughed. "So, the worst thing either you or your friend can do while your men are sorting things out is to try to speed up the process and drag them out into the light of day. Until they are ready, talking is the very last thing they want to do."

Eliza grimaced in frustration. "So what are we supposed to do in the meantime?"

Gary smiled. "Easy. Do something else. Anything else. Go to a movie. Go shopping. Just don't be there when the guys finally emerge. Trust me, your absence will get their attention but fast."

It was like a light went on inside the girl's head. "I think I get it," said Eliza, grinning broadly. "Awesome!"

Gary smiled back at the young teenager. Why was it that he could give romantic advice so easily to her and yet his own romantic life was such a disaster?

"Well, Eliza, I see you've commandeered another one of your mother's friends," said a cheerful voice behind them. Gary turned to see an attractive older woman, probably in her early sixties, with short, blunt-cut white hair and red-framed glasses, standing in the doorway. She wore a long blue denim jumper, a puffy white blouse, and a red apron tied around her waist. Her voice was strong and pleasant, and she had a plate of homemade chocolate chip cookies in her hands. This was the source of the good smells coming from the kitchen.

"Aunt Sophie, this is Mr. Craig. He's here to see Mom. He says men are weird and that I should go shopping," reported Eliza faithfully. Gary immediately stood up and extended his hand in greeting.

"Nice to meet you," said Gary a bit sheepishly.

Aunt Sophie's eyes and eyebrows widened so much that those small red glasses fell precariously close to the end of her nose. "Nice to meet you, too, Mr. Craig. Wish someone had given me such advice when I was younger," remarked Aunt Sophie dryly with a smile. "Mr. Baldwin called a little while ago and told us you were on your way over. I'm afraid Martha isn't here at the moment. She had a last-minute meeting on campus this afternoon. But please stay for a bit and have some cookies. I just made them." She offered the plate to Gary.

"Thank you," said Gary. "Here, let me give you this." He handed her the invitation. Having exchanged cookies, invitations, and niceties, they both sat down on the sofa.

The lady paused and looked at Eliza. "Shopping?"

Eliza grinned. "Can I take the car and go with Patty to the mall, Aunt Sophie? Please?"

The older lady handed her niece a cookie with a sigh.

"My car, I suppose?"

Eliza beamed at her aunt.

"Have you done all your homework?"

"Yes, all of it."

Aunt Sophie picked up a cookie and took a bite. "Alright," she said crunching. "I should say no, but I'm thrilled to have you off the phone for five minutes and in better spirits. You've been driving me crazy moping around here all morning. But be back here by seven. We've got that reception to go to tonight, thanks to this invitation. You wouldn't want to disappointment your new friend here by being late!"

The teenager thanked her aunt profusely, kissed her, waved goodbye to Gary, and then dashed off upstairs, her cell phone on speed dial.

Aunt Sophie looked at Gary and sighed. "I'm such a wimp," she confessed with resignation while taking another bite of cookie. "That girl has me totally wrapped around her little finger."

Gary nodded appreciatively. "Well, I can see why . . . Ouch!"

Sharp biting pinpricks of pain, like tiny steel needles, suddenly shot up from the bottom of his right leg. He looked down to discover a small black ball of fur attached firmly to the raw flesh of his ankle and lower calf. It mewed at him.

"Sheba! You naughty, naughty girl!" Aunt Sophie quickly got up and extricated the small kitten from Gary's wounded ankle. She placed the small animal on the floor. The creature paused for a moment, then it hissed at Gary, did a half turn-flip in the air, and raced out of the room and up the stairs.

"Oh, dear! Are you bleeding?" Sophie handed him a Kleenex from out of one of her apron pockets and knelt down to inspect the damage.

"I'll recover," said Gary wincing as he pulled back his sock to fully inspect his ankle. "So that's Sheba? Your nephew, Josh, warned me about her."

"Yes, that is our wild little kitten, seven weeks old and going strong. She belongs to Abigail, our wild little girl. Abigail's the youngest. She's five years old and going strong, too. She can turn cartwheels in mid-air just like that cat." Aunt Sophie watched intently as Gary blotted his bleeding ankle. "Fortunately for us, Abigail is having a quiet day today. She's outside playing her 'hiding and no seeking' game."

Gary rolled his sock back up and reached for a cookie. "Hide and no seeking?"

Aunt Sophie plopped back down on the sofa across from Gary. "Yes, a Johnson family twisted version of the traditional game. She hides and we're not allowed to seek — that is find her — for half an hour or so. If you find her before she's ready to be found, she gets very cranky and there'll be hell to pay later on, pardon my language. After leaving her alone for awhile, our job then is to walk around every five minutes or so, calling her name and looking in all the wrong places."

"How do you know when she's ready to be found?" asked Gary intrigued.

Aunt Sophie laughed softly. "Appendages begin showing, a foot here, an arm there. Trust me, if that child wants to hide, you'll never find her. We've had to put bolts on the basement and attic doors to make sure she doesn't hide in places she really shouldn't be in. But all in all she's pretty good about staying in boundaries, such as in the house or in the yard. She won't wander off too far, thank goodness. Today Abigail is hiding in the backyard . . . we think. I was outside unofficially checking on her when you arrived."

"Is that her only quiet game?"

"Well, the only one that's legal," answered Aunt Sophie, while looking up to the ceiling with a moan. "She has this naughty fetish for lipstick we are all hoping she'll soon outgrow. Pink and red are her favorite colors, although she's been known to steal coral and mauve. She sees lipstick as a designer form of crayon. Coloring is her other favorite pastime. She goes through a book a week. Eliza and I are considering padlocks for our purses. Tell me, do you like cats?"

"As a matter of fact, I do. I had a cat growing up named Boo-Boo. He spent most of his kittenhood chasing his tail."

"We have two other cats in the house," said Aunt Sophie proudly. "They're all named after famous queens! I have an adorable Tabby named Cleo. She's quite fat and never leaves the kitchen. She oversees all my cooking. Martha has an exotic white cat, a Ragdoll, named Victoria. She's a beautiful animal, with long hair and blue eyes, but she's a bit skittish around strangers. She hides in closets and under comforters when guests are here."

"What about Josh and Eliza? Don't they have any pets?" asked Gary.

"Oh yes," said Aunt Sophie dryly. "Eliza has a cell phone. And Josh has a computer."

Gary laughed. He really liked this old gal. She was kind and witty and she made one heck of a good chocolate chip cookie.

"How long have you lived with the family?" Gary inquired with interest.

Aunt Sophie picked up a cookie and crunched into it thoughtfully. "Four years. I came when Peter died, that was Martha's husband. Peter was my nephew by marriage. He was a trauma surgeon at the University Medical Center. He was killed in a Life-Flight helicopter crash."

"I'm sorry," said Gary. He felt a pang of sympathy for Josh outside. He had been four years without a father.

"Thank you. We really miss him. He was a good father and a good doctor."

Gary paused, then turned to look up at the large oil painting hanging over the fireplace mantle.

"That's quite nice," observed Gary as he admired the painting. "He looks familiar."

"He should. That's Thomas Jefferson, the other great man in Martha's life. One of Martha's law students painted that for her as a graduation-going away present. Martha has a thing for Monet, too. I think this one looks very Monet-ish, especially the face of the girl. The painting is supposed to show Jefferson at a garden in Versailles with his daughter Polly while he was serving as U.S. Ambassador to France."

"Oh, that's right," said Gary as he studied the painting more closely. "I forgot. Dr. Johnson is a Jefferson scholar."

"*The* Jefferson Scholar, if you want my unbiased opinion and that of many others here in town. Nobody outdoes Martha in that department. And she is Jefferson's descendent, you know, a distant cousin on her mother's side. I forgot how many generations back it is. There is a book over there on the bookshelf documenting the genealogy. Anyway, I feel so badly Martha wasn't here to meet with you! And really, it wasn't necessary to make a fuss and come all the way over to deliver the invitation."

"My boss, Ned Baldwin, insists I make fusses. He's a stickler for protocol, Mrs. Johnson."

Aunt Sophie laughed again, her eyes twinkling behind her red glasses. "Mr. Baldwin should have warned us that you were such a charmer, Mr. Craig."

Gary almost choked on cookie crumbs. "You think I'm a charmer?"

"Why, yes," said Aunt Sophie delightedly. "You haven't been here an hour and you've managed to get Eliza off the phone, Josh outside happily shooting hoops with a tall skinny fellow, and me out of the kitchen. Now if only you could talk Abigail out of the backyard, we'd be one big happy family."

"Should you go find her now?"

Aunt Sophie's looked at her watch and her face brightened. "I know. Why don't you take a turn? Look, but don't look too hard. I'll rustle you up a glass of iced tea or lemonade in the meantime. "

"Great, Aunt Sophie. We're thirsty!"

Gary and Aunt Sophie turned to see Blaze and Josh standing out in the hallway. Both of them were looking happy and sweaty.

"Mrs. Johnson, may I present my colleague, Mr. Blaze Phillips," said Gary.

"Hello, Mr. Phillips. Welcome to our home."

"We've been playing basketball," explained Josh excitedly. "Blaze showed me some real cool moves." Josh demonstrated bouncing an imaginary ball in the hallway. He looked over at Gary, the man who set this all up, with real gratitude. "Thanks."

"You're welcome," said Gary.

Josh looked at his aunt. "We came in for a drink. Will you make us some lemonade, Aunt Sophie? The real kind?"

The lady quickly got up from the sofa. "Of course, I will."

Gary stood up. "We really should be getting back, Mrs. Johnson. There's a lot to do before the reception tonight."

Aunt Sophie shook her head in protest. "Nonsense. You can't go without something to wash down those cookies."

Gary conceded. In all honesty, he wouldn't mind staying a few minutes longer, and the prospect of fresh-squeezed lemonade sealed the deal. Hopefully Ned wouldn't kill him if he returned a little bit late. "Alright, we'll stay a few moments longer."

"Wonderful," exclaimed Aunt Sophie with pleasure. "Everyone follow me."

She led the way back to the kitchen. She immediately directed Josh and Blaze towards a downstairs bathroom to wash up, then directed Gary to a doorway leading outside.

"Abby is out there," said Aunt Sophie.

Sophie began getting food and dishes out as an absurdly large orange tabby hopped up onto the counter top, meowing and pacing back and forth while supervising the cook's activities.

Following her directions, Gary turned towards the door. That's when he saw it. Hanging on the wall in a grouping of pictures was a photograph of Eliza, Josh, Aunt Sophie, and an angelic blond-haired little girl. They were standing beside another lady on the steps of the U.S. Capitol Building in Washington D.C. Gary leaned closer and felt his heart sink.

It was the woman whom Jack Parish had predicted — the stern, gray haired, grimacing lawyer, dressed in tweed, standing behind these darling children. Gary suddenly felt let down, disappointed, and well, astonished. How could such attractive vibrant children like Eliza and Josh be related to that?

Deflated, he stepped outside on the veranda. Gazing upon the backyard, he shook his head in amazement. The UVA Law School dean might be a drab old crony, but some hidden inner beauty had nevertheless extended itself into this garden.

A tall brick wall covered with a variety of flowering vines bordered the entire yard. Although autumn, Gary recognized massive wisteria and clematis vines along with some spectacular red honeysuckle and Carolina jasmine. He spied a rose bush or two climbing up the back wall. There was a circular gravel path surrounding a modest white gazebo in the middle of the yard. Around the edges of the walls were square plots of herbs and perennials, many giving off a final autumn show of purple, pink and yellow. Several red maple and dogwood trees stood near the vine-covered walls.

Gary stepped off the back porch and meandered around the garden. He wished he had his camera. As he paused for a moment to stand underneath a bright red maple tree, he suddenly heard a rustling of autumn leaves overhead. He looked up, just in time to see a small foot attached to a white lace sock and pink tennis shoe retreat into the thick orange red foliage above him. Gary smiled to himself and then side stepped over to the tree trunk. He cleared his throat.

"Hello there, Miss Maple Tree," said Gary, introducing himself in a clear business like voice, patting the bark gently. "What a nice garden you have."

The tree leaves rustled ever so slightly.

Gary leaned up against the trunk and conversed with the maple.

"You know, there was a maple tree just like you in my yard when I was growing up. My grandpa planted it there. Of course, my maple tree had yellow leaves in the fall, not bright red like yours. My tree was very special. My tree loved candy and liked for me to crawl up in her branches after school and tell her stories."

The maple tree giggled.

"Oh, how she loved my stories. I would tell her about pirates and Indians and fairytale castles and cursed princesses. I think she liked the princess stories best. We'd eat treats together, too. Would you like some candy, pretty red maple tree?"

There was a pause.

"Yes," whispered the tree.

"I thought so," said Gary nodding his head. He carefully pulled out the three remaining rolls of Lifesavers from his coat pocket and examined them out loud. "Well, let's see. I have peppermint and wintergreen and cherry Lifesavers. Which one would you like?"

"Cherry," said the tree.

"That was my tree's favorite, too," said Gary. He held the roll of cherry Lifesavers high above his head. Shyly, a small arm and hand wearing a pale pink cardigan sweater appeared out of the branches. The hand quickly snatched the candy and disappeared back again inside the fire colored leaves.

Gary gazed contentedly out at the peaceful garden.

"Thank you," said the tree.

"You're welcome," said Gary.

Chapter 5

Election Night

Tuesday Evening, November 7

"Someone is going to trip over those cables."

Jack Parish stood poised by a row of decorated buffet tables, holding a long black television cable in one hand and a mini cheesecake in the other.

"What cables?" asked Jack innocently, while putting the cable behind his back and putting the cheesecake quickly into his mouth.

"Those cables," said Gary testily pointing to the one Jack held and to several others nearby on the floor. "How many cables do you need to broadcast this thing anyway? I only see one big camera on the platform."

Gary referred to the small wooden and steel platform nearby constructed for television crews to set up their cameras. Due to the limited space in the Rotunda, only CNN, NBC, and Fox News had been allowed access inside the building. Other networks had reporters stationed outside and had made arrangement with these three networks to share the live feed.

"Some of those belong to Fox News," explained Jack. "And a few are phone lines and internet hook-ups and radio broadcast. Marshall is manning the live camera on the platform, and my man, Al, is handling the smaller camera for video clips and interviews." Jack pointed to the man standing at the far end of the room setting up a tripod near one of the drink tables. Al was Jack's trusty cameraman, the one who had chased several pretty UNCG nursing students around the block down in Greensboro.

"Well, your cable collection is too close to my buffet tables and your sticky hands are too close to my dessert trays. Move them. And no eating before the guests arrive," ordered Gary as he made a final visual check as invited guests began to arrive.

Everything was ready to go.

Two long tables were draped with red tablecloths. Sculpted ice centerpieces, one of the Statue of Liberty and the other of the White House, were surrounded by cut red and white flowers. Silver bowls filled with grilled shrimp, chucks of fresh cooked lobster, and deviled crab cakes were set around the ice pieces. Platters of roasted vegetables, a variety of gourmet pasta salads, sliced European cheeses, caviar, assorted crackers, and hot artichoke dip was placed beside the seafood. Finally, a variety of small delicate desserts was carefully arranged on the outer parts of the two tables. Drinks were set up at two separate open bars at other locations inside the Dome Room of Jefferson's Rotunda.

"The guests are arriving," argued Jack pointing to a group of people entering the room and simultaneously eyeing a dainty white chocolate truffle. "It should be legal to eat now."

"Fine. But I still want to know how many desserts you have had," said Gary inspecting a less-than-full dessert platter.

Jack gazed upwards and guiltily raised four fingers on one hand. Then he slowly added two fingers with the other hand.

"You're as bad as Blaze," complained Gary wearily. "I've banished him twice already." Gary stood with his hands behind his back looking up and down the food tables.

Jack smiled broadly and grabbed a chocolate truffle when Gary's back was momentarily turned. "By the way, where is your partner in crime?"

"Downstairs on the balcony," said Gary. "Ned put Blaze on 'Celebrity Patrol.' When I last checked, he was getting Sissy Spacek's autograph."

"Lucky devil," said Jack.

Gary nodded his head in agreement, looked down at his watch, and then helped himself to a mini cranberry scone. Jack didn't wait for an invitation but immediately followed Gary's lead, let go of his cable, and stepped closer to the table.

"Speaking of luck, how did this afternoon go?" asked Jack airily while reaching for another sweet. "Was I right? Was Madame Law School a looker or a loser?"

Gary avoided the reporter's question, picked up a plate, and spooned some red sauce onto the dish. "Here. If you are going to eat all of those, at least try dipping them in the raspberry sauce."

Jack stared down at the dish in amazement.

"Raspberry? I thought that was tartar sauce for the shrimp."

Gary shook his head. "You are utterly pathetic."

Jack dipped a mini cheesecake into the raspberry sauce and devoured it. "You're good at this, you know. You're also good at dodging my questions. If you get any better at that, I'm going to suggest you run for office. Now spill the beans. What did she look like?"

Gary huffed. "I really can't say. I mean technically I didn't get to see her in person." Gary picked up a cracker and sampled the artichoke dip. "I only saw a photograph of her in the kitchen and she looked . . . well, she looked . . ."

"Yes?"

"Awful."

Jack laughed triumphantly. "Ha! Told you so. When it comes to women, son, I'm never wrong."

Gary frowned. "I highly doubt that. But in this case, you win. She was as drab as you predicted. I was kind of shocked though after meeting her family. I mean, they were great. You'd love the old lady of the house, a feisty aunt named Sophie. She was a real card. Three beautiful children, too, although I only got to see two of them."

"Where was the other one?"

"Up a tree."

Jack glanced towards the door and smiled. "Well, I think the old gal and kiddies just arrived."

Gary turned to see Aunt Sophie, Eliza, and Josh entering. They immediately spotted Gary and came over to say hello.

"Good evening, Mr. Craig," said Aunt Sophie cheerfully as she extended her hand. "What a wonderful celebration! You must be so excited."

"Excited and tired," said Gary honestly. He turned and greeted the Johnson children. Eliza looked radiant and Josh looked miserable.

"Hi," muttered Josh. The boy did not look too keen at being there. Gary could sympathize. Being a boy at a formal reception like this would not be cool.

"Hello," said Eliza shaking Gary's hand. She looked exceptionally pretty.

"How was your trip to the mall?" asked Gary casually.

Eliza smiled back. "It was fun. And there were three phones messages waiting for me when I got back."

"Glad to hear it! Have you returned the calls?"

The girl resolutely shook her head no.

"Good. Wait another whole day," instructed Gary

"Will do," said Eliza grinning.

Aunt Sophie looked at Mr. Parish. "I don't believe we've met. I'm Sophie Johnson. And this is Eliza and Josh."

"Honored to meet you," said Jack in his best television voice. He beamed at them, turning on the old reporter charm. "I'm Jack Parish. Mr. Craig was just telling me about his little visit to your house today and how terribly disappointed he was in not meeting Dr. Johnson. Where is the good doctor anyway?"

If Jack Parish had been just a few feet closer, Gary would have elbowed him hard in the ribs.

Aunt Sophie's eyes widened in recognition. "Jack Parish? The reporter? Why, of course, you're the new one on CNN! I've seen you on television. My, you are even more handsome in person."

Jack flashed a fake modest smile and humbly bowed his head. Gary frowned and handed him a mini cheesecake.

Aunt Sophie continued. "Martha? Yes, she's here. She's downstairs with Abigail having her picture taken with Mr. Taylor by the Jefferson statue. The Taylors arrived when we did. Tell me, Mr. Parish, did you enjoy traveling around the country with Mr. Taylor and Mr. Craig?"

Jack nodded his head and pointed towards the food tables. "Believe me, Mrs. Johnson, it has been a fulfilling experience, especially with spreads like this one. Mr. Craig does a fine job, don't you think?"

"You did this?" said Aunt Sophie in awe.

"Awesome," said Eliza

Josh's face brightened slightly when he looked at all the food. Gary handed him and his sister each a plate.

"I do my best," Gary said modestly. "And I had help. Mr. Parish has been assisting me this evening with the desserts."

Aunt Sophie looked at Mr. Parish inquisitively. The reporter shook his head vigorously.

"Tasting only. I'm afraid I don't cook. I steal, sample, and order out. Speaking of sampling, I'm supposed to get some footage of guests arriving and their reaction to the election. We'll air the segment later on tonight. What do you say?" asked Jack looking at Aunt Sophie. "Would you be willing to do an interview?"

Aunt Sophie's face flushed pink. "Me? Well, I guess so."

"Great," said Jack. "And I'd like the kids in the spot too!"

"Sure," said Eliza enthusiastically.

Josh however looked stricken at the prospect. Television appearances for sports were one thing. Interviews? Never! Gary stepped over and put his hand on Josh's shoulder. "Just take the girls, Jack. I have a special project I'd like Josh's help on. That okay with you, Josh?"

Looking very much relieved, Josh nodded his head up and down. Jack led Eliza and Aunt Sophie across the room to where his cameraman was set up, leaving Josh and Gary alone by the tables.

"How about helping Mr. Phillips greet celebrities, Josh?" suggested Gary. "A couple of local Hollywood types are coming." Gary named them. Josh didn't look too impressed with that line up. Gary then added, "And a couple of sports celebrities are coming, too. Let's see. Some players for the Washington Redskins and Philadelphia Eagles are supposed to show up." Josh suddenly looked interested. "I think Darrell Green of the Redskins is coming."

Josh's eyes nearly popped out of his head.

"Darrell Green?"

Gary grinned. "Yes. Wait. Let me check to see when he's expected."

Gary looked around and spotted Ken Friedman standing by one of the drink tables, talking to another reporter. Friedman, their in-house techno wizard, had at least three palm pilots on his person at all times, one for his schedule, one for Taylor's schedule, and one for everything else.

Gary called Ken over and introduced him to Josh.

"Ken, what time is Darrell Green arriving?"

Ken pulled out his blue palm pilot, the one he kept Taylor's stuff on, and checked the time. "He's supposed to get here at 9:15, in about ten minutes. Is there a problem?"

"No, my friend Josh here is going downstairs to help Blaze out with celebrity patrol. I wanted him to meet Mr. Green and some of the other Redskin players."

"Well, I'm headed that way and would be happy to take Josh downstairs. I need to check on Donald. You know his allergies. Being around the old books up here is killing his sinuses. He went outside for an antihistamine break."

"Yeah, I saw him a few minutes ago. His nose was aglow." Gary looked at Josh inquisitively. "Do you mind?"

"No problem," said Josh happily. Gary saw them off, then turned his attention back to the reception, which was now in full swing. The Dome Room was beginning to fill as more prominent guests arrived, including the two Virginia senators and their families. Gary scanned the tables again and checked with several servers to see if they were set, then went looking for Ned to make sure he knew of the senators' arrival.

Gary found Baldwin standing inside one the cubicles of the Dome Room. In the early 1800s, the Rotunda served as the university library. Jefferson's clever design hid rows of tall bookcases directly behind tall white pillars extending down from the dome center. Standing in the middle of the room, the bookcases completely disappear from sight. Today, the room is used only for receptions and special lectures, but a number of old books are still kept on the pillar bookcases.

Ned's rule was he personally greeted all political folks, especially those in Congress. Gary approached his boss and paused, as Ned had his back turned and was talking quietly into his cell phone.

"Yes, we can meet tomorrow," said Ned in a hushed voice. "No, not at the hotel. Too many people there. Somewhere else . . ."

"Ned?"

Startled, Baldwin quickly turned around.

"I'll call you back," said Baldwin, abruptly ending the call. He quickly put his cell away.

"I'm sorry to disturb you," said Gary apologetically. "The Virginia senators have just arrived. I thought you'd want to know."

Baldwin nodded his head. He began to talk fast. "Oh, yes, that's right. They were scheduled to arrive just before the Taylors. That means Stan should be here as well. I should go check on him, too. It's a big night for all of us, Mr. Craig. Tensions are riding high, right? Well, I'd better go. By the way, the buffet looks splendid. You've done it again." With that, Ned darted off in the direction of Senator Warner, leaving Gary a bit puzzled. Ned was normally verbose, but not that blustery. He was clearly nervous, rambling on like that. How strange! Gary shrugged. Must be the excitement of the coming victory.

More people were arriving. In the midst of one particularly smart-looking group, Jim Myers made his entrance. The handsome blond was greeted with cameras flashing and reporters calling out questions. Myers stood proudly in the middle of the room and struck a perfect pose. Female reporters were dazzled. Long days at the White House Press Room were not going to be so bad with this handsome bachelor on the scene. Gary could not bear to watch. He decided to go and sample whatever dessert Jack Parish had left. On his way back to the buffet, he spotted her.

She was standing apart from the other guests, looking around the room with a critical stare. Her hair was darker in real life, a salt and pepper gray, pulled in the severest of knots on the nape of her neck. She was wearing a plain navy blue wool skirt and white blouse. A white cardigan sweater was draped around her bony shoulders. She wore no make-up whatsoever, and her small dark eyes were half hidden behind gold wire-rim glasses. She was alone. No surprise. Who would show up to the party with that? Gary wondered where the youngest daughter, Abigail, was. The child must have met up with Blaze and Lewis downstairs. He watched as the lady paused and then walked towards the buffet tables.

Well, no time like the present. Gary decided to go over to meet Dr. Johnson. She was carefully inspecting the shrimp as he approached and introduced himself.

"Hello," said Gary cheerfully extending his hand. "I'm Gary Craig. It's nice to finally meet you."

The gray-haired lady glanced up from the shrimp. She looked at him severely and then looked down narrowly at his outstretched hand.

"I beg your pardon?" Even the tone of her voice was scary.

Gary smiled back nervously. "Oh, I should explain. I work for the Taylor campaign. I brought the invitations for the reception over this afternoon. But I'm afraid I didn't get to meet you."

The lady's face finally lit up with understanding.

"Ah, of course. You're the one Sophie told me about." She critically sized Gary up again. "You're a bit too short to play basketball, aren't you?"

Gary laughed. "No, that would be my associate Mr. Philips. He's the tall skinny one."

The lady's eyes narrowed again. "I see," she said curtly, turning her attention back to the seafood platters.

You would think a lawyer and the dean of the UVA Law School would be a bit more social, thought Gary feeling annoyed, especially at such a political function. Gary tried again.

"You really should try the shrimp. We had them brought in fresh today from the Maryland shore," advised Gary in his most helpful voice. "It should be a good party tonight. And if the polls hold true, Stan Taylor will get elected."

"Yes," said the woman indifferently following Gary's advice and freehandedly sampling a shrimp.

"Stan Taylor will make a great president," added Gary.

The lady paused. "So they say. I didn't vote for him myself. I'm a Democrat."

There was an uncomfortable silence. Okay, so she didn't vote for Taylor. Then why bother to come to Taylor's victory celebration? More to the point, why should Gary even bother speaking with her if she was going to be so nasty? Her manner offended Gary, but this woman was a college classmate of Taylor's, so he should be nice, regardless of her personal politics. Gary politely started the conversation one more time.

"Well, regardless of your political persuasions, Mr. Taylor will appreciate your presence here tonight. By the way, I enjoyed meeting the children today. Josh was looking uncomfortable when he arrived so I sent him downstairs with Mr. Philips to meet and greet celebrities. And my friend Jack Parish of CNN is interviewing Eliza on camera. I hope you don't mind."

"Why should I mind?" she asked helping herself to some crab cakes. "Eliza can do whatever she pleases."

Gary was taken aback by the woman's aloof manner. Didn't she care what her own children were doing?

"Well, I just thought you'd want to know."

The lady shrugged her shoulders and moved on to the lobster.

Whatever Stan Taylor saw in this woman was beyond Gary. He politely continued. "I met Abigail this afternoon while she was up a tree in the backyard. I was hoping to see her tonight. Where is she?"

Looking bothered, the woman shook her head. "I really don't know, Mr. Craig, and it's really none of my concern."

Gary stared at the woman incredulously. He had heard enough. "None of your concern? What kind of mother are you? Don't you care where your little girl is?"

Finally the woman stopped putting food on her plate and looked up at Gary directly.

"My little girl? Mr. Craig, what in heaven's name are you talking about? Abigail Johnson is not my child."

"Dr. Johnson, of course she is your child."

The woman's eyes widened and the unattractive face suddenly looked frightfully amused. "I'm afraid you're quite mistaken. I'm not Dr. Johnson. I'm the next door neighbor, Mrs. Norma Carroll."

Gary stood there stunned. "But you were in the photograph in the kitchen. I saw you."

Mrs. Carroll thinly smiled. "Oh, that. My husband, Frank Carroll, is Dean of the College of Arts and Sciences. We were at a national meeting of college deans with Martha in D.C. last summer when that picture was taken. Frank is out of town this week or he'd be here tonight instead of me. Frank is the Republican in the family," she said with a sniff. "Martha and Sophie invited me to come along with them at the last minute."

"Well, if you aren't Dr. Johnson," said Gary, "then where is she?"

Norma Carroll tilted her head ever so slightly and replied, "I believe she's standing right behind you."

"Good evening, Mr. Craig," said a melodic voice.

Startled, Gary turned around. But sadly he forgot about Jack Parish's numerous television cables directly underfoot. Four of those cables, Gary's new black patent leather shoes, and the highly polished Rotunda wood floors proved to be a most unfortunate combination. In full view of public and press, Gary toppled over, falling flat on his face at the feet of the UVA Law School dean.

It was a singularly loud crash. Babble and laughter in the room abruptly ended. Mortified, Gary lay still on the floor, face down, wondering if he should just simply roll under the table and hide beneath the tablecloths for the remainder of the evening. It couldn't be worse.

"Well, well, well, Mr. Craig, I see Martha has knocked you off your feet. I honestly can say I am not surprised."

It was worse. That was Stan Taylor's voice.

Gary looked up and smiled weakly at the next president of the United States. Taylor was grinning merrily down at him. "Yes, sir," Gary said meekly while struggling to get up on his knees. "Sorry, sir. It was the cables, sir. I'll see that they are moved so no one else trips."

Taylor turned to his female friend. "See the effect you have on men, Martha? If I get elected, I shall personally send you over to the Senate with the White House budget proposal firmly in hand. The Democrats won't stand a chance against you. You can knock them over with your beauty and your brains."

"Very funny, Stan. Flattery will get you nowhere. Mr. Craig, I'm sorry if I startled you. I just wanted to thank you for bringing over the invitation and for being so kind to the children. They enjoyed your visit tremendously. Are you injured?"

He lied. "No, I'm okay," said Gary rubbing his bruised forehead. Gary's vision and attention, which had been temporarily blurred in the midst of his fall and embarrassment, now cleared and he looked up at Dr. Johnson. She was standing there holding the hand of a darling little girl. Both were blond, green-eyed, and absolutely lovely. Here was the mother of the children he had met today, and she was drop-dead gorgeous.

It was either a mild concussion or Dr. Johnson's extraordinary green eyes, but Gary suddenly felt light-headed. The room seemed to spin a bit. He sank back down on his knees to regain his equilibrium. He was still feeling somewhat off-center when Stan Taylor leaned over and gave him a hand up. Gary slowly got back on his feet.

Abigail looked up at her mother. "He came over today and gave me candy and told me stories while I was up in my tree," explained the five-year old matter-of-factly in Gary's defense. This seemed to clarify everything as far as she was concerned.

"Yes, sweetheart," said Dr. Johnson.

Stan Taylor laughed. "Climbing trees? Mr. Craig, your list of hidden talents never ceases to amaze me. If we have a victory tonight, I want you and your friend Phillips to come to the meeting at my house on Saturday. If you are as good at decision making as you are with catering and tree climbing, then perhaps you can help me pick a vice president."

"Yes, sir. I will be there, sir. Thank you, sir."

Taylor immediately walked off in the direction of another group of guests eagerly waiting to speak with him, leaving Gary alone with Dr. Johnson and Abigail.

"It really is nice to meet you, Mr. Craig," said Dr. Johnson sincerely offering her hand. "My aunt and my children were most impressed."

"It's nice to meet you, too," said Gary recovering but feeling a bit self-conscious.

"I'm hungry," announced Abigail on her tiptoes, looking at the desserts.

"In a minute, Abby. I think we should find Aunt Sophie and Eliza first. Do you know where the rest of my family is, Mr. Craig?"

"Yes, they are over there with my friend Jack Parish. He was interviewing them for a spot on CNN." Gary pointed over to where Jack and his crew were set up. Aunt Sophie and Eliza were standing there waving to Dr. Johnson. Then Gary noticed Jack Parish also waving at him, with Jack's television camera pointed straight in Gary's direction. The red light of the camera was definitely on. No telling how long the camera had been filming. Knowing Jack, it was all on tape.

Gary turned around and put his aching head in his hands.

"Are you sure you're alright?" asked Dr. Johnson with concern.

"I'm fine. I think I just need something to eat."

He handed Dr. Johnson a plate.

"Here," said Gary. "Have some cheesecake."

Chapter 6

The Vice President

Saturday, November 11

As predicted, Stan Taylor decisively won the election. Not since the landslide victory of Ronald Reagan had a presidential candidate garnered so many electoral and popular votes. It had been relatively early in the evening, well before midnight and before the results of the California vote had come in, that Taylor was declared the clear winner by the national news media.

With the election over, the main players in the Taylor camp paused for a much-deserved break, a few days off before beginning the huge task of organizing a transitional government. The Taylor family sequestered themselves at their Charlottesville home while their campaign staff went off in various directions. Baldwin and his wife flew down to Florida to relax in Miami Beach. His wife's family owned a condo there. McKay jetted off to London. During his military days, he had been stationed in England. He planned to visit a son still living there. Hooper was going home to Texas to visit his mother and to have a physical. Only Hooper would consider a thorough doctor's examination a recreational activity. With his new job at the White House, Donald would be requiring an entire new arsenal of medications for ailments, real or imagined. Ken Friedman flew home to Southern California with plans to visit the gods of Silicone Valley, with the hope of discovering some new techno toys to make his and everyone's life much easier. Myers flew up to New York City to buy himself a smashing new wardrobe. Washington's most eligible bachelor must be looking good for the inauguration.

Gary and Blaze quietly left Charlottesville early Wednesday morning in opposite directions for the three-day break. Blaze drove north to a relative's home in Baltimore while Gary went south to North Carolina. He would spend his time in the gentle care of his friends, Harriet and Mildred.

Mildred had Gary's backyard cottage sparkling clean with fresh linens and cut flowers when he arrived mid-morning. When he walked into the door of the main house, he was greeted with the comforting aroma of Harriet's homemade vegetable soup and sourdough bread. He was quite ready to be fed and fussed over. For three glorious days he slept late, ate too much, watched movies and puttered around his sleeping backyard garden, pruning back his rose bushes and pulling up the weeds remaining from summer. There was such solace in his small garden space. There he happily put all thoughts of presidents and politics completely out of his mind and focused on the simple pleasures of daily living.

Early Saturday morning, with a bag of Harriet's ham biscuits and apple walnut bread firmly in hand, Gary got into his car and drove the four hour drive on Route 29 North to Charlottesville. Taylor made good on his promised invitation for Gary and Blaze to attend the meeting at his Virginia home that afternoon. This was a significant request. Gary and Blaze were included with the smallest circle of Taylor operatives in a meeting where the new vice president would be selected. Wouldn't Jack Parish give an arm and leg to be there!

The Taylor family owned a magnificent horse farm west of Charlottesville in an exclusive area called Foxfield. Known for its high-class annual horse races and fantastic tracks, Foxfield was filled with large homes and country estates. Stan Taylor and his family lived in a hundred-year-old, white, two-story farmhouse located on a working horse farm, and that was where today's meeting was going to be held.

When Gary reached the long private driveway leading down to the house, he was immediately met by a host of television news vans and a full Secret Service detail manning the gates. Among the agents there were two young men that Gary particularly liked. John Clark and Sam Lewis were cousins from Atlanta, Georgia. They had thick southern accents, strawberry blond hair, bright blue eyes, and broad winning smiles. They had played college football together at Clemson and later joined the army together right after college. Their remarkable skills displayed on the training ranges and in the field did not go unnoticed or unappreciated by the federal government, and eventually they were recruited for work in Special Forces and then finally into the Secret Service.

Taylor had personally requested these cousins to be assigned to his White House detail. Gary knew better than to let the colorful southern drawl and infectious humor of these two young men fool him. Clark and Lewis were the best, and Gary was comforted knowing that they would constantly be by Taylor's side.

Gary turned slowly into the gravel drive and rolled down his window and waved at the agents.

"Good afternoon," Gary said pleasantly.

"Afternoon," Clark said with his palm extended. Gary pulled out his ID and handed it to Clark. Although a formality, Gary trusted and respected the agents' strict adherence to protocol.

"Runnin' a bit late today, aren't cha?" asked Lewis grinning, standing behind Clark.

"Late? What do you mean late?" protested Gary taking his ID back from agent Clark. "The meeting is at one. It is now only twenty till."

Clark shrugged his shoulders. "Hate to tell ya, but you're the last one to arrive. Even your buddy Phillips is here."

"Will I get shot at if I speed down the driveway?" Gary asked.

The agents barked with laughter and signaled ahead to the house via wrist transmitters that Mr. Craig had arrived, and then waved him on through.

Gary rolled the window back up and drove down the winding gravel drive, his car bumping and shaking over the uneven surface. It was a beautiful autumn Virginia afternoon. The November sun was high overhead and the dark purple mountains of the Blue Ridge rose up majestically against the western Virginia skyline. Wood-fenced pastures were located on both sides of the drive, and a number of horses were outside their barns, wandering lazily within the fenced pastures.

Several structures surrounded the Taylors' old farmhouse, including a large red barn and a small white picketed riding circle. A number of cars were parked right beside the white house, and Gary saw several other Secret Service agents out on the front porch, standing solemnly at their posts. Gary parked his car underneath a large oak tree and hurriedly walked up the porch steps and into the house. It was now ten to one. Technically he wasn't late, but he hurried inside. Taylor did not tolerate tardiness in his staff.

As Gary entered the house, he was greeted immediately by Gandalf, the Taylor's friendly greyhound, and Honey, their golden lab. Gandalf ran up to him and jumped, demanding a pet. Not to be left out, Honey also approached him bearing her favorite stuffed animal, Thumper, a toy white rabbit with long pink ears, tucked tightly between her teeth. Gary greeted and petted both dogs with enthusiasm. They were no strangers to him. Gandalf and Honey had traveled with Taylor and his staff on the campaign bus across the country.

"Now, now. Behave yourselves. Let Mr. Craig get his coat off before you attack him."

The President-elect's wife, Barbara Taylor, came into the foyer with a happy, bright look on her face. The future First Lady was an attractive woman in her mid-fifties with a slender build and medium height. She had dark, shoulder-length hair and the warmest brown eyes. She was intelligent, compassionate, had a great sense of humor, and was Stan Taylor's most devoted supporter. Theirs was a great marriage, and Gary was certain Barbara Taylor would make a fine First Lady.

"Hello, Barb," Gary said cheerfully. "You're looking radiant this morning."

"Thank you. It's amazing what victory and three days of sleep will do for you. Ned told me that you and Blaze were coming. I was getting a bit worried, though. You know how Stan likes to start on time."

"Yes, I know. I would have been here a bit earlier, but traffic was backed up on 29 at Lynchburg." Gary handed his coat to Mrs. Taylor, who opened a closet door and promptly hung it up. She then opened the front door and encouraged the doggies to go outside. Once that was done, she pointed to the dining room table.

"Everyone is gathered back in the family room. But Stan is on the phone upstairs with an international call, so the meeting hasn't started yet. You can't imagine how many calls we've had from leaders around the world. Most of them don't bother to consult their clocks and time zones either. The phone has been ringing at all hours day and night. We had to unplug it to get our three days of sleep in! Now, please, come get something to eat."

Gary walked up to the table, picked up a plate, and started fixing a burger.

"This is enough to feed an army, Barb. You made all this?"

Mrs. Taylor smiled pleasantly. "I had help." She waved her hand in the direction of the kitchen where muffled sounds of high-pitched female chatter and clanging dishes emanated. "My sisters, Ruth and Caroline, assisted in the cooking. Ruth and her husband Ed live on the property. They run the farm for us. Caroline lives down in Lexington. Her husband, Michael, teaches at Washington and Lee."

Gary selected a burger covered with melted sharp cheddar cheese and placed it on a sesame seed bun. "Well, it looks great."

Mrs. Taylor flushed. "It's just basic cookout."

"I like basic," Gary said, scooping up a big pile of German potato salad on his plate that even Blaze would be proud of. Then he helped himself to some potato chips. "Be sure to have some of the canned tomatoes. They're homegrown. Ruth and Ed always put in a vegetable garden each year."

"Thanks," said Gary, helping himself to the red veggies.

"I know you are quite a gardener, Gary. Do you grow vegetables, too?" Mrs. Taylor asked.

"Me? No, I stick to flowers. Although I have been known to grow some herbs in pots. Nothing like homegrown tomatoes!"

"This looks interesting," said Ned cheerfully as he entered the dining room with an empty plate in his hand. "My able assistant and the First Lady caught in a clandestine meeting beside the baked beans. Stealing away the hired help, Barbara?"

Mrs. Taylor smiled broadly and her eyes twinkled. "Why, Ned, what a lovely idea."

Ned chuckled. "That will cost you dearly. I'll take another burger before the meeting begins. And I hear rumors there's homemade peach ice cream?"

"True," Barbara said smiling, looking at Ned and then at Gary. Her face and her voice suddenly became serious.

"Actually, Ned," Barb said hesitantly, "if you don't mind, I would like to 'borrow' Mr. Craig for awhile, for the inauguration."

The First Lady's request caught Gary by surprise at a precarious moment while pouring a glass of iced sweet tea. Thankfully he managed not to spill it all over the table in front of his superiors. He carefully put the pitcher of tea down on the table.

Barbara Taylor smiled slyly at Ned. "Don't worry Ned. You won't be left out. I was planning to steal you away from Stan as well."

"Well, that makes me feel better," he said chuckling. "And just what do you plan to do with us?"

"I need both of you for planning the inauguration celebration, "said Barb enthusiastically. "Stan and I have been discussing themes, and we want to do something quite different, quite daring really, for the inauguration."Mrs. Taylor stepped forward and motioned for Gary and Ned to come closer. As they did, she leaned towards them and continued speaking in an excited whisper. "Last night, Stan came up with a wonderful idea. We want to take advantage of Charlottesville history and have the oath of office taken at Jefferson's home at Monticello!"

Gary could see the complex mental wheels in Ned Baldwin's head beginning to turn, thinking about the logistics, the expense, the security, and most importantly, the exclusive invitation list that would be involved in such an historic venture. Exclusive was the name of the game inside the Washington Beltway, and this extravaganza would certainly be that. The Washington crowd would be lining up for miles to secure tickets.

The look on Ned's face told Mrs. Taylor she had hit pay dirt. She proceeded on with confidence. "The swearing-in must be done at noon, of course, as outlined in the Constitution. Ned, you would be in charge of the entire event. If you agree to take it on, I'd like for you to contact the people at Monticello today. I know some of the people that work there. Then I can meet with you later this weekend to discuss other details."

"What about the traditional inauguration parade and inauguration balls?" asked Ned.

Barb Taylor picked up a potato chip and crunched on it thoughtfully. "We would fly up to D.C. by helicopter for those events after the oath of office and the reception."

"Reception?"

Both Ned and Gary responded in unison chorus. Mrs. Taylor's eyes sparkled.

"That's where you come in, Mr. Craig," she said pointing to Gary with her potato chip. "I want you to be in charge of that. The events you put together Tuesday night and in Greensboro were simply marvelous! I want you to do the same thing for us in January."

Now the wheels in Gary's own head began to spin. Ideas and menus flooded his brain. January! It would be cold. Outside reception with tents would be difficult but could be pulled off. It should be a brunch theme on the mountaintop at Jefferson's home before the ceremony, then a sit-down luncheon afterwards. For brunch, they could offer some hot drinks and pastries — French pastries to be exact. The White House chefs should be involved. For lunch, they would need to secure a location in town, perhaps at the UVA Alumni House. The prospect of this new assignment, however exciting, gave Gary mixed feelings. He was thrilled to be given the job. Yet it felt a bit odd. He expected his work at the White House to involve events of great political import, not organizing receptions and dinners. Nevertheless, he was a good scout and would serve where duty called. And honestly, he really did enjoy the recent assignments that made use of his domestic creativity. He looked at Ned first, who gave him an approving nod. Ned graciously accepted the invitation for both of them.

"Wonderful!" said Mrs. Taylor triumphantly. "I'll give you the name of a lady in downtown Charlottesville who does catering. Gary, you'll work with her and White House chefs on the menu selection and details of the set-up. I want white flowers, lots and lots of white flowers. I hope it snows. Won't that look pretty? White flowers in the snow?"

"Snow? Never!" Ned exclaimed as he finished putting his second burger together. "Neither rain nor snow will dare fall on our parade."

Barb laughed. "Parade? That reminds me . . ."

The sound of Stan's voice could be heard now from the back of the house.

"We better get in there," Ned said interrupting Mrs. Taylor mid-sentence. "Stan must be off the phone and ready to begin. Barb, we'll get with you on this after the meeting is over."

Gary hurriedly gathered up his plate and glass of iced tea and followed Ned to the back of the house.

The room they were meeting in was not part of the original farmhouse but was a modern addition that extended across the back of the entire main floor. On one end there was a big television and loveseat. On the other end of the room were a round table, dining chairs, and a fully-stocked wet bar and mini refrigerator. In the center of the room there was a large stone fireplace and a long, burgundy, overstuffed sectional sofa. The room was warm and cozy, with taupe colored walls, dark chocolate velvet drapes, and pine wood floors.

All the major players were gathered inside the room on this bright November afternoon. Gary paused and looked around the room at the men who would soon be running the country.

Standing next to the TV, fiddling with the remote to an impressive DVD system, was Ken Friedman. Here was a man born to tinker with anything electrical, computer generated, or battery operated. More than once he had saved a lost file on Gary's laptop. Ken was a genius with electronic gadgets of all kinds. His talents of fixing extended to people also, and for that reason he would be deputy counsel. Ken would be closely looking after Donald Hooper.

Speaking of Taylor's legal counsel, Donald was sitting on one of the plush sectional sofas. Physically a small man, Donald was nevertheless a powerhouse when it came to law and legal matters. He was a brilliant attorney and would work hard as counsel to the president. Hooper's Achilles heel was his high anxiety. Donald worried about everything, most notably his health. However, Gary noticed that Donald was looking quite chipper today. The trip to Texas and to his family doctor must have been just the ticket to put the rosy glow back into Hooper's ivory cheeks.

Sitting next to Donald was General Charles McKay, U.S. Army retired, the antithesis of the neurotic Hooper. McKay was a solid rock, a port in any storm, an island of calm amid troubled seas. Even McKay's build bespoke strength. He was a big solid man with broad shoulders. McKay was military all the way, a career man who had worked his way up the ranks inside the Pentagon. He was two years retired from the service when Taylor coaxed him to join the campaign. In this era of global terrorism, Taylor needed a military heavyweight on his team. McKay was that man and would become the National Security Advisor. Although Gary didn't know McKay well socially (who did?), Gary greatly respected the general.

The new president-elect was sitting quietly in a wooden rocking chair in front of the stone fireplace, reviewing some notes with Ned Baldwin and Jim Myers, who were standing nearby. Stan Taylor was an impressive-looking man in his late fifties, with dark brown hair streaked with little flecks of gray. He was of slender build, but his presence was powerful, a man full of positive energy, a natural born leader. Gary looked at Stan with a deep sense of admiration, knowing that a very good man was going to be president.

Beside Taylor stood his future chief of staff. Jim Myers looked dashing as usual in his designer jeans, designer brown leather shoes, and a thick, white, cabled sweater that matched his whitened teeth perfectly. On his right hand, Jim wore a gold ring with a ridiculously large ruby that flashed in the afternoon light. It was a ring he always wore, probably a family heirloom. Jim came from old money. With his straight blond hair and penetrating blue eyes, Jim looked every bit like a young version of Robert Redford. It was enough to make Gary sick.

Blaze was seated at the table with his laptop open in front of him. Gary went over and sat down with his plate of food next to his friend.

"Here," Blaze said handing Gary a shiny new camera. "Ned wants me to take notes and for you to take pictures."

"Me? Isn't Barb taking the pictures? She's the professional!" Gary protested as he bit into his hamburger. Mrs. Taylor was an amateur photographer, specializing in black and white pictures. Barb herself had taken most of the official pictures during the past year along the campaign trail.

Blaze shrugged. "Mrs. Taylor has stuff to do with her sisters in town. So here's her new expensive camera. Don't drop it."

"But I'm not a professional photographer," complained Gary. "I just take pictures of flowers. I'm not qualified to document a historic moment."

"Well, I'm no professional secretary. But I can spell."

"Who says I can't spell?"

"Spell *inaugural*," requested Blaze.

Gary put down his burger and picked up the camera. "Okay, so how does this thing work?"

Blaze laughed. "Figure it out and do it fast," he advised while helping himself to a potato chip off of Gary's plate. Then Blaze leaned over and whispered, "Whom do you want to see as VP?"

Gary shrugged. "I don't know. Peters is a hard act to follow."

"I'm pulling for George Kingsley."

"The African American congressman from Georgia?"

"Yeah," said Blaze enthusiastically. "He's totally cool. He's wowing them in the House, and I think Taylor should put a minority into the top spot! I might have overstepped my bounds a bit, but I e-mailed my idea to Taylor last night."

Gary stared at his friend incredulously. "You did what?"

Blaze nodded his head. "Shhh. I e-mailed him my idea. Ned will kill me when he finds out."

"Ned will kill you and he *will* find out," warned Gary.

They stopped talking when Stan Taylor stood up and called the meeting to order. Taylor first thanked everyone in the room for their hard work and then went over a few miscellaneous items of business, which included the set up of some transition teams. Blaze typed away and Gary ate quietly, taking an occasional picture now and then. Finally, when Gary's lunch and Taylor's random business items were both finished, the real issue of the day, the selection of a vice president, came to the floor. Stan sat back down in his chair and picked up a pad of paper and his pen.

"I want each of you to know," Taylor began soberly, "how grateful I am for your support during the last few weeks." He paused and looked around the room. He went on. "Eric's death has been difficult for all of us to bear, publicly and privately. I miss him more than I can say, as I know you do. More than anything, I wish he were here today to share this victory. So, before we get down to the business of finding his replacement, I'd like us to honor him with a moment of silence."

Taylor stopped talking and bowed his head solemnly. Blaze carefully typed Taylor's memorial comments as Gary lifted the camera and took a photo of the moment. This would be the picture they gave the press. After the brief pause of silence, Taylor raised his head and continued.

"Thank you. Now, we need to get to the main purpose of this meeting, which is the selection of our vice president. It's very difficult for me to imagine anyone taking Eric's place. This was our dream. Nevertheless, a decision must be made soon, and I want your input. We've developed a 'short list,' and the FBI has already vetted all of the top candidates, so there shouldn't be any surprises when we send the name up to Congress for ratification. The media has certainly had a field day trying to guess who it will be."

There was some snickering and laughter in the room.

Taylor continued. "So, to begin, I want each of you to recommend one person from the list. Then the group can discuss the pros and cons of that candidate, and we'll see if we can come to a consensus as to who would be the best choice. Donald, we'll start with you."

Donald sat up straight and spoke. "What about Governor Tom Patrick of Florida? Early in the campaign, we were worried about getting the Florida electoral votes. Patrick made that happen for us in a big way. He is smart, popular, and an effective governor. Plus he's been very successful in dealing with some of the economic issues facing his state. He'd be a great vice president."

"I'm not so sure," said Jim Myers promptly, jumping right into the debate. "Patrick is a good leader, no doubt about that, and we appreciate his support, but do we want an older man, in his early seventies from the retirement capital of the country? He would remind people too much of Reagan."

Myers' quick criticism seemed to deflate Hooper, who didn't respond. But Baldwin immediately stepped in. "And that's a bad thing? Reagan helped end the Cold War and changed world politics forever."

Myers leaned forward confidently. "True, Reagan is a respected president. I don't debate that point. But the final days of his presidency include images of him snoozing in the Oval Office while his staff and his wife's psychic advisors ran the show!"

Taylor thought for a moment. "Donald, I agree Tom is a good man but Jim might be right on this one. However, given Tom's successes with budget issues and his background in banking, he would make a fine Secretary of the Treasury. Would you agree?"

Donald seemed pleased with this compromise, and the rest of the group concurred. The President-elect called on Ned next for his recommendation.

"I like Congressman Ross Green of North Carolina. He's young and popular and doing some really good work on the Hill. He's a respected southern republican and he helped us also secure Missouri and Tennessee in the election. He'd be perfect."

Now it was Donald's turn to object. "That could be a tough call, Ned. The Democrats are raising holy hell over health care again, and Green's family has close ties with the tobacco industry. I think his mother was a Reynolds, as in RJR. That will never fly with the Democrats in the Senate."

"Too bad," observed Taylor. "But he knows a lot about business and workers. What do you think of nominating him for Labor Secretary?"

Again after further discussion the group agreed that Green's history might not draw such harsh criticism for a mere cabinet post.

Blaze continued to type and Gary snapped a shot of the intense discussion among his associates. Taylor looked next to Friedman. "Who do you recommend, Ken?"

Ken cautiously cleared his throat. "Uh, I was thinking a bit outside the box. This person is not on the current short list. He is someone down in Donald's home state of Texas, an attorney in Houston who currently serves as a judge. His name," said Ken glancing back down at his palm pilot, "is Carlos Hernandez."

"Hispanic?" asked Taylor raising his eyebrow with some interest.

Friedman nodded. "Exactly. Hispanics have become the largest voting minority in the United States. We need to recognize their vote. Hernandez would be the first minority ever to serve as VP. Imagine the response we would get from the press!"

"Rats. That was my idea," whispered Blaze as he typed.

"Shhh," ordered Gary sharply.

Once again the handsome new chief of staff put a damper on the nomination.

"Interesting idea, Ken, but I'm afraid it's a bit too far outside the box. Don't get me wrong. I like the idea of minorities being represented in our administration. Hernandez may be a good judge, but I think it's too risky raising this fellow, who hasn't served in a major elective office, all the way into the VP slot. However," he paused judiciously, "perhaps he could be considered for attorney general?"

The idea seemed to please both Ken and Taylor. The group agreed to place the name of Carlos Hernandez on the short list of people to be considered later for the important post at justice, and McKay added the Hernandez name as someone who needed to be cleared by the FBI.

"Charles, who do you like?"

The room was hushed, and Blaze stopped typing. Gary was anxious to hear whom the big man would nominate and, more importantly, if anyone would dare to contradict him.

"Senator Miles Trent of Pennsylvania. He was military. Worked with him for ten years in Europe and in the Pentagon before he entered civilian life and got into politics. He's serving in the Senate now. He's your man."

Taylor nodded his head in agreement. "I've seriously considered Miles myself. He's been one of our best supporters and helped deliver Pennsylvania and Ohio. He'd be good."

It looked like the plum was going to Trent, but then Myers spoke up again.

"Putting Trent into the VP slot wouldn't be the best use of his talents. Like Charles said, Trent has an amazing military background. What a tremendous asset to have both military and civilian experience. Given the growing threat of terrorism in the world, I think Trent would be a better fit for Secretary of Defense."

"Tell me again," whispered Gary softly to Blaze, "exactly why I don't like Jim Myers."

"Because he's powerful, smart as hell, richer than God, and a chick magnet?" answered Blaze without slowing his typing.

"Right. Thanks for reminding me."

"No problem."

It was painful for Gary to admit that Myers was right about Trent. And McKay was man enough to see it, too.

"You're right. Miles would be well received at the Pentagon."

"Are you in full agreement then?" asked Taylor.

McKay nodded his head in the affirmative. He was above all a good soldier, and it was done.

Taylor looked down at his notepad carefully, and then spoke.

"Getting back to Ken's idea about a racially diverse ticket, several people, including some in this room, have mentioned Kingsley from Georgia, as a possible vice president."

Taylor paused, looking around the room. Gary thought that Taylor winked at Blaze as he did so.

"However, after giving Kingsley some serious thought, I have decided his talents would be much better served in the Commerce Dept. I'd like to nominate him for Secretary of Commerce. Any objections?"

There were none, and that finally left Myers to nominate someone, and he wasted no time taking the floor. He stood up and strode confidently over to stand in front of the fireplace.

"I have the perfect candidate, Senator David Miller of New York!"

Jim paused to let the name fully sink in for a minute. Senator Miller was well known to members of this group. Miller had been an avid supporter of Taylor throughout the long months of the campaign. After a well-timed moment for reflection, Jim continued.

"Senator Miller is one of the most popular members of the Senate, a senior statesman in the beginning of his forth term on the Hill. Before that, he was well known and respected in the House. He's your man for VP!" Jim looked confidently at Taylor, hoping for his quick approval.

It was now Donald's turn to get back at Jim. "Now wait a minute. Isn't Senator Miller about the same age as Governor Patrick? Wouldn't age be a deciding factor against Miller as well?"

Jim Myers did not look at all pleased at having his choice being challenged, which made Gary immensely happy.

"Technically yes," Jim said slowly. "But Miller is a few years younger, in his late sixties, and more importantly, he looks a lot younger than Patrick. Like it or not, looks matter a great deal in politics."

No one argued that point, especially with Taylor sitting right there looking younger and healthier than many people his age.

"Tell me," asked Ned, "does Miller have any international experience?"

Myers smiled and jumped at the question. "Yes! I'm glad you brought that up, Ned. Miller does have experience in the international arena. First, many of you know his father was a big man in the military — a bit before your day, Charles. Miller traveled all over the world growing up." Myers paused and looked at McKay, who quietly nodded his head in the affirmative. Myers went on. "Miller is associated with the Council on Foreign Relations in D.C., and I believe he has worked some with Maurice Porter, our U.N. ambassador in New York City."

"Then it seems to me," Ned said, "given Miller's background in the international scene and his record as elder statesman, I think we ought to consider him for secretary of state instead." It was artfully done. Ned had pulled the rug right out from under Jim and before Jim could respond, the group chorused their support for Ned's idea.

"Great idea!" barked McKay. "He'll work well with defense and the Pentagon."

"Excellent idea, Ned!" said Friedman while looking up something on one of his palm pilots. "Miller is a senior member of the Senate's Foreign Relations Committee, too. That means he'll be up on important matters of state and can handle any problems in the Senate."

"Brilliant, Ned!" Donald said. "Miller is such an amicable man. He's strong, conscientious, and fair-minded. He'll make a great diplomat."

Taylor didn't say anything. He listened silently and seemed to enjoy the debate game while carefully taking notes. Myers looked frustrated and kept up his end of the argument. Blaze kept typing. Gary stood up, needing to stretch, and walked over to the doorway for a shot of the meeting from a different angle.

Jim said, "Gentlemen, gentlemen, please. I'm glad you recognize Senator Miller's vast experience and qualifications, and while I agree with you that Miller would make a great secretary of state, I really don't think we should exclude him from the pool of candidates for vice president."

Myers continued speaking, and as he droned on, Gary decided he didn't want to listen any more to the young prima donna. He lowered his camera and turned around to study the collection of black and white framed photographs displayed on the wall behind him. He had been in the Taylor home a few times but not had the time to take a good look at some of Barb's photographs. About twenty pictures of various sizes covered the wall. Some were relatively new. One was a shot of Stan after his victory in New Hampshire in the early primary. And one had been taken backstage after Stan's acceptance speech at the Republican National

Convention. Gary smiled to see a small picture of the dogs, Gandalf and Honey, sitting in the front seat of the campaign bus.

There were a few older photographs as well, pictures that Barb had blown up and framed. There was a lovely photo of Stan and Barb's wedding, the two of them standing by the cake. There was another smaller photo of an early Taylor Christmas with their children, grandparents, and pets gathered round a huge Christmas tree. Then a picture caught Gary's eye. A very young Stan and Barbara Taylor stood together on a beach. They were dressed in bathing suits and sunglasses of 70s fashion. Beside them were standing two other couples. Gary immediately recognized Eric Peters and his wife as one of them. Then there was a tall thin man with dark curly hair who Gary didn't recognize at all. Next to this man there was an attractive woman with long blond hair down to her waist, wearing a rather shockingly small bikini. She was smiling, holding up a can of soda in one hand and pointing to a tiara resting on the top of her head with her other hand. Gary leaned in for a closer look and was stunned to realize . . .

"It's her!" he gasped out loud in surprise. The debate behind him abruptly stopped, and the room became deadly silent.

"Who's her?"

Gary turned around to answer the President-elect, who was staring up at him.

"I'm sorry, sir. I didn't mean to interrupt. I just didn't recognize her right away without her clothes on."

Eyes in the room widened and a few sniggered at the statement.

Gary quickly tried to clarify. "I didn't mean to imply she was not dressed. She just looks quite different in a bikini."

"Most women do," said Ned with a broad smile.

"Naturally I didn't recognize her in the photograph," said Gary embarrassed. "I only met her once, just this past week, and then she was older and wasn't wearing a crown."

This was not getting any better. Myers bent his head and chuckled, and Ned sat back in his chair, arms now folded and looking quite amused. Donald and McKay exchanged glances, and Friedman actually put down his palm pilot. Gary felt his insides sink when Taylor got up from his chair and walked over to Gary.

"You still haven't answered my question," the future president admonished. "Whom are you talking about?"

Gary pointed tentatively to the beach picture. "Dr. Johnson," he said.

Taylor leaned forward and looked steadily at the photograph with surprise.

"That's right. You deftly fell at her feet the other night. Well, I'll be. I haven't seen that picture in years. Barb has been busy in her lab downstairs the past few days. She must have fixed that up and put it on the wall, probably in Eric's memory, to remind me of good times."

Gary asked, "Why the crown, sir?"

Taylor chuckled. "Oh, that! Well, you see, Martha and I had just been elected as student body officers in our senior law school class. Only in this case, she was president and I was vice president! You know the old saying, 'Behind every good man there stands a great woman?' We turned it around for our campaign to read, 'Behind every good woman, there stands a great man!' You should have seen the posters! They were hysterical. I was standing behind her in all kinds of crazy places in crazy poses. Eric and I later gave her that tiara in honor of her victory. She wore the darn thing at the beach and frequently in the law library during study sessions, as a not-so-subtle reminder that she was in charge, not me!"

Gary chuckled. "Too bad you couldn't turn it around now and let her be vice president for a change!"

Taylor turned toward Gary with a strange expression on his face. He looked at Gary, then at the photograph, then looked at Gary again. A smile slowly spread across his face, and he patted Gary enthusiastically on the back.

"What a marvelous solution, Mr. Craig! Once again you come to the rescue with a creative idea. And how foolish of me for not thinking of it myself!"

"Thinking of what?" said Donald anxiously, holding onto the edge of the sofa as if for dear life. The faint glow of pink in his face started to drain away.

Myers sensed what was coming and rushed forward, grabbing his president by the arm.

"Stan, wait a minute! You can't be serious. You can't just ask an ordinary citizen to be your vice president!"

"Uh, actually, he can," said Ken consulting one of his palm pilots, the big green one that held copies of federal government documents. "It's been done before. It says right here in the Federal . . ."

"But she's a woman!" cried Jim Myers.

"Yes, a brilliant, hard working, mother of three and internationally-known lawyer. She's also dean of the UVA Law School, a Jefferson scholar, and a woman who looks great in a bikini," replied Taylor. "Won't the United States public love that? Remind me, Ned, to ask Barb to make a copy of that picture for the press release. A female vice president will be something of a minority figure. Right, Ken?"

"Right, sir," answered Ken with some hesitation in his voice.

"And she's young and pretty, very important in politics. Right, Donald?"

"Yes, sir," muttered Donald weakly. "But she doesn't have clearance!" said Donald mopping his forehead with a wilted white handkerchief. "We'll have to get her vetted."

"Get her clearance, Charles," ordered Stan sharply. "We need to make sure there aren't any skeletons in her closet before she goes to the Hill for confirmation."

"Yes, sir," said General McKay while pulling out his cell phone.

Myers tried again. "Stan, please stop and think about this."

Stan Taylor walked over and sat back down resolutely in his chair. "Oh, I am thinking about it, Jim. I'm thinking about it very hard. I want Martha. I know her. I respect her. I trust her. And I will have her as my vice president come hell or high water! And I have you to thank for it, Mr. Craig."

All eyes were fixed again on Gary, some in appreciation, some in disbelief, some in utter fury.

"You're welcome, sir," responded Gary meekly. "And, now sir, if you don't mind, I think I'll go back to the kitchen to see how that peach ice cream is coming along."

Cell phone call sometime that afternoon . . .

"A woman! He picked a god-damned woman for Christ sake! . . . Of course I put forth our guy as a candidate. Taylor had everyone nominate someone. But my choice and everyone else's was knocked down somehow. . . . Who suggested her? I'll give you three guesses and the first four don't count. . . . Right, our Mr. Craig again, the guy who put that Colonial hoedown together in Greensboro. He is single handedly undermining all of our plans. Would it be possible to include him in our budget? Knock him off one evening? . . . I know, I know. We can't have too many hits, and we do have bigger fish to fry. But it would give me great pleasure to see him tossed over a bridge one dark night, straight down into the muddy waters of the Potomac River. . . . Who is she? Beats the hell out of me. She's some brainy academic; a friend of Taylor who looks like Miss America and thinks she's Thomas Jefferson. . . . We best keep a low profile until after the inauguration. Then we can reassess and see who this woman really is. Perhaps she can be influenced, properly contained, even controlled . . . ."

Chapter 7

The Inauguration

Thursday, January 20

The announcement of a woman as vice president sent shock waves through Washington D.C. and around the world. As a consequence, reporters were everywhere day and night, trying to get pictures of Taylor and Johnson together. Gary expected Jack Parish to call in his favor, but Parish didn't ask for a thing. He hung back with the rest of the gumshoes. Even if Jack had called, Gary didn't have a lot of news to share. Details on "the phone call" Taylor made to Dr. Johnson were sketchy, but Gary did hear, through Ned, it took some tough talking on Taylor's part to get the woman to finally accept the job.

Public reaction to Dr. Johnson's nomination was overwhelmingly positive on both sides of the political world. Thank God the FBI vetting went smoothly, and the ratification process on the Hill went fairly quickly as well. The Democrats asked lots of questions on social issues, but Dr. Johnson managed to answer well and appease them, holding a fairly centrist stance like Taylor on hot topics. Her main concerns were education and health care, topics the Democrats loved to champion.

Gary didn't have a lot of contact with Dr. Johnson during the vetting and ratification process. He was busy moving himself physically up to Washington while planning the inauguration with Baldwin.

Finally, the big day arrived, and up on Jefferson's mountain, a chilled but enthusiastic tour guide cleared her throat and began a well-rehearsed speech prepared for this historic occasion. More than a dozen reporters stood around her on this cold January morning, fingers frozen and pencils poised.

"In 1768, the top of this mountain was leveled off, and Mr. Jefferson began construction on the main house structure the following year in 1769." She pointed in direction of the large southern mansion behind her. "Monticello means 'Little Mountain' which describes this 867 foot hillside upon which Mr. Jefferson built his public home."

The tour guide, a fair-haired stocky woman bundled up in a brown wool coat and hat, pointed out two large L-shaped terraces extending from either side of the main structure. Cameramen and reporters dutifully followed the tour guide's expert hand movements. "Early American plantations had an outdoor kitchen, laundry, and stables, as well as servant's quarters, all located in separate buildings surrounding the house. Desiring to preserve the lovely view and landscape around Monticello, Mr. Jefferson creatively concealed these outside structures underneath inside these two large wooden terraces."

As he listened to the presentation, Gary restlessly stamped his feet on one of the hardwood floors and blew air into his icy hands. Although cold outside, it was a sunny January day, and the temperature was beginning to edge close to the forty-degree mark as they approached the noon hour, the time specified in the Constitution when a president is sworn into office. Gary's friend, Jack Parish, did not seem bothered one bit by the chilly air, as he pulled his microphone in and asked a question of the tour guide.

"Excitement has been building in the nation's capital about staging the inauguration here at Monticello instead of Washington D.C. How has the decision to move the ceremony to Jefferson's home been received here by your staff?"

The guide smiled and folded her arms authoritatively. "We've wholeheartedly embraced the idea. We felt the theme of President-elect Taylor's campaign was something Mr. Jefferson would support. And, of course, long before Dr. Johnson — I mean Vice President-elect Johnson — was selected, she was well known and well loved here at Monticello. How could we turn her down?"

Jack pressed on. "I understand Dr. Johnson and her late husband were generous patrons of the estate. Did that influence your decision in any way?"

The tour guide shook her head emphatically. "Let me assure you that the Johnsons' financial patronage of Monticello was not a deciding factor in granting permission to hold the ceremony here. It was a matter of history, something we deeply care about. The staff at Monticello unanimously agreed that Mr. Jefferson's home would be the ideal place to hold the historic inauguration for Mr. Taylor and for the first woman vice president, our own dear Dr. Martha Johnson . . ."

Mr. Parish interrupted. "Is it true that President-elect Taylor slept in Mr. Jefferson's bed last night?"

Gary couldn't help leaning closer to hear the answer to this question.

The fact that Taylor and Johnson had been extended an unprecedented opportunity to spend the night at Monticello made headlines around the world.

The guide smiled broadly. "Actually, Mr. Taylor declined that offer, allowing Dr. Johnson the pleasure of sleeping in Mr. Jefferson's home herself."

"Wow," muttered a cameraman from CBS under his breath.

The tour guide continued.

"We strongly feel that holding the ceremony here truly symbolizes the 'Back to Basics' theme of President-elect Taylor . . ."

At this point, Gary abruptly turned away. He already knew the campaign theme by heart, thank you very much. He had helped preach that doctrine many times over from New York to California and back again. Mercifully, the campaigning had ended. Now they looked forward to policy making and serving in the White House.

The move to D.C. was going well. Not surprisingly, Blaze had opted for a small but posh apartment in Georgetown, while Gary had chosen a modest little townhouse out in Sterling, Virginia, a charming suburb near the Dulles airport. Having spent the past year and half riding coast to coast in an overcrowded bus, Gary wanted to live within a ten-minute drive of the airport should he have the need to travel.

With the tour guide's interview continuing, Gary stepped onto the edge of the terrace and glanced over the railings to the northwest, taking in the breathtaking view of the Blue Ridge Mountains and the town of Charlottesville down below. This morning the mountains appeared tall and dark against the clear January sky. Then Gary turned around and gazed at the very crowded backyard of Monticello.

The large circular grassy portion of the yard (the famous view featured on the back of the American nickel) was covered by three large crimson red and white striped tents. Underneath the elaborate red canopies, members of Congress and special invited guests, two hundred and fifty in total, were gathering to watch Stan Taylor take the oath of office. A white tent-like awning was placed over the back portion of the house, covering a wood podium where the actual swearing in ceremony would take place. The stand was surrounded by two evergreen pine topiaries, an assortment of potted white silk hydrangeas, and vases of cut white roses. Gary had seen to it that Mrs. Taylor got her white flowers.

The national and international press was tightly packed on the L-shape terraces and on the walkways along the sides of the tents, positioned with their cameras and equipment. Down on the circular lawn, covered this morning with a gentle light frost, were ushers guiding arriving guests to their seats, with the Secret Service overseeing the affair literally from all angles. Overhead, military helicopters circled every five minutes or so for additional security. On this day, Mr. Jefferson's mountain would be a fortress.

The announcement that Taylor would receive the oath of office in the backyard of Monticello had had the exact response that Ned and Gary predicted. Although a few of Washington's elite initially criticized the event, soon shock and dismay gave way to the pride and the desire to get an invitation. Invitation requests poured into Baldwin's office, and the phone literally rang off the hook from November to January. So much for tradition!

Gary slowly glanced around the grounds once more.

He was quite pleased with the reception and the luncheon planned afterwards at the Michie Tavern down the hill. He had privately toured Monticello three times, twice being allowed in the upstairs area, which is not open to the public. He chose the music (traditional songs of the 1800s being played by a local Appalachian folk band), the flowers, the tablecloths, the chairs, and the paper for the invitations. For the first time, he had the pleasure of meeting and working with the extraordinary White House chefs. Together, they had selected the menu and table decor. And it had come together this week without a hitch. Looking around the grounds, Gary had a feeling of deep satisfaction. Everything looked beautiful.

Gary relaxed with a big yawn. His day had begun at three A.M. He rubbed his eyes and walked over to a long table set where various blends of expensive coffees and hot chocolate were being served. Elaborate pastries were also laid out on ornate silver trays. Centerpieces of American Eagles, designed by the White House chefs and constructed completely out of white and dark chocolate, adorned the tables. Guests would be able to enjoy a cup of hot chocolate and some pastry while waiting outside for the presidential party to arrive.

Blaze was standing nearby helping himself to a mini apple and pear tart. Gary picked up a cup and joined his friend.

"Good morning," said Gary yawning again.

"You mean good afternoon. And it's too early to be good," complained Blaze with an accompanying yawn. "Get any sleep last night?"

"About four hours," said Gary as he picked up a Napoleon.

"That's one hour more than I got," said Blaze as he picked up a steaming cup of coffee. "Man, I can't wait for the day when we can sleep in till six."Gary laughed and took a bite of his pastry. "I was glad the tents got up. Those local idiots delivering the wrong order of blue tents nearly gave Baldwin a stroke. Imagine how that would have looked on television." Gary shuddered as he took another bite.

"Let's not. Anyway, this whole thing will knock the nation's socks off. When it's over, I think we should take a long vacation," Blaze said. "How does Virginia Beach sound?"

"A warm beach anywhere sounds great, but I'm too tired to drive!" said Gary enjoying his coffee.

Blaze laughed. "No problem. We can flag down a helicopter and hitch a ride. Then we'll send Baldwin the bill! By the way, where is the boss?"

Gary looked around. He spotted Baldwin standing on a far end of one of the terraces, talking with a man Gary didn't recognize. They seemed to be engaged in a serious conversation.

"He's over there," said Gary pointing.

"Looks like he's practicing being press secretary. Uh-oh, I see the Supreme Court justices arriving. Better run and help their honors to their seats and get them some hot chocolate. Save me one of those little custard things."

Gary watched Blaze dash off to greet the judges and then turned to look at Ned. But Baldwin and the other man were gone. That was strange. Where had Ned wandered off to, right as the ceremony was about to start? Most of the guests had arrived. Ned usually was quite compulsive and hands-on about greeting important people. Gary recognized the Senate majority leader from Maine and his bejeweled wife, as well as the prime minister of Britain and the secretary general of the United Nations. Gary quickly handed his empty plate to a waiter, grabbed a napkin, and wiped off his hands and mouth. If Ned had disappeared, he had better go shake hands with the prime minister.

It was almost noon, time to start, and Gary could see that everything was in order, ready to begin.

"I can't see."

Two Secret Servicemen literally dropped to their knees and began searching while Aunt Sophie handed Martha a tissue from her oversized black handbag.

"Your mascara is running, dear," said Aunt Sophie.

Martha grabbed the tissue and dabbed the right side of her face carefully. "That's because something's in my eye," she said crossly. "An eyelash, I think. What a time to lose a contact lens! I'm blind as a bat without it." Martha turned and faced her doting aunt. "How do I look?"

Aunt Sophie frowned. "Like a weeping one-eyed raccoon. Give me the tissue." Martha handed it to Aunt Sophie, and the old lady began attending to Martha's smudged face.

"What happened?" Ken Friedman asked frantically as he and Donald Hooper hurriedly entered the open foyer of Monticello.

Agent Lewis, down on all fours, raised his head up and promptly addressed his superiors. "Her contact lens popped out when she rubbed her eye."

"Oh, no," cried Donald anxiously. "What are we going to do? Taylor and his wife are ready to go outside and the ceremony is supposed to start in less than ten minutes. We can't possibly delay the inauguration broadcast. The networks will scream bloody murder."

"I'm sure it's down there somewhere," said Martha hopefully. "I was standing right here when it came out."

"Hold still," ordered Aunt Sophie. "There's still some mascara on your face."

"Hold still," requested Ken at the same time. He knelt down and grabbed agent Clark by the ankle. Gingerly, he picked a crushed contact lens from the sole of Clark's heavy black shoe.

"This one is a goner, I'm afraid. Looks like you'll have to go out there visually impaired."

"Sorry, Ma'am," said Clark apologetically.

"It's okay," assured Martha in a forgiving voice. "At least I don't have to read a speech."

"That's right, so there's nothing to worry about," said Donald, trying to convince both himself and Martha. "Just stand very still and look appropriately solemn. Now Taylor will be at your left, so just concentrate all your attention in his direction."

"Well, that should be easy," Martha replied dryly, "as I won't be able to see anything to the right of my nose. Let me put on a little makeup, gentlemen, before I stumble my way outside."

Donald looked frantically at his watch. "Okay, get yourself squared away and I'll stall as much as I can. Taylor's in the next room. I'll go tell him about the problem. Maybe he'll want to go ahead and step out while we wait for you. It's not exactly protocol, but since this whole thing is new and a bit less formal, who will care?"

"I'll hurry," promised Martha. "By the way, all my children have scattered. I shouldn't have told them they could wander around before the ceremony. Where is Josh?"

"Outside," said Ken smiling, "talking to some marines."

"And Eliza?"

"Outside," said Ken, his smile broadening, "talking to some marines."

Martha shook her head. "Wonderful. Dare I ask about Abigail? Is she playing hide and no seek with the marines as well? I don't want to lose her in this crowd, gentlemen. There are too many excellent hiding places. We'd never find her."

"Don't worry, Martha. She's upstairs playing jacks with one of the tour guides," answered Aunt Sophie as she handed Martha a compact and a lipstick. "The guide wanted to show Abby the Oval Room upstairs. I agreed. I hope you don't mind. You were in the other room with Taylor greeting the Senate and House leadership. Abigail looked so restless, and it seemed a nice place for her to run around in while we waited for things to start."

Martha looked surprised. "Are they up there alone?"

"No, Madame Vice President," said Ken calmly. "A Secret Service agent is posted at the stairs, and General McKay went up there a few moments ago to check on her. I saw him come down just before I came in. General McKay told me they are quite secure."

"Secure?" inquired Martha with skepticism as she powdered her nose and check bones. "And with what did the National Security Advisor secure my child, Mr. Friedman? Handcuffs?"

"No, Ma'am," said Ken solemnly. "Cinnamon rolls."

"Excuse me, but I'd like a cinnamon roll and a hot cup of coffee to go."

Gary had barely taken a step in the prime minister's direction when he heard the woman's curt request. No mistaking that venomous voice! Reluctantly, Gary turned to face his ex-wife, Janet Marie Benson-Craig.

She looked absolutely smashing, of course. She was dressed in a stunning full-length white wool coat and white leather gloves, her auburn red hair falling carelessly across her shoulders. In the cold afternoon light, her lavender-blue eyes looked like iced lilacs. And her lips, that round perfect mouth of hers, were the color of winter cranberries. The effect was hypnotic. But the spell shattered the moment the cranberry colored mouth opened.

'Hello, love," she said coolly. "How's tricks?"

"Janet, what a surprise seeing you here. I don't recall your name being on the invitation list."

If I had, thought Gary, it would have been crossed off instantly.

Janet folded her arms and gave Gary an acid stare. "A mere oversight, I'm sure. Don't worry, darling, I didn't crash your little get-together. I was properly invited." She bent over, picked up a fruit tart, and stuffed it into her mouth. "Excellent. Make them yourself? Cooking was the one thing you were good at."

Gary ignored the insult. Instead, he picked up the entire tray and shoved it into her hands. "Those are very fattening, Janet. Here. Have a dozen."

Before Janet had a chance to respond, Gary excused himself and dashed off in the direction of Baldwin, who had finally reappeared and was standing near the podium. Gary greeted Ned and told him things were good at the reception tables. Baldwin thanked Gary and then looked at his watch. At that moment, Stan and Barbara Taylor walked outside of Jefferson's house and began waving and shaking hands and greeting a group of select dignitaries on the podium stage.

That wasn't right. Martha and her aunt were supposed to come out first, along with Donald and Ken. They were nowhere to be seen. Nor was McKay present. That wasn't right either. Gary was concerned, but with the Taylor party on the stand, Gary quickly stepped aside, back onto one of the side terraces. He wasn't alone five seconds before you-know-who showed up again.

"I'm crushed, dear heart. You ran off in such a hurry," Janet said scornfully.

"In case you didn't notice, I'm working," Gary replied curtly. "I suggest you run along and find your seat."

Janet pouted. "But you left before I had a chance to show you this." She took off her glove and held out her left hand, flashing an obscenely large marquise cut diamond ring in front of Gary's face. It was infinitely larger than the tiny round engagement ring he had given her the day they graduated from law school. He had worked and saved months to buy her that precious little diamond.

Gary brushed her hand away. "My deepest sympathies to the lucky man."

Pleased with herself, Janet proudly folded her arms. "Don't you want to know who I'm engaged to, who I came with?"

"Mmmm. Let me guess. Justice Barnes?" Justice Barnes, age ninety, was the oldest person serving on the Supreme Court, a crusty old fellow on oxygen and in a wheel chair.

Janet ignored his reply and took Gary by the arm, turning him towards the crowd. "I came with Congressman Daniels, the newly-elected and newly-divorced Senator from South Carolina."

"How nice." Gary tried hard to sound unimpressed.

Janet continued. "Evan comes from an old, wealthy family from Charleston. They live in the biggest old mansion you ever saw. I practically got lost in it the first time I was there! If you keep up with the news, Garykins, you'll know Evan is very popular in the other party. He's young, handsome, and powerful. Not at all like you, dearest. There's already talk on the Hill that he should run for president in the next election — an idea I plan vigorously to support."

Janet looked around the grassy area, spotted Congressmen Daniels, and wistfully waved in his direction. Daniels eagerly waved back. He looked like a lovesick hound.

"Gary?"

As if things couldn't get worse, now Jim Myers was standing beside them. As usual, Myers was looking well put together this morning in his dark gray wool Armani suit with matching long wool coat. Jim was also wearing an expensive pair of tortoise shell eyeglasses. Not that Myers needed the glasses. His vision was normal. But he wore these non-corrective glasses at opportune times to give himself a certain intellectual "power look."

"We're about ready to start," said Myers rapidly. "But there seems to be a slight delay with Dr. Johnson's party. How are things with the reception?"

"Fine," said Gary crisply, not wanting to chat.

Jim Myers nodded his head, and then suddenly noticed Janet.

"Be still, my heart. Gary, you've been holding out on me. Who is this magnificent creature?"

Janet smiled coyly at Jim.

Gary reluctantly made the introductions. "Janet, this is Jim Myers, President Taylor's chief of staff. Jim, this is Janet Benson-Craig — my ex-wife."

Jim looked at Gary in astonishment. Janet extended her hand with delight, which Jim immediately took hold and kissed.

"Pleased to make your acquaintance, Ms. Benson-Craig. Gary never told me his former wife was so ravishing. Gary, how did you ever let such a lovely woman get away?"

"It wasn't easy," muttered Gary.

"So much for taste," added Janet sarcastically while flashing another bright smile towards Jim. "I've heard so much about you, Mr. Myers! If I were not engaged to marry a United States senator, I would most certainly relish the idea of getting to know you better."

Jim Myers smoothly pulled out a business card and placed it firmly in Janet's hand. "Here is my card. Should something unforeseen prevent your happy nuptials, don't hesitate to give me a call. I'm very good at consolation."

"I'll bet you are!" said Janet winking.

Jim said goodbye and hastily made his way down to the front row, where Senator Miller, the future secretary of state, was sitting. Members of the local folk music group started playing music, a signal the ceremony was soon about to start.

Janet turned and gloated. "What a lovely, lovely man. Well, I'd better go take my seat. I wouldn't want to keep my senator waiting. Now don't forget, dearest, you won't be the only one going to Washington this year. Granted you do have a nice little unimportant job working at the White House. However, given the right political circumstances and the proper feminine persuasion — mine — and Daddy's money, Evan will someday be president and I'll be living at the White House with him."

Gary inwardly fumed. This was classic Janet. She just couldn't stand for him to have one tiny little victory. She had to come over and spoil it.

This was not the proper time or place for an argument, but at this point, Gary simply didn't care. He was on the verge of giving Janet a piece of his mind when, at last, the members of the Vice President's party suddenly appeared on the platform along with Donald, Ken, and General McKay.

Gary grabbed Janet's hand and held it tightly. "Sorry, Janet dear. The White House doesn't need any more women. We already have our fair share. Mrs. Taylor is going to make a splendid First Lady, and over there is an extraordinary and beautiful woman about to become the first female vice president of the United States."

Janet glanced over at Martha Johnson and huffed. "Well, I really don't see what's so extraordinary about her."

"No, I don't believe you would." Gary looked straight at Martha and waved.

Vice President-elect Johnson did not respond. Instead, she gazed blankly in front of her, past him, and across the yard. Aunt Sophie, however, smiled enthusiastically back and winked at Gary.

Janet laughed wickedly and patted Gary playfully on his arm. "Ah, I see you still have a way with older women. But don't fret, my precious, an intimate relationship with an older woman is very, very trendy."

"Oh, I see," said Gary slowly as the folk band began playing a Celtic style version of "Hail to the Chief." He turned and faced his ex-wife with a smile. "After the ceremony, Janet, I'll be sure to go over and ask Senator Daniels just how much he's enjoying it."

Chapter 8

The Press Conference

Thursday, March 17

After the inauguration, Gary settled down in his new life as assistant to Ned Baldwin, the White House press secretary. This meant Gary spent a lot of time in the West Wing. He did odd jobs for Ned and worked hard at keeping up with domestic and foreign news. He subscribed to five newspapers: *The Washington Post, The Washington Times, The New York Times, The New York Post*, and *The Wall Street Journal*. He signed up for several new magazines, and he watched as many cable news programs as he could. He had televisions installed in his office, and in his home office, kitchen, bedroom, and bathroom. Gary was now well connected.

He put in long hours, but the work was enjoyable. During the first few weeks, his interactions with Martha had been pretty limited, which was a good thing since he always felt a bit uncomfortable around her. He wasn't sure why that was — either it was the fact he made a fool of himself at their first meeting or it was the spell-binding effect of looking into those dark green eyes of hers. Regardless, she and her family lived in the vice president's residence (away from the White House), and Martha had her own suite of offices in the Old Executive Building across the street. If she did make an appearance in the West Wing, Gary had plenty to do to keep him distracted and out of her way.

One of Gary's favorite distractions, whenever he had a moment to spare, was the gardens at the White House. He was particularly interested, of course, in the Rose Garden, which flanked the Oval Office and the Jefferson Colonnade. It was mid-morning in March that Gary found himself squatting down in front of a very sick rose bush inside a pot just inside the White House lower floors. Beside him was his law school mentor and fellow rose-enthusiast, Dr. George Washington Campbell.

Dr. Campbell studied the bush closely. "She doesn't look so good."

"That's what I thought," said Gary.

"Pale there . . . and there."

"Life threatening?"

"Could be," said the expert cautiously.

Gary bit his lip. "What's wrong with her?"

There was a long pause. Dr. Campbell, a large Caucasian male in his mid-sixties, removed his tortoise-shelled glasses and shook his head. He gently pulled off a fading leaf from a potted pink rose bush and held it up for Gary to examine. "Viral infection. There's a new one going around the nurseries. Fortunately, it's treatable. I've got three miniature roses in my greenhouse with the same thing. Probably came from the grower where she was propagated." The man looked at Gary confidently. "I'll write down an organic 'home remedy' that I'm using that seems to help. Have the park service people spray her with it for a few weeks. Of course, being inside doesn't help the situation. Be sure to put her outside as soon as the danger of frost passes."

His diagnosis made, he looked outside the ground floor windows of the enclosed area connecting the house and the West Colonnade. "Why do they call that a rose garden, when the only roses in it are those nasty potted hybrid teas? I don't see any roses planted in the ground anywhere!"

"Well, it wasn't always like that," agreed Gary sympathetically. "I've been doing some research on the Rose Garden since I got here to the White House. At one time, a large glass conservatory covered the top of the entire West Colonnade. It reached out over this whole complex. There was literally a rose garden 'under glass,' with a misting fountain in the center and year-round roses blooming everywhere."

"Must have been beautiful," said Dr. Campbell carefully still clipping away at the tiny plant before him.

Gary closely watched his mentor and continued. "Theodore Roosevelt was responsible for major remodeling of the White House. The conservatories were removed during his administration. First Lady Eleanor Roosevelt had a passion for flowers, and she designed a Colonial garden at the turn of the century. It was filled with all kinds of plants — hollyhocks, sweet Ryan, sweet peas, phlox, and boxwood borders."

"Any roses?" asked Dr. Campbell while he carefully inspected the little pink rosebush again.

"I'm not sure. One would hope so. Anyway, First Lady Ellen Wilson replaced the Colonial garden with a more formal rose garden. There are pictures of it in one of the books in the gift shop. I'll show you later. I think you would have liked that garden, sir. It had long rows of roses planted in the ground . . . not in pots! It was during the Kennedy administration that the garden was redesigned and the crab apple trees and boxwoods were planted."

"It would have been a Kennedy," sighed Dr. Campbell, a long-time southern Republican.

Gary knew it was not a good idea to let Dr. Campbell start a political discussion. Such discussions were often quite lengthy. Not that Dr. Campbell would prevent you from contributing to the conversation. It wasn't that at all. It was just that he knew so much more than you did. Gary quickly changed the subject from Kennedys to flowers.

"It's not the White House gardeners fault, you know. Only the President or First Lady can initiate major changes to the grounds. Of course, such changes would have to be approved by the White House Historical Association."

"Just promise me that you'll try to get some different varieties of rose bushes planted around here someday," urged Dr. Campbell bitterly as he finished his work. He put his pruning sheers and gloves into a small black duffel bag and gathered up his dark brown winter coat and hat. "An Alba, a Bourbon, a Damask, a Gallica, or a Hybrid Perpetual, even a modern English Rose. Anything but a Hybrid Tea!"

Gary nodded vigorously in complete agreement. "I promise."

She was clearly outnumbered.

Martha Johnson leaned back against the tall mahogany grandfather clock that stood against the east wall of the Oval Office and silently observed the crowd of men gathered around the President. Members of the cabinet were on hand also, each waiting on Taylor as he readied himself for the much anticipated press conference. None of them were paying much attention to her except for Myers, who occasionally cast a winning smile and wink her way. Such flirtation she ignored. She didn't trust men who were that handsome.

She leaned further against the clock as she watched. Secretary Trent of Defense and General McKay were standing near the fireplace, talking army no doubt. Martha liked Secretary Trent. She wasn't so sure about McKay though. He was so quiet and always observing.

Donald Hooper and Secretary Patrick of the Treasury were sitting on one of the large overstuffed red-striped sofas. Red stripes? How ghastly! She paused to look around the room. It definitely could use a woman's touch. For starters, she would order a solid fabric for the sofas. That would soften the room and hopefully soften any negotiations taking place nearby. She looked down and frowned at the stark blue rug with the presidential seal beneath her feet. The particular shade of blue was rather obnoxious, something you would typically find in a daycare center or little boy's bedroom. She smiled to herself. If you believed the rumors about past administrations, a little boy's bedroom would be a correct description of the Oval Office.

Enough of that!

She smiled and brought her concentration back to the décor. A new rug was added to her mental shopping list, probably something in a deep berry red. She paused and looked up at the bright gold-colored drapes surrounding the Oval Office windows. What a ghastly shade of yellow! Those, given the opportunity, she would pull down herself.

She inwardly sighed and turned her thoughts to politics. The Democrats were pushing for a new tobacco bill, which had Donald and House Republicans in a complete tailspin. Fortunately, Secretary Green seemed to be doing a good job handling that, and this afternoon he and Ken were trying to calm Donald down. Donald was so easily agitated. Smart, but decidedly overactive in the worry department! The attorney general, Mr. Hernandez, was also present, holding Donald's hand while consulting him on the Justice Department's position on the issue. She looked at Donald with concern. He really wasn't looking well. The job must be getting to him. Perhaps he should see his doctor?

There were other options for the tobacco problem. Martha held the philosophy that no matter what the problem, there were multiple solutions. The trouble was that politicians and politics gravitated toward extremes, and only recognized two solutions — black or white, one or ten, my way or your way. Personally, Martha hated extremes. Difficult to see your choices from an extreme vantage point. She studied Green for a moment longer. She didn't know about him, either. He was quite popular in the new cabinet. Time would tell if he deserved that popularity.

President Taylor and Chief of Staff Jim Myers were conversing by the President's oak desk, an ornately carved piece given to Rutherford B. Hayes by Queen Victoria. Martha liked the desk, but then, she liked Queen Victoria. After all, her ragdoll cat was named after the famous British monarch. She could picture her cat Victoria perched atop that massive desk napping. Perhaps Stan would let her bring Victoria over one day for an Oval Office visit.

Taylor and Myers were in pre-game huddle, hashing out the final details of the press conference speech, where they would publicly announce several new programs to be added to the federal budget requests, items to be sent to Capitol Hill this week. So many things still needed fine-tuning. Had she been too quiet, too passive, in the budget meetings last month? She smiled to herself. Any woman with half a brain and experience with limited household budgets, bargain shopping, and coupon clipping could do a pretty good job at overhauling the nation's finances. What the government needed was a home shopping network. She smiled again. No, she would wait. No need to offend a room full of over-sensitive male egos right now. Wait till Congress gets hold of the budget and starts to argue the details. She would tactfully make her own recommendations in private to Taylor when the congressional committees worked out the final details in conference.

"Penny for your thoughts," said a mild voice.

Startled, Martha turned to see Secretary of State Miller standing close by. He had just entered the Oval Office through the rounded door beside the clock. Miller was a busy man and often arrived late to functions, but this foible didn't bother Martha in the least. Miller was her favorite. He reminded her of her deceased father. He was a medium-sized man with snow-white hair and light brown eyes. His voice was always calm and controlled, and his manner one of poise and distinction. Miller was the only one in the room who had really taken the time to get to know her well. In a paternal way, he had taken Martha under his protective wing while she was learning the ropes in Washington.

Martha grinned. "I was thinking about pennies."

Miller smirked. "Well, money is the topic of the day. Any thoughts on how we should be spending our pennies?"

Martha literally bit down on her lip. What a perfect moment to speak her mind. She stared briefly into Miller's questioning eyes while words of Thomas Jefferson ran through her mind. "Opinion is Power" Jefferson once told his friend John Adams. Why not share her opinions with Miller? She trusted him. She had ideas, good ones! And she was vice president for goodness sakes. She was supposed to bring her influence, her opinions, and her power, to this government. She opened her mouth, but then closed it again, noticing that all eyes in the room were now focused squarely upon her. They were staring, waiting for her answer. How unnerving!

Something in her gut told her to hold back. Woman's intuition was telling her that something was not right here. But what? She couldn't put her finger on it, but Martha trusted her instincts. Better keep a low profile and keep her opinions to herself, at least for a while. She inwardly collected herself, turned, and smiled prettily at Miller and the others.

"Well," she said in her best non-threatening southern accent. "I was thinking we should order some new china for the White House — Sevres porcelain? Jefferson obtained some during his stay in Paris. I've always been partial to the cornflower blue one myself. Do you think we could get General McKay and Secretary Trent to talk the Pentagon out of an extra few thousand?"

There was a collective sigh of relief from the men around the room, smiles and some light laughter. Miller's face relaxed. He took one of her hands, and patted it cheerfully.

"Let's go ask them!"

✷ ✷ ✷

"I appreciate your coming over today on such short notice, Dr. Campbell. I hope it didn't upset your research schedule too much." Gary and his mentor, having just finished an impromptu walking tour of the White House grounds, were standing outside in the Rose Garden, which was now filling up with reporters and invited guests. The March air was still chilly, but the sun was shining bright and warm. No one seemed too unhappy about holding a press conference outdoors. Taylor was a traditionalist. He'd hold a press conference in the Rose Garden during a blizzard.

Dr. Campbell half smiled. "My research would have been interrupted anyway. Violet's bridge club was coming over to the condo today for lunch and a game. It's her month to be hostess. You rescued me from a house full of cackling old women. I should be thanking you!"

"Well, anytime you want to putter around the Rose Garden, just let me know," said Gary sincerely.

"I wouldn't make such rash promises, boy. The next time you call and make an appointment, I'm bringing my shovel."

Gary laughed and then looked down at his watch. The press conference was going to start in about twenty minutes. Baldwin had been gracious enough to allow Gary time to spend with his former college professor, but he had better get back to work. Gary was just about to bid his old friend goodbye when a surprised female voice startled him.

"Dr. Campbell?"

Dr. Campbell and Gary turned to see the Vice President of the United States quickly approaching them with two massive Secret Service agents, Clark and Lewis, faithfully in tow. She looked stunning, wearing a striking hunter green wool coat and black leather gloves. Against that coat, her green eyes sparkled like May gemstones. Those eyes gave Gary a jolt. Fortunately, they were not focused on him. They were solidly fixed on Dr. Campbell, who was now (for the first time ever in Gary's memory) speechless.

"It is Dr. George Campbell, isn't it?" persisted Martha intently. The agents stood behind her expressionless.

Dr. Campbell politely coughed and extended a humble hand in greeting.

"Yes, it is. It's a pleasure to see you again, Madame Vice President."

"You know her?" Gary blurted out in disbelief.

Dr. Campbell nodded his head. "We met briefly once at a national convention years ago. Boston, wasn't it?"

The Vice President looked absolutely thrilled that he had remembered. "Yes," she said positively. "I attended your workshop on 'The Constitution in Modern Times.' It was a wonderful presentation."

"Thank you. Very kind of you to say."

"I can't tell you how happy I am to see you here," she said earnestly. "Tell me, what are you doing in Washington? Don't tell me you've left the university."

Dr. Campbell shook his head. "I'm on a two-year sabbatical from

UNC. My wife Violet has severe rheumatoid arthritis, and she needs new hips and knees, a total rehaul. We decided to come up here where she can be near her sister, Pat, during the surgeries and rehabilitation. So, I'm spending my free time at the Library of Congress, working on a new textbook while she recoups. And the folks at the Council on Foreign Relations are asking me to do some consultant work for them."

Martha clapped her hands enthusiastically together. The Secret Service agents continued to stand silently behind her.

"Really! Why, that's marvelous. I'm thrilled to hear about the new textbook. I've always used one of your textbooks in my first year law class. I'll e-mail the new dean, Dr. Jensen, and let him know another Campbell text is on the way. He'll be delighted."

At this point, Dr. Campbell actually blushed. Here was a man who put terror into the hearts of every first year student in his constitutional law class. Here was a man who prided himself on only giving out three A's in his entire academic career! (And Gary earned one of them!) Gary had never seen his ominous law professor so meek and mild. It was backwards. It was unsettling. It was, well, wrong.

"Madame Vice President, you flatter me."

The Vice President now looked curious. "If I may ask, what are you doing in the Rose Garden, Dr. Campbell? Were you invited to the press conference?"

Gary mustered up his courage and finally got a word in. "I asked him to come. I wanted his help with a sick rosebush over there inside the White House."

The steady green gaze finally turned directly on Gary. A strange expression came over her face as she studied him.

"You know Dr. Campbell?" she asked with wide-eyed amazement.

Gary didn't know quite what to say. Those eyes again! They were very distracting.

Dr. Campbell answered for him. "Why yes, Mr. Craig and I go way back. He was my teaching assistant during his third year. Did a research paper with me, too. His greatest claim to fame was getting an A in my first year constitutional law class. I've given out only three A's in my twenty-six years of teaching. He has one of them."

Martha's eyes grew even wider.

"Really?"

Gary finally found his voice. "I've got the final grade sheet framed in my office, next to my diploma. I'm not sure which took the most effort."

"I do," said Dr. Campbell grinning broadly.

"Congratulations," complimented the Vice President sincerely. "That is quite an accomplishment. I don't know anyone more respected in the academic community than Dr. Campbell." She continued to study Gary for a brief moment, and then she switched her gaze back to Dr. Campbell.

"If you're done with Mr. Craig, how about joining me up front? We're just about to start. I'd like to introduce you to the President after the news conference."

Dr. Campbell humbly accepted the Vice President's invitation, bid Gary a hasty goodbye, and walked off with her and the two bodyguards leaving Gary behind.

"Baldwin wants you," said Blaze crisply as he briskly walked up to his friend. "ABC's got their underwear all in a knot over their camera location. He wants you to sort it out."

"Now?" said Gary half dazed.

"Yesterday." Blaze paused to look around at the press gathering outside. Suddenly he changed topics. "Have you seen Donald?"

Gary shook his head. "Not for a while. Why?"

"I don't know. He looks sick."

Gary grimaced. "Donald always looks sick."

"I know that, Gary, but something's really off with him. He's more jittery than usual. He spent most of yesterday in his office with the door closed. Then he actually left the office at noon and went out for a long lunch! I think Ken went with him. Can you imagine? Donald never goes out to lunch. I mean, the man has no social life." Blaze's face brightened. "Hey, maybe Donald's got a new girlfriend and he's meeting her on the sly, with Ken as chaperone! That would cause him to stress out!"

"That would also stress out his overprotective mother!" was Gary's sage reply.

Blaze stopped the happy babbling and stared at his friend. "Speaking of funny looking, you are looking kind of pale yourself. If you're sick, I hope it's not catching. What's up?"

"She spoke to me."

"Who spoke to you?"

"The Vice President. She spoke to me. She actually paid me a compliment."

Blaze looked impressed. "Congratulations. Now, she's something else, real nice and quiet. She's the only woman I've ever met who doesn't have a million things to say about any and everything."

Gary solemnly nodded and bit his lip. "I know. That's what worries me."

Cell phone call later that day . . .

"I know you're worried, but trust me. She's been in office a couple months now and hasn't said 'Boo.' She barely opened her mouth this afternoon except to say 'good afternoon' and 'nice tie' and something about dishes. . . . That's right, dishes. She wants the army to buy her some. . . . I don't know. Blue ones from Paris. We finished our meeting in the Oval Office today on the budget and that's

all she had to say. . . . Beats the hell out of me. The only other time that woman opens her mouth is to put on lipstick. I swear she has more lipstick in her handbag than they've got at Macy's department store. Claims her little kid steals 'em and draws with them. Guess she has to carry around a year's supply. . . . Now to the matter at hand. I think it's is an excellent plan. It's been approved with the others? . . . Great. I'll get things rolling from this end. . . . No, there shouldn't be any real problems. Too bad we plan to keep her on. We could have an assassin write a note in lipstick and put the blame on her. We could get rid of both of them at once . . . . Sorry. Just a thought. What's important, I guess, is that she can be controlled. Trust me; she's as meek as mother's milk. Once Taylor is removed, I'll comfort the grieving new president and talk her into picking our man for VP as originally planned. Then, with his oversight and our control, it will be his job to tell her what to do. . . ."

Chapter 9

The National Cathedral

Thursday, April 7

President Taylor's budget was sent over to Congress. There it stalled, as usual, as the Senate and the House, the Republicans and the Democrats, in public and private discussions, ironed out the details. Promises were made on and under the table. Hands were shaken. Money flowed.

Other news events had kept Gary and the press secretary very busy that week. On April 1, the Japanese prime minister suffered a stroke and fell into a coma. Given the strong business ties the U.S. had with Japan, this news had Ned's office working closely with the State Department all week long. Miller had been at the Oval Office in meetings daily. By Tuesday the fifth, Mori Yoshiro had replaced Obuchi Keizo as prime minister. Then there was the governors' annual meeting. President Taylor had luncheons and afternoon meetings every day with various governors. The First Lady hosted the governors' wives luncheon upstairs in the White House. That and the case of the U.S. versus Microsoft kept things interesting in the West Wing. So when Thursday came, Gary was ready for the Easter holidays. That night Gary got off work early, showered and changed, and then went with Blaze to a special Easter concert.

"Surely, Surely, He hath borne our griefs and carried our sorrows."

The resounding voices of the Mormon Tabernacle Choir echoed throughout the enormous nave of the Washington National Cathedral, filling the church with the sacred sounds of music from Handel's *Messiah*. The world famous choir was giving a special Easter performance, with the President and the First Family in attendance. Many of the nation's governors, in the nation's capital for the annual meeting of governors, were also present. Baldwin and their office helped arranged the evening festivities. Once the invitations were mailed, Gary helped Ned arrange the live media broadcast of the concert on PBS, with Gary's new friend, Jack Parish, presiding.

The approximately three hundred choir members were seated in a semi-circle in the center section of the cathedral known as "The Crossing," where a large Jerusalem Cross was inset in the marble floor. The female choir members were wearing dark purple, floor-length dresses while the men wore black and white tuxedoes. Around them and beneath the Canterbury Pulpit, the ornately carved podium in the center of the church, were dozens upon dozens of white Easter lilies. Large white pillar candles burned brightly, casting flickering light and dancing shadows around the performers. It was an impressive sight.

Gary and Blaze were seated back in the main section of the nave, situated near a statue of Martin Luther King. From that position, they had an excellent view of the choir and the President.

Seated next to President Taylor was the presiding bishop of the Cathedral and Episcopal Diocese of Washington, the Reverend Jonathan Palmer. Palmer was an interesting character. A tall, charismatic gentleman, the bishop was bald with no eyebrows whatsoever. His head literally shone beneath the bright lights of the candles and cameras. He was an outspoken man, with a firm, strong voice and a distinctive Midwest accent. Bishop Palmer was originally from Michigan, Gary recalled, as he continued to watch the President and the bishop up in the High Altar. President Taylor sat quietly in a chair placed beside the bishop and listened serenely to the concert.

Gary sat back and watched his commander and chief with feelings of pride and great respect. He was certain that Taylor was destined to be a great president. His leadership would make a positive difference to this nation. Gary smiled with satisfaction. What an honor it was to serve with him!

"Hey, did you know there are over ten thousand pipes in the organ?" whispered Blaze in an awestruck voice into Gary's ear. Blaze had been studying the back of the large white and gold program.

"I know. It sounds wonderful."

"Hey, Mr. Gardener, did you see the Rose Windows over there?" Blaze was referring to the round stained glass windows in the north and south sections of the Cathedral.

"Shhh," ordered Gary severely. "They're getting ready to sing the sheep song. It's my favorite."

"Sheep song?"

"'All we like sheep, have gone astray.' Like your mouth."

Blaze quieted down, and Gary closed his eyes, relishing the beautiful music, the peace, and the stillness of the evening. It had been such a hectic week. Besides all the stuff with the Japanese prime minster, the Microsoft case, and this concert, Gary had been unofficially assisting members of the White House staff in the planning of Monday's annual White House Easter Egg Hunt.

As he continued to enjoy the sacred music, Gary pondered how once again, his old internal conflict was playing out. Gary was a classic Gemini, and he blamed that astrological fact for the cerebral civil war eternally raging inside his brain. His right and left-brain were equally talented, equally expressive, and equally desiring for control over his life. Consciously, his left-brain had been given official dominance and was awarded a formal education. He had gone to law school, like his father and like his grandfather before him. And admittedly he loved law. He loved the rigors of late-night research, the finding of facts, the discovery of details, the crafting of language, the intricacies of business, and the play of politics.

Unfortunately, despite all efforts to suppress it, Gary's artistic right brain continued to exert its own strong influence. That brain loved color, cooking, fabrics, flowers, and entertaining. His was the only law school dorm room filled with angel wing begonias and scented geraniums. Of course, Dr. Campbell later introduced him to rose gardening, and Gary had been hooked on heirloom roses ever since. Like prolific little dandelions, Gary's artistic nature had a way of springing up in whatever professional field he happened to be engaged.

After the stinging divorce, Gary tried to shut down his right brain, letting his left brain again reign supreme by throwing himself into law and then into Taylor's campaign. Much to his dismay, however, his reputation for putting together tasteful décor and delicious foods eventually spread throughout the White House. Now, with increasing frequency, a shy sideways glance and beckoning hand, a brief phone call, or a quiet e-mail was directed his way to share ideas and to request his opinion. Not that the White House staff needed any help! The ushers, the chefs, the florists, and the butlers were magnificent in their work on major White House functions. But they all recognized a kindred spirit in Gary, a man with a gift they could appreciate.

"For the Easter Egg Hunt celebration, Mrs. Taylor wants Robin Williams to read *Peter Rabbit* in the Blue Room. His agent also wants it filmed. Which network would you suggest?"

Even Anderson was asking his opinion these days, including his thoughts on the Williams reading. Cecilia Anderson was the White House social secretary who ruled over all social events at the White House with a pink velvet iron glove. Behind her back, most of the White House ushers referred to it as the pink iron fist. Privately, they disliked her brash manner and flamboyant taste, but she had arrived with the former president and continued to stay on and on — much to everyone's dismay. Despite her grace in front of the camera, Mrs. Taylor was a bit of a shy person and was not eager to replace Ms. Anderson (i.e. fire her). Honestly, Gary couldn't blame the First Lady for being scared of the woman. Anderson intimidated everyone.

Gary pondered other queries recently sent his way.

"What color would you pick for the First Family's Easter egg? The First Lady likes the cream one, but the social secretary, Anderson, is dead set against it. She's leaning towards the bright red."

"Madame Vice President wants to dress up for the historical interpreter's stage. She wants to appear as Martha Jefferson. But the Secret Service is screaming. She'll be totally exposed to the public. Can she do that?"

Gary folded his arms and pondered. Everyone saw Martha as a meek little mouse. Maybe she was. But he, for one, didn't buy it. Nope. There was definitely something about her, something more than met the eye. It bothered him. And it bothered him that it bothered him. Too bad she wasn't here tonight. Had other arrangements, she said.

"Thou shalt dash them, in pieces, like a potter's vessel!"

The tenor soloist had just hit his resounding high note, ending his song and signaling the beginning of the famous *Hallelujah Chorus*. As the organ began the familiar introductory notes of the song, the President and the congregation stood. Bishop Palmer seemed to have some difficulty getting out of his chair, so the President took him by the arm and assisted the bishop to his feet. The bishop smiled and patted the President's hands gratefully.

The choir and organist performed the majestic chorus perfectly, and a great round of applause resounded in the nave at its completion. It was when the congregation sat back down that Gary looked up at the High Altar and noticed that the President was still standing, gripping violently at his chest. A look of pain crossed the President's face. He reached out towards the bishop, gasping for air, as he collapsed hard onto the marble floor.

"Blaze! The President!"

The music abruptly stopped. People began yelling. Gary and Blaze were out of their chairs in an instant and rushed up the high altar. By the time they got there, General McKay had miraculously appeared, along with at least a dozen Secret Servicemen surrounding him and the President. McKay quickly knelt beside the President's crumpled body as he began shouting orders while the bishop stood back and silently began to pray. There were tears in the bishop's eyes. The choir stood motionless watching in horror. The nave was filled with anxious whispers and cries of alarm from the stunned congregation.

Gary let out a breath of relief as medics quickly arrived on the scene. The Secret Servicemen and McKay stepped back as two paramedics frantically began working on the President.

"No pulse," shouted a paramedic. His voice echoed loudly within the enclosed section of the stone church. A distinguished gray-haired gentleman from the Tabernacle Choir literally jumped out of his seat and rushed towards them, tearing off his black coat and rolling up his sleeves. Two Secret Servicemen immediately grabbed him, preventing him to get any closer.

"I'm a cardiac surgeon," he cried out. "Please, let me help."

McKay steadily looked at the man.

The man continued urgently. "I work at the University of Utah Medical Center and teach at the medical school. You can check my credentials. They are in my wallet. Please!"

McKay gave a brisk nod for his men to check the man's wallet. The Secret Servicemen quickly took the wallet out of the man's back pocket and tossed it to McKay. McKay flipped through it, then closed the wallet and motioned for the doctor to approach. The Secret Servicemen let him go, and the doctor quickly raced up to join the paramedics feverishly administering CPR to the President. Gary stood back and watched as the doctor took over.

"Still no pulse," the doctor said.

The doctor called for adrenaline. They pulled out a long needle and syringe.

Then he asked for the portable defibrillator.

"My God, he's going to die," said Blaze in a stunned whisper.

"No," said Gary firmly. "No, he'll pull through. He has to pull through." Gary closed his eyes and turned away when the doctor placed the electric pads across the President's bare chest. He could not watch. Instead, Gary looked at the anxious faces of the choir and congregation. He spotted Jack Parish and his CNN cameraman. The camera was on and Jack was talking excitedly into his microphone. Jack looked sick.

"Stand back. Again," ordered the doctor loudly.

He won't die. He'll live. He has to live.

He's my president.

"Again."

He's my friend.

"Again."

"Again."

Gary continued to stare into the sea of bright lights and worried faces, refusing to turn until he heard the doctor announce that it was over.

There was nothing more they could do.

President Taylor was pronounced dead.

Blaze reached out and put a strong arm around Gary's shoulders as his friend silently lowered his face into his hands in utter disbelief.

Taylor was gone, and everything was lost. Everything they had worked for, believed in, just died. Gary looked up and silently prayed.

God, what will happen now?

* * *

She picked up the bottle of Wild for Gardenia Foaming Milk Bath. "Thank heaven for bubble baths!"

Martha yawned and pulled the thick white terry cloth bathrobe tightly around her as she sat on the edge of the marble bathtub and turned on the spigots. She poured a generous amount of the scented milk bath into the tub and checked the temperature of the water to see that it was not too hot. She continued to sit, watching the bubbles form, grateful for a night completely alone. Alone as a vice president was ever allowed with a full Secret Service detail constantly underfoot, she bitterly thought. But tonight her armed posse had been ordered downstairs, with a strict warning that she would personally shoot anyone who dared disturb her privacy. They were no fools. Her detail had immediately run for cover. Aunt Sophie and the children were down in Alta Vista, Virginia, for the Easter holiday, visiting Sophie's older sister Lillian, so Martha was free to completely relax and enjoy her night off. She deserved some pampering this evening, after spending the majority of the afternoon entertaining the governors' spouses at a luncheon and meeting at the White House.

Being the vice president was not such a bad assignment, Martha mused as she watched the white foam slowly rise in her tub. It was quite perfect, really. She worked with important people on important issues. She got to travel and to visit with various service and educational organizations. She attended lots of luncheons. Thank goodness for Richard Simmons exercise videos or she'd be the size of the Smithsonian by now! And she did all this without having to be the real focus of attention, the main one in the spotlight.

Martha liked working in the shadow of President Taylor. They were a good team. She liked him, and she liked his ideas. So let him get the glory, the fame, and the nagging press corps. Not that she couldn't take center-stage or handle the pressure, but she preferred to remain the quiet smiling figure standing behind the man. True, she liked politics and always considered herself politically savvy. But since she had no political ambitions of her own, this experience would come to an end all too soon and then she and her family could return to their old way of life.

Her bath ready, Martha turned off the water, stood up, and moved over to the sink. Her cat, Victoria, was curled up in a ball asleep on the countertop. Martha leaned over and gently patted the white cat on the head several times. Victoria regally rolled her head around and yawned. She was enjoying the peace and quiet as well.

Martha picked a silver and turquoise barrette and pulled her blond hair up. She looked in the mirror and examined her face. It looked dry and flaky, a result of winter weather. Well, nothing like a mudpack to clear the skin and clean out those clogged pores. She reached into the

Body Works bag sitting on the counter and pulled out a white jar. She liberally applied a greenish-brown mud to her face. Thus adorned, she lit a vanilla-scented candle on the countertop, turned off the lights, turned on the CD player for some quiet piano background music, took off her robe and slid down into the steaming tub. Martha closed her eyes and relaxed in the steamy hot water.

Ah, alone at last.

Less than a minute later the door to the bathroom burst open, and a frantic Secret Service agent ran into the room and turned on the lights.

"Madame President!"

Martha sat up and screamed.

The Secret Service agent looked at her face and screamed.

Terrified, the cat hissed, jumped off the counter, and promptly ran around the agent's legs and out the bathroom door.

The young man hurriedly put his hand across his eyes as his face reddened. It then occurred to Martha that she was significantly underdressed. Gratefully, she was sitting in the middle of a bubble bath. She looked down. Regrettably, too many of the bubbles had melted away. She calmly reached for a towel.

"You realize, don't you," said Martha testily as she got out of the tub, "that now I really will have to shoot you? I left strict orders not to be disturbed."

"Yes, Ma'am," said the agent anxiously, his hand still tightly over his eyes. "I'm sorry to disturb you, Ma'am. But there's news. It's about the President."

Martha paused in the middle of putting on her bathrobe. What had the agent called her? Madame President? An inward chill ran through her wet body as she pulled her robe tightly around her waist.

"I'm dressed now. Open you eyes and mouth, please," she ordered sharply, "and tell me what's happened."

Agent Smith let his hand fall and looked up at her despairingly. He didn't have to say it. From the look on his face, she already knew.

"President Taylor is dead. He had a heart attack and died at the National Cathedral ten minutes ago."

The news hit Martha exceedingly hard, and she suddenly felt dizzy, like she was going to throw up. She quickly sat down on the edge of the tub and covered her mouth. Intense feelings of sadness and unbelief flooded her. He couldn't be gone. Stan was so young, so healthy. He wasn't supposed to die. He wasn't supposed to leave her. The realization of what that meant also hit her hard. She could hardly breathe. But she must.

Breathe.

Agent Smith swiftly stepped over and put his hand on her shoulder.

"Are you okay? Do you need anything?"

Martha shook her head and concentrated on inhaling air.

"No, I'm alright," she finally said in a hoarse whisper. There were a number of loud noises now coming from downstairs. The downstairs phone was ringing. Voices were shouting. Someone was running up the steps. Cars were arriving outside. Car doors were slamming. Agent Smith picked up a white hand towel laying on the countertop and slowly handed it to her.

"Madame President, you'll need to wash your face off. The Chief Justice is on his way over to give you the oath of office. He has a police escort. He'll be here in a few minutes."

Martha took the towel and held it tightly to her chest.

"Thank you, Agent Smith."

"You're welcome, Madame President."

Cell phone call two weeks later . . .

"Sorry it's been so long since I've called. Things have been rather hectic around here with the funeral. . . . No, no suspicions about the heart attack whatsoever. But I'm worried about taking action again too soon. Are you sure Reverend Palmer needs to be dealt with?. . . True. He is the only loose end. And I know how you hate loose ends. . . . Yes, wasn't that touching? Some picture, huh? The first female president of the United States sworn into office standing in her kitchen wearing a bathrobe and her hair up in a towel! It played like a Hollywood script. Only to be outdone, of course, by her upcoming official move to the White House residence on Mother's Day. . . . Nope, our little lady hasn't moved a muscle in the process of selecting her own VP, and the word is she won't until she's moved in and settled down. . . . Don't worry. I'll be in the Oval Office, by her side constantly. . . . Oh, by the way, nice job on the Stand Out issue. With the media focused on Taylor's funeral, no one in the press took much notice of the explosions at their Texas compound. With all the tight security here at the White House, explosives are quite useless. Pity. I love explosives, don't you?"

Chapter 10

The China Room

Mother's Day, Sunday, May 8

Next to ending his marriage, the four weeks between Easter and Mother's Day were probably the toughest in Gary's life. Emotionally, he was in shock. It just didn't seem real. Every morning he got up not believing that Stan was gone. His death left Gary feeling empty, lost, and devastated.

Nevertheless, Gary had to put his personal pain aside and go to work tirelessly with Ned in planning the state funeral. They met with the widow daily. Barb was a trooper, holding up as best as could be expected, with her children coming and staying in residence. The press was unbelievable, with American and foreign reporters flocking around the White House in droves. Gary, Blaze, and Ned had to handle the swelling press corps, with Ned giving his noon press conferences daily and with Gary and Blaze handling all the phone and e-mail requests. The day of the funeral arrived, a warm April day in Washington with the cherry blossoms in bloom, and a horse-drawn carriage took the body to the Capitol Rotunda. It lay in state for two days, and then it was taken back down to Charlottesville where Stan would be laid to rest in a family cemetery.

At the same time, the West Wing had to shift gears and prepare for the arrival of a new president.

Madame President.

And it was here that Gary's special talents were called upon once more.

★ ★ ★

"Well, you've done it again."

Jack Parish stood beside Gary while watching a throng of chattering women milling about the South Lawn, well-dressed guests witnessing the official arrival of Martha to the White House. The air was saturated with excitement, style, and expensive perfume.

Martha, her Aunt Sophie (who would be filling the role of "First Lady"), and the President's children had arrived an hour ago in a long string of black limousines and Secret Service vehicles. Crowds of well wishers lined up and down Pennsylvania Avenue to wave and catch a glimpse of the nation's first female president. The arrival of the First Family was captured, frame-by-frame, at the White House entrance, by a sea of national press photographers and international paparazzi.

Planning this event was difficult. Martha was sensitive to the situation and was against holding such a large and formal celebration. She didn't think it proper, as she and the nation still mourned the loss of President Taylor. But Baldwin and Myers were adamant and she had finally given in. So today, history was made with accompanying fanfare. The move into the White House was taking place on Mother's Day, with many famous wives, mothers, and daughters from around the world in attendance.

So far, the event was turning out well. Martha and her family had ceremoniously arrived, Martha had given a very short speech, and now the new First Family was socializing with their guests on the back lawn of the White House. Gary was quite pleased.

"Thanks for the compliment," said Gary simply, "but you know perfectly well that I wasn't completely in charge of all this."

The "all this" that Gary was referring to was the transformation of the circular White House back lawn into an enchanted garden place. Given the circumstances, pink was selected as the prevailing theme. In addition to numerous white, wooden folding chairs, an assortment of potted ivy topiaries and large vases filled with fragrant bouquets of pink flowers and white orchids were scattered around the edges of the asphalt circle. Round tables with salmon pink tablecloths (adorned with arrangements of white gardenias and pink candles) were placed between the topiaries. Large terra cotta pots planted with pink rose trees aligned the grassy circle. Overhead, on the South Portico, a string quartet played pieces by Bach, Mozart, and Handel. Inside the Kennedy Garden, now cleared of the modernistic Clinton-era statuary, food tables were set up with tabletop water fountain centerpieces and countless bottles of pink champagne and pink lemonade. Martha herself even wore a handsome pink silk suit.

"Cecelia Anderson was officially in charge," added Gary while taking a sip of champagne.

"That war horse?" exclaimed Jack. "Hmmph! I'm surprised all the tables weren't draped in black."

Gary quieted his friend with a stern finger to the lips. Although he secretly agreed with the reporter's assessment, this was no time for snide comments about the brash White House social secretary. Cecelia Anderson held the post of social secretary for a number of years. She was a native of Boston, a transplant to Manhattan, and now it seemed a permanent fixture of Washington D.C.

Anderson was known for her bold fashion sense, which included an almost religious adherence to wearing basic black. To work, she wore expensive black skirts, black silk pants, or tailored black dress ensembles. Occasionally she wore a white blouse. Against this plain palate however, she wore large bright pieces of costume jewelry (of which she owned plenty). To top her look off, her short-cropped hair was dyed an overwhelming shade of red.

Jack's scathing critique of Ms. Anderson continued. "How can you stomach that woman! I'm glad Madame P decided to keep the rest of Taylor's administrative staff, but she'd be doing us all a big favor if she gave the acidic Miss Anderson the boot."

"Jack, hush," scolded Gary firmly, although he enjoyed Jack's running commentary. "Anderson does a good job. Although, if I had my druthers, I would put Adams in charge," added Gary thoughtfully.

Jack frowned. "Adams? Who the heck is he?"

"You know, Cecilia's assistant."

Jack looked at Gary puzzled.

"Sorry. I'm not placing him."

"He's got dark hair, wire rim glasses, medium height, and carries a clipboard."

Jack barked with laughter. "Oh right, him. Plain and quiet as a mouse. Poor guy! Imagine working side by side with Anderson eight hours a day. Eewww. Anyway, pal, my spies (which are everywhere) inform me you were discussing today's menu and floral arrangements with our new First Lady."

"Okay, I did give Mrs. Johnson a few ideas on Hawaiian orchids. My friend Mildred knows the right people on the Big Island who are growers . . ."

"Aha!" interjected Jack triumphantly. "I spotted your touch, old buddy. Nice job. But you did forget one itsy bitsy detail."

Gary blinked in surprise. "And what was that?"

Jack sipped his champagne slowly and grinned. "You forgot to get yourself a date. However, never fear, I can help you out in that department. I'll just go out into this luscious crowd and pick someone out for you."

Gary laughed heartily. "Guess your spies don't know everything, Jack. I actually do have a date, and here she comes now!"

A short, plump lady with graying hair approached them. She was wearing a pale peach silk suit and a white orchid corsage. She smiled proudly as she greeted Gary and Jack.

"Harriet, may I introduce you to my friend Mr. Jack Parish. Jack, my dear friend and Greensboro landlady, Harriet Simmons."

"Greetings, Mrs. Simmons," responded Jack with his hallmark television smile and deep voice. When called upon, Jack could instantly turn on his celebrity charm.

Harriet blushed and shook hands with the flashy reporter.

"So nice to meet you, Mr. Parish! I've seen you on television." Harriet beamed at Jack sweetly. "I'm having such a wonderful time! There are so many people here. I'm having problems figuring out who is who."

Parish stepped forward and carefully took Harriet by the arm.

"Allow me, Ma'am. I'm well versed in celebrity. I can guide you while providing some White House tree trivia. This location, officially the President's Park, is known for its trees. Let's see. Well, to our immediate left, standing by the old Jackson magnolia is our National Security Advisor, General Charles McKay, drinking his iced tea (sweet tea with lemon to be exact) while speaking with former British prime minister, Margaret Thatcher. One can only wonder as to what these two powerhouses could be discussing.

"To their left, standing almost hidden beside the Kennedy magnolia, is our ever-anxious counsel, Donald Hooper, enjoying a private chat with Dr. Joyce Brothers. It boggles the mind to consider what ailments Mr. Hooper is describing to the famous doctor. Gary, your office will get a bill from her for services rendered. Now, to our right, over beside the Reagan oak, Ned Baldwin is busily talking with the female members of the Senate. He is speaking with Barbara Boxer, Kay Bailey Hutchinson, and Olympia Snow. How bipartisan of him! There seems to be another gentleman waiting to talk to Ned. Can't place him, I'm afraid. Oh, beyond Ned, Ken Friedman has gathered around himself a number of female athletes. He's chewing the fat with Venus and Serena Williams, Peggy Fleming, and Michelle Kwan. And there," added Jack spinning around, "is our darling chief of staff, Jim Myers, standing on the circular lawn, hard at work impressing some female royals. He is simultaneously hitting on Sarah Ferguson, Duchess of York and Queen Noor of Jordan. I hope the red-headed duchess will give the laddie a swift kick in the shins."

Harriet laughed at Jack's remarks. Encouraged, Jack continued.

"Eliza and Josh Johnson are mixing it up with Hollywood superstars. Eliza is chatting with Reese Witherspoon, and Josh doesn't look too sad to be talking with Julia Roberts, Jennifer Garner, and Cameron Diaz. My, my, looks like our young man has finally discovered the fairer sex! I don't see the little kid, Abigail, anywhere. From what Gary has told me about the little bugger, she probably climbed up a tree somewhere. And last but not least, standing on the lawn way back near the Jefferson mounds, is Martha, talking to Oprah Winfrey and Whoopi Goldberg! And that, my dear children, is the photo op of the day. Pardon me while I round up my overworked and underpaid cameraman, Al, and drag him over there for a photo shoot. Ta!"

With that, Jack dashed off in search of his photographer, leaving

Gary and Harriet alone. Gary led his friend over to the East Garden area, known as the Kennedy Garden, where refreshment tables were set up. They came to a table where First Lady Sophie Johnson stood exchanging a few words with White House chief usher, Alan Morgan. The reception was scheduled to end soon, and Mr. Morgan was discussing some specifics concerning today's move into the White House.

Gary waited until Morgan left before introducing Harriet to Aunt Sophie. The two women hit it off immediately. Gary listened with enjoyment to their chatter until a flash of red and a streak of black entered his peripheral field of vision, and he steadied his nerves for the onslaught he knew was coming.

The long slender arm of Cecilia Anderson brushed forcefully past Gary towards Harriet and Mrs. Johnson, and the not-shy social secretary broke right into the conversation, pushing Gary aside in the process.

"Mrs. Johnson, just wanted to check in. The reception appears to be going quite well. I hope you are pleased," she said smiling broadly while turning towards Harriet. "And I don't believe we've been formally introduced. I'm Cecilia Anderson, social secretary, and you are?"

Harriet blinked nervously and extended her white-gloved hand.

"I'm Harriet Simmons from North Carolina. I'm with Mr. Craig." She pointed in Gary's direction.

"Ah, yes, of course. I recall your name on the list." Cecilia Anderson paused while placing her hand dramatically up against her forehead in a sweeping motion, as if in great concentration.

"I remember. You are Mr. Craig's former landlady I believe? And you live with another woman by the name of Long, the lady who gave us suggestions on flowers for our reception?"

"Why, yes, that's right!" exclaimed Harriet in amazement. "Her name is Mildred Long and she's my sister-in-law. That's quite amazing."

Cecilia placed a modest hand to her not so modestly exposed sunlessly tanned chest and sighed. "Thank you. I do pride myself on remembering details. Is Mrs. Long here as well?" she asked, scanning the East Garden intently.

"No, I'm afraid not. Mildred was planning to come," explained Harriet, "but at the last minute she was called away on business. Mildred judges in orchid shows worldwide. An international show was scheduled overseas, but one of the American judges became ill and couldn't make it. Mildred was asked to fill in at the last minute. She was just heart broken that she couldn't be here today! She was so looking forward to it!"

"I shall see to it personally that she gets a note from the White House thanking her for her assistance with the reception flowers . . ."

Suddenly Cecilia Anderson stopped talking. She stared down at the table full of silver platters with a look of horror on her face. She reached over and picked up a small decorative plate with dark green lettuce leaves and three mounds of a white mixture surrounded with petite sesame crackers. She held it out as if she were holding a dirty smelly sock.

"And what, pray tell, is this?" she asked Gary with displeasure.

Gary looked down at the plate. "Chicken salad."

Cecilia's eyes narrowed. "And what is it doing on *my* table?"

Before Gary could answer, Aunt Sophie quickly stepped forward.

"I'm afraid that it's my fault. I put it there. Actually, it's my own recipe," confessed Aunt Sophie honestly. "It's a dish our family has on special occasions. I prepared it last night and had one of the agents bring it along and place it on the table."

This should be interesting, thought Gary happily. Anderson was caught dead in her tracks, for the First Lady was technically her boss.

"How sweet," replied Cecilia quickly recovering with the politest strained voice. She paused and offered a thin smile to Aunt Sophie. "Naturally we try to honor all the preferences and traditions of the First Family. However, you must agree that you are new to this arena and not yet familiar with the protocol for entertaining on this scale. May I recommend that that we take the chicken salad upstairs in the family residence today for a private reception with your family afterwards? I'm afraid this dish just doesn't fit with today's menu."

Aunt Sophie looked mortified. Incensed, Harriet immediately stepped up and took the plate right out of Ms. Anderson's hand.

"How rude!" exclaimed Harriet indignantly. "There's nothing wrong with this chicken salad. You haven't even bothered to taste it! I did and it's delicious. If you ask me, it should stay." With that, Harriet took the plate out of Anderson's hands and placed the plate resolutely back down on the table.

Cecilia Anderson, her lips tightly pursed, picked the plate right back up. All politeness in her voice vanished.

"I don't recall asking you, Mrs. Simmons. And I say it goes."

Now Gary lost his temper. He stepped forward and took the plate out and held on to it firmly. "The chicken salad is a Johnson family tradition and today is a Johnson family celebration. I was the one who gave approval to Mrs. Johnson for having her salad here, and I say it stays."

Cecilia Anderson glared at Gary with a look of utter contempt. "You approved it? Oh, really? Very well, Mr. Craig, the chicken salad shall stay. And I'll see to it personally that you will go instead."

With that threat hanging in the air, Cecilia Anderson stormed away, leaving Aunt Sophie, Harriet, and Gary behind in her wake.

Harriet put her arm around Aunt Sophie and patted her shoulder consolingly. "What a horrid woman! Don't you pay attention to a single word that old windbag says. The chicken salad is just fine. If Mildred had been here, I'm sure she would agree and would want the recipe. We could make it for our Methodist Sewing Circle next month!"

Aunt Sophie smiled at Harriet and blinked back a few tears. Clearly, Cecelia Anderson had upset her.

"Harriet," said Gary softly, "why don't you take Mrs. Johnson over there to get something cool to drink?"

Harriet brightened. "Yes, of course. Leave her to me, Gary. Now come along, Mrs. Johnson. You need something to calm your nerves. So do I. And let me tell you more about Mildred's orchids. You should see the new purple ones that are in bloom now! So lovely! Perhaps Mildred will send one up special for you and Madame President."

Harriet led Aunt Sophie to a table serving the pink champagne. Inwardly Gary was seething. Needing a moment to calm down, he left the Kennedy Garden and slipped inside the ground floor of the White House, walked through the round Diplomatic Reception Room, and entered the China Room where he could be alone for a few moments.

Gary stood in front of a glass wall case displaying dinner plates from past presidencies. He stared blankly at the plates trying to calm down. Slowly his anger cooled, and, as it did, his apprehensions began to rise.

He didn't regret standing up to Cecilia Anderson, not one bit. Harriet was right. She was an old windbag, and it was high time somebody around here put her in her place. He smiled imagining the entire White House staff applauding his actions. But Anderson's malicious threat against him still resonated in his ears. Could she say or do something to Ned or worse, to the President? Would he indeed be fired over this?

Gary shuddered. It was bad enough having your ex-wife fire you in the middle of breakfast. But if he got fired again, here at the White House of all places, he wasn't sure his ego could take it. Painfully Gary could clearly picture the smug look on Janet's face if that were to happen! Would it be on the national news? Would Jack Parish cover it?

Suddenly Gary felt a small hand take his own and grip it tightly. He looked down to see Abigail Johnson standing beside him.

"I'm five years old," announced Abigail.

Gary looked at the pretty blond-haired little girl and smiled. "That makes me about thirty five years older than you are," answered Gary.

Abigail nose wrinkled up. "That's old."

"It is," agreed Gary. "Today it feels very old, in fact."

While still holding Gary's hand tightly, Abigail turned her feet inward so that the tips of her black patent shoes touched. "You came to my house and talked to me and my tree. Can you do this?"

Without falling over, Gary successfully turned his feet inward with toes touching. "I can and I did. How is your tree?"

Abigail next turned her feet outward like a ballet dancer. "Okay. Can you do this?"

With difficulty, Gary turned his feet outwards. "There are some lovely trees outside of this house, too."

"Uh, huh. I'm going to live here," observed Abigail wistfully, letting go of Gary's hand so she could twirl around in a circle. "Do you live here?" she asked while spinning around.

"No, I just work here. But sometimes it feels like I live here." Gary reached into his pocket and pulled out some spearmint Lifesavers. He popped one in his mouth and offered the little girl one.

Abigail instantly stopped twirling and took a piece of candy. Then she pointed up to the china cabinet.

"Those are pretty!"

"They belonged to other presidents who once lived in the White House," answered Gary.

Abigail stepped up to the wall cabinet.

"My mommy is president. Are Mommy's dishes in there?"

Gary grinned at the child. "Not yet."

"I want to see them," ordered Abigail. She turned to Gary and raised both her arms, a gesture indicating she wanted him to pick her up. Touched by the child's request, he leaned over and gently lifted her in his arms. He held her carefully as they walked around the room. They looked inside the cases, and he read the names on the china plates. Suddenly Gary heard Martha's lilting voice.

"There you are, Abigail! I was worried you had climbed up a tree and we'd never find you!" Martha came and stood by them. The President looked lovely standing near the large oil painting of Mrs. Calvin Coolidge. The gold-framed portrait of the former First Lady seemed to be smiling down in approval at the female American president. Martha looked at Gary and Abigail with amusement, holding a small black cat in her hand.

"Abigail, your kitty has arrived."

Abigail wiggled out of Gary's arms and gleefully jumped down to the floor.

"Sheba!" exclaimed Abigail as she danced over to her mother with outstretched hands.

Martha handed the purring black ball of fur to her daughter.

Abigail held the kitten up for Gary to pet.

"We've already been introduced," said Gary.

Martha instructed her daughter to go back outside as there were photographers wanting a picture of her holding her kitty. Abigail dashed out of the room, leaving Gary and Martha alone.

"I see you've won my younger daughter's trust, Mr. Craig. You should be quite flattered. Not many men have so easily obtained her favor."

Gary felt himself flush with her compliment.

"Well, I do love children," he owned honestly.

"I can see that," observed the President with admiration. "Since the two of you have bonded, I should caution you to watch what you say around her. Abigail has photographic memory." Martha paused. "Her ability is not public knowledge, by the way. I would appreciate you keeping it to yourself."

"Absolutely," replied Gary at once, mentally reflecting on past conversations with Abigail in the China Room and in the backyard of the Johnson home. Gratefully he didn't remember saying anything that could come back to haunt him. Then another thought hit him. "I assume she reports what she overhears directly to her mother?"

"Every word," said Martha.

"I see," said Gary enlightened. "That's quite an effective undercover intelligence operation."

Martha chuckled. "Yes, isn't it? A deadly weapon given my daughter's affinity with the game of 'Hide and No Seek,' wouldn't you agree?"

Gary nodded his head. "Thanks for the warning."

Martha paused and glanced around the room. Compared to other rooms in the White House, this one was simply done with its cream walls and a large red rug covering the wood floors. The modest sized fireplace was framed by a white marble mantel with two female Grecian figurines. Overhead, there hung a lovely English regency cut-glass chandelier.

"I like this room," she reflected as she stepped towards one of the glass cases. She took a moment to study several plates on display there. "I wouldn't change a thing. Would you?"

Gary was flattered to be asked his opinion. "No, I would not."

She looked at Gary intrigued.

"What do you like about this room?"

For the first time, Gary noticed he wasn't feeling acutely embarrassed or mesmerized by this woman's presence. Instead, he felt quite at ease. "Well, I really like the red rug. Red's my favorite color, so I guess I'm a bit partial to red decor."

Martha looked pleased. "Aunt Sophie likes red, too. She'll be happy to know someone shares her sentiments." She paused for a moment, stepped back towards the Coolidge portrait, and sat down in one of the two high-back chairs placed there. She motioned for Gary to be seated, which he did promptly.

"I wanted to have a private talk with you, Mr. Craig. First of all, thank you for your contributions to the reception outside. It was splendid. Aunt Sophie truly appreciated your input, especially with your friend's orchids. They were real showstoppers. They helped make the South Lawn look like a fairyland!"

"I really didn't do that much," said Gary modestly, doing his best not to sound too thrilled by her praise.

"You are a talented man, Mr. Craig, and everyone in the White House appreciates your skills. I've noticed. The ushers, the chefs, the butlers, they all talk about you."

She noticed? Gary felt a warm wave of feelings. "Well," conceded Gary mildly, "I admit I do like putting things together."

Martha paused, leaned forward abruptly, and changed topics. "There is something else that I need to discuss with you. Something I'm afraid is quite awkward. I understand that there was a little spat outside in the Kennedy Garden a few minutes ago."

Gary swallowed hard, and the warm feelings vanished. This was it. Just as he predicted, Anderson had gone straight to Martha with her complaint. Despite the President's compliments on the reception, Gary feared his days at the White House were numbered.

"Uh, yes. There was a slight disagreement between Ms. Anderson and the First Lady."

Martha raised her eyebrows skeptically. "Disagreement. About?"

"Chicken salad," said Gary weakly.

Martha looked at Gary narrowly. "I see. Tell me, Mr. Craig, exactly what is your opinion of the social secretary?"

Gary didn't like being quizzed so closely by the new commander in chief. He didn't want to be openly critical of a White House staff member, even of someone as awful as Anderson. He would have to come up with something neutral to say.

"Ms. Anderson? Ms. Anderson is . . . I would say . . . she is one of the most forthright individuals I've ever met."

The President threw back her head and laughed out loud. Her dark green eyes glistened back at him with merriment.

"Spoken like a true politician! Forthright? In the ever-polite South, I believe that would translate into bulldozing." She grinned at him. "Well, I think the woman is the most arrogant and the rudest person I've ever met."

Gary's mouth fell open.

"You do?"

"I do," said Martha. "I've never liked her."

Gary gasped. "You haven't."

"No, I haven't," said Martha airily as she put her hand under her chin. "Which is why I just fired her."

Gary's mouth fell open again.

"You canned Anderson?" He couldn't help it that his voice sounded absolutely cheerful.

Martha leaned back in her chair, crossed her legs, and nonchalantly brushed her pink silk skirt. She gazed up at the ceiling with a reflective look on her face. "Yes, and I don't believe I've ever seen the chief usher look so utterly happy. I thought Mr. Morgan would hug me right then and there. I believe that reporter friend of yours, Mr. Parish, caught it all on tape. Perhaps he'll give you a copy." Martha then leveled her green gaze at Gary. "I have asked Ms. Anderson to pack her things and clear out her office by six o'clock this afternoon."

Bottles of leftover pink champagne would be flowing inside the White House kitchen tonight, thought Gary happily.

Martha then rested her elbow against her leg. She leveled a stare at Gary. "With Anderson gone, I'll need a new social secretary. Aunt Sophie and I just talked about it, and we want you to fill the position starting immediately."

To borrow one of Harriet's phrases, you could have knocked him over with a feather. Gary looked at the President in astonishment. She ignored him and kept chatting.

"I've spoken to Mr. Baldwin, of course, and while understandably he hates to lose you, he has agreed to your promotion. You'll have to hit the ground running, I afraid. Commerce is planning to renegotiate our trade deals with Canada and Mexico, and the Canadian prime minister and the president of Mexico will be here for talks in two weeks. I'll need working luncheons set up with both men right away. And I'd like to set up a new system for hosting small weekly dinner parties in the upstairs family residence for various members of Congress. I want to get to know members of both parties individually and become familiar with the needs and concerns of their constituents. And of course, there is the state dinner slated at the end of summer for the new German chancellor and his wife and the new German ambassador to the United Nations. You'll need to contact the office of our U.N. ambassador, Maurice Porter, on that. I actually know Maurice from my old UVA days. He went to school with President Taylor and me. Stan had him in the U.N. spot and I plan to keep him there. Start working with him and with Miller and the State Department on the dinner immediately. And then there is the Fourth of July. I really want something smashing for that holiday . . ."

Martha finally paused and looked at Gary, who was still in a state of shock.

"Mr. Craig, are you alright? You will agree to take the position, won't you?"

"Yes, of course, Madame President," said Gary dutifully.

"Excellent," declared Martha with pleasure. She stood and extended her hand. "For a moment there, I thought you might turn me down."

Who would ever turn her down? Certainly not Gary Craig! He managed to quickly get to his feet and shook her hand. "Thank you, Madame President. I promise to do my best to serve you and the country."

The President looked grateful. "I'm sure you will. Oh, I see the chief usher has arrived with the rest of our cats. Good, everyone else is here, too." Aunt Sophie, Jim Myers, General McKay, Secretary Miller, and Eliza arrived in the China Room at that moment.

"Welcome home!" said Myers smoothly, smiling broadly at Martha as he walked up beside her. He was looking great in another new suit, this one dark navy. Myers was also wearing a pink silk shirt, matching the President's outfit to a T. How disgusting.

"We've been looking for you. Come. Let me escort you to the residence."

"We are ready when you are, Madame President," added Miller proudly. He walked over and put his arm around Martha's shoulders. "You really wowed them out there, by the way!"

Martha blushed. "Thank you, David. However, I'm sure I'll need your help to keep them wowed."

"I doubt that. You'll do just fine!" encouraged Miller with a wink.

Morgan politely coughed, getting everyone's attention. The happy man, sans Anderson, stood in the doorway with a radiant smile on his face. He was holding two cat carriers, one in each hand. White fur poked out of the bright purple carrier while hungry yellow eyes gazed out of the wire window of the silver gray carrier. Standing behind Morgan was a tall handsome African American young man, dressed in a black suit. He was one of the distinguished White House butlers.

"Your pets, Madame President," announced the usher.

"Thank you, Mr. Morgan. My cat Victoria is in the purple carrier. She'll stay in my quarters. Is there a small kitchen upstairs?"

"Yes, Madame President."

"Oh, good, Cleo will live there. She likes to be near food at all times. Would you carry her upstairs for my aunt, Mr. Morgan?"

After firing Cecilia Anderson, Gary was pretty sure Morgan would be happy to carry the pet carriers all the way to Maryland. "Certainly," he replied. He then introduced the young man standing next to him. "Madame President, this is Dwight Cook, our new upstairs butler. He'll be handling the needs of your family. I'll make sure that he gets Miss Cleo squared away while I get Miss Victoria settled. And be sure to have some of Mr. Cook's famous hot chocolate!"

Mr. Cook smiled. "My mama's recipe. She swears by it!"

"I'll have a cup this evening," said Martha pleasantly.

Miller glanced quickly at his watch. "I have a phone call to make, but I'll join you all in a minute. Make me a cup, too, Mr. Cook."

Miller left, and Morgan and the young butler followed him, proudly bearing Cleo and Victoria in their plastic cages.

Aunt Sophie looked at Gary appreciatively. "Mr. Craig. I've invited your kind friend Harriet for a cup of tea. Josh and Abigail have already taken her upstairs to the residence. I hope you'll join us?"

The world as Gary knew it a few moments ago had vanished, and Gary found himself walking with President Johnson and the First Family through the Diplomatic Reception Room to the elevators leading up to the private family quarters on the second floor of the White House. He spoke not a word as Martha and Jim Myers discussed the agenda for the next morning and while Aunt Sophie and General McKay quietly discussed hiring a nanny for the children.

The elevator door shut, and Gary rode upstairs marveling, as if he were in a dream.

Chapter 11

The Blue Room

Friday, May 27

The social secretary's primary responsibility was to oversee White House special events. The job was huge, and Gary came to work each day feeling a bit overwhelmed. The White House was an enormous, complex place. The building itself consisted of six floors, seven staircases, three elevators, and 132 rooms. There were twenty-eight fireplaces with ornate mantels that were each decorated during holidays. White House staff had thirty-five bathrooms to keep clean and sixteen guest rooms to offer to important overnight visitors.

A piece of history that Martha loved about America's most famous house was the fact President Thomas Jefferson wrote the article for the newspaper that announced the competition for the building. The building, designed by the winner of the competition, James Hoban, was laid out to be 165 feet long and 85 feet wide. However, it was Adams, not Jefferson, who first lived in the house. Jefferson helped fill the house with furniture in the Louis XVI style. Interestingly, the house was not always white. Gray was the original color.

As Gary soon learned, no single branch of government claimed the White House as its own. In fact, it was a complex operation, and all major areas of the White House and the presidency were divided up. The Defense Department handled a complex phone system, with an estimated 50,000 calls per day coming into the White House. The motorcades, consisting of up to 27 cars, were handled by the army. The president's helicopter was managed by the marines while the air force operated the president's plane, an aircraft known to the world as Air Force One. (Gary was hopeful that someday he would get to ride on that!)

The National Park Service kept the White House grounds, which included the famous Rose Garden and Kennedy Garden. There were also a number of historic trees, all planted by previous presidents, that had to be cared for by the park gardeners. The National Park Service also oversaw the purchase or donation of any new furniture to the building. The Secret Service protected the President and her family, as well as providing security for outside appearances by the President.

The Mess, the exclusive cafeteria where workers from the administration in the West Wing took their meals, was run by the navy. (This cooking area was separate from the White House kitchen, where numerous chefs worked tirelessly to prepare meals for the First Family. This kitchen had five full-time chefs and a number of support staff.) Official state dinners, such as the one coming up for the Germans, was handled by the State Department. The social secretary, in conjunction with the ushers, had to work with all of these entities to smoothly run the day-to-day operation of the White House with its many important social events. This morning was no exception.

"The meeting will take place here Monday at 10:00 sharp. The Mexican president and President Johnson and their translators will talk privately from 10:00 until noon. A private luncheon for them with the First Family and the wife of the Mexican president will then follow at noon in the Family Dining Room."

Gary stood in the middle of the majestic Blue Room, one of the three historic staterooms at the center of the White House's main floor. The Blue Room was one of three large oval rooms in the executive mansion; the others were the Diplomatic Reception Room below on the ground floor and the Yellow Oval Room in the family residence above. The Blue Room décor was French-Empire style, a design adopted by President James Monroe who furnished the room with classic gold gilded settee and chairs. Seven of the original chairs were still there. Since the Clinton presidency, the room had been updated with rich yellow gold walls and lush dark blue draperies at the windows. Motifs of eagles, stars, and classical Greek figurines adorned this impressive stateroom.

Standing beside Gary was his assistant, Ryan Adams, a quiet competent man who had been Cecelia Anderson's assistant. Ryan actually had spent more time in White House service than Anderson had, having worked with three past presidents. Yet, unlike his former boss, Ryan did not seek the spotlight. He preferred to remain in the background. Right away, Gary found he got along well with Ryan. His new assistant was unpretentious, unassuming, and content to be a good worker bee. Ryan always had his trusty clipboard in hand, busily taking notes. He was never without it, meticulously making lists of things to do.

"Is President Johnson sure she wants to hold the meeting in the Blue

Room?" inquired Ryan softly. "The Green Room is much more intimate and is used more often for such meetings."

Gary shook his head confidently. "Yes, I'm sure. I raised the issue with the President this morning before her meeting with the secretary of state and the cabinet. She insists on using this room, saying it has the ambience she wants. She has important issues to discuss concerning the trade agreements. This room exudes importance, hopefully underscoring her feelings about the issues."

"Very good, sir," replied Ryan dutifully while writing it down.

"I've approved the luncheon menus you drafted. Give the chefs the green light. I understand the Mexican president's wife likes strawberries. Make sure there is something special with strawberries for dessert. Perhaps red should be the color theme of the table? We could use the Reagan red china."

"Agreed," said Ryan jotting another note. "I'll have the florists create an arrangement with bold red flowers."

"Sounds perfect," said Gary.

Gary and Ryan were interrupted as Aunt Sophie briskly entered the room accompanied by an unusual looking young woman. The young lady was quite pretty and looked to be in her late twenties. But unlike many sophisticated ladies working inside the White House, she was oddly dressed, wearing a broomstick skirt made of a gold Indian cotton fabric, a white peasant blouse, and a brown British tweed blazer. She carried a bulky tapestry bag over her shoulder that was large enough, Gary thought, to serve as an overnighter. Her thick curly hair was light brown, shoulder length, and quite out of control. She wore round black glasses and a very dark shade of red lipstick. On her feet, she wore dark brown Birkenstock sandals and thick white socks.

"There you are, Mr. Craig," said Aunt Sophie cheerfully. "I wanted you to meet Miss Jane Michaels, the children's new nanny. Jane, this is Gary Craig, the White House social secretary and his assistant, Mr. Ryan Adams."

"Hello," said Gary offering his hand in greeting. "Welcome to the White House." Ryan murmured a faint hello.

"Hello," said Jane with a clear English accent, firmly shaking their hands. "Pleasure to meet you both."

"Would you like to sit down?" asked Gary, pointing to one of the gilded chairs by the fireplace.

Miss Michaels shook her head. "Oh, no. I'd prefer to stand really. I was sitting all cramped in a plane last night. The overseas flights are most dreadful. They are so overcrowded these days, even in the business section. So many people chatting! It was quite impossible to sleep."

"I'm sorry to hear that. Well, I'm sure Mrs. Johnson and Mr. Morgan will get you settled in your room upstairs right away. I hope you will like it here. The White House is a very busy, very public place.

There is always something happening. But don't let it overwhelm you. You'll adjust soon enough. We all do. If you have any questions or needs, don't hesitate to call upon me or Mr. Adams or one of the chief ushers."

"How very kind you are," said Jane sincerely. She smiled, although looking very tired. She glanced momentarily around the majestic room. It was impressive.

"I better get down to the florist shop," said Ryan dutifully. "Miss Michaels, welcome to the White House!" He turned and promptly left the room.

Gary continued to study the young English woman. Despite her funny outfit, she seemed nice enough. And if Aunt Sophie had hired her, Gary trusted the nanny's references were impeccable.

"Tell me," asked Gary making conversation, "Have you been to the United States before?"

"Mmmm, yes. But just on holiday. This is my first assignment to actually live in the States. For the last five years, I've been working in Windsor, near London," answered Jane.

"Are you from London?" asked Gary with interest.

Jane shook her head and pushed her oversized glasses up the ridge of her nose. "I was born in Yorkshire, near the moors close to Harrogate. Most of my family lives abroad, but I have a brother that still lives and works in England. I'm here quite all on my own actually."

"Well, I don't think you'll get too homesick while working here. President Johnson and Aunt Sophie will make you feel right at home, and I'm sure you'll love the children," added Gary smiling, thinking happily of Eliza, Josh, and most of all, Abigail.

"I'm sure Jane will do a fine job," said Aunt Sophie confidently.

"Well, I do hope to be up to the task. I'm quite anxious to meet the children. Can I see them now?" asked Jane.

"I'm afraid they're out," replied Sophie apologetically.

A small body of black suddenly streaked across the room, right past Gary and Jane's ankles, and disappeared into the Red Room.

"However, there goes one of your other charges," added Gary dryly.

Jane's eyes widened. "Indeed!"

Aunt Sophie laughed softly. "That's Sheba, Abigail's kitty. I hope you aren't allergic to cats, Jane. We have three."

"Oh, no. I think they're splendid. I had a pet kitty when I was a little girl."

Aunt Sophie looked relieved. "Good. When we go upstairs, I'll introduce you to my cat, Cleo. She's the oldest and fattest and not as fast on her feet, a real sweetheart. Martha's cat, Victoria, has elected to stay in the West Wing mostly and shouldn't be a bother. But be warned. Sheba is a very free spirit . . ."

"With sharp claws," said Gary finishing the sentence. "May I recommend thick socks and a year's supply of band aids?"

"I understand perfectly," said Jane pushing her glasses again up her nose.

They were now joined by General McKay and Blaze Phillips who entered the Blue Room, having just finished with the cabinet meeting in the West Wing. Aunt Sophie made the formal introduction of Jane to McKay and Blaze.

"Nice to meet you," said Blaze happily with wide eyes and a smile on his face.

"Good afternoon, Miss Michaels," said McKay stiffly, looking and sounding very much like an old army general. He looked at her with a narrow, critical eye.

"Oh, hello, General," said Jane enthusiastically. "How wonderful to meet you at last. I understand I have you to thank for getting this position."

Gary looked at both of them in surprise. "Really?"

Aunt Sophie nodded and explained. ""General McKay and his wife lived in England years ago, and they were quite familiar with the fine agency representing Jane. When I expressed my desire for a true English nanny, the general was kind enough to use his connections to contact them!" Aunt Sophie beamed at Jane.

"Anything to help Mrs. Johnson," said McKay honestly, although his expression seemed to indicate some concern about the agency's selection.

"Well, General, I am most grateful," said Jane Michaels to McKay, "and I would genuinely like to shake your hand." She quickly stepped forward but en route stumbled on the red rug underneath and crashed right into the general. In falling, she reached out and grabbed his arm, stepping down quite hard on his right foot with her thick shoes.

"Ouch" cried McKay loudly, wincing in agony and jumping away backwards. The huge military man hopped around on his good foot, holding his injured one in the other.

"Oh, dear! How very clumsy of me," declared Jane. "These shoes are absolutely insufferable. I'm forever tripping about in them."

"Are you all right, General?" asked Aunt Sophie anxiously.

"Corn," muttered McKay through gritted teeth, his eyes watering.

"You poor man," said Aunt Sophie. "Corns can be so painful. I had one a few years ago and suffered severely with it."

"That will never do," declared Jane solemnly. "Especially for a military man like yourself. Really, how fortunate I should show up today. The British pride themselves on their feet, you know. What your foot needs is a good soak. Nothing better than twenty minutes in a warm bath of peppermint tea! It's an old family remedy. My mother swore by it. Luckily, I have some here right in my bag." Jane immediately opened her large carpetbag and began rummaging around.

McKay looked at her, aghast.

"Soak my foot in tea? Lord, woman, you must be joking!"

"Oh, no, sir, I'm perfectly serious. It will set you to rights in no time.

Wait a moment." She continued digging around in her handbag, spilling lipstick, pencils, a toothbrush, a green pillbox, and an opened bag of English crackers on the floor in the midst of her search.

McKay looked horrified at the prospect.

"Thank you, Miss Michaels, but no," insisted McKay firmly. "It's nothing really." He then tried to put his aching foot back down on the floor, but winced in pain once more.

Jane Michaels looked up at him triumphantly holding a flimsy tea bag in her hand.

"Got it! Now, General, surely you don't intend to hop around all afternoon with that foot unattended to!" In showing him the tea bag, she inadvertently dropped the handbag down on his other foot.

"Aaahh!" yelled McKay wincing.

"There you are, then. Just leave your feet to me." Jane knelt down and began gathering up her purse and fallen items off the floor.

"I'd rather not," complained McKay through clenched teeth.

"I think you should, General," urged Aunt Sophie, taking McKay firmly by the arm. "Come along with us upstairs. The children are out for the rest of the afternoon taping a special televised tour of the National Zoo. We'll be undisturbed. I'll make you a hot cup of coffee while Jane attends to your toes."

Outnumbered and outflanked, the former army general finally gave in and was led limping out of the Blue Room, hemmed in closely by Aunt Sophie and Jane. Gary and Blaze watched in amazement as they left.

"I don't believe it! General Charles McKay bagged by an English nanny!" exclaimed Blaze incredulously. "We should tell that Jack Parish. He could run a story on it! Did you see the look on McKay's face?"

Gary nodded with a smile. "The general was clearly out of his league. He is used to dealing with terrorists. Being commandeered by two strong women is a different matter altogether."

"Where's the nanny from anyway?" asked Blaze.

"Outside of London," replied Gary.

Blaze laughed merrily. "Well, move over, Mary Poppins. This girl's got you beat! Wait till Ned sees her!"

Gary chuckled. "Better yet, imagine Donald's response. Can you see him having lunch with Jane and the children?"

Blaze rolled his eyes. "I better have Ken order more sedatives."

"Right. We wouldn't want Donald to run out."

Blaze lowered his voice to a soft whisper. "You know, seriously, I think Ken does have some sort of medical thing going on. I overheard him talking on his cell the other day with somebody about the dangers of mixing medications. Wonder what that's all about?"

Gary sighed. "I don't know. Maybe Donald's nervousness is rubbing off on Ken. Being the President's personal attorney nowadays would give any good lawyer a nervous breakdown. Ready for lunch?"

"Always," said Blaze. "You can catch me up on things in North Carolina."

"Big news there," said Gary happily. "Harriet has had a third date with the new neighbor, a plumber named Bert."

"Has she cooked for him yet?" asked Blaze.

"Yes, she's had him for dinner."

"The man's a goner," predicted Blaze. "He'll propose immediately." His stomach growled in agreement.

Gary sighed. "Alright, alright! Let's go feed you. By the way, how are things going in the West Wing this week?" asked Gary as he and Blaze left the Blue Room for lunch, walking down the red-carpeted colonnade of the Cross Hall within the Entrance Hall leading towards the west staircase. Gary and Blaze walked beneath the soft yellow lights of two cut-glass chandeliers, passing the imposing portrait of President Eisenhower as they talked.

"Utterly stressful," said Blaze. "You've heard the reports in the news. North Korea is blustering again, formally denying rumors they have a nuclear weapon. We know otherwise. They'll either use it or sell it if we don't meet their demands for additional financial aid. That, of course, is what they really want, but people are worried they'll still sell the materials to other terrorist states. The reports in the PDB are rather frightening."

"The what?" asked Gary.

"You know, the President's Daily Brief."

"Right."

"The NRO has sent unmanned spy planes and satellites over to look, but we don't have solid evidence yet the weapon actually exists. We're trying to orchestrate a new SIOP for the situation. The DDO seemed quite worried today during our meeting."

"Do you realize," observed Gary sourly, "that since you've been working in the West Wing, you've begun speaking in code?"

Blaze looked at Gary apologetically. "Sorry. It is becoming a habit. NRO is the National Reconnaissance Office. They are a super secret bunch, part of the State Department, who handle satellite intel. SIOP is the code name for the nuclear war plan we had for years to deal with the former Soviet Union. We are creating new ones for current terrorist states. The DDO, of course, is the Deputy Director of Operations in the CIA, in charge of espionage."

"And to think my main worry this morning was to decide which crystal goblets to use for the luncheon with the Mexican president," replied Gary quietly. "You can have the West Wing, Blaze. I'll stay in the East Wing, thank you very much."

Blaze's stomach growled again. He shook his head in agreement. "Maybe I should put in for a transfer."

"What was President Johnson's reaction to the whole situation?" asked Gary curiously as they began walking down the west staircase. "How did she handle it?"

Blaze whistled. "Cool as a cucumber! She didn't blink an eye. The consensus was that we needed to begin a covert operation over there, perhaps getting a controlled asset on the ground. She gave the order for the 'finding' straight to Miller like she was ordering a burger and fries at McDonald's. No sweat! Miller is taking 'the finding' over to the Senate Intelligence Committee this afternoon. I think her decisiveness surprised most the cabinet members. I think they expected her to fall apart, you know, get all emotional or something."

Gary paused as they reached the bottom of the step. "I know we haven't known her for long, but something tells me there's more to this woman than meets the eye." Gary turned and faced his friend. He emphatically pointed his finger in the direction of the West Wing. "People over there have grossly underestimated her. You just watch, Blaze Phillips! Give her a little time to settle in to her new role, and there will be no stopping her!"

Chapter 12

The Green Room

Thursday June 2

"You've got to stop her!"

Gary slowly sipped his coffee while trying to appear calm. Emotions were riding high in the Green Room, and it was hard not to pick up on the tension in the air. Gary put down his cup and tried Harriet's tactic for handling any crisis. He picked up a silver plate and offered cookies.

Sitting across from Gary were three of the most powerful matriarchs in Washington society, respectable ladies not to be trifled with. Charlotte Elizabeth Donovan, Kate Yardley, and Vera Osborne were senior members of the illustrious White House Historical Association, the organization responsible for running the White House gift shop and, more importantly, for overseeing the preservation and presentation of the staterooms within the executive mansion. The three women were sitting in the Green Room, each handsomely attired in pastel silk suits with matching hats and handbags. Shoes, of course, were dyed to match. The leader of the group, Mrs. Donovan, added to her elegant ensemble a luxurious fur wrap draped loosely around her plump shoulders. Mrs. Yardley and Mrs. Osborne were furless, but both were fairly dripping in diamonds.

Mrs. Donovan quickly brushed the proffered plate of cookies aside. She would not be diverted.

"I will not be diverted," said Charlotte Donovan decisively with a sniff. She picked up a single piece of paper lying on her lap and waved it directly at Gary. "The First Family has always been given much leeway in modifications to the house's décor, but this list is beyond anything ever honored in the past. Again, Mr. Craig, we appeal to you to stop her!"

Mrs. Yardley and Mrs. Osborne said nothing but sat snugly beside their vociferous leader on the striped settee and nodded their heads in staunch unity.

Thankfully Gary was not alone in facing the all-female posse. Sitting next to him in rich green upholstered chairs were his loyal assistant, Ryan, and the chief usher, Mr. Morgan. Ryan sat with his clipboard in hand, taking notes as usual. Morgan sat gloomily with his arms crossed, staring over at the portrait of an elderly Benjamin Franklin hanging above a white marble mantel. The usher appeared to be appealing to Mr. Franklin for some assistance. Gary gently put down the cookie plate and held out his hand to Ryan, who promptly gave Gary a xerox copy of the White House memorandum that had Mrs. Donovan and her friends in such a snit.

"Well, then, Mrs. Donovan, exactly which of the requests are you most concerned about"

Mrs. Donovan put on a pair of multi-colored reading glasses and looked down at the paper with disdain.

"I'll start at the top. President Johnson wants to paint the Blue Room blue."

"Yes."

"But its walls are yellow."

"Were the walls ever blue?" asked Gary politely.

"Oh, yes," offered Mr. Morgan. "President Van Buren in 1837 began the Blue Room tradition, and blue fabrics covered the walls from 1902 till 1962 . . ."

"He didn't ask you," said Charlotte, cutting him off. "The point is the walls are creamy yellow now and have been for years. Next, look at item number three. President Johnson wants to put a piano in the Red Room! A piano in the Red Room! What in heaven's name for?"

Mrs. Donovan stared hotly at Gary and Morgan. Gary decided not to answer. Let the lady vent.

Mrs. Donovan continued. "There is a Steinway grand piano in the East Room. If she wants a concert or desires to play the piano herself, she can walk down the hall and pound away to her heart's content!"

"The East Room Steinway is an excellent instrument, "observed Mrs. Yardley. "It has been used in concerts many times."

"That's right!" echoed Mrs. Osborne timidly while leaning over and selecting a cookie.

"President Johnson doesn't play the piano herself," replied Gary bluntly. "She is a musician, but she plays the violin and the harp. She keeps her violin in her private office in the West Wing."

Mrs. Donavan raised a skeptical eyebrow.

"Well, if she is a violinist, then why on earth does she want a piano in the Red Room?"

Ryan cleared his throat and humbly offered the answer.

"Mrs. Donovan," said Ryan tentatively, "President Johnson's request to place a piano there has to do with history. You are aware, I'm sure, of President Johnson's affinity for Thomas Jefferson. Jefferson originally used the Red Room as a music room. President Johnson is simply trying to put it back the way Jefferson had it years ago."

It was a good answer and not one that Mrs. Donovan, a proud member of the Historical Association, could easily argue against. She of all people would not go against tradition. Adam's answer gave Mrs. Donovan a moment's pause.

"I see," she said frostily as she, too, finally reached for a cookie. Seeing her leader giving in to the refreshments, Mrs. Yardley followed suit and generously helped herself. Charlotte crunched thoughtfully and then looked down again at her paper.

"What about all the changes to the upstairs? The Historical Association is primarily concerned with stateroom preservation, but we feel it is appropriate to voice our concerns on the proposed changes to the upstairs residence. They will change some time-honored traditions of the house. For example, look at this. President Johnson is giving the Queen's Bedroom to her little girl to sleep in? Why, it's positively shocking."

Gary struggled to keep a straight face. The idea of Abigail sleeping in the majestic bedroom where queens from various countries had slept brought to mind a number of hilarious images, but he kept them to himself and answered Mrs. Donovan with the facts as he knew them.

"The move is a practical one," said Gary clearly. "Abigail is a very young child, and the President doesn't want her youngest daughter to sleep up on the third floor with the other children. President Johnson wants her youngest child on the same floor to keep an eye on her." It was a view shared by Aunt Sophie, Nanny Jane, the ushers, the upstairs maids, the downstairs maids, Ryan, the Secret Service, the Park Police, and rest of the White House staff as well, thought Gary to himself.

"The room is already pink!" added Morgan helpfully.

Charlotte Donovan looked narrowly at them both.

"I know what color the Queen's Room is. It's a good thing the child isn't a boy or you'd be painting that blue, too! Now, I see here," she rattled the paper at them again, "that President Johnson is planning to give the Lincoln Bedroom to that ragamuffin nanny, Miss Michaels! She cannot be serious! Important guests coming to the White House always stay in the Lincoln Bedroom. Where, pray tell, will those guests be staying in the future?"

"On the third floor," said Gary promptly. "There are plenty of nice rooms up there."

"Quite suitable rooms," agreed Mr. Morgan.

Charlotte Donovan huffed. "Am I to understand, Mr. Craig, that kings, presidents, and rulers of nations will be asked to sleep upstairs while the hired help will be sleeping in Lincoln's bed?"

Gary bit his lip. Time to mention one item not listed in the original memo. "Uh, no," he said hesitantly. "President Johnson will be sleeping in the Lincoln bed herself. She is having it moved to her bedroom today. In fact, we're swapping out the beds. The one currently in the President's bedroom is being moved down to the Lincoln bedroom for Miss Michaels' use."

Charlotte Donovan's eyes practically popped out of her head. Thank heavens, thought Gary, she was finally speechless.

Taking advantage of the rare moment, Kate Yardley bravely spoke up for the committee. "But what about the Lincoln bedroom sleepovers?" she asked aghast. "Lincoln Bedroom sleepovers are traditionally given to big campaign contributors as a reward for their generosity."

"There won't be any more sleepovers," said a female voice firmly. "I have made it clear to Mr. Craig and Mr. Morgan that the White House will no longer be used as a campaign contributor hotel."

All three women turned in astonishment. President Johnson was standing there with Abigail; both were dressed in matching floral dresses. Martha was holding Abigail's hand. Abigail was holding a coloring book and clear plastic box filled with crayons in her other hand.

"Madame President!" Charlotte Donovan gasped, now recovering her voice.

"Good morning," said the President cheerfully. Seeing Gary, Abigail quickly let go of her mother's hand and raced forward and plopped herself down on the floor directly at his feet to begin coloring. The three ladies immediately stood up as Martha approached them with an outstretched hand.

"Mrs. Donovan, Mrs. Yardley, Mrs. Osborne, I hope you don't mind my joining you this morning."

Mrs. Donovan, Mrs. Yardley, and Mrs. Osborne shook her heads and said they didn't mind at all.

"I've been looking forward to meeting all of you," said Martha candidly. "Your work at the White House is well known and much appreciated. In the brief time I have lived here, I'm astounded at the good condition of the White House. It is a tribute to your successful oversight."

"Why, thank you, Madame President," said Charlotte Donovan sincerely. "You are too kind." Kate Yardley and Vera Osborne smiled and thanked the President for her recognition.

Morgan quickly arose and gave his seat to Martha. She sat down and invited the party to do so. "I would have been here earlier, but I had a meeting in the West Wing that went way over the time allotted. There is a little problem in Haiti that needed my immediate attention."

"Of, course," said Charlotte understandably. Mrs. Yardley and Mrs. Osborne looked sympathetically at each other. One couldn't ignore Haiti.

Charlotte spoke up. "Madame President, I . . . we are quite honored for you to attend our meeting, but we wouldn't dream of imposing upon you, especially if you have pressing matters of state to attend to."

"No imposition," said Martha simply. She paused a moment while Mr. Morgan prepared her a cup of coffee and handed it to her, which she accepted gratefully. She took a sip and looked at the ladies intently. "I know my list of proposed changes is rather long, but you must know how passionately I feel about the history of this house. Knowing what pride you take in your work, I view this passion for history as something we have in common. So I hope you'll understand my desire to honor President Taylor's legacy and his wish to honor our early American heritage. I only want the house itself to reflect that ideal."

"Of course," said Charlotte in a new subdued voice. Mrs. Osborne and Mrs. Yardley's heads bobbed up and down.

"That is why I wanted to ask for your help."

"You want our help?" Charlotte sounded both surprised and flattered. Very flattered, in fact. Gary began to relax. The mood in the room was changing.

Martha leaned forward and took Charlotte's hand firmly in her own. "Absolutely. Who else is as qualified to oversee the project than you, Mrs. Donovan? Take the proposed changes to the Yellow Oval Room. Right now it's a bright yellow. But originally, in President John Adams' day, it was done in crimson. I understand there were elegant mahogany chairs and crimson damask sofas. I would like to see it restored to its original color. To do that, we need someone like you, Mrs. Donovan, with your skill and taste to properly accomplish the task. You would know, I assume, the best artisans, craftsmen, and historians to research and recreate the original motifs?"

"Why, certainly" said Charlotte with a sniff of assurance. "I know all the right people."

Martha smiled and squeezed Charlotte's hand. "I knew you would. Then I can count on you to head up the project, with Mrs. Yardley and Mrs. Osborne acting as your assistants? I'm afraid it's rather a big commitment."

"Of course!" cried Mrs. Donovan enthusiastically. "We would be delighted. I agree it will be a big job, but I assure you that together Vera and Kate and I can handle it!"

Mrs. Donovan turned to her associates, who whole-heartedly pledged their support to Martha.

Satisfied, Martha thanked them and arose. Everyone in the room also stood up. "Excellent. Would you ladies care to join me for a private lunch upstairs to further discuss the plans? There are many details to go over."

The women graciously accepted. President Johnson turned to Morgan, who was looking somewhat startled at the dramatic turn of the tide.

"Mr. Morgan, would you kindly show our guests upstairs to the Family Dining Room and tell the kitchen I'll have three guests for lunch?"

"Yes, Madame President!" With that, Mr. Morgan briskly led the women out of the Green Room, leaving Gary alone with Martha, Abigail, and Ryan.

"That was well done," observed Gary once the ladies were out of earshot.

"I thought so, too," said Martha. "But we aren't out of the woods yet."

Gary looked at Martha in surprise.

She continued. "Charlotte Donovan is no one's fool, Mr. Craig. She is one very smart and very powerful lady. My compliments to her were genuine. If I had been simply flattering her, she would have sensed it immediately and would have been insulted. No, Charlotte is the real McCoy, but she acquiesced to our scheme because she is smart and because she really cares about this old house and its history."

Martha paused a moment and smiled. "Mrs. Donovan is a woman that can be trusted. I believe she'll do a good job to create the changes I envision for the mansion."

"Are you going to tell them about changing the Monroe Room to a Jefferson Room anytime soon?" asked Gary.

"No, I think I'll wait a bit," said the President wisely. "They've had all the change they can handle for one day."

"Good idea. In the meantime, I'll put in the calls you requested to the White House warehouses to see what furniture pieces and paintings we can assemble from the late eighteenth century."

Gary paused and looked at Martha with a puzzled expression. "Weren't you wearing a navy blue suit this morning?"

Martha nodded with a grin. "Yes. How nice of you to notice! Mr. Adams sent me a last-minute e-mail and suggested I change into something more flowery. This old thing was last year's Easter dress. I hoped it sufficed."

"Perfect," said Ryan softly.

"Your timing and attention to detail were excellent as always," said Gary gratefully to his assistant.

Ryan looked positively embarrassed. "Just doing my duty. Now, if you don't mind, I'll run downstairs to the kitchen and speak with the chef about lunch. I think something rich in chocolate would be helpful in calming Mrs. Yardley's nerves."

After Ryan left, Martha asked Gary to sit down again.

"I'm afraid I have another huge favor to ask of you," she said apologetically. "It's seems I'm always asking favors of you. This one is really way over the top, not at all part of your job description, so please say no if you are not available."

She paused to take a sip of her coffee. "It seems that our nanny had a bad night last night. Aunt Sophie tells me that Jane has been having a terrible time sleeping. First it was jet lag. Now it's her sinuses and insomnia. Anyway, she was up half the night and is totally exhausted. I have a meeting with White House council this afternoon, right after I meet with the ladies upstairs. So I was wondering if Abigail could spend a little time with you while Nanny Jane takes a short nap? Normally, I would have Sophie or the children help out. But Sophie is out after lunch for the rest of the day, and the kids are visiting friends in Charlottesville. I know, I know, there are plenty of maids and butlers and Secret Service agents around, but, well, Abigail likes you. And I would be more comfortable knowing she was with you. Would you mind?"

"Here. You can color," added Abigail to the invitation, handing Gary a large purple crayon. "You can do this page with the bears. I don't like bears."

Gary looked at Martha for a moment, gazing into those green eyes of hers. How did she know? Did she sense that one of his life's greatest disappointments was not having a precious little daughter of his own?

"It's the best invitation I've had all week," said Gary happily to Abigail and the President of the United States. He sat down on the floor next to the child and took the crayon. He looked up at Martha. "I'd be more than happy to watch your daughter anytime."

"Thank you," she said gratefully, her eyes sparkling. "I knew I could count on you. I'll come back as soon as the meeting is over. Abigail, be good. Have fun, you two!"

She left, and Gary proceeded to color the bears purple as ordered. Abigail pulled out a yellow green crayon and began coloring a flock of flamingos with it.

"I think flamingos are pink," suggested Gary.

"My flamingos are green," said Abigail.

"Okay. So, what have you been doing today," asked Gary brightly.

"I had a picnic in Mommy's office," replied Abigail as she seriously worked on her flamingos.

"What did you eat?"

"I had a peanut butter sandwich and potato chips! I ate under Mommy's desk. My mommy has a big desk."

"She certainly does," agreed Gary.

"Lots of people came to Mommy's office. The big general came and told Mommy about nuclear weapons in North Korea. He said 'the listening post in Alice Springs was not sufficient, and the NSA wants to open a new one in Borneo.' He told Mommy 'I want a Black Ops team to be dropped in North Korea overnight, which will cost 20 million dollars in executive funds to pay for the mission.'" Abigail looked up a Gary. "What's a listening post?"

Gary stared at the little girl in amazement, remembering Martha's previous warning of the child's photographic memory and ability to tattle. The actual display of her remarkable ability and its ramifications in this political setting was quite unnerving.

"A listening post is a secret place where you can listen, kind of like your maple tree back home. Now, Abigail, I want you to promise me something, okay?"

Abigail nodded eagerly, reaching for a bright blue crayon to color the flamingo legs.

"I want you to promise me you won't tell anyone what you hear in Mommy's office or anywhere else in the White House. Tell no one except your Mommy or Aunt Sophie . . . and me. Okay?"

Abigail stopped coloring and looked up at Gary with a big infectious smile.

"Okay, Uncle Gary."

She continued coloring, blissfully unaware the effect of her new appellation was having on Gary.

"What color do you want me to do the trees?" asked Gary obediently.

"Orange," ordered Abigail.

Gary picked up the plastic box holding Abigail's assortment of crayons and was startled to discover an expensive tube of lipstick buried deep among the crayons.

"What's this?" he asked pulling out the lipstick.

"It's pretty," replied Abigail.

Gary frowned. "Yes, it is pretty. But where did you get it?"

"Eliza's purse," was the mumbled answer.

Gary shook his head sternly. "Abigail, hasn't your mother told you not to take lipsticks?"

Abigail ignored his question and began coloring the fluffy clouds a lovely shade of magenta. Gary opened the lipstick. It was a becoming shade of coral. He sighed and began coloring the trees.

Chapter 13

The Red Room

Wednesday, June 15

The conversion of Charlotte Donovan to Martha's camp turned the tide. The proud ladies of the White House Historical Association promptly lined up behind their beloved leader and joined Martha in her overhaul of the White House interior. And Charlotte wasn't kidding when she said she knew all the right people. The right people showed up in droves. Over the next two weeks, Donovan's army marched through the executive mansion — decorators, artists, carpenters, painters, antique dealers — offering their sage advice and assistance. Gary and the ushers followed along, taking notes and making arrangements for the restoration of each room. The task appealed to Gary and made his work enjoyable.

Today, however, was a miserable day.

Gary sat at his desk in his cramped second floor East Wing office and looked out his window. It had been pouring rain off and on for three days straight, and the local weatherman was predicting two more days of the same abysmal weather. The Washington D.C. skies were dark and gray, and the summer air was hot, humid and oppressive.

The gloomy weather matched Gary's mood, and the only thing that brought a brief smile to Gary's face this morning was watching two reporters and their cameraman dash from the northwest gatehouse across the wet front lawn to the North Portico steps. The reporters made it unscathed. The cameraman fell.

At least the White House itself shone steadily against the dark lowering skies, a symbol of hope amid a political world growing ever more skewed and skeptical. The sight perked Gary up. A soft knock at the doorway to Gary's office indicated Ryan had returned from Starbucks with a hot cup of Gary's favorite coffee.

"Your café mocha," said Ryan dutifully, handing Gary a tall steaming cup.

"God bless you," said Gary sincerely taking the drink. He was truly in need of a strong morning jolt. Sipping his coffee, Gary looked over his lengthening to-do list. "Are the invitations back from the White House calligraphers?" asked Gary.

"Yes," replied Ryan crisply, "but the final invitation list is not back from the State Department yet."

"Wonderful," said Gary glumly. "All we need is a delay in getting those invitations out. Put in a call to State, Ryan, and see if you can kindly, gracefully give them a shove?"

"Will do," said Ryan promptly, making a note on his clipboard and glancing down at his watch. "I'll call after our MPM. At ten-thirty."

Gary glanced up at Ryan with a puzzled look.

"MPM? Don't tell me Blaze has been teaching you to talk in code."

A rare smile appeared on Ryan's face.

"A Madame President Meeting," said Ryan grinning like a kid. "You know, special meetings for people up in arms over the President's new ideas."

Gary sympathetically nodded his head and took another sip of coffee.

"We seem to be having a lot of those lately. She is creating quite a stir."

"Indeed she is, sir," agreed Ryan tapping his pen nervously against the top of his clipboard.

"Why do they all come running to me?"

"They know she likes you, sir."

"Oh, I don't know about that. Her kids like me though. And so does the cat."

Gary reached down and petted the small black ball of fur curled up next to his computer monitor. Over the past few weeks, Gary and Sheba had come to a truce and an understanding. Gary was to pet the cat several times a day, and the cat was to no longer attack his unarmed ankles. The ball of fur stretched out and purred blissfully.

"Okay, which departments of government would President Johnson be stirring up this morning?" asked Gary with resignation.

"The Park Police of the National Park Service, the Secret Service uniformed division, and the SAIC."

"No more code! Spell it out."

"Special Agent in Charge with the Secret Service" answered Ryan.

"Ah," said Gary enjoying the warmth and aroma of his hot drink. "The three departments in charge of protecting the White House grounds and members of the First Family."

"Yes, sir, them. They got the list announcing President Johnson's changes for the grounds two days ago, and they called first thing yesterday morning in a tizzy. I made them wait a day. Hopefully tempers have cooled down now. There are too many attending to fit inside your office, sir, so I took the liberty of arranging the meeting in the Red Room. I also took the liberty of calling Mrs. Donovan yesterday afternoon and invited her to attend."

Gary didn't mind scheduling a meeting outside his office. It was about the size of a kitchen pantry. People seeing the White House on television really didn't grasp how small most of the rooms actually were. Offices in the East Wing were no exception.

Gary was pleased with Ryan's choice of the Red Room. Of the three public staterooms on the main floor, the Red Room was Gary's favorite, with the walls of warm crimson and elegant gold draperies at the windows. Gary worried that Martha would change this particular room back to yellow, the original color of the room during James Madison's presidency. It had been known as the "Yellow Drawing Room," the spot used by Dolly Madison in which she held her Wednesday night receptions. Happily, Martha planned to keep the room red. It would be a nice place to sit on this rainy, drab morning.

Gary was a bit surprised to hear about Mrs. Donovan's invitation.

"Why invite Charlotte?" said Gary sipping his coffee.

"Well, since she's switched sides, you must admit that she's become a powerful ally. I thought her presence might be persuasive."

"True," said Gary honestly. "Charlotte's presence won't hurt, as President Johnson is not available this morning to drop in and sway the unhappy male audience. And who knows? Maybe the portrait of Dolly Madison in the room will add an additional dose of feminine persuasion."

"Yes, sir," said Ryan hopefully. "A woman's touch often does the trick. Might even be calming. Judging from the tone of the phone calls yesterday, these men will definitely need some placating."

"Marvelous. Get me some Advil, Ryan. I will probably have a headache before lunch." Gary sighed, pulling out a copy of the memo that went out the day before and looked back again at the pouring rain. "President Johnson has people madder than hornets in changing so many things. They don't like it. They don't like it one bit! And I'm afraid she's got most of them quite worried . . ."

"We're quite worried," confessed Mr. Frank Peach candidly to Gary, as he stepped inside the Red Room. Mr. Peach was a senior officer of the National Park Service Park Police, which have the responsibility of the maintenance of the White House grounds. Mr. Peach was a tall, dark haired man in his late fifties, who normally was pleasant and easygoing.

Today, Mr. Peach's expression was frazzled, reminding Gary of Donald Hooper. The officer pulled out a wrinkled handkerchief and wiped his sweaty brow.

Two other men were standing with Mr. Peach in the Red Room. Mr. Leo Patterson, a distinguished looking African American, worked for the Secret Service uniformed division. Like D.C.'s metropolitan police, this branch of the Secret Service had the responsibility of protecting the White House and other federal administration buildings, such as the Old Executive Office Building next door.

Next to Mr. Patterson was agent Rick Pullman, a senior officer in the Secret Service and one of thirty-five special agents assigned to the First Family at the White House residence. In his early forties, the man was a poster image of a broad shouldered and solemn faced ex-marine. Agent Pullman, unlike Mr. Peach and Mr. Patterson, did not look the least bit worried. He looked annoyed.

Gary acknowledged the male trio by nodding his head in greeting. He then introduced his assistant and Mrs. Donovan, who had just arrived. Gary motioned for the group to sit down on surrounding chairs and two empire sofas. Gary's assistant chose to remain standing next to Gary. The three men calling the meeting appeared very tense and serious, but Mrs. Donovan remained pleasantly cheerful and seated herself next to a silver tea service that had been rolled into the formal stateroom on a cart. Gary sat back on one of the sofas and allowed Charlotte Donovan to gently take over. She welcomed the three gentlemen graciously and began pouring tea.

"Worried? I'm so sorry to hear that, Mr. Peach," said Mrs. Donovan. "What has you so concerned?" Gary smiled. As if she didn't know. Ryan had informed Gary this morning that he had briefed Charlotte on the situation in detail late yesterday afternoon via e-mail.

Mr. Peach politely took a cup of tea from Mrs. Donovan and took a sip.

"This memo she put out! We are stunned, simply stunned at all the projects President Johnson has planned for the grounds!" exclaimed Mr. Peach frantically. He put down his tea and then pulled out a folded piece of paper from his coat pocket and waved it excitedly at Gary. "Have you seen this?"

Gary opened his mouth to speak, but was interrupted.

"Why, of course he's seen it!" replied Mrs. Donovan serenely while opening the sugar bowl. She looked at Mr. Peach with an almost bored expression. "We've all seen it." She then smiled reassuringly at the park policeman who did not look very reassured. She continued.

"I completely understand your feelings, Frank. When President Johnson announced her plans for changing the interior of the White House, I was initially shocked and taken aback. Change is difficult, to be sure. But now I'm on board and you soon will be, too. You'll see. Actually, I envy you a bit. As wonderful as I think President Johnson's ideas are for the staterooms and residence, her ideas for the grounds are even more exciting. So, you mustn't let the improvements upset you so. Here. Have some sugar with your tea. It will settle your nerves."

Frank Peach begrudgingly allowed himself to be appeased by Charlotte's assurances and accepted several lumps of sugar for his tea. Gary looked at Ryan, and they exchanged a quick glance. Ryan had been right to invite Charlotte. She had deftly maneuvered Mr. Peach into their corner.

Mr. Patterson politely cleared his throat and spoke up next. "Mr. Craig, Mrs. Donovan, I — that is we — in the uniformed division — will of course follow the President's directives." He glanced quickly over at Mr. Peach with a sniff. "But there are issues of expense and security that need addressing and that may indeed delay the initiation of any such plans." Mr. Patterson gently took the list away from Frank and began to expound upon his concerns. "I refer to the three major construction projects on President Johnson's list. First is the restoration of the greenhouses. Is she planning to rebuild the greenhouses exactly as they were in early 1900? If so, that will add significantly to our security concerns."

"Agreed," said Agent Pullman darkly. "It would be unsafe. If President Johnson were to walk across the lawns and through the greenhouses at night, she would be an easy target. A marksman could reach her through clear glass walls. We cannot allow that to happen!"

Agent Pullman stared coldly at Gary and the group. Gary felt depressed. President Johnson really wanted the greenhouses, and Gary particularly liked the project. He would enjoy growing a few plants there himself. He didn't want Agent Pullman to nix the idea.

Charlotte, however, seemed completely unruffled by the agent's sour remarks. She totally ignored the Secret Serviceman's chilly stare and spoke lightheartedly to the male assembly.

"Gentlemen, gentlemen! What a bunch of big worrywarts you all are! President Johnson wouldn't dream of rebuilding the greenhouses without fully and adequately taking issues of security into the equation. No, no, no! Give the woman some credit. To specifically answer Mr. Patterson's question, President Johnson wants to have the greenhouse built on the west side of the house, south of the West Wing near her office and the swimming pool. I believe we have a map of the proposed site. Mr. Craig, would you care to show them the blueprints now?" She smiled confidently at Gary with a twinkle in her eye and shifted the conversation back over to him.

Gary promptly pulled out copies of a one page xeroxed map from a folder lying on his lap and passed them out to everyone in the room.

"We share and anticipated the same concerns for security. As you can see, the site of the new greenhouse will be on the southwest portion of the property. This site is surrounded by a number of existing trees. Those trees will provide natural shelter for the location. In addition, President Johnson consulted with scientists at NASA and has learned of a new glass material that is both bullet proof and resistant to explosives. The new greenhouses will be constructed with this specialized material to insure President Johnson's safety."

Agent Pullman clenched his jaw tightly and nodded his head in concession. "Fine. The glass solves one issue. But get us the specifications as soon as possible from NASA. I'm sure we'll want to conduct tests of our own before giving final approval." Gary turned to Ryan, and Ryan made note of it. Agent Pullman continued. "But that doesn't address the issue of mobility. How does she expect to get inside the greenhouse? Walk across the lawn alone in broad daylight? She'll be a sitting duck!"

Charlotte looked directly at the Secret Serviceman with a sparkle in her eye. "That's easy as pie, Agent Pullman. We'll simply build her an underground tunnel, to go along with the rest of the crazy tunnels running around this place."

Agent Pullman stared at Mrs. Donovan for several moments, inwardly fuming, his face turning a shade of red that nearly matched the walls. He got out of his chair and stood at attention. "Madame, you should not say such things in public. That will not do. Officially, there are no secret tunnels at the White House!" he declared sharply in firm denial.

Mrs. Donovan chuckled softly and handed the agent a cup and saucer. "Of course! Anything you say. And I'll remember that, Agent Pullman, the next time I'm in the basement of the Treasury Department. More tea?"

Agent Pullman curtly declined the tea and went over to stand stoically by the white mantle of the fireplace, to listen and to sulk at a safe distance.

Two down, thought Gary happily. One to go.

That exchange over, Mr. Patterson resumed his review of the outdoor plans. "Next is the rebuilding of the Jefferson Arch, which is a nice gesture and not too difficult. But who will pay for this one? Frank and I discussed it, and he feels the greenhouse can come out of his budget, as it can contribute directly to the flowers and plants used both inside and outside the house. But the arch doesn't fit into his budget or my own."

Mr. Patterson sat back and sipped his tea, apparently confident that he and he only had bested Gary and Charlotte. Gary bowed his head as if in contemplation. This was a lie. He already knew the answer, but Charlotte was having such fun. He would allow her the joy of volleying the project right back into Patterson's court.

"I'm so glad you bought that up, Leo. Here, have some lemon. I faced the exact dilemma with President Johnson's plans for the residence only last week. The White House Historical Association has sufficient funds to cover some of the expenses, but not all. Imagine my surprise when President Johnson let me in on a little secret . . ."

Charlotte gave Leo a well-timed pause. People in Washington liked nothing better than little secrets. She gave the men time to imagine what such a little secret might be. Clearly she captured their attention.

Charlotte leaned forward and spoke in a hushed whisper. The men leaned forward too. "This isn't to leave this room, Leo," which meant the entire staff of the uniformed division, the Secret Service detail, and all the White House staff would know all about it by suppertime, "but President Johnson told me in greatest confidence that her deceased husband was quite a wealthy man. Yes, he was a successful doctor and all that, but I mean he had money. Big money, Leo," Charlotte said, spacing those last three words out slowly and carefully for maximum effect. "His maternal grandmother was a DuPont and left the Johnson family a sizable fortune."

Charlotte sat back triumphantly and watched the news sink in.

Sink in, it did.

Mr. Patterson's and Mr. Peach's faces at first looked shocked, then contemplative, then rather pleased. Certain she was on solid ground, Charlotte proceeded with more juicy details. "Dr. Johnson left his wife and his children a substantial trust. The size of this fund is the secret, gentlemen, but let me assure you it will more than adequately meet our needs. Since the ideas of President Johnson exceed the usual allotments of your annual budgets, President Johnson has graciously offered to underwrite all the extra expenses for the Jefferson Arch and remodeling of the upstairs residence." Charlotte Donovan paused momentarily to demurely sip her tea, and then gently added, "And my husband and I will be making a rather hefty donation to these projects as well."

Leo Patterson raised his eyebrows in surprise. "How generous of you, Charlotte. But I don't understand," said Mr. Patterson obviously bemused. "President Johnson has said nothing of this, has given no indication whatsoever to anyone that she was such a wealthy woman!"

Charlotte smiled knowingly. "The really wealthy people rarely do."

Charlotte's revelation immediately altered the expression and demeanor of the group. At this, Gary was not surprised. In Washington, politics and money went together hand in hand. The two spelled power. Suddenly Martha was a woman who had plenty of both. Patterson and Peach exchanged a satisfied glance that told Gary they were both squarely on board.

Mr. Patterson softly coughed and cleared his throat once again.

"Ahem. Well, well, well, yes, I see. Uh, thank you so very much, Mrs. Donovan, for clarifying that particular point. This, of course, understandably changes things. Puts things in a different light, so to speak."

"So to speak," echoed Charlotte sweetly.

"Most definitely," agreed Mr. Peach now taking back the paper and looking down at the list. "Now, I don't want to sound — how shall I put this . . ." he looked up at the ceiling, ". . . indelicate? But will Madame President also be paying for the new State Banquet Hall underneath the outside Ellipse? That project, as you can certainly see, is the largest undertaking of the three, a bold and massive undertaking to be exact. It will be enormously costly."

Mr. Peach was referring to the grandest project on Martha's list, the construction of a large reception and formal state dining room to be built partially underground, beneath the large round grassy area known as the Ellipse on the South Lawn. Blueprints had the room constructed below ground, with shrubbery and plants and a fountain placed on the room's roof to maintain the illusion of the current grassy circle. Since the South Lawn slants downward toward the Mall, the underground room would have skylights and a staircase entrance from the south side. Access to the new room from inside the White House would be from two new underground walkways, one directly from the West Wing and the other extending from the staircase on the east side of the house on the ground floor.

"Indeed," said Mr. Patterson in full support. "This project is the most needed, the most practical, and the most expensive. The current State Dining Room is ridiculously small. As everyone knows, it severely limits the size of formal state dinners. Why, we can hardly fit two hundred guests in the existing space! Building a new State Dining Room, with additional kitchen area and storage, will greatly enhance special functions. If I'm not mistaken, I believe the new facility will hold up to five hundred at a seated dinner. A vast improvement, I'm sure you'll all agree?"

"Actually, we were thinking this space could serve an additional function," added Agent Pullman quite reluctantly. All the heads in the room promptly turned around to the Secret Service agent. "In the age of terrorism, we are more and more concerned about holding outdoor events in the Rose Garden. If Madame President goes through with all these plans, we'd like to suggest that this new space also function as an official conferencing and ceremonial area. Such a space will be easier to secure and monitor, more so than the current outdoor rose garden receptions. So, of the three projects, this was the one we definitely supported."

"Why, Agent Pullman. What a marvelous idea!" said Charlotte clapping her hands together. "Mr. Adams, write it down."

Ryan wrote it down.

Mr. Patterson coughed again. "But again, where will the money for this project come from? It will cost millions. Surely Madame President isn't going to underwrite the entire project herself, is she?" He looked at Gary and Charlotte expectantly.

"Ah, good question," observed Mrs. Donovan demurely. She turned and faced Gary and gave him a little wink that only he and Ryan could see. "I better let Mr. Craig explain. I believe he has all the details on the financing of this particular project."

Gary took a deep breath and motioned to his assistant. Ryan walked over to a nearby table and picked up a brown mailing envelope. He pulled out a square white marble tile and held it up for the men to see. "This project will be paid for by private donations, gentlemen. Madame President wants to partly bill the project as a memorial to American veterans, past and present. The floors of the two walkways will be covered with white marble tiles like this one with names of veterans inscribed upon them in gold lettering. You've probably seen such memorial walkways in gardens and on university campuses. Anyway, she plans to have the White House press secretary make the announcement and then have the project placed on the White House web page. The cost for each marker will be somewhat expensive, but she expects the American public will jump at the chance to help improve the White House and be a part of American history while honoring a loved one here at the president's house."

"The project will not receive any federal funding?" Mr. Peach asked incredulously.

"Not a penny," said Gary.

"No federal dollars?"

"Not a one," said Charlotte.

"She can't do that!" exclaimed Mr. Patterson in alarm. "Mr. Craig, you must tell her she can't do that!"

Mrs. Donovan quickly put down her cup and stood up. "Don't be silly, Leo. Why of course she can! Building memorials through private donations is done all the time and is very popular with veteran groups. Look what they did in Bedford, Virginia, building the D-Day Memorial. If little old Bedford, Virginia, can build a huge D-day Memorial back in the secluded hills of the Blue Ridge Mountains, then I think Madame President and the White House can surely raise enough money to build a new dining room on the South Lawn. Anyway, half the money will be raised through public donations."

"And the other half?" asked Leo skeptically.

Mrs. Donovan spoke quite softly. "The other half we already have."

The room went silent. The men in the room looked completely stunned.

"Someone gave half of a hundred million dollars?" Leo exclaimed taken aback.

"Yes," said Charlotte nonchalantly. "Mrs. Camilla Dawson has donated the first fifty million."

You could have heard a pin drop in the room.

Frank Peach spoke in a hushed whisper. "Camilla Dawson? The woman who just gave the Smithsonian twenty-five million dollars last year to underwrite a new exhibit on the First Ladies and caused such a brouhaha?"

Mrs. Donovan paused to gently wipe the side of her mouth with her napkin. "The very one."

"But Charlotte," said Leo with mounting anxiety, "won't that cause serious concerns about access and conflict of interest?"

Charlotte waved her hand in the air and shook her head. "Nonsense. Camilla, a dear friend of mine I'm happy to say, clearly stated she wants no such thing. The only thing she cares about is offering educational opportunities to young people, and a small portion of her contribution will go to help foster the White House internship program — which, I'm sure you'll all agree, needs some revamping, pardon the pun, after the last administration. Now, that should take care of everything on your list. Any more questions? No? I didn't think there would be. Then this meeting is adjourned."

Mrs. Donovan looked down at her watch, then abruptly turned to Ryan and asked him something about wallpaper for one of the upstairs bathrooms. Her stance indicated the meeting was indeed over, and the men in the room didn't seem to want to belabor the point. Mr. Peach and Mr. Patterson stood up. All three men shook hands with Gary and said they would be in touch. After the men left the room, Charlotte immediately turned back around to face Gary and smiled.

"My, my, wasn't that fun?" she said beaming, lightly pushing back the hair from her forehead. "Reminded me of my younger days when I played tennis."

"You must have been a terror on the court! I'm certainly glad you are on our side now, Charlotte," replied Gary candidly, putting his empty cup and saucer down on the teacart. "You brought them right around, although I think Mr. Patterson at the end was getting cold feet."

"Cold feet?" said Charlotte chuckling. "I think his feet were frozen!" Charlotte gathered her purse and gloves and then patted Gary confidently on the shoulder. "Don't worry about Leo. His bark is worse than his bite. And Frank shouldn't give you any more problems. Wherever Leo goes, Frank is sure to follow. However, just to make sure, I'll just have a little word on the side with Frank's wife, Gwen. She plays in my bridge club. And I'll have Camilla Dawson give both of them a personal call. That ought to smooth over any fragile male egos. Now, if you boys will excuse me, I must run along. I'm supposed to meet a very famous, frightfully expensive, and wonderfully handsome young designer upstairs in ten minutes. He's helping us with the new crimson draperies in the Oval Sitting Room. I'm so glad we changed the color from yellow to crimson. It makes the room so much warmer. Now, if you need any thing else, don't hesitate to call."

"Thank you, Charlotte. You're amazing," said Gary gratefully.

"I know," said Charlotte batting her eyelashes madly at Gary. "Ta ta, boys!" And with that, the grand lady of Washington society waved her hand and sailed out of the stateroom.

Gary collected his file while Ryan gathered up his clipboard and materials.

"One thing still bothers me," observed Gary plainly staring out the doorway after Mrs. Donovan.

"What's that, sir?"

"I have this funny feeling that had we given Mr. Patterson, Mr. Pullman, and Mr. Peach the exact same speech, the exact same information, they wouldn't have had the same reaction to us as they did to her."

"No, sir."

"Why is that, Ryan? Why do women have such an effect on men?"

"I don't know sir," said Ryan. "I gave up trying to understand that a long time ago. It's better just to accept it, sir."

"Very wise of you, Ryan."

"Thank you, sir." Ryan looked down at his watch. "We've finished a bit early. I need to go out and run a few errands. Would you like for me to bring you back some lunch?"

"No, thank you, Ryan. I have lunch plans."

Ryan gave Gary a surprised look but didn't quiz him for any further details.

"Will you take my stuff back to the office?"

Ryan nodded, then suddenly walked over to one of the windows and extracted a black ball of fur from a rich golden drapery and held it out at a safe distance. It hissed at him.

"Yes, sir. However, I better take this," he looked at the black kitten with distrust, "upstairs first. It followed you in here. I don't think it should be left unsupervised."

Ryan firmly took Sheba in one hand and Gary's files in the other and left the Red Room, heading upstairs via the Grand Staircase in the Entrance Hall. Gary went off in the opposite direction, heading for the West Wing. He walked down the stairs and then outside through the white-columned walkway beside the Rose Garden. There was finally a break in the rain, and a rare patch of blue appeared in the clouds above. Gary felt cheered as he knocked on the locked glass door leading out to the West Wing.

An African American guard who sat at a round table with a green marble top arose and came to the door. Gary flashed him the badge that hung around his neck, a security protocol, and the man smiled and unlocked the door.

"Morning, Mr. Craig."

"Morning, Sam," said Gary. "Looks like we're going to get some sunshine out of those clouds today."

"Sure does," agreed Sam heartily. "About time, too. My grass needs cutting."

Once inside, Gary paused and leaned his head inside the White House Press Room, which was just inside the doorway on the right. The room was the one where the daily White House press conferences were held, where Ned made announcements and fielded questions from reporters. Ned would be speaking that afternoon at 1:00, but the Press Room was not yet too crowded. Most of the reporters were literally out to lunch. Happily, Gary did find his friend Jack Parish inside, sitting in his seat, eating a thick peanut butter and banana sandwich and drinking a vanilla Coke.

"Ah, it's the White House concierge come to visit a poor White House hack! Sit down, Fred, and have a sandwich," said Jack offering half of his lunch to his friend.

Gary smiled and shook his head. "I believe I'll pass. How are you, Jack?"

Jack took a drink of Coke and leaned back lazily in his seat. "Bored as hell. Just waiting around for your man Ned to come out and throw us some tasty tidbits on what's happening in North Korea. Got any info on that score?"

Several reporters sitting nearby perked up, looked and leaned over slightly in Gary's direction, hoping for an inside word.

Gary shrugged his shoulders. "Sorry. Can't help you on politics. They don't tell me anything. You know my work is limited strictly to food and flowers."

The other reporters in the room quickly turned away and went back to eating or napping or talking on their cell phones.

Jack rolled his eyes and gave Gary a look of disbelief. Jack knew better but would play along. "Too bad. I could use a good story, followed by a nice long vacation. Speaking of vacations, my Aunt Dorothy sends her regards. She and her Texas posse decided to take their show on the road and are whooping it up on a holiday cruise in Alaska. Pity the poor fishermen."

Gary laughed. "Sounds like fun."

Jack smiled and then leaned over and spoke in a hushed whisper. "She sent me some newspaper clippings on those explosions at the compound where your terrorist friends lived. Nasty business. Seven bombs brought the whole place down burning over their heads. My thinking is that whoever hired them terminated their business, if you catch my drift. So, you're safe from the Stand Out, pal, but keep your eyes open and your doors locked."

Gary nodded his head and swallowed hard. "Thanks. Give my best to your auntie. My friend, Mildred, is also traveling abroad. She's doing some heavy duty international orchid buying. She's been in and out of the country for the past few months. Harriet says the Fed Ex man comes almost every week with packages of plants. On my next vacation to Greensboro, Mildred wants me to help her design a new extension onto her greenhouse."

"Lucky you. At least they feed you down there in North Carolina. By the way, how's the cook?" asked Jack finishing off his pitiful peanut butter sandwich.

"Harriet? Happy. She's seriously dating a plumber named Bert. Things seem to be going quite well. Harriet tells me Bert has gained ten pounds and she has a brand new white cast iron kitchen sink."

"Sounds like a match made in heaven."

Gary sighed. "Yeah. Personally I wouldn't know much about that."

Jack laughed out loud and took a final swallow of his Coke. "Neither do I, pal. Neither do I!"

Gary said goodbye and left the Press Room. Passing the gigantic guard stationed at the green desk, he quickly walked up a ramp to another locked door. He knocked on the door, which was opened by another blue suited uniformed Secret Service agent. Once cleared there, Gary then walked down a long hallway, past the large Cabinet Room on his left and then into an open area with a desk and a secretary, a short, plump, no nonsense African American woman named Fran.

Fran looked down at him severely through trifocal glasses and a mass of dreadlocks.

"You're late," she said.

You didn't mess with Fran.

"I was in a meeting," said Gary promptly and with an apologetic smile.

Fran frowned and pointed to a doorway next to her desk. "Go ahead. She's inside waiting."

Gary took a deep breath and opened to the door into the Oval Office. Martha was sitting at her oak desk. This desk was one of the prize possessions of the White House, a piece of furniture that was given to President Rutherford B. Hayes by Queen Victoria. Her namesake, Victoria the cat, was presently curled up in a ball on the desktop near the famous red phone. Martha was reading a thick file when Gary entered the Oval Office. Immediately she looked up and smiled.

"Oh, good. There you are." She closed the file and stood up. Victoria also arose, stretched up into an inverted U shape like a Halloween cat, and promptly jumped off the desk and dashed off underneath a nearby sofa. "It's been a long morning. Meetings and more meetings and now I've got the pleasure of reviewing some very technical specs and cost estimates on proposed unmanned drones from the air force. It's what the military refer to, I believe, as 'light reading' before lunch."

Gary winced. "I'd rather read my cookbooks. Time for you to take a break."

"Those seem harder and harder to come by these days," said Martha wearily. She smiled warmly and walked around the desk. "Well, are you ready?"

"Absolutely," said Gary sincerely.

She looked at Gary appreciatively. "Wish I could go, but I have a security briefing with Secretary Miller over lunch. Thank goodness for him. He's such a help with this crisis brewing in North Korea. The North Koreans threw out the U.N. inspectors again and have broken all treaties. South Korea is fuming. Lord knows what Japan and China and Russia will do. This meeting today is quite important." As if on cue, there was a subtle knock at the door. The door opened and Jim Myers stepped inside the Oval Office.

"Madame President, we're ready. Secretary Miller is in the Cabinet Room with the DCI, Secretary Trent, and the chairman of the Joint Chiefs of Staff." Jim stared at Gary with a startled look. "Afternoon, Mr. Craig. I wasn't expecting to see you here. Everything on schedule for the State Dinner?"

Regrettably Gary shook his head. "We're on schedule. The State Department is not."

Jim grinned and nodded his head in understanding. "Sounds like business as usual. No problem. I'll have a word with David and see if I can't get things moving along. Madame President?"

"On my way, Jim. Gary, she's back in my private office. Make sure she's back in the residence by two. If she misses her nap, she'll be in a foul mood before bedtime. And don't let her out of the van. No hiding and no seeking at McDonald's."

"Sure thing," said Gary.

After Martha left with Jim, Gary walked back through a small door and narrow hallway leading into the President's private office. There he found Jane Michaels sitting on a sofa, reading a book to Abigail. Seeing Gary, Abigail jumped down from the sofa and greeted Gary enthusiastically.

"Ready for lunch?" asked Gary happily.

"Yes," said Abigail clapping.

"She's been ready since breakfast," said Jane yawning and putting down Abigail's book.

"Another bad night?" asked Gary.

"Dreadful," said Jane yawning again. "I was up half the night!"

"Well, try to get a nap in while we're gone."

"I going to have a hamburger and French fries!" declared Abigail excitedly.

"As you wish," said Gary quoting *The Princess Bride*.

Jane looked at Gary skeptically. "How are you two going to pull this off? I daresay the Secret Service chaps might not like your little adventure."

"Ah, but there I have connections, Miss Michaels."

Gary motioned for Jane and Abigail to follow him. Jane stood up, picking up Abigail's book and a small paperback novel, and together they went back into the Oval Office. Waiting for them there were agents Clark and Lewis. Both men were standing at attention, wearing dark sunglasses and broad smiles.

"We have a black van waiting outside with the finest detail the Secret Service has to offer."

"I say," said Jane in awe. "Top secret covert operations."

"Exactly. We won't be allowed out of the van to eat, mind you, but we can picnic in the van with our detail. Agent Clark will man a lead car and agent Lewis will be manning our van. Sure you don't want to join us, Miss Michaels?"

"Tempting, Mr. Craig, but I really do need that nap. Actually I've just received a new novel in the mail. Some reading and a good lunch should put me to sleep!"

Gary glanced down at the paperback in her hands.

"Trevor Allyn? The Scottish spy novelist! He's great! I've read some of his stuff."

Jane raised her eyebrows and nodded. "You have? He is a most exciting author! I'm his most devoted fan really. Now, Abigail, be a good girl and mind Mr. Craig."

"Okay," said Abigail wiggling.

Gary took Abigail firmly by the hand and followed the agents out towards the waiting van.

"So, Abby, have you been coloring in Mommy's office today?"

"Uh-huh," said Abigail tapping her feet loudly on the new black and white marble hallway, an evidence of Charlotte Donovan's decorating flair. Abigail was wearing her shiny black patent leather shoes and white lace socks for the special occasion.

Tap. Tap. Tap.

"Did they talk about North Korea, sweetheart?" asked Gary as they got into the van. A bit of warm sun peeked out from behind the dark oppressive clouds and shone on the wet lawn, making the grass sparkle like it was covered in diamonds.

"Yes, Uncle Gary," said Abigail.

"Good. Let's get a Happy Meal and you can tell Uncle Gary all about it!"

Chapter 14

Poolside and The East Sitting Hall

Wednesday, June 22
The Fontainebleau Hilton, Miami Beach

He was burning up.

It was 4:30 in the afternoon, and the white Florida sun was beating down relentlessly overhead. He wiped his brow and bald head with a limp towel and then took the last swallow of his iced tea. He looked at the crumpled towel in his hand and tossed it down on the cement in disgust.

God, he was bored.

God . . .

He had stayed inside for most of the day as ordered, avoiding notice and the hot midday sun. He had slept and watched television. There was nothing else he could do given his situation and the heat. It was totally insane to be in Florida in the middle of June. But what choice did he have?

He got up and walked over to the edge of the enormous outdoor pool at the Fontainebleau Hotel, the largest pool he had ever seen. The sparkling aqua structure twisted and turned in a U-shape, with a rock island located in the center. Water gushed down over the rock upon a couple of swimmers playing underneath. The man stuck his toe in the pool. Cold. He jumped in, enjoying the shock of the chilly water upon his hot sweaty body. Thankfully the pool was not crowded. At this hour, families staying at the hotel were inside getting ready for dinner, and the young single tourists, sunburned to their satisfaction, were downing drinks at happy hour. Grateful to be alone, he dove underwater and swam around. He relaxed, swimming then floating for a while, feeling invigorated.

Refreshed he left the pool and went back to his lounge chair and dried off. He sat down and faithfully reapplied his sunscreen. To his dismay, his legs and body were disgustingly white. They would be, of course, after years of wearing dark suits and the heavy robes of the clergy. It was embarrassing. At least his body was in fairly good shape. He had purchased a treadmill a few years ago and had exercised and watched his diet carefully. If only he were staying in Miami longer! He would look pretty good in a Florida tan.

But there would be no staying and no going back now, not after what he had done.

He picked up the book he had brought down from his room, a mystery from Patricia Cornwell, and tried reading, but he found it difficult to concentrate. He restlessly put the book down on a small table next to his chair where he had placed his drink and his sunscreen and put his sunglasses back on. Then he lay flat on his back, closed his eyes, and tried to divert his mind by enjoying the hot rays warming his exposed skin. But it didn't work. He couldn't stop thinking about the horrible events that had led him to this place.

It began a year ago with the tragic death of his brother-in-law, killed in a horrible car accident. His little sister, his only family, was left a young widow with three small children. Then six months ago, she herself had fallen ill with a severe episode of dizziness. Her doctor did tests and discovered that she had a brain tumor — a slow growing, malignant, inoperable brain tumor. She was told chemotherapy and radiation was not an option. The doctor gave her one-year, maybe two years at best, to live.

What to do? She would die and he didn't have the means to support her three children. Desperate, he had gone to the presiding bishop of his church for help. But church leaders replied with their polite denial and deepest regrets. They expressed great empathy for him and his sister and would do what they could to assist in the short term with encouragement and prayers, but they could not commit to any long-term significant financial support to three children. How could they? Bishop Palmer's sister had married a Catholic and converted.

The refusal angered him, infuriated him, enraged him. How dare they turn him down? He had given his whole life to the church, to serving God, to serving others in their own suffering and trials. Now look what God had done for him and his sister in their hour of need!

It filled him with bitterness, a deep bitterness as destructive as his sister's tumor, slowing growing, slowly eating away and eroding his faith.

Desperate, Bishop Palmer then turned to the Catholic Church. He contacted the Vatican himself. But the Vatican promptly turned him down as well.

Then "they" showed up.

They appeared at his office one day, with no appointment, asking to see him. They seemed to know about everything. It made him shudder to imagine exactly how they knew. But they did know and came quietly with an offer. It was a horrible solution but a simple answer to his problems and crisis of faith, an answer that also offered a very great deal of money, and a failsafe plan of escape.

And all he had to do was commit murder.

He exhaled deeply and reached for the soggy towel to wipe the beads of sweat from his brow. He applied more sunscreen on his shining head, which was now turning red in the sun. He should have brought a hat down to the pool.

God, it was hot.

God . . .

Well, it was almost over now. He followed their orders and did what they asked, and soon he would be free to live a new life away from the church, away from America, away from everything. He would meet with them later tonight and get the rest of the money promised him. Then tomorrow he would fly to South America, where he had good friends and a place to stay. There was nothing to fear now. Everything had gone according to plan. Most importantly, his sister would have the best medical care money could buy and her children would be provided for.

However, he hadn't completely followed all instructions to the letter.

They had insisted that he not announce his resignation until he was out of the country, that they themselves would handle the announcement of his retirement and his move to South America. But one person he had to tell himself. Mrs. Witherspoon had been his private secretary for over twelve years, a faithful employee and dear friend. Society would view him as a miserable traitor, nothing more than a cold-blooded killer if they knew the truth, the horrible truth he must live with secretly for the rest of his mortal existence. But somehow he imagined that dear, sweet, loyal Mrs. Witherspoon would understand his plight, his wretched choice, and feel sorry for him.

His seared conscience fiercely held on to this one comforting thought, to the image of his devoted secretary believing in him no matter what. So he had left her a letter, placed in the bottom drawer of her desk where she hid her purse while working. Thinking her boss was gone on a week's vacation to Florida, Mrs. Witherspoon had taken a week of vacation herself, a visit to her sister in Arizona. She would not discover the letter till he was out of the country and the announcement of his decision to live and work abroad made public. But she would find the letter and know of his appreciation for her service and his regrets for resigning. He had even left her a generous check and a gift of an expensive gold bracelet. Why not? He certainly could afford it now.

Troubled by the unhappy combination of external heat and internal guilt, he got up again and went for another swim, this time spending a good twenty minutes in the pool. Then he got out and went straight to the outdoor bar and ordered a chilled margarita. His religious occupation hadn't allowed him to touch a drink of alcohol for years. But that barrier was gone now. Sobriety didn't matter anymore.

Armed with a drink for courage, he returned to his chair, only to find he was no longer alone. A group of five old women — retirees? — had arrived and were seated right next to him. Three ladies, dressed in bright Palm Beach attire, were sitting at a round table and were sipping strawberry daiquiris while setting up a well-worn board game of Scrabble. One of them was fiddling with a laptop computer. The oldest of the women was seated in a lounge chair next to them. She looked like quite a character. She was very petite lady wearing a bright purple and white flowered Hawaiian muumuu and matching purple cat eye sunglasses. On her nose was a white blob of sunscreen. She looked quite content and oblivious of him as she drank a long neck beer while reading the latest edition of *The National Enquirer*. In the chair right next to his was an attractive woman, one more suitable to his taste. She was tall, slim, graceful in appearance, wearing a classic black bathing suit and matching sheer black cover-up. She appeared relaxed, reading a Martha Grimes novel. She wore a wide-rimmed straw hat and dark sunglasses. She was also drinking a margarita.

He liked this gal. Giving her the once over again, he decided she was just his cup of tea. The only thing he didn't like about her was the blue tint of her gray hair. His mother had used blue rinse when she went gray. He hated it. But he guessed most women with graying hair resorted to it eventually. He noticed all the women in this small group had gray hair with a slight distinctive tint of blue.

He tentatively walked back to his chair and sat down. The woman in black smiled and spoke to him.

"Good afternoon," she said pleasantly.

"Afternoon."

She closed her book and put it down, then took a sip of her drink.

"It's terribly hot, isn't it?"

"Extremely! But I hear the weatherman is calling for thunderstorms later tonight. That should cool things down a bit."

"Thank heavens. I would pay money for some rain after a day like today!" She smiled again and sipped more of her margarita. Then she raised up her sunglasses and looked at his face intently.

"Pardon me for saying this. I know it's rather forward. But I noticed you just came out from the pool. Have you been outside very long in this heat? You look a bit, well, worn out," she said.

Her statement took him by surprise. Was his inner stress showing?

Frankly, he didn't know what to say.

"I'm sorry. I was just wondering if you were feeling all right. This sun is so hot, one can overdo it very easily," she added hastily.

His feelings? That question hit close to home. What was he feeling? Nothing, of course. He was doing his best to freeze all feelings, to be totally numb inside. For at this stage of the game, if he allowed himself the luxury of feelings, he would be overcome with remorse, self-loathing, and absolute terror. Feelings would be dangerous.

He looked at the lovely lady in black and lied. "Thank you for your concern, Madame. I assure you I'm feeling just fine. It's just the heat."

She smiled blandly at him, perhaps not convinced by his answer.

"Of course," she said speaking in a much lighter casual voice, "this heat is dreadful. We all must be out of our minds to be Miami in the middle of summer. It's like an oven out here." She fanned herself with one of her hands. "I, for one, would have preferred taking a vacation up in Cape May. I love New Jersey at this time of year. But it is Maddie's 70th birthday, and what Maddie wants, Maddie gets." She pointed at the funny little woman dressed in purple.

"Amen, sister," said Maddie lifting her beer high in the air. The old broad leaned forward, lifted her sunglasses, and gave him a wicked wink. "Elvis stayed here you know."

"So did Lucille Ball," added the lady dressed in lime green at the Scrabble table. "Maddie, put down that tabloid trash and come join us."

Maddie grimaced and shook her head resolutely. "No, Livvy. I want to drink my beer and read this article about Barbra Streisand. Did you know that Babs is going to get a nose job by the same doctor that did Michael Jackson? I don't think she should trust her honker to that surgeon."

Livvy rolled her eyes and huffed.

"Don't believe everything you read, Maddie. You're old enough to know that! Slim, do you want to play with us?"

The classy lady in black shook her head.

"No, thanks. I'd rather sit and talk with this nice gentleman."

"Alright. I'll just lose to Gerty on my own. Does the nice gentleman have a name?" She looked over at him with wide eyes and blinked.

"Jonathan," he said automatically, then stopped short of saying his last name. Too late he remembered the instructions of keeping a low profile until he left the country. He had used his real name in registering at the hotel, but he guessed he shouldn't be flaunting it out in public. He would improvise.

"Jonathan Smith."

The lady in lime continued chatting airily, pointing and making introductions. "Nice to meet you, Mr. Smith. I'm Olivia, that's Gertrude, the champion Scrabble player of the universe. That's Eileen with her wireless computer. She never goes anywhere without it. And you've met Madeleine and Slim. We're military widows who vacation together. Are you here on vacation, Mr. Smith, or are you here on business?"

"Both," said Jonathan.

"How nice," said Olivia. She paused a moment to put down her word tiles. "Here's my word, Gertrude. F-A-U-X. Why is it I always get that wretched X? Not too bad, though. Put down fourteen points for me, Eileen."

Eileen nodded and entered the points on her computer spreadsheet.

"Good play, Olivia," observed Eileen. "My turn."

"Do you come here often?" asked Olivia while sipping her strawberry drink.

"No," said Jonathan honestly. "This is my first and probably last trip to Miami."

"Oh, really?" asked Slim showing slight interest. "Why is that?"

Jonathan hesitated, not sure how much he should be telling absolute strangers. But then, what did it matter? They were just a bunch of old ladies, some of which, taking a hard look at Maddie sipping her Bud Light, had had too much to drink.

"I'm leaving the country tomorrow. I'm going to live abroad."

"How exciting!" said Olivia. "I've always wanted to live in France myself. I love the castles and the trains and French food. Eileen, you're taking too long. Hurry up and put down a word."

Eileen promptly obeyed and put down three tiles, playing off an S from another word. "F-I-L-S."

Maddie cackled out loud. "Are you girls playing in French today? I thought that it was illegal to use foreign words."

"It is!" said Livvy shrewdly. "But we are anyway. It's our best strategy to out score Gert. That's seven points for you, Eileen. Better luck next time. So, Mr. Smith, does your business take you out of the country? Did you get a transfer?"

"No," said Jonathan hesitantly. "I'm afraid that I've decided to retire. And I shall miss my work. Until recently, it was very fulfilling."

"I know just how you feel, Mr. Smith," said Olivia sincerely in response to his solemn demeanor. "Retiring can be both an exciting and a sad experience. One doesn't know what to do with all the free time at first; but trust me, you'll be busy soon enough, wondering how you ever had time to work! Gertrude, it's your turn. Make your move and kill us all."

Gertrude said nothing but calmly took all of her tiles and placed them down on the board, playing off of Livvy's U.

"Q-U-A-D-R-I-L-L-E. Let's see, that's nineteen for the word. Then I had a double word score, which makes it thirty-eight. And then I get fifty points for using all of my tiles that's eighty-eight points for me."

"I really hate playing this game with you," muttered Livvy. She put down a single vowel, an E, to make her next word. "BE. That's a big four points for me. Hurry up and win, Gertrude. So we can go to dinner."

"I'm hungry," announced Maggie loudly. "I want Tapas."

"We had Tapas last night," complained Eileen while typing scores into her laptop. "How about the Bleau View Restaurant tonight? They have Mediterranean food."

"It's my birthday," reminded Maddie in a testy voice. Old Maddie sounded very cross.

"Yes, dear. Calm down. It certainly is your birthday. And we shall eat at the Tapas restaurant again tonight as you wish," declared Slim assuringly. She turned to Jonathan. "Would you like to join us, Mr. Smith?"

The dinner invitation was very appealing, as was she.

But he could not. They were coming tonight. They would be expecting him. He would have to decline. He sighed. There would be time for socializing later. Better leave before he changed his mind.

He put down his drink, gathered his towel and book, and stood up.

"Thank you most kindly, but no. I'm afraid I already have plans for the evening. Enjoy your dinner, ladies, and happy birthday."

Quickly, before they could respond, Reverend Jonathan Palmer of Washington D.C. turned around and walked away.

Slim watched quietly as Mr. Palmer retreated inside the hotel. The women with her also watched him leave.

"You almost had him," observed Maddie bluntly. She put down her empty bottle of beer, a bottle that was actually filled with ginger ale.

"Almost isn't good enough," said Slim frowning.

"Well, at least we know he's leaving the country," said Olivia.

Slim nodded her head in frustration. "Unfortunately, we don't know where he is going."

"Yes, we do," said Maddie brightly. She pulled out a single white piece of paper folded up inside her *National Enquirer* magazine and handed it over to Slim. "He's going to San Paulo, Brazil, tomorrow at 6:00 A.M. It's a Delta Airlines flight. And tonight he's staying in room 477."

Slim opened the paper and examined it. It was a carbon copy of an airline itinerary. On the top of the paper was scribbled his hotel room number.

"Where in heavens name did you get this?" she asked in amazement.

Maddie folded her arms in satisfaction. "Easy. While you, Slim, were busy monitoring our fish splashing around in the pool and were getting your drink at the bar, and while you three little darlings had your backs turned while setting up that blasted board game, I took the opportunity to rifle through his stuff. He was using his airline ticket as a bookmark. And I took the extra key card to his room. It's nice that hotels routinely issue you two cards these days. It makes the job of breaking and entering so much easier." She flashed the card for all the women to see.

Slim looked at her friend in admiration.

"Madeleine, your skills as a pickpocket and common thief never cease to amaze me."

"Why, thank you, my dear," said Maddie with pleasure. "That's the nicest thing you ever said to me. I've earned a real drink now. I'm going to the bar to get a glass of champagne while you call this in. Oh, by the way, ladies, that was a bit risky with the wordplay, don't you think? Faux Fils? False Son? False Father? I'm surprised the dear reverend didn't cotton on to you naughty girls straight away. But I loved the quadrille thing, Gertrude. How appropriate! When the four of you get through dancing with Mr. Palmer, he'll not know what hit him!" She merrily got up and left for the bar.

Slim signaled for Eileen, who promptly came over and handed her a cell phone. In exchange, Slim handed Eileen the stolen paper.

"Hack into Delta Airlines," ordered Slim authoritatively. "Get a reservation for the seat next to his in first class. Bump someone off if you have to, but send whoever you bump some complimentary tickets, a gift from a grateful government for their trouble. We must have someone on board the same flight tomorrow morning."

"Will do," said Eileen promptly, as she returned to her laptop. Slim took the phone, dialed, and waited for a single tone and voice prompting.

"Code name Blue Hair," she said and then waited. "Let me speak to the major." Slim paused, waiting for another connection. She sat up and ran her fingers through her soft gray hair, tinged with a blue rinse like that of her companions. Olivia and Gertrude put away the Scrabble game, came over and sat on the edge of her lounge chair to await further orders. A deep male voice soon came online.

"We've made initial contact," reported Slim sharply to her CIA superior. "And it's not good. He's leaving the country tomorrow. He claims to be retiring and moving to Brazil. We're sending you the flight information now via internet. We will continue to monitor . . ."

☆   ☆   ☆

Thursday, June 23
The East Sitting Room

It was a scene of perfect domestic tranquility.

Well, sort of.

Members of the First Family were gathered together inside the East Sitting Hall that evening. Actually a wide hallway in the upstairs residence between the Queen's Bedroom and the Lincoln Bedroom, this private space served presidential families as a cozy sitting room. The room, painted a warm yellow, was filled with several pieces of dark mahogany furniture. Dominating the room was the majestic half circle east window, framed with rich lemon silk taffeta draperies that hung gracefully and caught the light of the cut-glass chandelier hanging overhead.

This evening Aunt Sophie sat quietly in her own antique rocker, working her daily crossword puzzle. One perk of living in the White House was the access to many national newspapers delivered daily. Members of the West Wing staff, having learned of Aunt Sophie's affinity for crossword puzzles, cut them out and had the butlers deliver them upstairs each evening. The plump Cleo was stretched out at her owner's feet fast asleep. The White House chefs were daily sending up treats for the first cat as well.

Nanny Jane sat in one of two overstuffed armchairs, reading her new Trevor Allyn spy novel and noisily crunching smoked almonds. She sat comfortably in her baggy linen black pants, white peasant blouse, and light blue crocheted scarf carelessly draped around her neck. Eliza was curled up on one end of the mahogany sofa underneath the window, painting her toenails and talking on her cell phone. Eliza was using a bold shade of lavender nail polish that Nanny Jane bequeathed her oldest charge. Josh was sitting at the other end of the sofa, hard at work winning a game of cards.

"Got any nines?"

Sitting on Gary's lap, Abigail held up her cards for review. Abigail sometimes got her sixes and nines mixed up. Gary studied the cards and shook his head, much to Abigail's delight.

"No!" said Abigail triumphantly to her brother. "Go fish!"

Josh huffed and picked up a card from off the mahogany breakfast table that stood in front of the sofa and large window.

"Got any fives?" asked the little girl. Abigail was partial to fives, since that was how old she was.

Josh moaned and handed over three cards. Abigail giggled and put four fives down in a pile on the table.

"I'm winning," she announced proudly pointing to the table. "I have more stacks than you do."

"I noticed," said Josh dryly.

"Abigail, don't gloat, dearest. There's a good girl," cautioned Nanny Jane as she slowly turned a page in her novel.

"How come she always wins?" complained Josh bitterly looking down at his hand.

"Girls often do," said Gary while holding out a long piece of blue yarn over the arm of his chair. Sheba, hunkering down in the middle of the Oriental rug, watched the yarn intensely, wiggled her backside back and forth in preparation, and then pounced.

"Well, it's not fair," said Josh handing over two more cards when Abigail asked for twos. It was her final move. Abigail won.

"It never is," said Gary.

"Eliza," said Jane looking up momentarily from her book, "you've been on that phone more than a half hour, love. Your mum doesn't want you to talk so long. Sign off and go tend to your brother."

"Alright," agreed Eliza without much resistance. "Katie, I've got to go. I'll call you tomorrow." Eliza said her goodbyes, put down her fingernail polish and cell phone, and got up from the sofa. "Come on, Josh. Let's go upstairs and play one of your end-of-the-world, shoot 'em up video games. You always beat me at those."

Josh's face instantly lit up.

"Cool!"

Josh and Eliza went over and gave Aunt Sophie a good night hug, then left the Sitting Hall to go upstairs to their third floor bedrooms. Gary moved over to the sofa that had been vacated by Eliza. Sheba, Gary's new shadow, moved with him, jumping up on the sofa and plopping herself down beside him. She started washing her paws.

"What's a ten-letter word that stands for arsonist, ending in a y?" asked Aunt Sophie staring at her puzzle.

Gary shrugged his shoulders. He wasn't very good at crossword puzzles. He didn't have a clue.

"Firebuggly?" he offered.

Aunt Sophie stared up at him narrowly through her red glasses.

"That's not a word," she said.

"Incendiary," replied Jane casually, chomping absentmindedly on her almonds.

Aunt Sophie looked up at her with surprise, then took her pencil and tried the word in her puzzle.

"That's it, Jane. Well done."

"How did you know that?" asked Gary with amazement while rubbing Sheba behind the ears. "Do you work crosswords too?"

Jane held up her book and laughed. "No, I'm afraid not. There was an arsonist in this book, in chapter three. He was a rather extraordinary fellow who set off a pair of bombs in Australia. The fires burnt two city buildings to the ground, but led to the arrest of several shady characters dealing in international arms trading. Such a good chase scene, too. Very thrilling." She looked up at the window dreamily. "Yes, he is quite an extraordinary fellow indeed."

Just then a weary Martha and General McKay entered the room. Abigail jumped up and ran to her mother, who scooped her daughter up in her arms and gave her a big hug.

"Hi, sweetheart," said Martha.

"Hi, Mommy. Uncle Gary is helping me play cards and Nanny Jane is reading a book about a man who blows up things."

Martha looked over at Gary with a big smile.

"That's nice, Abigail. Good evening, Uncle Gary!"

"Good evening, Madame President," said Gary standing up immediately. "Evening, General."

"Hello," said McKay gruffly. He looked very tired and very tense. He plopped down in a chair next to Aunt Sophie and stared out the window with a grim look on his face.

Martha stared at Gary inquisitively. "Did my family entrap you again, Mr. Craig?"

"No, Madame President. Not at all," said Gary honestly. "I love playing Go Fish, especially with little girls named Abigail."

The little girl looked up at Gary and beamed.

Auntie Sophie put down her paper and smiled lovingly at her niece.

"Don't blame the children, Martha. It's my fault. I asked Mr. Craig to come up just as he was leaving for home so we could go over a few items concerning the state dinner and the Fourth of July party. Plus I wanted to discuss more changes to the Oval Sitting Room. Charlotte Donovan wanted his opinion on fabric for the sofas. Abigail and Josh subsequently roped him into playing cards."

"Guess I'll have to further modify your job description, Mr. Craig, and start paying you overtime!" said Martha with amusement. She looked down at her daughter. "Did you have a good time?"

"I won," added Abigail proudly.

"Good for you, Abby," said Martha with pleasure as she set her daughter down. "And where is my son? Moping?"

"He's upstairs licking his wounds," explained Jane setting her book down on her lap and pushing her thick glasses back up her nose. "But no worries there. He and Eliza are playing video games. She'll lose on purpose to save his ego. She'll sort him out soon enough."

"Poor fellow," said the general turning his head and attention back to the group.

Martha smiled and nodded her head. She kicked off her pumps then went over and sat down in the chair by the table where Gary and Abigail had been playing cards. She tilted her head back and closed her eyes.

"Hard day?" asked Gary mildly while petting the black cat. Sheba had finished her bath and was snugly curled up in a ball next to Gary purring.

"You can't imagine," said Martha wearily. "But a good day. We made real progress on the North Korea front. Secretary Miller and I were able to broker a tentative agreement for more talks and negotiations. He'll fly out soon to handle the rest of the talks in person. I think with his help we'll be able to get the North Koreans to back down on their threats to escalate their nuclear weapons program, at least for a while. Long enough for us to make sure they don't sell the weapons they already have to terrorists. Iran is another issue. But we'll save that for another day." Martha sighed. "Secretary Miller is extraordinary. I'm very lucky Stan choose him for secretary of state. I couldn't have made it through today without him."

"I think, Madame President, you don't give yourself enough credit," observed the general. "You held your ground very well. Miller can make backroom deals, sure enough, but your straight talking got him there. Don't underestimate yourself, Madame President. You were brilliant."

"Thank you, General," said Martha sincerely with a blush. Then she sighed. "And then, of course, there was the news about Bishop Palmer."

Gary looked up startled. "The bishop at the National Cathedral? The one who was there the night President Taylor died?"

Martha nodded her head sadly. "Yes, it is. I'm afraid he's dead. The news just came over the wires into the Oval Office before we came up. It hasn't hit the media yet, but Ned is downstairs getting a briefing on the details. It will hit on the cable news channels shortly."

Jane looked up from her book intrigued.

'How shocking! Was it an accident?" she asked.

General McKay shook his head and grimaced. "Not sure yet. He drowned. He was vacationing down in Florida. Hotel workers found his body this morning floating face down in the pool."

"One should never swim alone," observed Aunt Sophie definitively. "The poor man! To have been with the President when he died, and now this!"

"Poor man indeed," echoed Jane quietly.

There was silence. The news of the bishop's death gave Gary a jolt. It brought back again vivid images of President Taylor's death, a mix of intense feelings of shock and sadness and loss. Suddenly he felt cold inside.

"This is horrible," said Gary bitterly. "First Eric, then President Taylor, and now Bishop Palmer. There have been just too many deaths."

There was another long pause, and Gary became acutely aware that all eyes were focused on him and on what he had just said.

"Yes, Mr. Craig, you are quite right," said the general tightly. "There have been far too many deaths."

Gary glanced uncomfortably over at the general, and McKay looked back at him with an intense stare, saying nothing more. What was the general thinking?

"Well, enough of work and seriousness for one night," declared Aunt Sophie brightly, changing the conversation while putting down her newspaper. "I think we should celebrate your success with the negotiations, Martha. How about some homemade cherry pie and vanilla ice cream to cheer us all up?"

"Yummy!" said Abigail clapping her hands.

"Sounds divine," said Martha. "Let's eat and talk about something else. I know! The new Jefferson Arch is coming along nicely. I heard this morning it will be completed before the end of July. Perhaps, Mr. Craig, you could give us more of the details and tell us how the fund raising is going for the new State Dining Room. Mrs. Donovan is doing a splendid job on getting the word out on that. Ned had several calls today on some big donations, some very wealthy people in Texas and California wanting to contribute. Abby, let's get into your pajamas and wash your hands first before eating our dessert." She stood up and took her youngest daughter by the hand. She cast a smile at Gary. "Don't go away! We'll be right back." Then she and Abigail left to go to the Queen's Bedroom.

Jane put down her book and got up from her chair.

"I'll pop upstairs and round up Eliza and Josh. They'll be wanting pie, too," she said. "Then, I'll come down to the kitchen to help you, Mrs. Johnson." With that, Jane promptly left the room.

"Excellent," said Aunt Sophie also rising from her chair. "I'll call Mr. Cook and see if we can get some of his famous hot chocolate. Abigail doesn't like hot chocolate, but the rest of us do. She can have lemonade instead. General, you'll join us?"

"Madame," said General McKay somberly. "I make it my policy never to turn down an offer of homemade pie. My dear departed wife, Isabelle, God rest her soul, used to bake pies for me on Sundays. It's a pleasure I'm afraid I haven't enjoyed in a very long time."

"Well, I hope Isabelle will approve of my baking. And you'll have some too, Mr. Craig?" asked Aunt Sophie pleasantly.

Gary hesitated. He certainly wanted to stay but feared he might be outstaying his welcome. Plus he wasn't sure if he should allow the lines between work and pleasure to become so blurred. The feelings of affection for this family were growing stronger by the week, and that was a bit unnerving. And, he reminded himself, he was a White House employee. He was here to do a job, not to socialize.

Gary shook his head and declined. "No, it's so late. I really should be going."

The look on the First Lady's face told Gary she wouldn't be taking no for an answer. "Don't be silly," argued Aunt Sophie. "Martha asked you to stay, and I simply won't let you leave on an empty stomach."

So much for sticking to virtuous principles. Gary immediately gave in the tempting offer. "Alright, I'll stay."

"Wonderful," said Aunt Sophie. "I'll get the plates and glasses out. When Jane comes back down, she can cut the pies while I'll dish up the ice cream."

"Give her a knife?" exclaimed General McKay in horror. "You'll do no such thing, woman. She'll trip and fall and kill someone before the night is through. As head of national security, I insist on slicing the pie myself. You'll give the nanny a big spoon and I'll pray she won't jab it into my eyes while she dishes up ice cream. Now, Mrs. Johnson, let's order up the chocolate milk! Lead the way to the kitchen, Madame."

Aunt Sophie laughed. "You're in charge, General." She stood and smiled at Gary.

"Mr. Craig, make yourself at home. We'll be back in a jiffy."

The general and Aunt Sophie left the room. Cleo got up, stretched, and followed them to the kitchen. Gary was left alone sitting on the sofa with his new four-legged friend, Sheba.

It was so quiet.

So very quiet.

He picked up the stack of playing cards and shuffled them carefully, thinking again about his job and his growing ties to the First Family. Over the past few weeks, he felt the deepest sense of satisfaction, a growing feeling of being truly needed and appreciated. It was wonderful. Yet part of him felt a bit frightened, an uneasy feeling of vulnerability as his heart opened up to these children. Such fear was natural, he told himself, after what he had been through. After the crushing disappointment of his failed marriage and not having a family of his own, he was hesitant to be so vulnerable again.

And speaking of vulnerability, what about her? Gary shuddered slightly and put the cards down.

It was best not to entertain thoughts about that at all. True, her green eyes were mesmerizing, her mind sharp, her face beautiful, her leadership strong, her motherhood magnificent. She was a dream come true. But she could never be his dream. No, they were just good friends. Better to keep it that way. Besides, he knew deep inside she would never consider anything else.

He turned from his thoughts and gazed out the large window, out at the peaceful city lights twinkling along the streets of the nation's capital. He looked down at pedestrians out walking in the night. A young couple was strolling hand in hand up Pennsylvania Avenue. A young man passed them, going in the other direction, riding a skateboard. An old lady with a large shopping bag walked behind the couple. A police car drove down the street. There was very little traffic.

Another long day was coming to a close.

Gary felt tired, yet he felt content.

He felt at home.

He looked down at the small black cat and rubbed the creature behind its ears again. Sheba turned her head up and yawned.

"What do you say, Sheba? How about a game of Go Fish?"

Chapter 15

The East Room

Monday, July 4

Another week passed, and Gary's schedule was crammed full of deadlines, meetings, luncheons, problems, crises, and (of course) inquisitive reporters. Gary arose early each day, ridiculously early in fact, to get to the East Wing and try to get ahead of the growing pile of papers on his desk. He was amazed that not once did he beat his assistant into the office. Ryan's door was always open, light on, the smell of coffee in the air, as Gary climbed up the narrow steps leading to his East Wing cubbyhole.

The news of Bishop Palmer's death made a splash in the newspapers and cable news talk shows. One reporter for the *Washington Post* sinisterly noted the three deaths all occurred in one year, than asked, was the Taylor presidency cursed? Doomed? Gary expected Jack Parish to cash in his chips and to call for the promised inside scoop. But no, not a peep out of Jack. It made Gary wonder just what did that crazy reporter consider a big news story anyway? Who knew? Gary certainly didn't.

When the morning of July 4 finally rolled around, Gary indulged himself and slept in late! He awoke that morning with the rare and glorious experience of sunlight pouring into his bedroom! It sure beat dragging himself out of bed at 4:30 in the morning in the dark.

Gary lazily opened his eyes to a brightly-lit room. He lay comfortably nestled inside his overstuffed featherbed and thick down comforter, enjoying the luxury of the moment and the surroundings. His room was simply done, with stark white walls, burnished silver lamps, and white pine furniture. His massive sleigh bed was piled high with cozy pillows in a variety of white silk and quilted fabrics. The one splash of color in the room was a large Georgia O'Keefe print of a teal poppy hanging behind his headboard. The only other decorative piece in the room was a marble water fountain mounted on the wall, with a sculpted white lion in the center. The gentle, relaxing sound of falling water helped Gary fall sleep at night.

Gary yawned and reached for the remote on his night stand. He aimed it at the TV opposite the bed. He turned on the television and began scanning the channels for the morning news. Working at the White House required one to stay abreast of current events. Gary was happy to see that the situation in North Korea was indeed calming down, the stock market was going up, CBS ratings were down, Martha's approval ratings were up, and a new Johnny Depp movie was opening that weekend.

Gary continued surfing the channels when his phone rang. It was Harriet.

"Good morning, sleepy head. Happy Fourth!"

"Good morning, Harriet," said Gary pleasantly. "How are you?"

"Wonderful!" exclaimed Harriet. "Are you enjoying your day off?"

"It's not really off. I have to go in later, but yes, I'm enjoying it immensely," said Gary yawning again and stretching. He finally sat up in bed. "I could get used to this. Any special holiday plans for today?"

"Oh, yes," said Harriet brightly. Gary could hear kitchen sounds rattling in the background, clinks and clanks of pots, pans, and dishes. "Bert and I are making a picnic lunch and driving down to Seagrove to do some pottery shopping. I want to get some more of the blue dripped pieces from Holly Hill."

"Sounds awesome. Will you pick me up some apple cookers," requested Gary. "And see if they can ship them directly here. I'll pay you back."

"Will do. I'll also send you something from O'Quinn Pottery. I know you like their stuff, too. They have a new green glaze I think you'll like. So, what are you going to do to celebrate today?" asked Harriet.

"This morning I'm going to putter around my back porch container garden. You should see all the stuff I've been able to grow in pots! Then Blaze and I are going to a movie this afternoon and then to the party at the White House tonight."

Harriet squealed with delight. "A White House party! How exciting! Anyone famous going to be there?"

Gary laughed. "No, it's not that kind of party, Harriet. Nothing like a state dinner or congressional ball or the reception you attended! This is something rather fun that Madame President planned and I got to execute. The President wanted to do something special for everyone who works at the White House, both the East and West Wings. So, she is putting on a White House barbeque for all employees and their families. The White House chefs got to make my famous barbecue, of course."

"Oh, Gary, what fun! Tell me more," gushed Harriet breathlessly.

"Buffet tables will be set up in the State Dining Room, as well as tables and chairs throughout the main floor hallway, Entrance Hall, and East Room. For the children, there will be game tables set up in the Diplomatic Reception Room downstairs and some Disney movies showing in the East Wing Theatre. There will be a dance afterwards."

"A dance! You're such a good dancer, too," observed Harriet proudly. "Maybe I'll get to see you on television!"

"No, no!" said Gary laughing. "No press allowed, although I did cave in and invite my friend, Jack Parish, to attend, with strict orders to leave his weird cameraman at home. When Jack heard we had Brooks and Dunn and their band providing the entertainment, he wouldn't leave me alone until I invited him."

"That was very kind of you, Gary. I like Mr. Parish. He's a nice man."

"I'll tell him you said that," said Gary yawning. "He'll be thrilled. He thinks you're pretty swell, too. What's Mildred doing today?"

"She's out in the greenhouse working on a big order. She got back a few days ago from her last trip. She's still jet lagged, poor thing. She's glad to be home for a while and working with her orchids again. Gary, you should see the flowers she brought home this trip! Oh, they are just gorgeous. She brought some very large red ones from Africa and South America and Hawaii. And guess what? She has some delicious whites from Hawaii that are fragrant, and some deep purple ones from South America that will simply knock your socks off! She plans to cross a few and create some new varieties. The word is out, and already she is getting orders."

"Tell her to put me down for a white. And tell her to call me on my cell phone when she finishes her work. I'd like to say hello and wish her a happy Fourth."

"Okay. Goodness gracious, look at the time! Got to run, Gary dear. Have fun at the dance tonight! Goodbye!"

Gary said goodbye to Harriet and hung up. He rubbed the sleep out of his baggy eyes, got out of bed, and headed for the bathroom. Gary indulged himself in a long, hot, steamy shower, overdoing it a bit with lather and off-key singing. After drying and dressing, he fixed himself a southwestern omelet and read *The Washington Post* and *The Washington Times* while eating his breakfast. It was 10:30 when he finally got outside, pulled on his garden gloves, and began weeding and pruning the herbs growing in his terra cotta pots.

He worked outside for about an hour and a half when he heard the front doorbell ring. Gary pulled off his dirty gloves and went inside to answer the door. He looked through the peephole and saw a familiar white head of hair and dazzling white smile on the other side. The owner of both was waving a mini American flag. Gary threw open the door in greeting.

"Jack! This is a surprise! What on earth are you doing out here?"

Jack smiled broadly. "I was in the neighborhood and thought I would drop by and see how the other half lives."

Gary eyed his friend skeptically. "In the neighborhood?"

Jack raised an eyebrow and feigned shock. "You doubt me?"

"Always," replied Gary smoothly, opening the door wider and inviting his friend inside.

"Good man," said Jack nodding approval. "You've finally caught on. Actually, I really was in the neighborhood. Two colleagues of mine just got assigned a six-month stint in London (God save the queen). I volunteered to drive them out to the airport. Got anything to wet my whistle? Beer?"

Gary shook his head emphatically. "Sorry. I'm on the wagon."

Jack's eyes widened. "I didn't know you fell off."

"I haven't yet and don't plan to ever," said Gary somberly. "After watching two uncles and a best friend in college struggle with booze, I decided never to go along for the ride. I'm afraid the strongest thing I have is diet Coke."

Jack shrugged. "Okay, Leroy. Bring it on."

Gary laughed and directed Jack to the outdoor patio. He got the soft drink ready and gave it to his friend. Jack plopped himself down on a black iron chaise lounge and propped his feet up.

"So, are you and your sidekick what's-his-name ready for the shindig tonight?" asked Jack lazily.

"Ryan. His name is Ryan, and yes, we are as ready as we'll ever be. We worked demons this week." Kneeling in front of a pot of chocolate peppermint, Gary sat back momentarily. "I feel a bit guilty though. I really should be in the office this morning, but Ryan absolutely insisted that I take the day off and volunteered to come in and oversee the last minute prep all day by himself. And he's right. Everything essentially is done. Ryan is so dependable. I couldn't ask for a better assistant."

"Lucky you," said Jack putting on his sunglasses. "That's what I need, a nice quiet assistant."

Gary laughed. "That shouldn't be too hard to find. Anybody working for you wouldn't get a word in edgewise!"

"You got that right, Fred." Jack folded his arms across his chest and leaned his face up towards the warm morning sun and sighed deeply. "My wicked Aunt Dotty overnighted me a care package for this party. Wait till you see! First of all she sent me some authentic, honest-to-God cowboy boots. They are made of black leather with these awful red and turquoise butterflies painted on the front. They have sharp pointed toes. I can barely walk in the things, much less dance in them! Then she sends me this black leather belt with the name 'Jack-Bob' tooled across the back. I think all men in Texas have names with Bob and Joe tacked on at the end. And then she sends me a brand new white cotton shirt so full of starch that I swear it can stand up on its on. I hope I'll be able to move the arms forward enough to drive into the city."

Jack then clasped his hand behind his head. "God, I'm tired. I'm worried I'm getting too old for this gig. I mean, man, the ups and downs of the last four months have drained me dry."

Gary silently nodded his head in agreement, as he began pulling off dead leaves from a large lime-scented geranium.

Jack took a swig of Coke and continued. "First of all, the death of Taylor was totally surreal. I've never covered anything like it and doubt I will again in my lifetime. Oldtimers at the network have been reliving the Kennedy assassination, and it's been a downer at the news station, let me tell you! Then Madame President's move into the White House on Mother's Day was a real trip. That was an up — draining but an up all the same. And then this funeral for Palmer, was that weird or what?"

Gary stopped pruning and looked at his reporter friend inquisitively. "Weird? In what way?"

Jack took another sip of Coke and sat straight up. "Well, Madame P. herself drops everything, including her touch-and-go North Korea situation to attend the funeral of this local priest, who has no real political connections whatsoever. Why? What was Palmer to her, to anyone else for that matter?"

"I guess she went because of the connection to President Taylor. Remember, Reverend Palmer was with him the night he died."

Jack looked at Gary narrowly. "Okay. I'll buy that. But then Jim Myers shows up proudly escorting Madame President like the prim and proper peacock that he is at this high-profile funeral. And wasn't he all tender and attentive? Did you see how he took her arm as they walked into the church and how snugly he sat beside her during the service, how he carefully put his arm around her waist when they were consoling the poor pastor's sister and children? What in blue blazes is going on there?"

"Nothing is going on there!" snapped Gary quickly, forcefully clipping back a potted rosebush's stem as he spoke.

Jack looked at Gary with a slight grin on his face. "Touchy. My, my! Are we a bit jealous or do you always manhandle your plants in that fashion?"

Gary put down his pruning shears and picked up some potting soil and shoved it forcefully into the pot. "Jealous? Me? Don't be ridiculous. Madame President and I have a strictly business relationship. We are just good friends."

"Oh, sure. Anything you say. So, if you two are "just friends" and if everything is above board, why on earth do you babysit her little kid all the time? I mean, every time I turn around, I see that little blond imp at your feet, coloring or tap dancing or jumping rope."

Gary huffed irritably. "I don't keep Abigail all the time. I keep a friendly eye on her, an hour or two here or there, in the afternoon, when Nanny Jane has had a bad night and can't sleep. Nanny Jane gets insomnia pretty bad. Since coming to America, she's up and roaming the halls late at night. I think her sinuses are bothering her, too. Aunt Sophie or Eliza insists that Jane take an afternoon nap, a 'kip' I think she calls it, after she's had a bad night. So, when Aunt Sophie or Eliza are busy, I volunteer and let Abby stay in my office."

Jack smiled wickedly. "Well, take my advice, chum, hurry up and cast a more friendly eye on her mother. Jim Myers certainly has."

Gary rolled his eyes and began angrily pruning the innocent potted white rose bush again in earnest. "Jim Myers casts his eye on lots of women, and lots of women have their eyes on him, too. The White House interns, secretaries, and female reporters fall at his feet daily. Enough on Myers! It's too depressing. Let's get back to something more cheerful, like the funeral. Was there anything else that happened to make you say it was weird?"

"Now that you mention it, yeah! Very odd! It was right after the funeral, when everyone was talking to Palmer's family. This little old lady comes up to me and wipes her eyes and blows her nose and starts rattling about his holiness. Said she was his devoted secretary. She said, 'I know you, you're that reporter on television.' A brilliant deduction since I was holding a microphone and standing beside Al, my cameraman! Anyway, the old bird then rambles on something about what a shame it was that the benighted bishop should die just when he decided to retire and leave the country."

Gary looked up at his friend in astonishment.

"Retire? The report we got said Palmer was on vacation in Florida."

"Exactly," replied Jack smugly. "That's the story we got as well, that Palmer was down South, having some fun in the sun. I didn't think men of the cloth were allowed to do that. If so, maybe I should sign up. Anyway, the old bat probably got her P's and Q's all mixed up, but what's interesting is the fact that she backed her story up by showing me the gold bracelet the old man bought her as a goodbye gift. I'm no jeweler, Mack, but I can tell you our preacher man didn't buy that trinket at a local Wal-Mart."

Gary got up and moved over to a large potted bush of pineapple sage that badly needed some watering.

"That is strange," he mused. "So why do people think he was vacationing?"

"Well, I was interested enough to do a little checking," said Jack confidentially. "But it didn't pan out. It seems that Palmer told everyone — his neighbors, his underlings at the church, his newspaper boy, his doctor, his dentist, his yard man — he told all of them that he was going to Florida for a bit of R&R. Like I said, the old gal probably isn't playing with a full deck. Come to think of it, she didn't look like she had a full deck to begin with. And who knows? Maybe his holiness was trying to impress her with expensive gifts. Not the first time that's been done around this town."

"No," said Gary chuckling softly as he watered his thirsty plant, "it most certainly is not."

Jack suddenly took off his sunglasses and looked around, sniffing. "What smells so good?"

"It's the oregano in the pot beside you, Jack," said Gary.

Jack leaned over and smelled the leaves.

"You grow spaghetti back here?"

Gary shook his head impatiently. "No, goofy. I grow the spices for spaghetti."

Jack looked up with a triumphant grin on his face.

"Great! When do we eat?"

For the President's Fourth of July party, permission was given to pull out all the stops. There were two themes: "The Signing of the Declaration of Independence" was the first and "Old Fashioned Texas BBQ" was the second. For this Independence Day celebration, White House florists, Nancy Clarke and Ryan Hixson, set up an Independence Day tree in the Blue Room, like a Christmas tree, and decorated it with ornaments representing all fifty states in the union along with red and white striped ribbon garlands. A large glittering blue star sat glowing on the top of the tree that reached to the ceiling. In the Green Room, the fireplace mantle was decorated with massive garlands of red apples, yellow sunflowers, miniature navy blue cowboy boots, and green and red chili peppers. White House plumber, Andrew Stewart, and his crew constructed large figures of the founding fathers to stand inside the Cross Hall to greet guests and their families as they arrived.

In the State Dining Room were two gingerbread creations, one of the signing of the Declaration of Independence with blown candy figurines, and the other a chocolate cowboy rodeo. The rodeo was Abigail's favorite. She was caught twice trying to eat one of the horses. Large wreaths of berry red crabapples and green magnolia garlands filled with white flowers and red, white, and blue stars filled the room. An ice sculpture of the Liberty Bell, surrounded by more sunflowers and yellow roses, was positioned in the middle of the buffet table.

That evening, the magnificent bohemian cut-glass chandeliers inside the grand gold-and-white East Room were brightly lit and casting their sparkling light down upon the guests. Country singers, Brooks and Dunn, and members of their touring band were set up on a makeshift stage where a Steinway grand piano normally stood, right beneath the portrait of George Washington (the one that Dolly Madison rescued before the British burned the White House in 1814). President Washington seemed to welcome all, with his hand outstretched while members of the White House family and their loved ones were clearly enjoying friends, food, and country music.

Martha herself was proving to be the belle of the ball. Already she had danced around the East Room's parquetry floors with all the members of her senior staff, earning the applause of her guests. She began the dance with the general, who proudly led her out on the floor for a dignified Texas Two-Step. President Johnson had enthusiastically joined a fancy line dance with Ned, Ken, and Blaze, who all had a hard time keeping up with their superior. To everyone's amazement, Donald Hooper (a Texas native) had outdone them all, cutting up the dance floor with Martha in a boot slapping, heel stomping, dress-twirling polka. Gary had never seen Donald's face that shade of pink before. The President had also danced with her favorite member of the cabinet, Secretary of State Miller. Like a proud father, Miller led Martha out to the dance floor and masterfully twirled her around the room in a lovely waltz. Cameras flashed. It was the photo op of the night.

Martha was now in the clutches of her chief of staff, who held her tightly around the waist and was proudly spinning the commander in chief across the dance floor in another Texas Waltz. They floated around the dance floor, gaily laughing. The sight made Gary feel like throwing up into the gold damask draperies behind him. He looked away and concentrated instead on serving up punch, a task he had assigned himself and Jack Parish.

"Name your poison," said Jack cheerfully to the upstairs butler, Dwight Cook, who approached the punch table where Jack and Gary where standing. Dwight was the newest of the highly-respected White House butlers serving in the upstairs residence. Dwight was a tall, slender African American, very handsome and distinguished looking. He was the first in his family to land the coveted White House position. Many of the other butlers, also African American and D.C. residents, had been working in the White House for decades. For many, it was a family affair, fathers and sons serving in the White House year after year.

"Leaded or unleaded?" asked Gary pleasantly.

"Oh, I better take the unleaded," said Dwight wearing a big grin. "I'm on duty later on."

"Good lad! Leaves more of the leaded for me." Jack filled a clear crystal cup and handed the red punch to the young man, who thanked him and took a sip.

"Mighty fine, sir. I think my mama would approve." Smiling, the young butler retreated to join several of his fellow butlers.

Gary looked over at his reporter friend skeptically. "If you drink any more of that stuff, the Secret Service will have to drive you home."

"Killjoy," muttered Jack, putting down the cup.

Gary ignored his friend's complaining and looked around the room. He noticed Blaze talking with Secretary Kingsley of Commerce. Kingsley pulled out his wallet and handed a card over to Blaze, then whispered something into Blaze's ear. Blaze nodded and then they shook hands. Then Kingsley walked away.

There was a break in the music, and Charlotte Donovan strode up to the punch table. She was clad in an outrageous (and Gary judged very expensive) cowboy outfit, a full, calf length, ruffled denim skirt and a gold silk blouse that matched her gold boots. An overly sequined gold cowboy hat topped off the outfit. Charlotte came alone, sans husband.

"Hello, boys," she greeted them breezily. "Is this the stag line?"

"Afraid so," owned Gary happily. "You look ravishing this evening, Mrs. Donovan."

Charlotte blushed with a smile. "Why Mr. Craig! You devil you!"

Gary offered the Washington socialite some punch, which she graciously refused.

"No, thank you. I prefer to dance. Would you like a dance, Mr. Craig?"

"Sorry," objected Gary decisively. "No dancing for me tonight. I'm chained to my post. Where is Mr. Donovan? Doesn't he like to dance?"

Charlotte sighed disappointedly. "Yes, Mr. Donovan is a fine dancer, but sadly he's away on business. Somewhere in the Amazon, dancing with snakes I think. Well, then, it will just have to be you, Mr. Parish."

"Me? Why me?" gaped Jack in astonishment.

"Because, young man, you are the best-dressed bachelor in the building!"

Jack smiled proudly and held out his hand to the Washington socialite. "Can't argue with you there, Madame. Man the fort, Duckie. I'll return shortly if I don't trip and break my neck in these God-awful boots."

Amused, Gary watched as Jack and Charlotte took to the dance floor. Martha was still out there with Jim Myers. Myers wasn't giving up his dance card with her anytime soon. Jerk.

The tension of the moment was eased as Miller came up for a refill of punch.

"Fill her up," said the old gentleman happily. "I need something to wet my whistle."

"Plain or spiked?" asked Gary with a grin.

"Better make it plain," said the secretary regretfully. "My Mrs. Miller is over there watching. She's got me on a strict diet that limits my drinks."

"Here you go, then," said Gary handing the glass to Miller.

Miller took a few swallows and turned to watch Martha and Jim dance around the floor.

"Isn't she something?" pondered Miller proudly. "She's handling her role as president brilliantly ."

"I agree," said Gary sincerely. "And I know she appreciates having you on board."

The old man smiled modestly. "I try. I shouldn't say this, but I can't help feeling like a dad watching out for his daughter. I hope she doesn't mind my standing close and giving her some fatherly advice now and then."

"I know she doesn't," replied Gary with certainty.

Miller finished his drink and put the glass down on the table. "That's good to hear. She really thinks a lot of you, son. Well, maybe together, we all can get some important things done while she's in office. Uh-oh. Better run and take Mrs. Miller for a spin. She's looking a bit restless. Have a good evening, Mr. Craig. Don't work too hard."

"I won't," said Gary. He sipped his unleaded punch and stared sullenly as he watched Miller take his wife by the hand and join the action. He felt a soft tap on his shoulder. Someone else, another lady on staff, he thought, was probably wanting to dance.

"I'm sorry, I don't feel like dancing," said Gary bluntly.

"Nor do I," said Agent Lewis softly.

Startled, Gary turned around. Agent Lewis was standing behind him, back in the shadows of the thick gold curtains.

"Sorry to disturb you, sir, but General McKay would like a private word with you in the Rose Garden. Now, sir."

"Now? But I'm serving."

Agent Lewis quickly stepped forward and motioned to another agent, a female, who suddenly appeared from out of nowhere.

"Yes, sir. We'll have this agent cover for you while you're gone. If you'll follow me, then?"

Looked like Gary didn't have much choice. Intrigued, he obediently followed Agent Lewis out of the East Room, down the staircase, and across the hall and outside through the Jefferson Pavilion into the Rose Garden. The night was clear, and Gary saw General McKay standing in the middle of the garden, past the trimmed boxwoods and crab apple trees. Agent Lewis pointed towards General McKay then took up his post, guarding against anyone else wandering outside.

"Good evening, General," said Gary as he approached the large man. "I understand you wanted to see me?"

General McKay turned and looked at Gary pensively. He nodded his head and took out two dark colored pipes from inside his jacket and handed one to Gary.

"Yes, Mr. Craig. I thought you would like to join me outside for a smoke."

Gary stared at the pipe awkwardly. "Um, General, I'm afraid I don't smoke."

General McKay smiled smoothly. "Nor do I, Mr. Craig." He carefully held out his pipe and pushed down on the base of the pipe. A faint red light, one that would appear as a flame from a distance, began to glow from inside the barrel. Then he pushed the base of the other pipe and handed it to Gary. General McKay held his pipe up to his mouth as if he were smoking it and explained. "These are electronic jamming devices, Mr. Craig. They prevent anyone from eavesdropping or recording our conversation. That would include Agent Lewis's friends inside the Secret Service monitoring room, but since I am the National Security Advisor, they will first check their equipment before daring to barge into our discussion. I've made sure that Agent Clark, who is part of the monitoring team this evening per my orders, will delay their arrival as long as possible. I predict we'll have about twenty minutes before they get here. Please hold your pipe up to your mouth before you begin speaking."

Bewildered, Gary obeyed and then stared at General McKay confused. "I don't understand what this is about."

General McKay took a long deep breath and exhaled. "No, you wouldn't. This concerns the President and her safety, and I've reluctantly come to the decision to tell you my suspicions. Although, honestly, I admit I don't want to bring you in. I don't like trusting people, Mr. Craig. I'm in the business of not trusting people. Not anyone!"

Gary swallowed nervously. "But you're going to trust me? Why?"

The general pinched his lips together tightly and narrowly gazed into Gary's eyes. "Two reasons, Mr. Craig. First of all, logic! You were the one who suggested that Taylor nominate Martha Johnson as his vice president. Consequently, you are literally the person that put her in the White House. So logic tells me you are not the one who might try to remove her."

Gary's eyes widened in alarm. "Remove her? You mean, kill her?"

General McKay bit down hard on the tip of the fake pipe and soundly nodded his head. "Oh, yes, Mr. Craig. That is exactly what I mean. And may I remind you that everything that I am about to tell you is classified. You are to tell no one. No one. Is that perfectly clear? Especially that reporter friend of yours!"

Gary quickly nodded his head in agreement. "What's the other reason for trusting me with this information?"

General McKay took the pipe out of his mouth and glanced up at the clear July moon that shone gracefully overhead. "Because of your love for the children, especially your connection with the little girl and her love for you. I have a daughter, Mr. Craig. Did you know that? Two boys and a precious little girl. As a father I learned early on, you can't fool children. They are quite clever, you know. They can see through adults, instantly see through their lies and façades. A child knows when you are lying to them. If you truly were dangerous, were a threat to Madame President, Abigail would know." Then he added darkly, "And then I would know."

Gary readily accepted the general's explanation but not so readily his concern. "So why are you worried about Madame President's safety?" asked Gary skeptically. "Presidents constantly live under danger. It's an every day fact around here. Death threats are commonplace. Why the heightened concern?"

General McKay squared his shoulders. "Because, young man, we have evidence they already broke through our security twice. They killed Eric Peters and they killed Stan Taylor."

This news shook Gary to the core. He stared at General McKay in disbelief. The general took his arm and pulled him in closer, talking rapidly in a hoarse whisper. "There is a lot to tell you, Mr. Craig, and I don't have much time. So, let me go back to the start, to Eric Peters' death.

"Eric was in perfect health the day he died. He had a physical that week with no sign whatsoever of heart disease. So, his heart attack struck me as extremely odd. Six months later President Taylor also drops dead of a heart attack. Two heart attacks in two relatively healthy men? A mere coincidence? I think not."

"But there were autopsies done," argued Gary critically. "Wouldn't a deliberate killing be detected?"

General McKay shook his head. "Not necessarily. There is historical precedence of such things. It's been done before. After World War II, during the Cold War, Soviet spies developed a lovely little cocktail that took out our agents quite effectively. They used prussic acid, a naturally occurring form of cyanide, a colorless substance with a faint odor of almonds, and mixed it with a delivery drug DMSO. DMSO is a common substance used by vets to give medications to animals, like horses. It was very slick. A Soviet agent could walk up and shake hands with a CIA agent, touching the American agent's bare skin with the prussic acid and DMSO mixture. A few minutes later, the drugs would cause a massive coronary, and there would be little or no traces remaining in the body at autopsy."

"Wouldn't it kill the Soviet agent, too?" asked Gary incredulously.

"No," said the general sharply. "The carrier himself was given the mixture over time before the hit; he developed an immunity to the lethal substance."

It seemed too unbelievable to Gary to be real, like something out of a James Bond movie. "But that poison acted quickly," observed Gary tensely. "It wouldn't give the agent much time to get away. Wasn't Peters alone in his hotel that morning when his heart attack happened?"

McKay looked at Gary appreciatively. "Your senses do you credit, Mr. Craig. That is correct, and that is why I didn't suspect anything right away. But with Taylor's death, I began to wonder. Suppose someone had developed a new version of this mixture, a weaponized poison with a built-in time delay of a few more minutes before causing death? That would explain it.

"After Taylor died, I made inquiries beginning with Peters. Eric was indeed alone in his hotel room when he died. Eric suffered with chronic back pain, and during travel he had to do regular exercises and get back massages to remain pain free. He often had a hotel masseuse work on his lower back before going out for a day of speeches and campaign rallies. My investigation revealed that Eric had a back massage very early before breakfast that day, just before he died."

Gary stared at the general warily. "So what did the massage therapist have to say about all this?"

General McKay tapped his electronic pipe briskly in the palm of his hand. "Unfortunately, we weren't able to question him. The fellow who worked on Peters died one week later. His car accidentally fell off a steep rocky ledge somewhere along the Pacific Coast Highway and exploded into flames. There wasn't much of a body left for the county coroner to examine."

Gary drew in his breath sharply. This was horrible. The general, however, was not done. There was more, much more.

"When I got that information, I looked more closely into Taylor's death. At first I was stumped, for Taylor died in a public place, shaking the hands of many people before listening to the concert. But then it dawned on me to look for the last person he had contact with before dying, for if the prussic acid-DSMO substance was still on his hand, others in the audience would have also had contact with it and died as well. They didn't, so it had to be the last person to touch President Taylor."

Gary followed and concurred with McKay's deduction. The scene of that Easter night, the stark images of the concert in the Washington Cathedral, replayed slowly in Gary's head. He saw the gleaming rose window overhead, visualized the burning candles at the altar, heard the sounds of the magnificent choir in evensong, saw the President taking his place on the stand beside the Washington bishop. Gary suddenly gasped. He knew.

"Bishop Palmer?" he cried incredulously.

McKay's eyes shown at Gary, in an expression that let him know that he was correct. McKay then looked at his watch and continued talking in a rapid pace.

"Yes, Mr. Craig. Bishop Palmer, who left town on an apparent vacation, then suddenly ended up dead in a hotel swimming pool. The police autopsy showed that Palmer actually died from a blow to the head, but that information has been suppressed. Fortunately, I already had Palmer under surveillance when he left town. I sent a Black Ops team down to Miami to watch him." McKay paused, smiling briefly to himself. "The agents I sent down are quite an amazing group. Perhaps I'll tell you about them someday. Anyway, they made initial contact before Palmer died. They monitored his actions at the pool and in room 477 where he was staying, and learned that he was not on vacation after all, but that he was planning to retire and to leave the country for good! He was headed for Brazil when he met his untimely demise."

Gary gasped. "Leaving the country? That's exactly what Jack told me!"

"What?" snapped McKay harshly.

Gary hurriedly explained. "Jack Parish, the CNN reporter. Like you noticed, he and I have become pretty good friends." This news immediately drew a frown from General McKay.

"It's okay. Jack is cool — weird, self-centered, spoiled — but cool. Anyway, he came by the house this morning and told me something about this, about Palmer retiring. Parish was at the bishop's funeral where Palmer's secretary came up and started rambling. She told Jack about finding a letter from the bishop, one he hid in the office before leaving, telling her he was retiring and leaving her a very expensive gold bracelet as a goodbye gift. Jack was pretty impressed by the jewelry but brushed the lady's comments aside. He thought she was flaky."

"Interesting," mused General McKay gravely, biting down hard on the tip of his pipe. "It goes nicely with what I learned from the bishop's sister. I paid her a private visit the day after the funeral. She just discovered that her decreased brother left her a large estate, a sum of over a million dollars in cash. He had never indicated to her that he had such wealth. The sister's husband died this past year, and she herself was diagnosed with a terminal brain tumor. Both she and her brother believed she would be dying soon and leaving her small children with little left to sustain them. She told me her condition had been a great concern both to herself and her brother."

Gary stared at the general.

"An inoperable brain tumor? But I saw her at the funeral. Aside from her obvious grief, she looked in perfect health."

"My observation as well, Mr. Craig," said McKay positively. "Which is why I took the liberty of insisting that the bishop's sister visit a neurosurgeon at Bethesda Naval Hospital, at our expense. The X-rays came back negative. She has no tumor, no cancer whatsoever. She never did. It was all made up. It was all a lie."

"A lie? Why would someone lie about a thing like that?" exclaimed Gary angrily.

McKay shook his head in disgust. "Motivation, Mr. Craig. It was a fabrication to force our dead bishop to do something he would never do normally, something quite horrible, something like murder."

Gary stepped back, feeling light headed and sick to his stomach. If McKay's allegations were true, this was beyond corruption and greed. This was evil, pure evil. "Have you checked to see if the hospital made a mistake? What did the sister's original doctor say? The one who diagnosed her with cancer in the first place?"

"Ah, that. Sorry. He wasn't able to add to my investigation, since that doctor is dead too, the victim of a recent hit and run. So, you see, Mr. Craig, the statement you made few nights ago, 'There have been too many deaths' is quite true. Too many people have died, I think, to guard against revealing a terrible plot. There is one more thing I must tell you, something few people know about. The day my agents in Florida alerted me to Bishop Palmer's death, I did some checking, including a review of his phone records. I was startled to find one call of supreme interest. Someone called Bishop Palmer the day before he left town. The call was made from here, Mr. Craig." McKay pointed his pipe behind Gary, in the direction of the West Wing.

Gary gazed steadily at the lighted Oval Office. Despite the heat of the hot July night air, Gary felt the sensation of cold dread running down his spine.

"Do you know who made the call?" muttered Gary heavily, unwilling to believe someone he knew, someone he worked with, trusted, could be entangled in such a web of deceit.

"No," said McKay darkly. "It was made in the Cabinet Room, with a phone easily accessed by anyone working in the West Wing. I've checked the logs for the day, and all the major players were in house."

"Major players?"

"The people who were at the Taylor's house the day he picked his VP. This is what I think the plan was. Someone wants control of the White House, someone with money and power and great ingenuity. They removed Peters, then they planned to have someone inside the Taylor camp guide the President in the selection of his new vice president. Once that person was in place, Taylor would also be knocked off. Then their man would be president, running this country directly under their control."

Gary gazed at the lighted Oval Office windows as the general's words slowly sank in. His gut told him the general was right. Regrettably, Gary had another piece of the puzzle to share.

"There is more," said Gary flatly.

"More?" The general sounded startled.

Gary told the general about Stand Out and the information that Jack Parish had confided in him the day of the election.

"Well, well, well! It all fits, doesn't it, Mr. Craig. Whoever is behind this silenced the Texas group before they could make waves. All right. I'll have my people do some searching into the situation with Stand Out, including Parish's story about the cash and purchase of Dallas property."

"Madame President knows about your theory?"

The general nodded his head gravely.

"Yes, I have kept her informed along the way. And she is aware of our conversation tonight."

"If the original plan failed, why are you still concerned about President Johnson's safety?" asked Gary earnestly.

"Because she hasn't turned out to be the lame duck, meek-as-a-lamb president that they hoped she would be. They counted on her being someone they could control and influence. That's a laugh. Look how she's turned this place upside down." The general pointed his pipe at the big hole in the middle of the South Lawn grounds where the new Dining Room was under construction. He continued. "Her refusal to appoint a new VP spoils their plans, and they might soon lose patience and decide to get rid of her all together. I need your eyes, young man," said the general, leaning close and whispering urgently. "I can't be everywhere. The other people at that meeting at Taylor's house — Ned, Jim, Donald, or Ken — are the main suspects. They were the ones who made suggestions to fill the VP slot. I need you to keep an eye on them and report to me anything strange or unusual you might see happening."

Gary thought for a moment, remembering that day on the Taylor farm. Something occurred to him, something he was very reluctant to say.

"General, you have listed four suspects. There is another."

The general's eyebrow lifted slightly. "Who would that be? Me, I suppose?"

Gary smiled weakly at the general. "Actually, you would make the best suspect, the one I would choose. You have the military background and the international connections and the know-how to pull something like this off. But no, I know it isn't you. I was thinking about my friend Blaze."

The general laughed. "Blaze Phillips? That's impossible. Whoever did this had a nominee for the VP slot. Mr. Blaze did nothing that day but eat and type."

Gary bit his lip. "You're wrong there, sir. He did have a candidate. He e-mailed Taylor the night before and suggested Kingsley. And Taylor appointed Kingsley to the cabinet, like the other nominees. But you're right. It couldn't be Blaze," added Gary hastily. "He's no traitor!"

"They never are at first. Alright, I'll add him to my list."

"What about Ambassador Porter?"

"Maurice? No," said the general promptly. "Maurice Porter wasn't at the meeting at Taylor's house. Taylor didn't put forth his name for vice president."

"Hem," coughed Agent Lewis loudly, a signal someone was approaching. McKay quickly deactivated his pipe, took Gary's pipe and shut it off, and put both away.

"Remember," he warned softly, "keep you eyes and ears open and tell no one."

Seconds later Agent Pullman and two other agents came striding into the Rose Garden.

"Sir, is everything alright?" He addressed the general urgently.

"Why, yes," answered McKay casually. "Mr. Craig and I were outside having a smoke. Something wrong?"

"Yes, sir. There was a total loss in audio surveillance."

General McKay looked up. "Really? Agent Lewis, contact the monitoring room and see if this is so."

Agent Lewis spoke quietly into a wrist microphone. Shortly the reply came through his earpiece.

"No, sir. Agent Clark reports the audio is now working properly."

General McKay smiled at Agent Pullman and pointed to the moon. "Probably a bad mixture of solar flares and fireworks. Carry on, Agent Pullman."

Agent Pullman glared at Gary unhappily.

"I didn't know you smoked, Mr. Craig," snapped Pullman curtly as Gary walked past him.

"Only on special occasions," replied Gary.

McKay grabbed Gary by the arm and dragged him back inside the White House. They walked upstairs to the State Room level where they ran right into Aunt Sophie, Jane, and Abigail standing in the Cross Hall near the statue of Betsy Ross. The girls were drinking red fruit punch and enjoying the country music floating out of the ballroom. Abigail squealed and clapped her hands when she saw Gary and McKay approach. Aunt Sophie smiled warmly at them.

"Hello, you two. We were wondering where you had run off. Care for some punch?"

"No, thanks," said Gary, trying to put on a good face after such a serious discussion. "I've already had my limit."

"I'll have some later," said McKay, "when I have some of Mr. Craig's famous barbeque."

"Uncle Gary, watch me, watch me!" the five year old ordered. She stepped out away from the group and started twirling around in circles, the edges of her blue checked skirt flaring out. It made Gary dizzy just looking at her. Cameras flashed. Reporters in the area caught the moment on film.

"Good job!" said Gary.

Abigail skipped over and grabbed Gary's hands. "I want you to dance with me!" demanded Abigail.

"Sorry, sweetheart, Uncle Gary doesn't feel like dancing tonight," said Gary regrettably.

Determined not to dance alone, Abigail marched back and took Jane by the hand and ordered her nanny to twirl around with her. Jane looked appalled at the request.

"Oh, don't be ridiculous, Abby!" said Jane sipping her punch. "I couldn't possibly."

"Go on, Jane!" urged Aunt Sophie laughing. "I'll hold your drink."

Nanny Jane sighed and handed over her cup full of punch. "Very well then."

She stood next to Abby and took hold of her flaming red broomstick skirt, and at Abby's command, began twirling with her little charge. Abby had no problem twirling and twirling around to the beat of the music. Jane's adult vestibular system, however, was not as steady as Abigail's and after only four spins she fell off balance, collapsing straight into Sophie, who was knocked over into the general. The two cups of punch that Sophie was holding splashed all over the general's face and white shirt. Noise in the hallway abruptly died down as guests turned and stared. More cameras flashed.

"Oh, how very stupid of me!" winced Nanny Jane apologetically. "I'm terribly sorry. Let me get you a napkin, General."

"Thank you, but no," muttered McKay. He pulled out a white handkerchief and started wiping off drops of red punch from his bushy eyebrows. "Madame, have you ever considered going into the military? I'm quite certain a week with you on the front line of any battlefield would send the enemies scattering."

"Charles, enough," declared Aunt Sophie sharply. "It was an accident. Come upstairs, and we'll get that shirt of yours cleaned up."

Jane stepped up and offered her assistance. "Oh, do let me help, General. I'm wonderful at cleaning shirts. My mother had a great method of getting out stains . . ."

McKay looked at Jane aghast.

"Kindly leave me and my shirt alone!"

"Charles, come along and stop complaining. Abigail, you come too! It's your bedtime."

"Save me," whimpered McKay as Aunt Sophie firmly led him away. More cameras flashed. Abby gave Gary a quick hug, and then she and Jane followed the others up the stairs to the family residence.

Gary watched merrily as they walked away. The din of the crowd soon rose again, and Gary stood alone pondering the conversation with McKay in the Rose Garden. All the glitter around him suddenly faded in importance. Something was wrong here. Something was terribly wrong. Things were not as they seemed.

Gary was so engrossed in his own thoughts that he didn't hear his name being called. He then felt a delicate hand placed on his right shoulder.

"There you are. I've been looking for you everywhere. They're about to do the last song of the evening," said a familiar voice gently. "Would you dance the last dance with me?"

Gary turned around and looked at Martha in astonishment.

"Me?"

She smiled gracefully, her dark green eyes flashing.

"Yes, you, you silly goose. Whom else would I dance the last dance with?" Gary's ban on dancing was quickly tossed aside.

Gary tentatively took Martha's hand and led her back into the East Room where guests and the band were waiting. Brooks and Dunn started singing their classic song "Maria," and Gary and Martha stepped out alone onto the dance floor. She smiled as he shyly placed his hand around her waist, and slowly they began dancing. Gary's brain was spinning, so many things were flooding his mind and heart — catching sight of Jack Parish by the punch bowl, broadly grinning and giving him the thumbs up sign; the view of Jim Myers standing by the doorway with a sour look on his face; the sweet scent of Martha's jasmine perfume filling his senses with pleasant feelings he hadn't felt in a very long time; and the stark reality that someone in this very room wanted to kill the beautiful woman he held tightly in his arms.

☆ ☆ ☆

Cell phone call later that night . . .

"What the hell is taking you so long? You've talked with her, reasoned with her, worked with her, and now danced with her. It's time she started dancing to our tune for a change . . . What is she waiting for, an invitation? Well, then give her one! That's what we're paying you for . . . I don't care about that. It's time to take off the kid gloves and start pressuring her. Otherwise, we might just start pressuring you . . . Yes, I thought you would see reason. Now, get to work. God, there's nothing I hate more than an obstinate woman!"

Chapter 16

The Social Secretary's Office

Monday Night, July 18

Gary stared at the alarm clock on his night stand. The clock flashed 12:45 A.M.

Gary normally fell asleep easily, curled up snugly inside his fluffy down comforter listening to the sounds of his wall-mounted waterfall. But tonight sleep evaded him, for his mind kept replaying the scenes of the Fourth of July party. After tossing and turning for over an hour, Gary finally gave up, got up, and put on his thick navy terry robe and slippers. He went to his kitchen, pulled out a white coffee cup, and microwaved some hot water. After making himself some chamomile tea with honey and lemon, he went to his living room and sat down and turned on the television.

Gary stared mindlessly at the screen while he sipped and surfed. There was not much on. There were two old John Wayne movies and a Ginger Rogers movie playing. Gary had seen all three before. There was a telethon on a religious station, a live broadcast of the BBC on PBS featuring a story on global warming, a documentary on hurricanes on the weather channel, and numerous infomercials for cookware and exercise equipment.

Were insomniacs overweight?

He glanced down at his waistline. Maybe so.

He continued to channel surf, pausing at the shopping channels QVC and HSN to see what was on sale. The Perlier people from Italy were on HSN, Prince Skip and Princess Amanda, talking enthusiastically about a special kit of White Almond bath and body products. Looked good to

Gary. Thinking some shopping might be a comfort, Gary picked up the phone and ordered three kits, one for himself and one each for Harriet and Mildred.

Cheered somewhat by retail therapy, Gary put down his cup of tea and reached lazily for the yellow steno notepad and pencil he kept in the side drawer of his massive white pine coffee table. He then lay down on the sofa with the pad resting on his bent knees. He took the pencil, chewed it thoughtfully on the end for a moment, and then made a list of all possible suspects in the White House murder case. He placed five names on his list.

> Jim Myers
> Ned Baldwin
> Donald Hooper
> Ken Friedman
> Blaze Phillips

Recalling his conversation with the general in the Rose Garden, Gary reluctantly added one more name to the list.

> Charles McKay

Okay, he had six suspects. Each was at the Taylor meeting and nominated someone for the VP slot, and each had access to the phone in the Cabinet Room in the West Wing. Next, Gary put down beside each man's name the person they nominated for VP and the resulting position in government to which that nominee was appointed. Gary ended up with a neat table with three columns.

Jim Myers	Senator David Miller	State
Ned Baldwin	Congressman Ross Green	Labor
Donald Hooper	Governor Tom Patrick	Treasury
Ken Friedman	Judge Carloe Hernandez	Attorney General
Blaze Phillips	Congressman Kingsley	Commerce
Charles McKay	Senator Miles Trent	Defense

If McKay's assertions were correct, one of these six men made the call to Bishop Palmer before he left for Florida and was part of a plot to kill Peters and Taylor and to gain control of the White House. Now they just needed to figure out which one on the list was the guilty party.

Studying the names, Gary smiled. Jim Myers was right at the top of his list. Freudian slip? Well, it didn't take a psychiatrist to explain it to him. Nothing would please Gary more than to have it be Jim. Come to think of it, Myers did make an excellent suspect. He possessed power, wealth and fame, and people like Jim Myers were never satisfied with what they already had. They wanted more. Myers was unquestionably self-centered, arrogant, and ambitious. Surely, the combination of those base human qualities, left unchecked, could turn one into a classic murderer. With zest, Gary underlined Myers name, place three stars beside it, and even added an exclamation point.

Then Gary considered the name appearing beside Myers, that of Senator David Miller. Gary huffed and chewed on his pencil. The fact that Jim had nominated Miller as VP was not a strong indication of guilt. Everyone in the White House and on the Hill admired the respected elder statesman from New York. The former senator was something of a political legend, someone Martha trusted and relied on. She even viewed Miller as a surrogate father. Gary had seen on a number of occasions with his own eyes how protective Miller was of Martha. Besides, look what Miller had achieved with Martha on that dicey North Korean deal. Would someone hellbent on destroying the presidency help her win accolades from the world leaders for successfully handling the sticky Korean situation? No. Of course, one could argue that Miller could be a fake, a phony, not be the great man Washington and the White House believed him to be. Gary sighed. Possible, but not probable! Of all the VP nominees on his list, Miller was the best known and least likely to be involved in anything as sordid as murder. If Miller were guilty, Gary would eat his pencil.

Nevertheless, Gary reflected on his interactions with Jim over the past few months, trying to think of something, anything, that would suggest guilt. Nothing came to mind. Gary reluctantly erased the underlining and exclamation point beside Myers name, but for the sheer spite of it, he kept the stars on the paper. It made him feel better.

Gary considered the next name on his list, Ned Baldwin. Gary reached for his tea and sipped it slowly. Other than Blaze, the least likely person to commit high treason would be Ned. Gary had known Ned and his wife for years. Ned was a true blue Republican. It simply couldn't be him. Then Gary remembered the cold day back in January, at the inauguration, when he observed Ned and a stranger talking before the ceremony began. Ned disappeared for a while that day, minutes before the swearing in took place. For Ned, that was an uncharacteristic breach of protocol. And Ned was a stickler for protocol. What would entice him to step away at that important moment? Could Ned have been discussing future assassination plans with the unknown hit man?

Nope. No way, Jose. Yet, Gary did overhear the odd phone call of Ned's the night of the election. Ned appeared quite anxious as he arranged to meet someone the next day, plus he was flustered when he spoke with Gary afterwards. What about the matter of Stand Out in Greensboro? Ned had been in on Gary's plan to get the FBI and police secretly involved in the demonstration. If Ned was part of the group trying to kill Taylor, why didn't he warn Stand Out? He had time to do it. Gary frowned. Well, maybe Ned chose to do nothing. If he had warned

Stand Out to suddenly change their plans, he could have been implicated. Begrudgingly Gary placed a question mark by Ned's name and a note referring to the overheard call and the meeting at Monticello. It seemed unlikely for Ned to be the guilty party, but his actions and whereabouts warranted watching for the next few weeks.

Gary considered Donald next.

Oh, please, giveth me a break!

Gary grinned broadly as he sipped his tea. Okay. Let's imagine for a moment the world's greatest hypochondriac taking part in international espionage bent on killing the president of the United States? Right! Donald Hooper was afraid of his own shadow, all germs, all Democrats, Dan Rather, James Carville, and the IRS, although not in that order. Hooper wouldn't even dare return a library book late, much less commit capital crime. Gary put down his tea and stared at Donald's name. But suppose all the nerves, the fuss, the worry that Donald displayed day in and day out was merely a show, a well-rehearsed act? Suppose Donald played the part of a highly stressed obsessive-compulsive attorney, when in reality he was a smooth talking cold-blooded killer?

Sorry. No one was that good of an actor.

Except maybe Dustin Hoffman.

Cautiously Gary put a question mark by Donald's name and noted the need to investigate the lawyer's background and if possible, past medical history.

Ken Friedman's name was next. Gary tapped the edge of his pencil definitively on the notepad and smiled with satisfaction. Now he was getting somewhere! If anyone made a good suspect, next to Jim Myers of course, it would be Ken. Consider his qualifications! Friedman was armed with a vast knowledge of political facts, possessed great organizational skills, had a cool demeanor under stress, and was highly skilled in electronics. Such talents would surely qualify someone for espionage. Yet Gary thought and thought but failed to recall anything incriminating in Ken's behavior recently. The only thing he came up with was the reported ordering of the pharmacy journals. Friedman's sudden interest in medications might link him to poisoning. Was he searching for a new combination of drugs to slip into Martha's morning coffee? Or was he simply trying to find new sedatives to slip into Donald's diet Coke? Tough call, but Gary put a star beside Ken's name.

Gary refused to seriously consider his good friend Blaze as an actual suspect. If he knew anyone's character well, if he trusted anyone at the White House, it was Blaze Phillips. The man was a complete innocent. Blaze wouldn't hurt a fly. But could Blaze Phillips, the young idealist, be swayed into doing something wrong for the right reasons, for something he deeply believed in? One of Blaze's best traits was loyalty. Suppose the people behind this plot were connected to Kingsley, and Blaze was acting out of loyalty to Kingsley and their secret cause. Would that push Blaze over the edge? Gary remembered seeing Blaze and Kingsley quietly exchanging cards and handshakes at the Fourth of July party. Blaze normally was quite verbose about current events in his life, but he hadn't mentioned anything at all to Gary about his interactions with Kingsley. Was Blaze sealing a secret deal with the former southern congressman?

Gary shook his head, tired and disbelieving.

Finally Gary considered the last name on the list, General Charles McKay. Gary had said it straight to the general's face that night in the Rose Garden — McKay made the best suspect in terms of prior experience in intelligence. McKay had military training, top-secret clearance, former employment at the Pentagon, and no telling what connections with covert operations with Central Intelligence. Was it possible that McKay was a double agent working at the White House? Then why tell Gary about the plot? Perhaps to set the stage to implicate others should the operation fold or become exposed? McKay could easily turn to Gary as a witness of his own innocence and his concern for Martha's safety! And how clever to employ Gary as another set of eyes and ears to watch the other West Wing players in case they got too close to the truth!

Gary put down the paper and pencil in disgust and got up off the sofa. He took his dirty cup and saucer to the sink, rinsed them off and placed them on the metal drain board. Truth was he trusted McKay. He couldn't explain why, but he did. His gut told him to trust McKay, to trust him completely in fact. So, in summary, the best suspect he trusted, the worst suspect (the one he wanted most to be guilty) looked the most innocent, and none of the other suspects had enough evidence against them. Some detective he made!

As he walked back to bed, Gary rubbed his tired eyes in frustration. He didn't have much to go on. But he could rectify that. In that moment, Gary resolved to no longer be a passive bystander. If someone were a threat to Martha, he would not sit idly by and let them harm her. He would take action. He would look. He would listen. He would pay attention, and he would start asking questions. Certainly, no one would suspect him, of all people, to be working undercover. They only saw him working with tablecloths and flower arrangements. And if he discovered the truth, he vowed he'd see whoever it was brought to justice.

Armed with that happy thought, Gary crawled back into bed, turned off the light, and fell soundly asleep.

"Let's go over the menu for the German state dinner," instructed Gary sharply. It was Tuesday morning July 19, and he was sitting at his computer in his small East Wing office with the cat Sheba curled up in his lap purring contentedly. Ryan stood near the door, holding his clipboard stuffed full of papers.

Ryan cleared his throat and began reading. Gary listened while scratching Sheba behind the ears.

"Traditional German dishes will be served, per Madame President's request. The appetizers or *vorspeise* will feature a collection of various hors d'oeuvres. So far, the list includes fried herring balls, seasoned petite salmon fillets cooked in olive oil, bratwurst with imported crisp rye breads, small onion pies, handmade salted pretzels with a variety of imported mustards, and a tray of mini hazelnut and praline cookies."

"Remind me to save up my Weight Watcher points that week," observed Gary sarcastically, as he continued to pet Sheba. The black cat yawned and looked adoringly up at Gary. Ryan smiled at Gary's wry comment and continued.

"Next course will be soup, or in German, *suppe*. For that we have slated *rote gruetze*, a traditional fruit soup."

"Delicious. Make sure the chefs get the best fresh fruits available," added Gary authoritatively. "Call our favorite Florida and California growers. And don't forget the Utah fruit tree folks. Their apricots and cherries are excellent."

"Will do," said Ryan promptly, dutifully making notes. "Now, for the main course or *hauptspelse*, we will have *rheinischer sauerbraten*, a superb beef roast stewed in fine wine. Speaking of wines, Madame President wants to feature some American wines. Since you yourself don't drink, I've arranged for Aunt Sophie to sample some American wines this afternoon during our meeting with the chefs and chief usher. Let's see now, for side dishes, called *beilagen*, we will have *gedunsletes rotkraut*, stewed red cabbage, and seasoned Spaetzle noodles."

Sheba meowed her approval.

"Wonderful," said Gary in agreement. "Dessert?"

"Right! We will feature imported coffees and assorted petite cake tortes. We will also serve a traditional Black Forest German chocolate cake, a recipe from Aunt Sophie's own kitchen. I understand Ms. Johnson has been baking test cakes upstairs in the family residence this past week and gave samples to the butlers and maids, much to their delight."

"No wonder they've been in such a good mood. Dwight Cook has been grinning all week. What's Roland doing?" asked Gary with keen interest. He was referring to the White House's famous pastry chef, known for his amazing dessert creations. "I hope we aren't overworking him, with the July Fourth party last week and Christmas planning also in the mix."

"Are you kidding? He's in heaven! For individual guests, Roland is creating his version of a *blechkuchen*, which is a traditional flat layer cake covered with seasonal fruits. I haven't seen the prototype yet, but I hear it is surrounded with handmade German chocolate leaves filled with a luscious orange cream covered with specially prepared fruits and handmade fruit sugar candies. Roland is also making another gingerbread masterpiece for the State Dining Room. This time he is creating a gingerbread version of the famous Bavarian Neuschwanstein Castle of crazy King Ludwig."

"Abigail will love that!" commented Gary happily. Sheba meowed again and then jumped down and scurried out the door.

The curtains by Gary's window rustled ever so slightly.

"What was that all about?" asked Ryan startled.

"Oh, nothing," said Gary casually. "Summer breezes, that's all. Probably spooked Sheba. I should keep that window closed and bring in the small desk fan from home instead."

Just then a young, red-headed summer staffer named Edward, a student from the University of New Mexico, came in with a large bag from Chick-Fil-A and a carton of drinks.

"Here you go," said Edward putting the paper bag and drinks down on Gary's desk. "Three Chick-Fil-A sandwiches, one eight-piece nuggets, three large fries, two diet Cokes, one pink lemonade, and lots of ketchup. The change and the ketchup are in the bag." His duty done, Edward saluted and immediately left.

Ryan stared down incredulously at all the food.

"I'm having lunch with Blaze," said Gary.

Ryan's face instantly cleared.

"Oh," said Ryan understandingly.

Just then, Agent Pullman barged into Gary's office, rudely pushing his way past Ryan. Pullman was out of breath and his face was flushed.

"Can I help you?" asked Gary calmly raising his eyebrows.

Agent Pullman scowled. "I'm looking for that imp. Is she here?"

"If you are referring to Abigail, she is not an imp," corrected Gary crossly, opening the food bag and helping himself to a French fry.

"Have you lost her?" questioned Ryan surprised. "She should be wearing her little sensor pad. All members of the First Family are required to wear them so that their whereabouts are known at all times to the Secret Service."

Agent Pullman held up a small black pad stuck to his forefinger. "You mean this one? I found it stuck on top of one of the bison's heads on the State Dining Room fireplace."

Gary pressed his lips together hard, suppressing a laugh while maintaining a serious expression. Ryan looked shocked.

"What about the overhead video cameras? Shouldn't they be able to track her?"

Agent Pullman glared coldly at Ryan. "In theory, yes. But, as I understand it from an apologetic White House Park Police, the cameras were originally calibrated for humans over four feet tall, not for short and elusive five-year-olds."

"Oh dear," said Ryan worriedly.

Gary gazed at the frustrated agent thoughtfully. "So, Abigail has managed to bypass all the Secret Service's infrared technology, electronic eyes, audio surveillance, and high tech pressure sensors?"

Agent Pullman made a choking sound and nodded.

"Well, she'll turn up soon enough," replied Gary loftily. "It is almost lunchtime."

Agent Pullman refused to be consoled. He continued his argument. "I most certainly hope so. My biggest concern is that she'll wander off, perhaps outside the house, near the construction site for the new State Dining Room under the Ellipse. Have you seen the hole outside lately? It's huge! Suppose she falls in and breaks her neck, on my watch?" The agent pulled out a wrinkled handkerchief and wiped his furrowed brow. "I'll be fired and lose my pension because a kindergartener was playing hide and seek in a construction site!"

"Well, if she wanders too close to the hole, perhaps the SWAT team on the roof can intercept," suggested Ryan helpfully.

Agent Pullman sneered. "That's not funny."

Gary fought hard not to laugh. Pullman had had enough.

"Agent Pullman, I can assure you that Abigail is not outside and won't fall into that big hole. She does like to play her hiding game, but she stays strictly within the boundaries of the house. Beside, she knows very well she would be in big trouble if she went outside unsupervised." Gary said this last line slow and clear. Only he noticed the edge of a pink tennis shoe withdraw quickly behind the thick folds of the office window's long velvet curtains.

"Perhaps you should check her mother's private office," suggested Gary helpfully. "Abby has been playing a great deal with her in the West Wing this week."

"Yes, I know," the agent said sourly. "I already checked there."

"Check again," advised Gary. "She does move around a lot."

"You're telling me," said Pullman grudgingly. "Alright. But if you see her, please take her upstairs immediately and deposit her with the crazy British woman."

"Will do," said Gary sincerely. "She will be upstairs soon. You'll see."

The curtains moved ever so slightly in disagreement.

Agent Pullman left. Ryan also took his leave to go to his own office, to make some calls and to eat his own brown bag lunch before the afternoon meeting with the First Lady. Once he was alone, Gary opened the food bag and took out the chicken nuggets and one French fry order. He placed them beside the lemonade. He opened several plastic ketchups and squeezed them out onto a napkin, and then he took a few more ketchup packets out and left them unopened on the desk. Then he gathered up the bag and drinks and spoke to the curtains before leaving.

"I've left your lunch on the desk. Eat all of your chicken nuggets, not just the fries. You can play some of the computer games that I loaded on my computer for you till I come back. Promise me you will stay here, that you won't go outside, and that you won't go near the big hole unless you are with Nanny Jane or me. Promise?"

"I promise," said the curtain.

"Good," said Gary. "Oh, and nice job on putting your patch on the fireplace. Next time, hide it underneath the piano in the gold ballroom."

The curtain fluttered and giggled.

"I will, Uncle Gary."

Gary bid the curtain goodbye and securely closed his office door.

There were two popular spots inside the White House where Gary and Blaze could eat their lunch. One was the White House Mess, where most of the West Wing folks took their meals. The other location was for the staffers, a place underground called the Mezzanine. Literally a sub-basement level between the ground floor and the basement of the White House, the Mezzanine consisted of a small storage area (where tables and chairs and red carpets for special events were stored) and a small kitchen and dining area used by the chief ushers, maids, and butlers. The place was not fancy by any means, but not just anyone could dine there. A certain pecking order prevailed inside the White House. Ushers and those working in the family residence received more privileges than those who worked outside on the grounds. Eating in the Mezzanine was one of those privileges, and Gary, as social secretary, was allowed to eat his meals there.

Gary and Blaze enjoyed their chicken sandwiches, fries, and drinks. Conversation was mostly about updates from North Carolina (details of Harriet's exciting love life with the plumber Bert) and Chicago Cubs baseball. After they finished eating, Gary decided it was time to talk politics.

"So, what's up in your neck of the woods? Anything exciting I should know about?" asked Gary trying not to sound too interested.

Blaze took a sip of his Coke and nodded his head. "You can say that again."

"Oh, really?" Gary said blandly, finishing his fries and wiping his mouth with a white napkin.

"Yeah. Big time. According to Ned, the last cabinet meeting was pretty hot."

"I'm all ears," murmured Gary softly.

"Well, there was a ton of talk about coal mining, something about the environmental dangers of strip-mining in the West Virginia mountains. The Interior and Commerce secretaries had a row over that one. Despite their arguments, Madame P stepped outside the traditionally Republican "big business" position and sided with the environmentalists. Ned nearly had a stroke. He told me later a move like that, one outside party lines, could cost Madame P some critical support from party conservatives. Ned made the sarcastic comments that Greenpeace would declare the President Woman of the Year!"

"How nice," replied Gary with a bored yawn. "Anything else?"

"Hmmm. Let's see. Oh, yeah. The attorney general was up in arms over the new immigration bill before Congress, the one Taylor started before he passed away. Tricky subject. The goal is to watch the borders but still let underprivileged people from other countries into America. Ken supports the attorney general in tightening the borders and had tons of boring legal stuff to say with a zillion references. I thought he'd never quit talking."

"What was Madame President's opinion?"

Blaze moaned heavily. "She doesn't have one yet. She says she wants to study the issue longer. It about drove Ken and Donald crazy. I tell you, Gary, Hooper is about to lose it. I think he needs I.V. Valium. He was a nervous wreck this morning, more so than usual. His hands were literally shaking during the meeting. He went out to lunch today, left early! Imagine that, Donald leaving early! Anyway, Madame P won't budge on immigration yet, just like she's not budging on the VP deal."

Bingo. Gary hit pay dirt.

"And what's up with that?" he queried nonchalantly.

Blaze shook his head and rolled his eyes.

"Nothing. Nada! Zip! Everybody, *and I mean everybody*, gave a full court press on that subject, but the lady won't lift a finger. Says she mulling it over. I still think she should pick Kingsley. He's the best in the cabinet for the job. I sent her another e-mail after the meeting. Don't tell Ned."

Gary looked at his old friend and ventured out on thin ice.

"You really like Kingsley. I noticed you two talking at the Fourth of July party. Are you two good friends now?"

For a brief instant, Blaze looked very uncomfortable. But he recovered quickly and answered.

"Friends with Kingsley? Naw! I was getting something for Ned. He wanted Kingsley's business card with a new fax number on it. That's all."

"I see," said Gary. And he did see. For the first time in their friendship, Blaze Phillips had lied to him.

Blaze looked restlessly down at his watch and jumped up.

"Oops. Better run. Got an appointment across town to go to. Never a dull moment in this job! Thanks for the lunch. I'll call you." And with that, Blaze dashed off, leaving Gary in the dust.

Gary took his time and finished his drink. Then he cleaned up the table, threw away the trash, and went over to speak briefly with Morgan at a nearby table, confirming some wine selections for the state dinner. Gary also stopped and chatted with a few upstairs butlers, including Dwight Cook, who were playing a very serious game of Monopoly. From their report, the game had been going on for a week, and Dwight was making a killing. The other butlers pointed to Dwight's numerous hotels on Park Place. It was good fun. After socializing a bit, Gary checked his own watch and left to start his fact-finding mission.

He exited the Mezzanine and walked up the stairs to the ground floor. He had just entered the hallway when he ran smack dab into Nanny Jane, Eliza, and Josh, along with Agents Clark and Lewis. Jane was dressed in one of her trademark broomstick skirts, this one a soft peach with white pearl beading. She wore an overly large peach linen blouse and a fringed brown leather vest with a matching purse that hung over her shoulder. Her hair, frizzing madly in the summer humidity, was piled atop her head. Stray pieces of hair trailed down on her shoulders. Topping off her look, Jane wore round animal print sunglasses. The kids were dressed down in blue jeans and UVA T-shirts.

"We've been shopping," announced Eliza happily, indicating several bags in her hands.

"And went out to lunch and the video store," added Josh, holding up his own purchases.

"Excellent," said Gary. "How did you guys manage it? I didn't think your Secret Service detail would allow you to mingle in public!"

Agents Clark and Lewis, still wearing their dark sunglasses, grinned at Gary. "We have ways," said Lewis casually.

Jane laughed. "Indeed! They called ahead to have a few shop owners at Tyson's Corner open for us an hour early. We had the whole store to ourselves. It was mall heaven."

Eliza smiled broadly. "Jane then took us to a fancy little boutique in Georgetown. They have a designer from London! Mom says Abigail and I can a have special dresses made for the state dinner."

"Fantastic! How did it go?" asked Gary.

"It was awesome," exclaimed Eliza. "I met the designer, and he took some measurements. Jane gave him Abigail's information. He's coming here with some drawings and samples next week! I can't believe Mom said yes!"

"Of course she did," observed Jane candidly. "She knew how peevish you would be if she had said no!"

Eliza feigned shock. "Me, peevish?"

Nanny Jane rolled her eyes. "Yes, you."

"Aunt Sophie ready for our meeting?" asked Gary laughing.

"Will be. She's been working on another German chocolate cake recipe this morning," said Jane. "I'm going to be two dress sizes larger I am afraid by the time the state dinner arrives."

"I won't," said Josh happily patting his stomach.

Eliza frowned. "It will catch up with you someday," she warned. "Hey, did Abigail ever show up? We wanted to take her shopping with us, but she went off hiding and no seeking this morning, and we didn't have time to go find her. Mom called us on our cell later and said Abby was in her office. I wonder where she is now?"

"She was hiding in my room early this morning," said Josh frowning. "She might be there again!"

Gary started to tell them about Abigail's current whereabouts, but Jane quickly interrupted.

"Oh, she'll turn up," said Nanny Jane with confidence. "She always does, that one. And I'll have a word with her about staying out of your room, Josh. A young man like you needs his privacy. Very well then, you two run along upstairs and let your detail have a break. Go on and do hurry. I'll be right behind you."

"Will you come up tonight for supper?" Eliza asked Gary, refusing to leave as directed. "The designer gave me some fabric swatches to look at. I'd like to have your opinion which to choose for the dress."

"Yeah, then we could play my new video game afterwards," added Josh perking up with excitement.

Again, Gary felt immediately torn. His feelings for these children were getting stronger and stronger, and he would love nothing better than spending a cozy evening with them. But his fear of finding himself into a position of getting hurt was also building. But, given the possible danger lurking inside the White House and the fact that General McKay had asked him to keep his eyes open, maybe he should accept such offers. Gary wasn't sure what to do.

"Well, I don't know," said Gary hesitantly. "I wouldn't want to impose."

Jane laughed softly at him. "Impose? How slow you are, Mr. Craig. You're practically part of the family. Do come. The children would be so pleased. And your friend, Charlotte Donovan, is coming to dinner as well. The remodeling of the Oval Sitting Room is completed, and Aunt Sophie invited Charlotte to celebrate the transformation. I think General McKay is coming as well to sample Sophie's latest cake recipe. So you see, it's already a party. The more the merrier really!"

Hearing that Charlotte and McKay were coming to dinner made Gary feel much more at ease. There was safety in numbers, right?

"Okay," said Gary. He then looked sternly at the youngsters and barked at them. "You heard Jane. Get going!"

Eliza and Josh laughed and went immediately upstairs. Clark and Lewis departed. Nanny Jane, however, lagged momentarily.

"One more thing, Mr. Craig" she said in an offhanded whisper as she adjusted her peach skirt. "Do send Abigail straight upstairs soon. Aunt Sophie would like her in residence this afternoon. Abby's new dance teacher is coming for tap lessons late today. God, have you seen the new tap shoes? I could hardly get them off her feet last night. She kept tapping in the Cross Hall! Drove poor Mr. Morgan a bit batty, I'm afraid. Anyway, the little dear needs a kip before her lesson. And since I was up again last night with my sinuses, I think I'll join her."

Gary stared at the nanny.

"How did you know Abigail was with me," he asked in amazement.

Nanny Jane smiled serenely. "I'm a British nanny, Mr. Craig. It's my job to know such things. Cheers!" With that, Jane twirled around and left.

Gary watched her leave, appreciative but confused by the nanny's skills of deduction. How could she be so daft, so clumsy, and yet so devilishly clever? Were all women like this, a puzzling combination that didn't add up?

This ageless riddle was not something Gary could reason out now. He was on another mission. He quickly changed mental gears and walked to the West Wing, ready to investigate.

He headed for Donald's office first, knowing from Blaze that Donald was out. Gary wanted to hear what, if anything, the secretary had to say. Secretaries were a wealth of information. Gary found Donald's secretary at her desk working at her computer. He greeted her and breezily asked where her boss was. The elderly lady, good at multi-tasking, did not stop typing as she replied crisply that Mr. Hooper and Mr. Friedman were out to lunch and wouldn't be back till two. Gary thanked her. He then went to Ken Friedman's office with the same purpose. Upon his repeating the question, Ken's secretary curtly replied that Ken was out to lunch.

"With Mr. Hooper?" asked Gary innocently.

A funny look came across the secretary's face. She shook her head firmly in the negative.

"Mr. Friedman is not with Mr. Hooper," was her reply.

Gary asked next if she knew where Ken was. The secretary promptly declared that she had not been at her desk when Mr. Friedman left, but her calendar indicated that her boss had an appointment across town. Her answers were vague, and Gary didn't believe he could get anything more out of her.

Gary stood at Ken's office area pleased with the information and made a mental note of the secretaries' discrepancy. It wasn't much, but it was more than he could discover by searching either Don's or Ken's offices.

Although Donald was obsessive compulsive over his health and politics, his approach to housekeeping was quite the opposite. Donald was a clutterer, a pack rat. His office was filled with stacks of letters, newspaper clippings, faxes, law journals, cardboard boxes, old and new files, Post-It notes, note cards, cassette tapes, DVDs, CDs, gum wrappers, magazines, and news videos. This chaotic assortment did not include Donald's stash of personal health items, including bottles of vitamins, herb supplements, cough drops, elderberry juice, saline nose spray, tissues, cool mist vaporizer, thermometer, and portable blood pressure monitor. Only a small pathway existed from the doorway around the desk to Donald's chair. Gary would never be able to find a clue in Donald's office, even if it were laying out in plain view.

Ken's office was also full to the brim. However, Ken's clutter was organized and neatly packed away in floor to ceiling boxes, bookcases, and file cabinets. There were masses and masses of books (some of them rather large), professional journals, newspaper files, computer disks, and note card file boxes. This material was meticulously labeled and alphabetized. Anything of importance to the murder case in this office would be securely hidden away. In code!

Gary got nothing more from Ken's secretary. But a brief glance of a stack of medical journals on the edge of her desk confirmed Blaze's mention of Ken's research. He left the office knowing one of the two secretaries was lying, and Gary bet it was Ken's secretary who was fibbing.

Gary went to the press secretary's office next and discovered both Ned and his secretary were out to lunch. What luck! The door was left often. Gary entered the office quietly and approached the desk. Unlike Donald and Ken, Ned was a neat freak, keeping his office clean and pristine at all times. Even the trashcan was emptied on the hour, and all trash was shredded. The flat computer screen displayed *The Washington Times* website. Nothing interesting there, except the daily Garner cartoon. The phone message pad was empty. Gary sighed discouragingly and was about to leave when he spied a single folded piece of paper in the black mesh trashcan by Ned's desk. It must have caught the edge and was left by mistake. Gary tentatively reached for the paper and opened it.

It was a list, one of many that Ned made daily. It contained a number of names and phone numbers for Ned to call. Most names were clearly marked as government departments or representatives, many of them on the Hill. Ned must be calling around on some hot issue, probably connected with the appropriation bills. There was a note about a meeting with Martha that afternoon and the time for today's press conference, nothing unusual there. Then Gary noticed initials at the bottom of the list, ones not familiar to him. No phone number, but a note had been scribbled beside the letters.

"Problems with negotiations. Call secure line to discuss original contract. Take action if necessary."

Gary folded the note and carefully placed it back inside the trashcan in the position he had found it and quickly left Ned's office. Gary took a moment to make note of the message on his own notepad. That done, he steeled his nerves, and headed for the chief of staff's office.

Gary went there hoping it, too, would be empty, but no such luck. Myers was in his office, and his secretary, a pretty blond thing in a plaid mini skirt, was busy filing her nails and talking on the phone. Not missing a beat with her phone call, the secretary waved Gary in with a smile. He found the chief of staff at his desk, dressed to the nines as usual and answering his e-mail. Myers looked up startled as Gary entered the sacred domain.

"Why, Mr. Craig, what a surprise! Have a seat while I finish this." Jim pointed to the chair in front of his desk. Myers quickly completed typing his e-mail message and sent it. "There. That's done." Myers faced Gary with a questioning look.

"What can I do for you, Mr. Craig?"

Gary had not come unprepared. If a reason to visit a West Wing office was asked for, he had one ready. Gary drew out another sheet of paper from his pocket and handed it over to Jim.

"I'm finishing up the invitation list for the German state dinner. I thought you might like to take a look at it before we give a final copy to Madame President."

Jim took the list and quickly glanced at it.

"Certainly. I'll be happy to review it. There might be a name or two left off." The subtle insult was not missed, insinuating incompetence on Gary's part. Surely Gary must have missed something. Myers read the list quickly and smiled.

"Ah, there is one change I can tell you about. On the space beside my name, you can make a deletion."

"You're not coming?" asked Gary, trying not to sound too hopeful.

Myers laughed. "Me, miss this administration's first state dinner? I wouldn't dream of it. No, you can remove the "and guest" part beside my name."

"I see," replied Gary promptly. "You are planning to come alone then."

Jim gave Gary a funny look.

"I guess you haven't heard then? I'll be Madame President's escort for the evening."

No, Gary hadn't heard that, and the news hit him squarely in the stomach. With much effort, he managed to keep a disinterested voice.

"That's nice. She asked you?"

Myers carefully laid the guest list down on his desk. "As a date? Technically, no she did not. Aunt Sophie is coming as Madame President's companion and First Lady. But I'll be present to serve as a male companion should the need arise. I doubt Martha will want to dance with Sophie after the dinner. So, seat me beside the President at dinner and at the concert."

"I'll get right on it," said Gary sourly. "I'll let my assistant and Mr. Morgan know of the arrangements."

"Excellent. In fact, why don't you send that shy assistant of yours by my office later this afternoon? I'll give him this list with my edits directly." Jim turned to his computer screen and began clicking on his e-mail, indicating the discussion was over.

Gary's emotions were churning inside, making him act against his better judgment. Myers had hit him with a bombshell. Fine. Now it was his turn. Gary cleared his throat and tossed out a comment.

"Yes, there was one more thing I wanted to ask you. It relates to President Taylor and Eric Peters. Odd that both of them died of heart attacks when they were in such great physical shape? Aren't you worried about that?"

Myers abruptly stopped answering his e-mail.

"You know?" he blurted out.

Gary stared straight at the chief of staff and replied.

"Yes, I know all about it."

Myers looked startled. Gary could see the mental wheels churning speedily inside of Myers' head. But Myers recovered, exhaled, put his finger to his lips, and got up from his chair. He walked over to the door, told his blond girl Friday to hold all calls, and then securely shut the door. Myers sat back down and spoke.

"I suppose someone told you? You have a source?"

Gary nodded his head. "A good one."

Myers nodded his head also, as he ran his fingers through his thick blond hair.

"Of course you do. Something this important wouldn't be kept a secret for long. Well, nothing I can do about that now. But what is important is that we have containment."

Gary stared at Jim Myers incredulously. That man's brazen lack of concern for anyone but himself was unbelievable. Now it was Gary's turn for an outburst.

"Containment? Containment??? You can't possibly be serious! This issue is one of national security. The nation has the right to know what is happening."

"Not necessarily," answered Myers smoothly, pressing his hands together and resting his chin upon them. "Granted, it is a delicate situation, but if it is handled right, I see no reason for the information to ever see the light of day."

"How can you say that?" Gary argued indignantly. "Two men have died, Mr. Myers! I won't stand by and see it happen again!"

Myers smiled at Gary placidly, calm, cool, and collected.

"Yes, it is a life or death situation, I admit. But my doctor has assured me that with diet, medication, and proper exercise, my cholesterol levels will soon return to normal. And how thoughtful of you, Mr. Craig, to be so concerned about my health."

This bizarre statement brought Gary up shortly.

"Your cholesterol?"

"Yes, my cholesterol. With Stan and Eric dropping dead in their tracks, you were quite right. I've been terribly worried, especially after getting the results of blood work from my physical last week."

Gary was speechless. Jim blithely continued.

"I'm scheduled for a follow-up exam next week for a stress test, but I'm hopeful the medication my doctor prescribed has already started to kick in. Besides, I'm a lot younger and healthier man than Stan and Eric were, so the odds are in my favor for a good outcome. Don't you agree?"

"Of course," murmured Gary, his head spinning.

Jim Myers sat back confidently in his chair and tilted his head to one side.

"Something the matter, Mr. Craig? You were interested in my cholesterol, right?"

"Ah, yes," agreed Gary quickly.

Myers flashed Gary a thin satisfied smile. "Well, Mr. Craig, I would appreciate it very much if you and your informant would keep this matter private. My medical condition shouldn't impair my ability to work, and most of all, I wouldn't want my public image to be tarnished. You know how nasty rumors get started, especially in this town. We wouldn't want people to get the wrong idea about my physical stamina on and off the job." At this point, Myers winked at Gary.

Gary held his fingers behind his back, crossed.

"No, we certainly wouldn't want that."

Jim stood up and extended his hand toward the door, indicating it was time for Gary to leave. "Thank you again for your concern. I'll let you know how the tests turn out next week. I hate to be rude, but I have some important calls to make. Don't forget to have your assistant come by to pick up the guest list."

Myers ushered Gary to the door, and then suddenly stopped. "Oh, one more thing, Mr. Craig. Since you seem to have such a hypnotic effect on Madame President's children, I was wondering if you could do something about the little one sneaking around here. I saw the little monster skipping out of Ken's office right after he left for lunch. It's unnerving how she gets around undetected."

"Yes, it is," agreed Gary dryly and quickly bid Myers a good day.

Gary left the office furious. It killed Gary to have to pander to that man's exalted ego. The fact that Martha would be attending the state dinner with that person by her side was enough to make him toss his cookies. It was more than maddening. It was outrageous!

At the same time, Gary walked away a bit shaken at the exchange of words. Was Myers trying to cover something up? His statements were plausible, but suppose Myers was the source inside the White House behind the murders? Had Gary recklessly tipped his hand, revealing their concerns over Taylor's death?

There was no time to waste. Either way, Gary needed to find out the truth about Myers' story, and he knew just the person who could do the finding out for him. He left the West Wing offices and walked straight to the Press Room. He looked in and spotted Jack, slouched down in his seat talking on the cell phone. Gary got the reporter's attention.

"A word. Now!" said Gary curtly.

Jack quickly ended his phone call and joined Gary out in the hallway.

"What's up, Doc?" asked Jack curiously.

"Tell me," asked Gary in a whisper, "exactly what is a 'leak' and technically how does it work?"

Jack's eyes instantly widened. "What a leading question! I may faint. Well, typically, someone like you will come to someone like me and tell me some dirt that I and the country don't know about. The more sordid, off color, or illegal, the better! I subsequently cross my heart, hope to die, and stick a needle in my eye if ever I reveal my source. I then run directly to my producers and spill the beans. Comprende?"

"And you protect the identity of the informant?" asked Gary intently.

"Till death do us part," said Jack holding up paper and his pen.

Gary looked around. No one was in the narrow hallway, and only Sam, the big guard, was at the desk, and he was busy reading the newspaper. Gary stepped closer and spoke quietly. "I have it on good authority that the White House chief of staff is not in the best of health. Washington's most eligible bachelor may have a significantly high blood cholesterol level that doctors are quite concerned about. Follow?"

Jack was writing madly. "Following you all the way, Fred."

Gary continued. "Given the heart attacks of Eric Peters and President Taylor, the doctors are taking no chances, and additional cardiovascular tests are scheduled for Mr. Myers later this week. With a heart condition, one would logically infer (although I don't know for sure) it might affect Mr. Myers' performance on the job and other aspects of his overall physical prowess. Get the drift?"

Jack grinned broadly as he scribbled. "Yeah. It's rapidly heading downstream!"

Gary put his hands into his pockets and concluded. "Total conjecture on my part, but if someone was in such poor health, should he continue serving in such a high-level White House position? Of course, it's not up to me to discover if these rumors have any merit. I leave that job to those more qualified than I to do the digging."

Jack finished writing and beamed at his friend.

"Thanks, mate. I'll run home and grab my shovel. Remind me never to get on your bad side, will you? Pardon me while I call this in. Chow!"

The reporter gleefully ran off. Gary took a deep breath and went outside, through the Jefferson colonnade beside the Rose Garden into the main house. He had only a few minutes to spare before his afternoon meeting upstairs with Aunt Sophie and Morgan.

One thing remained for Gary to do. He hastened back to his office and opened the door, finding Abigail sitting at his desk dipping her French fries melodramatically into a huge mound of ketchup. Apparently Abigail had opened the rest of the packs all by herself, and the result was a disaster. Traces of ketchup were smeared across his desk, his leather chair, his computer monitor, the little girl's face, her pink dress, and both elbows. Sheba was curled up on the edge of his desk, keenly watching the ketchup maneuvers.

"Abigail! You're a mess!" cried Gary with a huge exasperated sigh. "You need to be more careful, honey."

Abigail carefully put down her French fry.

"Can you lick your elbows?" asked Abigail. "I can." She then demonstrated this unique talent.

"That is truly amazing," said Gary crossly, taking a handkerchief out of his pocket to clean up, wiping off her face and hands. He picked up the small cat and sat down on the edge of his desk. "Abigail, listen to me. Were you hiding in Mr. Friedman's office this morning, the man with lots and lots of books in his office?"

"Uh huh," said Abigail sticking her little finger back into the ketchup and then licking it off her finger.

"Did Mr. Friedman come back to his office while you were hiding in there?" asked Gary intently.

"Uh huh," said Abigail taking up her drink and sipping it loudly with her straw.

"Put your drink down and pay attention. Did Mr. Friedman talk on the phone?"

"Uh huh," said Abigail, putting down her drink. She then took a French fry and used it like a pencil to draw circles in her ketchup. Gary impatiently took the fry away from her.

"Abigail, enough food games! Look at me. I want you to tell me what Mr. Friedman said on the phone. Tell me exactly what he said."

Abigail looked up at Gary and smiled sweetly. "Okay, Uncle Gary."

She paused to lick her thumb. Then the little child with a photographic memory leaned back in the big leather chair and recited word for word what she had overheard.

"We have a serious problem here, and I'm calling as instructed. I must see you immediately, this afternoon if possible. Things are not going well. In fact, I fear we will soon reach a crisis point. I've done everything I know how to address the situation — but my efforts have been to no avail. If something positive doesn't happen soon, we'll have to intervene . . ."

Chapter 17

The Upstairs Oval Room
(Formally the Yellow Oval Room)

Tuesday Evening, July 19

"Shoot the Moon."

Charlotte Donovan pronounced the winning game phrase after obtaining the last set of cards, revealing she had all the hearts and the queen of spades. There was a collective groan around the card table from Martha, Aunt Sophie, and General McKay, who were subsequently forced to add fifty points to each of their scorecards. America's National Security Advisor looked narrowly at Charlotte and scowled.

"That was a low blow," muttered the general.

Charlotte laughed heartily, took the cards, and dealt another hand for a new game of Hearts.

The First Family and their friends were gathered upstairs in the Oval Sitting Room after enjoying dinner together. Amid the complaints and cheers from the adults playing cards, Eliza was lying aimlessly on the floor, her bare feet propped up on one of two sofas newly upholstered in crimson plaid. Some swatches of dress fabric were lying next to her, which she was describing in detail to a friend over the phone. Eliza was to be interviewed by *Time Magazine* in a few weeks, and she was having trouble picking the dress color for the accompanying photo shoot.

Abigail was sitting in the middle of the floor, engrossed in a game of marbles. She shot them one by one across a new Oriental rug with her black cat, Sheba, pouncing in hot pursuit. Gary and Josh were sitting comfortably on the other sofa positioned in front of the television installed on the wall above the nineteenth-century Italian marble fireplace. They were playing a *Lord of the Rings* video game, hunting Orc monsters in the night battle at Helm's Deep.

Nanny Jane was also present, sitting cross-legged on the sofa reading her spy thriller and eating a second piece of chocolate cake. Martha's white cat was sitting atop the mantle with a paw poised dangerously close to a Louis XV golden urn.

The card game, the phone call, and the video game ended approximately at the same moment, and the adults moved over to the center of the room to join Gary and the kids.

"We won!" announced Josh proudly.

"So did I," added Charlotte smiling blithely at McKay.

General McKay plopped down miserably on the sofa near Nanny Jane. "Move over," he grumbled.

"Aren't you the grumpy one? You forgot to say please," Jane responded dryly, putting her cake plate down on the floor and shifting over ever so slightly.

The general ignored her and eyed Charlotte instead. "You are a fierce competitor, Mrs. Donovan," he declared gruffly. "If the White House is ever under siege, I know to whom I shall turn for reinforcements."

Charlotte laughed gaily and reached for a nearby phone. "Don't take it so hard, General. I think, perhaps, some of that yummy hot chocolate made by that young butler is just the thing we need to cheer the general up. What's his name again?"

"Dwight," answered Jane promptly while turning a page of her book.

"Right, him" said Charlotte. She picked up the phone and placed the order, then sat down in a gilded chair.

The general looked down at his round protruding waistline and moaned. "More chocolate? I believe I've reached my limit for one evening."

Nanny Jane lowered her book and stared incredulously at McKay. "Limit on chocolate? Why, General, there's no such thing."

The general folded his arms and huffed. In this house, he was clearly out-manned, or in this case, out-womaned.

Martha pulled up a chair and sat down near Mrs. Donovan.

"Enough, you two!" she ordered cheerfully. "Sophie, pull that chair over there and join us for a chat. Charlotte, I must say the renovations in this room turned out just spectacular!"

Charlotte looked proudly around the Oval Room, now painted a deep rich shade of crimson. Adding to the new color scheme, tasseled silk draperies hung in the three windows leading out to the Truman Balcony and expensive fabrics of various shades of red, gold, peach, and pink covered the furniture. Aunt Sophie came over to her chair holding a large navy tapestry bag. She sat down and pulled out her yarn and knitting needles to work on a scarf.

"Thank you, Madame President," said Charlotte. "It did turn out well, although, we've had enough complaints about changing it. The room was yellow for almost two hundred years, since the days of Dolly Madison. But now it's the way your ancestor, Mr. Jefferson, had it, and I think he'd be proud."

"I agree," said Aunt Sophie heartily, gazing up at Martha's impressionistic picture of Jefferson in Paris, now hanging magnificently on one of the walls in the room.

Charlotte's eye fell on a tall vase of blue, purple, and white larkspur on a nearby table.

"Those are nice," she observed with admiration.

"Yes, they are," said Martha blushing. "Jim sent them over today. He wanted to cheer me up after a long stretch of work on the budget. Wasn't it thoughtful of him?"

Gary silently gritted his teeth. Oh, yes, so very thoughtful indeed. Self-serving is more like it!

"Victoria, *no!*"

Eliza jumped up from the floor and rushed to the fireplace in time to catch the golden urn being pushed off the ledge.

"Naughty girl!" scolded Eliza.

The cat stared at her with a blank look and blinked, a gaze devoid of any guilt. Cats don't do guilt.

Eliza put the urn back securely on the mantle and lifted the large white cat onto her shoulder. "Mom, I'm tired. I think I'll take Victoria up to bed with me."

"Very well," said Martha. "I'll come up and get her later before I turn in. Sweet dreams my dear."

Eliza went over and gave her mother a kiss on the cheek, and then did the same with Aunt Sophie. Then, to Gary's surprise, the teenager came over and gave him a big hug.

"Can you help me pick out the fabric for my dress tomorrow?" asked Eliza anxiously.

"Come by around noon. We'll figure it out together," said Gary with pleasure.

She gave him a sparkling smile and left. Josh also got up, yawning.

"I'm cooked. I'm going upstairs, too. Night, Mom. Night, Sophie. Night, Jane. Night, General. Night, Uncle Gary."

Having said his goodbyes, Josh promptly followed his older sister upstairs. This left Abigail, who showed no signs of retiring whatsoever. She had finished her game of marbles and was now sitting squarely at Gary's feet, hard at work coloring in her new color book of famous First Ladies and their inaugural gowns. She was currently engrossed in coloring the dress of Eleanor Roosevelt a ghastly shade of lime green. Gary was pretty certain that color never made it to Mrs. Roosevelt's closet. Sheba was sitting beside Abigail, washing her front paws. Gary looked down at Abby's plastic box of crayons and was pleased to see no tubes of lipstick in the mix. Perhaps his lectures on the subject had finally taken hold.

"Abigail, are you ready for bed?" asked Aunt Sophie sweetly.

"No," said Abigail.

Nanny Jane put her book down and apologized. "Sorry about that. It's my fault really. I let her have a rather long nap this afternoon. Abby, dearest, how about a nice warm bubble bath?"

Abigail looked up at her nanny warily. It was a tempting offer, but not good enough.

"I want to stay," replied the five-year-old obstinately. She picked up a tangerine colored crayon and began coloring Mrs. Roosevelt's hair.

Martha and Aunt Sophie looked at the willful little girl and exchanged knowing glances.

Martha tried. "Why don't you take your bubble bath and then Uncle Gary will come down and read you a bedtime story."

Now that was more like it! Abigail immediately put down her orange crayon and looked up at Gary expectantly.

"Will you really read me a bedtime story, Uncle Gary?"

Gary nodded his head in the affirmative. Abigail relented, got up, and placed her coloring book and box of crayons squarely in Gary's lap.

"Keep these," commanded Queen Abigail as Nanny Jane took her charge by the hand.

"Have a nice bath," said Gary. "We'll read about Charlotte's web and Wilbur when you're done."

"And I want a George the Monkey book, too," said Abigail, amending the deal.

"Okay!" said Gary.

Abigail beamed, and Nanny Jane led the little girl out, leaving the adults alone. Once alone, Martha and the general exchanged quick glances. The general then picked up the television remote, turned to the CNN news channel, and turned the volume up. Martha leaned forward, and spoke quietly.

"It's time to hold a family council."

Her words hung poignantly in the air, and Gary sat straight up, putting the crayons and coloring book aside while looking at Martha and the general apprehensively.

Martha continued. "We need to talk about the dangerous situation we're facing, and, pardon the expression; it's time we laid all of our cards on the table." Martha looked directly at Charlotte.

"Understood," said Charlotte softly.

Gary looked at Mrs. Donovan amazed.

"You know, too?" asked Gary astounded. He turned to the general. "You told me not to tell anyone."

"I told her," confessed Aunt Sophie. She put down her knitting and looked at Charlotte and the general perplexed.

"It was per my orders. Charlotte had to be told," replied the general in a stern voice.

Charlotte cleared her throat. "General, perhaps I should explain. There was good reason to inform me, Mr. Craig." She paused, taking a deep breath. "The general had to tell me about the murder of Eric Peters and President Taylor because of my husband's connection with intelligence. You see, my husband is an informant for the CIA."

"And a very good one," added the general decisively.

"So, that's why your husband has been out of the country so much!" said Gary enlightened.

Charlotte nodded. "Exactly. My husband's business really does require him to travel a great deal internationally. It has for many years now. Consequently, the CIA approached him about ten years ago and recruited him into service. At first, he was just a carrier and did little jobs, not very dangerous. But, — and this will sound quite biased — my husband is a very smart man and very adventurous by nature. He's turned out to be quite a good agent." Charlotte smiled proudly. "My husband and I have known the general for some time now, through the general's past work at the Pentagon. So, when the general became suspicious of Peters' and Taylor's deaths, and more recently, the death of Bishop Palmer, he contacted my husband and secretly commissioned him to do some low-key investigative work while he was overseas. I, of course, had to be told."

Gary swallowed hard. "Are you a spy too?"

Charlotte laughed merrily. "Me? Heavens, no! I am what you see, a bossy rich woman who likes to decorate and have her own way. I'm still a little bit embarrassed at our beginnings, Mr. Craig, being so argumentative, but I trust that's all water under the bridge now. Anyway, I'm in for the duration and so is my husband!"

"And we're grateful for your support," said Martha reaching over and grabbing Charlotte's hand. She then spoke to Gary. "Which brings us to what's happening in the intelligence community. The general is pursuing leads abroad. General?"

General McKay took over. "Right. An agent of ours was sent down to Brazil where Bishop Palmer was headed, and leads there suggest a European connection. Mr. Donovan is currently in Brazil and will head over to London soon to follow up on that trail. I should know more details in a few days."

Martha continued. "Given what we know about the deaths of Peters and President Taylor and from what Mr. Craig learned about the Stand Out demonstration in Greensboro, we are fairly certain we are dealing with a very powerful, covert organization, one that is highly structured and funded. We believe their mission is to take control of the White House. Gratefully, the data does not indicate the group is connected with any third-world terrorist organization, like Al-Qaeda. That's the good news. The bad news is the evidence we have that someone inside the West Wing is involved in this scheme."

"It's so hard to believe!" declared Aunt Sophie emotionally, her knitting needles flying. "To think someone we know and work with every day could do such a thing!"

"Happens more often than you think," reflected McKay cynically.

"The White House connection," said Martha thickly, "is known by very few individuals. It must stay that way as to not alert the individual before we have a chance to discover his identity. Only the people in this room and select agents have been told."

"Agent Clark and Agent Lewis," clarified McKay. "If you need help for any reason in this matter, you can contact them directly."

"Good choice," owned Gary with satisfaction. They would have been his choice, too.

"Other than that, I'm afraid we don't have much else to go on right now," reported Martha candidly.

Gary felt his insides tighten. He better tell them what he discovered. "Well, actually," he said awkwardly, shifting his position on the sofa, "I did some discreet inquiries of my own this afternoon."

Four sets of eyes fixed themselves upon Gary. Aunt Sophie stopped knitting.

"You did what?" barked the general loudly.

Gary wilted beneath the hard military stare. "I went over to the West Wing during my lunch break today and visited the offices of all the prime suspects."

The general's eyes narrowed.

"Prime suspects?" Martha looked at Gary incredulously. "You've actually made a list?"

"Yes, it's the people who recommended candidates for the VP slot that day we met at Taylor's farm."

"How brave you are, Mr. Craig!" muttered Aunt Sophie as she knitted.

"Don't encourage him, Sophie," warned the general gravely. "That was a dangerous thing you did, young man. In the future, please consult with me before you take any unauthorized action."

Aunt Sophie ignored the general's rebuke. She smiled approvingly at Gary. "Oh, hush, Charles. I think it was very noble."

General McKay grimaced. "Noble or not, it was a dangerous thing to do, Mr. Craig. You must be careful! I don't need you getting killed as well. Okay, that said, did you learn anything?"

"Well, yes," said Gary tentatively. "A few things, beginning with my friend Blaze." Gary then reviewed for them a summation of what he had found: Blaze's new connection with Congressman Kingsley which Blaze lied about; the conflicting mysterious luncheon appointments as related by Hooper and Friedman's secretaries; Friedman's sudden interest in medical journals; and the odd note in Ned's trash can.

"I also intercepted a weird phone call from Ken Friedman's office," added Gary hesitantly.

"Intercepted?" General McKay sat up in alarm.

Aunt Sophie looked up at Gary, her eyes sparkling.

"Oh, Mr. Craig, did you bug Ken Friedman's office with a microphone, like they do on television?"

"Sophie!" cried the general.

Gary smiled and shook his head emphatically, then looked at Martha for some guidance on this topic. "Nothing that high tech. I had a more simplistic means."

Martha didn't miss a beat. She laughed softly.

"What Mr. Craig is alluding to is my youngest daughter's photographic memory, a fact I would prefer to be kept private, Charlotte. Abigail can repeat verbatim what is said in her presence — minutes, hours, days, even weeks after the conversation takes place."

Charlotte Donovan's eyes nearly popped out of her head. "Lord have mercy on us all. Remind me to watch what I say around here."

"Enough of that. What exactly did you discover with Friedman's phone call?" quizzed the general, bringing the discussion back to the investigation.

Gary pulled out a piece of paper and handed it over to the general. "I wrote it down. There."

The general read the note grimly and then passed it on to Martha. She read it out loud for the others to hear.

Martha had an unhappy look of resignation on her face. "I didn't know about this. Abigail didn't tell me."

"She's been busy exploring the White House, and this time it paid off," said Gary.

Martha nodded. "Well, I guess we can say Ken Friedman is our chief suspect."

"I'm afraid so, with Donald Hooper next in line, however unlikely that may sound," added the general reluctantly. "It appears he is involved in the outside luncheon meetings with Ken. I've also noticed that Donald has been more nervous lately. I'll put undercover agents on both of them to track their afternoon and evening outings."

Martha gave Gary a curious look. "What about Jim Myers? He was at the meeting at the Taylor farm. Did you find anything on Jim?"

Gary bit his lip. After the general's scolding, he wasn't about to give a play-by-play account of his strange exchange with Myers. The general would kill him. Besides, the talk with Myers turned out to be a dead end. Gary decided to say nothing and leave it to the press to sort out. Jack and his chums were pretty good sorters.

"Nope, not a thing."

Martha smiled in relief. "Of course not. I know he's young and overbearing at times, and he can rub people the wrong way. But he is very dedicated to me and this administration, that I am sure of."

Gary didn't like the sound of that at all.

Martha concluded. "Very well, then. The general will keep a close eye on Ken and Donald, and that means we should also have Secretary Patrick and Attorney General Hernandez watched closely as well. We must proceed with caution. Now, I'd like to talk about one more thing. The general, Aunt Sophie, and I discussed it this morning, and we want both of you to move into the White House residence, beginning tonight."

Gary and Charlotte gasped in unison.

"Whatever for?" cried Charlotte in disbelief.

"For your safety, Charlotte. If someone were to discover your husband's role in this matter, they may well come after you as a means to derail him. You would make an excellent kidnapping victim. Your cover for moving into the residence is easy enough to provide. I've officially asked you to move in temporarily to oversee the ongoing renovations to the House."

Mrs. Donovan thought a moment and agreed. "All right. I'll give up the daily commute from Rock Springs. I'll go home and get my things this evening."

"With a police escort, Madame," added the general firmly. "They will drive you and assist you in packing as well. And you are not to go inside your home till they have done a sweep of the residence."

Mrs. Donovan's eyes widened. "Yes, General. Whatever you say."

The room got quiet and everyone turned to look at Gary, who was still taking in Martha's request.

"Why am I included?" he asked bluntly.

"That should be obvious," was Martha's reply. Her eyes sparkled at him warmly. "Anyone I work with knows your value to my family. Consequently, one way to get to me would be through you. And I simply won't have it. I know it's awkward and inconvenient but please say yes."

Gary sadly noted that she didn't say "Your value to me" but her voice was sincere and plaintive. How could he refuse those pleading green eyes?

"Yes," said Gary.

Martha let out a sigh, looking quite relieved. "Excellent. Your cover story is we've asked you to move in due to the extreme workload of the upcoming state dinner. I'll have rooms prepared for both of you up on the third floor. Josh and Eliza will be absolutely thrilled to have the company." She picked up the phone and called down to Morgan's office to give the orders.

Just then there was a subtle knock on the door, and the butler Dwight entered, pushing a rolling cart with white mugs and a pot of his famous steaming hot chocolate.

Aunt Sophie quickly put down her knitting and got up.

"Oh, good, Dwight. Right on time. Just the thing we need after a long day. Pour the hot chocolate, and then Charlotte and I will take some up to the children. Oh, wait! We forgot to get something else for Abigail. She doesn't like hot chocolate."

"A child who doesn't like chocolate?" said Charlotte with surprise.

Aunt Sophie laughed. "She only eats her chocolate cold. Very picky that child! Dwight, can you make some pink lemonade for her?"

Dwight flashed his big smile while pouring the hot drink into the mugs. "Oh, yes, Mrs. Johnson. Right away." He finished serving the adults, and then quickly left.

Aunt Sophie and Charlotte picked up two mugs and left the Oval Room chatting excitedly about knitting and cross stitch and the fact that Charlotte was moving in. It was plain to Gary that Aunt Sophie would enjoy the companionship of a woman her age in the White House.

"God! Listen to this!" exclaimed McKay, with the remote in hand again. He turned up the volume. The screen flashed a breaking alert bulletin. The tan face and flashing white teeth of Jack Parish appeared standing on the lawn of the White House with microphone in hand, breaking the news.

"Sources at the White House have just confirmed that chief of staff Jim Myers may be seriously ill. Alarming rumors surfaced inside the West Wing this afternoon that the young chief of staff has a bum heart and was examined recently by physicians who are concerned about the young man's health and ability to continue serving in office. Myers and his staff declined to comment this evening on the veracity of the story, but according to sources inside the administration, Mr. Myers received poor test results on his heart health earlier this week. This is startling news, just several months after President Taylor died of a heart attack. Doctors are planning to monitor Mr. Myers . . ."

"Did you know about this?" asked McKay sharply.

"No. I had no idea. He hasn't said a thing. Oh, God, do you think someone has tried to poison him as well?" exclaimed Martha anxiously.

"Doubtful," said the general positively. "If Jim had been exposed to the same combination of prussic acid and DSMO, he would not be alive. If he is having heart problems, it's just a coincidence."

"I don't like coincidences," said Martha.

"Nor do I," said the general frowning. "It won't hurt to do some checking."

McKay turned off the television set and said he would go downstairs to make his own inquiries on the story. He promised to also go to the Secret Service office to confirm the arrangements for Charlotte and Gary to move in. The general departed, leaving Gary and Martha alone.

Admittedly, Gary was feeling a tiny bit guilty about Myers. Martha looked pretty upset. Perhaps he should say something.

"Don't worry about Jim," said Gary. "I'm sure he's just fine."

"I hope so. I really don't think I can take much more of this!"

"Have some hot chocolate," suggested Gary helpfully.

Martha picked up her mug of hot chocolate and took a sip.

"Tastes good," she said closing her eyes. "Just what I needed."

Gary followed suit. The warm sweet liquid warmed and comforted him.

"Not bad," was his expert opinion.

"How about a stroll on the Truman Balcony?" invited Martha. "Let's see how the big crater in my backyard is coming along."

Gary followed Martha out onto the balcony that overlooked the South Lawn and the east end of the Washington Mall with its famous monuments. He stood next to the President to gaze out onto the darkened yard below. The round grassy circle known as the Ellipse sported an enormous hole in the ground, surrounded by bulldozers and mounds of dirt, piles of brick, and stacks of cement bags.

"Lovely, isn't it?" said Martha wistfully as she sipped her drink.

"Yes, it's a very nice pit," said Gary.

Martha laughed and pointed left towards the Kennedy Garden. "No, silly, the new Jefferson Arch and serpentine walls. The Arch is finally up. One thing is missing though," mused Martha critically staring down at the garden. "The new walls look barren. You've been telling me for some time now we should have real roses, old roses, planted again at the White House. Why don't you contact Dr. Campbell and the two of you put in an old-fashioned rose garden?"

No request could have made Gary happier. He felt like jumping off the balcony and running down the South Lawn shouting for joy.

"I'll call Dr. Campbell first thing tomorrow. He'll bring his shovel."

"Good," said Martha. "Will the roses take long to establish?"

"Not necessarily. We can put in some ramblers that will grow in no time flat. And I'll put in a Mermaid rose as well. She has large yellow single flowers with some thick, wicked thorns. She'll add to the wall's security."

"Sounds perfect!" Martha continued to stare down at the garden below, lost in her own thoughts. Gary stood quietly beside her for a while and relished the moment of comfortable silence between two like-minded people.

Suddenly she spoke in a hushed sad voice.

"I shouldn't be here, you know."

"What do you mean?" he asked startled.

She stepped back and looked at him solemnly.

"Taylor should have picked someone else. Why pick me? I didn't ask for this. I love politics, it's true, but I had no political experience or political ambitions. I agreed to his request, but I thought I would only be the partner in Stan's shadow. Now he's dead and I'm president, knowing that someone inside the White House is guilty of murder. And everyone is pressuring me to pick a vice president. The decision needs to be made soon, but until I know for certain who is guilty, I will not give such a powerful position away!" Then she bent her head. Gary noticed a single tear running down her cheek.

Gary put down his mug on a nearby table, and put his arm around her shoulder. He calmly handed her a handkerchief.

"Go ahead. Cry. You need to get it out."

She took the handkerchief and let loose her feelings. He kept his arm securely around her as she gave full vent to all her grief and frustration. He said nothing, just held her tightly and gazed out across the darkened South Lawn until the torrent of emotion finally subsided.

"Thanks," she said sniffing. "I've needed to do that for some time now."

"I completely understand," Gary said sympathetically. "I could do with a good cry myself. I'm afraid I'm not very good at it."

Martha wiped away her remaining tears. "Thomas Jefferson once said, 'The appointment of a woman to office is an innovation for which the public is not prepared. Nor am I.' Perhaps he was right. Perhaps I have no business being here."

"I wouldn't say that," said Gary decisively. "If President Jefferson were here, he'd be your biggest fan. This is not the time to second-guess yourself. You're doing a great job."

"Thanks," she said handing him back his handkerchief. "It's just so overwhelming. With all this cloak and dagger, I'm becoming quite paranoid, especially for my children's sake. It's hard to know whom to trust. I'm really worried about the children's safety, even in this fortress. I'm at a loss as to what to do next."

Gary shoved the handkerchief back into his pocket and gazed steadily at her. "I don't know a lot about your man Jefferson, but I do know one of his sayings by heart, one that might be apropos for this situation."

"Which one is that?"

Gary smiled mischievously. "'A little rebellion now and then is a good thing.'"

Martha's eyes grew wide in wonder.

"Gary Craig, what in the world are you suggesting?"

Gary turned and looked out across the darkened South Lawn, out past the tall black iron gates, down onto the awe-inspiring Washington Monument, white and majestic and glistening in the summer moonlight.

"It's time you did what every other woman I know does in the face of personal crisis, what perhaps unconsciously you've been doing with the interior and exterior renovations to the House for the last few months." He turned and addressed President Johnson for the first time by her given name. "Martha, I think it's time you cleaned house."

Chapter 18

The Cabinet Room

Friday, July 22

Music was playing off in the distance.

The sound of a lone violin drifted lightly upon the wind. It was a haunting melody that invited him to follow.

He heard someone calling his name.

Following the call, Gary walked down a narrow graveled path that led out into an open grassy field, surrounded by weeping willow trees. To his right, children were playing. There was a Maypole decorated with brightly colored ribbons. Little girls in white dresses danced merrily around and around the pole. Eliza and Abigail were among the children. Abigail was holding on to a pink ribbon as she circled the Maypole. Purple flowers were woven into her hair. Harriet was at a nearby table cutting a three-tier wedding cake. Nanny Jane and Mildred were standing next to the table watching the children while talking quietly among themselves. Mildred was holding a blood red orchid.

Gary turned and saw a line of young soldiers marching across the green field dressed in eighteenth century Revolutionary War costume. Agents Clark and Lewis were in the center of the line, each carrying a musket. Josh was marching next to them, playing a drum. General McKay was out in front carrying an American flag. He heard gunshots ringing off in the distance.

Gary walked on, following the sound of the violin to the edge of a steep embankment. A wide dark river rushed below.

He saw her on the other side of the riverbank. There was Martha standing beside President Thomas Jefferson. Jefferson was playing the violin. Martha held out her hand, beckoning Gary to come.

She was the one calling his name.

Martha! I'm coming. Martha, wait for me.

Gary looked down at the water, churning, black, dangerous. There were jagged rocks in the midst of the rapids. How could he reach her? He could see no bridge or boat to ferry him safely across, and he could hear the gunfire getting closer. He looked again at the rocks. He would have to jump. It was the only way. But he could die if he missed the opposite bank.

He jumped out into the chasm.

He was falling down, down into the dark water below.

Falling down into the deep.

Sinking into the cold crystal river.

There was pressure against his chest.

He couldn't breathe.

His face was wet . . .

Gary awoke with a start, abruptly opening his eyes. It was pitch black in the room, and it took a moment to orient himself. Where was he? Oh, right. He wasn't at home. He was upstairs in the White House. He relaxed a moment and closed his eyes again. It was just a stupid nightmare, just a bad dream. Go back to sleep. But then he became aware of a real weight sitting on his chest, making it hard to breath. He opened his eyes again. Sheba was lying on top of him staring. Gary sighed and stared right back at her. The black cat leaned forward and gingerly licked his chin. His face really was wet. Gary began petting the kitty on the head and softly scolded her.

"Naughty girl! You scared me half to death!"

Sheba purred contentedly and licked his hand.

Gary glanced over to his bedside table. The alarm clock read 3:30 A.M. Gary suddenly sensed he was not alone. He reached over and turned on the bedside lamp. Abigail, in her pink-footed pajamas, was standing at the foot of his bed. A faded pink blanket was draped over her right shoulder and a thumb was in her mouth.

"Abigail, what are you doing up here?" asked Gary.

The thumb came out briefly.

"I'm scared," said Abigail.

Gary sat up in his bed, pulling up the comforter and pillows snugly around him.

"Why are you scared, sweetheart?" he asked yawning. "Did you have a bad dream, too?"

"There is a monster in my room," explained Abigail edging up closer to Gary.

Gary yawned again. It was much too late for monsters.

"Abigail, honey, there isn't a monster in your room, I promise."

"Yes, there is," objected Abigail obstinately. "I saw it. It's inside the curtains. Josh and Eliza saw a monster last night in their rooms, too."

Given concerns about someone breaking into the White House, Abigail's comment got Gary's attention fast. He rubbed his eyes and looked at the little girl intently.

"Josh and Eliza have seen the monster?"

Abigail's head bobbed up and down. "Uh huh. They told me all about it. Eliza saw it in the hallway, and Josh saw it his room. Josh says it lives here and scares people. He says it's Lincoln's G-H-O-S-T."

Gary frowned. Okay. It wasn't a terrorist inside the White House after all, just old Abe. Gary knew about the romantic stories of Lincoln's ghost residing at the White House, roaming the halls late at night. Some overnight guests positively swore that they have seen the tall former president in the Lincoln Bedroom or walking along the Cross Hall. Such stories were myth and legend, of course, but Gary was angry that Josh and Eliza had repeated the stories in Abigail's presence. Given the child's photographic memory, such story telling was only asking for trouble.

"Did Josh tell you what a G-H-O-S-T is?" asked Gary.

"No," said Abigail impatiently. "Come on, Uncle Gary. Hurry. You have to come get it."

The little girl began pulling the thick comforter aside.

"Okay, okay, okay," said Gary. He stood up, put on his bedroom slippers, and took Abigail firmly by the hand.

"Thank God you can't spell."

There were a number of routes from the third floor to the second floor residence. The elevator unfortunately ran on the west side of the building, which opened up directly near Martha and Aunt Sophie's rooms. Not wanting to disturb the President or First Lady, that way down was not an option. So, Gary and Abigail went down the main staircase, which was on the east side of the mansion. It led straight to the Queen's Bedroom and Lincoln Bedroom. Gary held Abigail's hand as he carefully walked down the dark stairs through East Hall. There were deep shadows all around, in the nooks and crannies of the hallway, lots of places for a tall bearded ghost to hide. No wonder the little girl was scared.

With Abigail standing in the open doorway to the queen's suite, Gary turned on the lights and dutifully checked for drooling ravenous creatures lurking underneath the bed (twice), inside the closet, inside the bathroom, and behind two large sets of heavy curtains. He even looked up the fireplace flue and inside her toy box. Finally satisfied that the coast was clear, Abigail crawled back in her bed, insisting that Uncle Gary sit with her until she fell asleep. Gary dutifully pulled over a rocking chair, and in his very off-key voice, he softly sang the mockingbird song to Abigail. Finally, the little girl was softly snoring.

Gary was now completely wide awake.

He sat contentedly for a few moments, watching Abigail blissfully sleeping, and recalled his strange dream. Maypoles and minutemen? Leaping across ravines to Martha and Thomas Jefferson? Gary shook his head and yawned again. Perhaps he should see a therapist. Donald could give him a referral. There should be plenty to choose from in the capital. People had to be slightly nuts to work around here!

In his edge of his peripheral vision, Gary caught sight of a sudden movement in the dark hall. A slim shadow moved quickly across the open doorway. Gary blinked his eyes and looked again. The shadow was gone, but his heart began to pound. Were his eyes playing tricks on him?

Could it actually be a ghost? Lincoln's ghost?

First checking to make sure that Abigail was soundly asleep, Gary got up slowly from the chair and crept cautiously forward. He thought he saw a flicker of movement again and was almost at the door when he accidentally stepped on one of Abigail's plastic baby dolls lying on the floor. The doll made a sharp crying sound. Gary jumped. He distinctly heard a sound in the hallway, a door closing? He tried moving forward again, but he tripped and fell over a roller skate, landing hard against the doorframe, jamming his left big toe. He let out a cry that rivaled the baby doll.

A light inside of the Lincoln Bedroom across the hall turned on.

Nanny Jane suddenly appeared in the hallway, dressed in a crumpled blue terrycloth bathrobe (several sizes too big) with a white towel wrapped around her head.

"Good Lord, Mr. Craig, is that you?" she asked.

"Yes, it's me," said Gary apologetically getting up off the floor. His toe ached.

"Are you quite all right?"

"I'm fine. Just stubbed my toe."

"You gave me quite a shock," complained Nanny Jane. "What on earth are you doing downstairs at this time of night?"

"Abigail came upstairs and woke me up. Said she saw a monster in her room, Lincoln's G-H-O-S-T. We have Josh and Eliza to thank for that."

She folded her arms with displeasure. "Honestly, how very vexing those two! I shall have a word with them straight away in the morning."

"Thank you. Abigail's imagination doesn't need any encouragement. Sorry if I woke you."

Nanny Jane shook her head vigorously. "Oh, no, I was up reading actually. Couldn't sleep again I'm afraid. Insomnia. And I've had a most unpleasant upset stomach. I suppose I'm not used to eating such a steady supply of rich food."

Gary smiled at Jane sympathetically.

"I'll see if the cooks can whip you up something tomorrow very British and very bland."

"How very kind you are, Mr. Craig," said Jane. "I'd be most grateful."

"Try and get some sleep," advised Gary sincerely. He bid the nanny goodnight and made his way back up the large staircase. Once on the third floor landing, he anxiously peered around and down the hallways, but there was nothing to see near his room or that of Mrs. Donovan or the other children. He went to his room, crawled back in bed, and resolutely turned off the light. Martha's paranoia was getting to him. The family was absolutely safe inside the White House. With the high tech security, Secret Service, and Park Police force on guard, only a real ghost could penetrate the inner sanctum of the family residence.

Gary told himself this repeatedly as he closed his eyes. But sleep was a long time coming, and Gary lay in bed for a while, awake and feeling quite certain that someone more corporeal than a ghost had walked the halls of the White House that night.

One advantage of residing inside the White House was missing the long commute into D.C. each morning. Not having to battle the insane traffic of the 495 Beltway translated into an extra hour of sleep, which Gary definitely needed today.

He was just waking up when his bedside phone rang. It was Harriet.

"Good morning," said Gary sleepily.

"Good morning, Gary dear," gushed Harriet brightly. "Did I wake you?"

"I was just up," said Gary yawning

"I'm sorry to call so early, but I have the most exciting news! Bert popped the question last night. We're engaged!"

The announcement caused Gary to sit upright in his bed.

"Harriet, congratulations! I'm so happy for you!"

"Thanks. I can't believe myself. Imagine this happening to me, a woman my age!"

Gary smiled. "No one deserves it more. Tell me everything."

"Well, you know how my kitchen faucet is always so leaky. I had Bert over for dinner last night — we had pork chops and cauliflower with cheese sauce and fried apples — and that old faucet was acting up again. It was after dinner and Bert was helping me clear the table and he spied the faucet dripping. He went out to his truck and got his tools and started working on it. Then he stood up and said, 'This here faucet sure is a tricky thing, Harriet. You need someone like me to take care of it for you.' I said of course and asked him how long he thought it would take. Bert said, 'The rest of my life.' Then he dropped down on his knee right then with the wrench in his hand and asked me to marry him."

Gary sighed. "A romantic plumber! Women across America will envy you! Have you set a date?"

"Oh, sometime around Christmas or New Year. We don't really want a big wedding though. We're too old for that. We just want something simple, a small church wedding with a few good friends and family. But even that will take some planning. Now I have something special to ask you. You're like a son to me, Gary, and I want you to do me the honor of giving me away."

"Absolutely!" cried Gary happily. "I would be thrilled. Now it's my turn for good news and invitations. I would like to invite you and Mildred up as my guests to the upcoming state dinner with the German chancellor and the new German U.N. ambassador and their wives."

"Oh, Gary, how good you are to us. Of course, we'll come. Mildred is just home from another travel abroad. Poor dear. She's in bed knocked over by jet lag. She just got back from Scotland last night."

"Scotland?"

"Mmm, yes. Some rich Scottish lord got it in his mind to grow orchids and decided Mildred was the only one in the world who could help him get started right. Wouldn't take no for an answer. Wouldn't wait either. Wanted her to come across the pond, as they say, straight away. The Orchid Society paid for her expenses, thank goodness. So she dropped everything and dashed over. It was a quick trip and now she's back and got an awful head cold. The castle was very damp and drafty, I'm told. I guess the lord of the manor doesn't spend money on anything practical like air conditioning."

Gary laughed. "Well, have Mildred call me tonight when she's up and around. I want to hear more about her trip. About the state dinner, I hope Bert won't mind sparing you for an evening. I'm afraid space is tight and I couldn't get him an invitation."

Harriet chuckled. "Bert won't mind. He's very supportive. He'll get by a few nights without me. Maybe he can work on that crazy kitchen faucet again while I'm gone!"

"Listen," said Gary looking at the alarm clock again on his nightstand. "I need to run, but I want you and Mildred to come up for a day or two before the dinner. You can stay at my condo. And as my wedding present, let me take you shopping for your wedding dress."

At this, Harriet burst in tears.

Gary rang off and got out of bed. Sheba was in his room again, this time napping at the foot of the bed. The black cat had become his shadow. She got up, too, and ambled after him into the bathroom. Sheba sat down on the white bath mat and took her own bath as Gary showered, then she jumped up onto the toilet seat and supervised as Gary shaved. After Gary dressed, he picked up Sheba and went downstairs to join the First Family and Charlotte for breakfast in the second floor President's Dining Room. Gary really liked this room. Predominantly gray-blue in color, the room featured a wallpaper of murals of the War of Independence. Curtains of blue and green silk damask framed two windows. In the center there was a larger dark wood Sheraton pedestal dining table.

The table was full of adults gathered for breakfast. Gary sat down at one end, with Nanny Jane sitting to his immediate right. She was enjoying eggs and toast while immersed in a London newspaper. At the other end of the table, Martha sat with Jim Myers at her right. Martha's cat, Victoria, was in her lap. Martha looked lovely, wearing a classic navy suit and white blouse. Her blond hair was pulled back behind her head with a clip. She looked up and mouthed a silent good morning to Gary when he arrived, then continued her meeting with Myers. They were talking in hushed voices, busy looking over an agenda for the day that Jim had brought up and, of course, reviewing the PDB (President's Daily Briefing). With the increase of terrorist attacks around the world and with the specific threat against Martha's life, Myers and McKay and Martha reviewed the PDB together each morning over breakfast.

Myers' presence at breakfast was annoying to Gary. Myers held his own daily meetings with chief staffers every morning, going over newspapers and identifying important news items and topics of concern. But now, he had wormed his way upstairs, reviewing the PDB over breakfast. Myers presence meant Martha had to work while eating, so Myers was getting the bulk of her time and attention. The chief of staff was looking perfect as usual in a new black suit. How many suits did that man have? Gary looked down at his old brown one. It looked a bit dated and dingy. Perhaps it was time to do some shopping himself. He would buy himself a new suit or two when he took Harriet out shopping for her wedding dress.

General McKay was also at breakfast. He was sitting at Martha's left. He was quietly eating his eggs and toast, his nose buried deep inside a copy of *The Wall Street Journal* as he had already reviewed the PDB. It gave Gary a feeling of security to have the general around. McKay wasn't afraid of terrorists. Terrorists, if they had any brains at all, would be terrified of him. The only thing McKay seemed to fear was Nanny Jane, in whose hands a shoe, handbag, or glass of punch became lethal weapons. Sitting between McKay and Nanny Jane (keeping the distance and the peace) was Charlotte, who was enjoying a western omelet and chatting with Aunt Sophie, who was seated across the table beside Mr. Myers. None of the children were present.

"Where's Abigail?" asked Gary sitting down by Jane.

"Her Majesty is having breakfast in bed," replied Jane dryly.

"I see. Perhaps putting her in the Queen's Bedroom was a mistake."

"Indeed," said Jane crunching on her buttered toast.

The butler, Dwight, appeared miraculously the moment Gary sat down. Dwight's timing and ability were always impeccable. The young butler poured Gary a cup of coffee and asked for Gary's breakfast order.

"I'll have what she's having with a side order of bacon, extra crispy," said Gary pointing to Jane's plate. Dwight flashed Gary a formal smile and departed with the order.

"Where are Eliza and Josh?" asked Gary after Dwight left.

"They are serving HRM in bed as their punishment for scaring her with stories about Lincoln's G-H-O-S-T. I've ordered them to serve breakfast and to be playmates the entire day."

Gary stared at Jane in astonishment.

"You are good!"

Jane looked up briefly from her paper.

"Yes, I know."

Jane offered to share a portion of her London newspaper with Gary. "Here's the life section and the sports pages, if you care to read about football. Spain gave us a brutal beating. I've got the theatre section. There's a new Broadway play starting in London. Sounds perfectly dreadful, which means it will be a big hit!"

Dwight magically appeared again with Gary's breakfast. Gary settled to read while eating. He read reviews of recipes for beef carpaccio and potato crepes with caviar in silence while half-heartedly eavesdropping in on Aunt Sophie and Charlotte's discussion. The topic was the transformation of the Monroe Treaty Room into a Jefferson Library. The Historical Society had balked again at the news until, Charlotte noted with glee, it was decided to move the Monroe artifacts down to the entrance hall of the new State Dining Room under construction. Aunt Sophie's contribution to this exchange of gossip was the news that members of Jefferson's family and executives at Monticello had come up with items of furniture and books belonging to the former president that they were willing to put on permanent loan to the White House. Photographs of some of the furniture items would be arriving today for review. Charlotte also wanted Aunt Sophie to help her go through the catalog of items in the White House warehouses to see what, if any, original Jefferson material was located there.

Charlotte and Sophie were in the midst of discussing wall color when Martha and Jim Myers stood up from the table to leave for the West Wing. Martha carefully let Victoria down to the floor and then bid her family and friends goodbye. She briefly flashed Gary another distant smile as she left. Since inviting him to move in, she had emotionally pulled away again, and their exchanges were very formal during work hours. Myers followed her out, too closely thought Gary unhappily. Victoria also followed, her tail fluffy and raised straight up high in the air. The white cat walked proudly past Gary, nose in the air, ignoring him.

General McKay put away his newspaper and took a final sip of coffee.

"Best get to work myself," he grunted. "Needed down in the Situation Room. Shouldn't keep the NSA people waiting. They aren't a patient bunch."

"Good hunting," wished Charlotte merrily. "Catch a few terrorists."

"Yes, have a nice day, General," said Aunt Sophie. "You will join us for dinner tonight?"

General McKay looked a bit sheepish, not a normal look for the man.

"Sophie, are you sure? I don't want to wear out my welcome."

"Nonsense," replied Aunt Sophie solemnly. "That can never happen. Dinner is at eight."

Cheered, the general accepted. Then he did the oddest thing. He came around the table to where Gary was sitting and dropped a folded piece of paper by Gary's plate and then left without a word.

Gary opened the note. It was short, handwritten by Martha.

"A 'Little Rebellion' starts today.
Cabinet meeting 10:00
Please attend."

☆　☆　☆

With the cabinet meeting added on to his morning schedule, Gary needed to get to his office early. He quickly finished his breakfast, bid the ladies good day, and hurried downstairs and over to the East Wing. He arrived to find his trustworthy assistant already there, sorting and stacking files and papers and mail on his desk in three even piles.

"Christmas, state dinner, everything else," said Ryan promptly pointing to the stacks on Gary's desk. "Matters needing immediate attention are on top," he added crisply. "Be sure to look at the Christmas tree contest applicants. The tree selection for the Blue Room must be determined this month. Once we select the farm, Mr. Morgan will fly out and select the actual tree to be used this year."

"Sounds great. Thanks for the sorting. You're a lifesaver," said Gary sitting down at his desk and eyeing the paper towers closely.

"Oh, and I found this under your chair," added Ryan handing over a tube of burgundy lipstick. "I could be wrong, but it looks like the shade Mrs. Donovan wears."

Gary shook his head in disgust. "Abigail strikes again."

"Abigail still lifting lipstick, sir?"

"Hmm. She considers them designer crayons. And you know her affinity for coloring."

Ryan made a moaning sound. "Yes, sir. She colored in all the blocks on my wall calendar last week."

"Sorry, Ryan. I'll see that your calendar is replaced and I'll talk to Abigail about it, although it doesn't seem to do any good. She has a mind of her own." Gary stared at the stacks on his desk. "Well, I'll tackle these for an hour or so, then I'll head over to the West Wing for the cabinet meeting."

Ryan raised his eyebrows in surprise. He looked down and studied his clipboard.

"I don't have you down for a cabinet meeting this morning, sir."

"No, sorry. Last minute thing. MP just called it for 10:00 A.M."

Ryan bit his lip looking alarmed, nodded, took out the pencil behind his ear, and started making adjustments.

"Of course. West Wing business takes precedence. I'll make the necessary changes to your schedule. Shouldn't be a problem. How nice that Madame P would invite you to the cab meeting. Need anything else for Secretary Miller and the state dinner?"

Gary shook his head. "No, it's okay. Wait. A couple of days ago I . . . uh, I went over to the West Wing and met with Jim Myers. He said he would contact you about updating the invite list. Did he call you?"

Ryan looked irritated.

"Yes, sir, I was duly summoned."

"He gave you an amended list?"

Ryan rolled his eyes.

"Oh, yes, indeed. He gave me a long list of recommendations."

Gary smiled.

"You don't like him either?"

Ryan nodded his head in agreement. He paused a moment, gazing reflectively out the small window in Gary's office. When he finally spoke, his lips were tightly pursed.

"I think it fair to say that Mr. Myers is one of the most annoying, immature, and arrogant men I have ever had the privilege of associating with while serving at the White House."

"Bless you," replied Gary gratefully.

"You are most welcome, sir. Anything else? Pardon me for saying, but you look tired this morning. Something wrong?"

Gary hesitated.

The pressure and paranoia of the situation weighed heavily upon him, and he would gladly welcome a confidant, someone to confide in. Ryan had his complete trust. He was severely tempted to spill it all, but he realized McKay would have a stroke if he did. Instead Gary decided to share just some of the peripherals.

"To tell you the truth, I didn't sleep well. Abigail had a nightmare of sorts, something about monsters and ghosts."

"She's five, sir. It's par for the course."

"True. Tell me, you've worked at the White House for a long time. Have you heard anything strange happening on the upper floors?"

Ryan's face broke out into the rarest of smiles.

"Lincoln's ghost, sir?"

"Uh, yes," said Gary a bit embarrassed.

"Don't feel bad, sir. You're not the first person to get spooked while staying at the White House. Actually, quite a few of the upstairs staff swear they have seen the ghost. Scared a new maid pretty badly once while she was changing sheets in the Lincoln Bedroom. She refused to ever go back. The butlers find him rather fun. They started the tradition of leaving a cup of hot chocolate for Mr. Lincoln in his bedroom on Christmas Eve. Don't know where Dwight will leave the tray this year."

"Dwight is resourceful. I'm sure he'll figure something out."

"Oh, yes. Mr. Cook is quite capable."

"Ryan?"

"Yes, sir?"

"Do you think it possible that someone, besides a ghost, could ever get upstairs in the White House?"

Gary's calm assistant looked startled at first by the question, but then his face appeared amused.

"Well, the answer to that question is yes and no, depending on the time frame you are referring to. Years ago, before Middle East terrorism and sex scandals hit the Washington newspapers, people snuck into the White House all the time. Staff snuck people into the residence through the treasury tunnels for sleepovers in the Lincoln Bedroom. Sometimes butlers were even allowed to bring girlfriends over for a romp in the presidential hay. But those days are over. The world and Washington have forever changed. Now you couldn't get a flea inside the White House without Agent Pullman and his boys taking notice."

"Only to be foiled by a five year old," added Gary.

Ryan sighed miserably.

"Yes, sir." With that, Ryan departed and Gary busied himself with his never-ending stacks of e-mails and letters and phone calls, cheered a bit by Ryan's humorous comments.

Gary lost track of time while working through the mounds of paper on his desk, so he ended up arriving a bit late to the cabinet meeting. As he came into the long room on the east side of the West Wing, he saw all the members of the cabinet seated around the oblong table. Martha sat in the middle of the table on the east side, a place traditionally reserved for the president in many past administrations. The cabinet room was devoid of the press, but the major West Wing staff members were present, including Jim Myers, General McKay, Ned, Blaze, Ken, and Donald. Gary walked in right as Martha formally began speaking. She looked up quickly as Gary entered the room and acknowledged his presence with a brief nod and steady look.

"Thank you all for coming on such short notice. I have just one agenda item and I will be brief."

Martha looked around the room and cleared her throat. Gary took note of the expressions of the West Wing group. Ken and Donald looked concerned, Ned looked interested, McKay looked calm, Jim looked puzzled, and Blaze looked clueless.

"First of all, I want each cabinet member to know how much I truly appreciate his or her good work, both in the Taylor administration and in the brief time that I have served with you. The circumstances of my coming to the presidency have been stressful for everyone, and I appreciate the smooth transition we have experienced over the past few months."

Martha hesitated. You could have heard a pin drop in the room. There was a foreboding sense that something not good was about to happen. It did.

"Which makes what I am about to say all the more difficult. When I became president three months ago, I stated that I would keep on all of President Taylor's cabinet appointments. However, circumstances have suddenly altered. For reasons of my own, I have decided to make a complete change and make new appointments for each major department of government. Therefore, I am asking each of you to step down. I would like a letter of resignation from each one of you on my desk by 5:00 this evening."

There were audible gasps in the room. Donald looked like he was about to pass out. Ken grabbed him by the elbow and quickly pulled him out of the room. Jim looked as if a truck had hit him. Ned looked stunned. And surprisingly, Blaze looked angry.

Miller, sitting beside Martha, was the first to speak.

"Madame President. This is all so . . . sudden. Have we done something wrong, to lose your confidence?"

A look of pain was on Martha's face as she gazed at her beloved secretary of state, a father figure to her in the recent months. She boldly shook her head and clearly fought back a tear as she directly answered his question.

"No, David. Nothing wrong. I have my reasons and I need you to respect them." She hastened to add, "Your under secretaries will immediately take over your responsibilities until I can make new nominations and have them cleared by the Senate confirmation process. However, David, since we are in the midst of the North Korean negotiations, I will ask for you to stay on a few more weeks. If that is okay with you?"

The kindly-looking old man smiled humbly and nodded.

"Yes, Madame President, whatever you wish."

"Thank you," she whispered sadly. She sat up straight and addressed the group again. "There is one other exception. U.N. Ambassador Maurice Porter will remain at his post. Now, we will need to discuss some specifics in the transition plans for all departments during the next hour." Martha then looked down at her list and turned to the labor secretary for discussion. At this point, Gary got up and left the room.

As he left, he caught a bit of conversation from Ken and Donald just down the hallway.

"I can't take it anymore! It has to end," exclaimed Donald anxiously.

"Shhh," warned Ken firmly. "Come to my office. Now."

Donald whimpered. "I can't continue. Things are out of control . . ."

"Quiet!" urged Ken. "We'll call him . . ."

The two men walked out of earshot, leaving Gary wondering at their discussion. Suddenly, he felt someone grabbing his arm and abruptly turning him around. It was Blaze.

"You knew about this, didn't you?" he said angrily.

"Blaze, it's okay. Calm down."

Blaze's temper flared.

"Answer me! You knew she was going to do this, didn't you?"

"I knew she would be taking some drastic action, yes. But I didn't know all the details . . ."

"Why didn't you tell me?" charged Blaze, his voice pitched higher and louder than Gary ever remembered hearing before. "Don't you trust me anymore?"

"Blaze, I couldn't say anything. Madame President took me into her confidence."

"Oh, sure, everything is fine for you. You get the big job. You get to move into the White House. You get the attention. What about me! This ruins everything for me! Everything!"

Now Gary was getting upset. "What does it ruin, Blaze? Talk about trust. You've been my best friend the last few years. I know you. And I know that you've been holding out on me too, hiding something. What? What is it? What haven't you told me?"

Blaze looked at Gary, his face contorted with a dangerous mix of emotions, hurt and anger and confusion. They glared at each other, neither one flinching, neither one backing down. Finally, Blaze threw his head back in exasperation.

"I've got to go," he said bitterly. He turned and started walking away, but Gary stepped forward and grabbed his friend by the arm.

"Don't go. Talk to me, Blaze! Please. I'll listen."

Blaze pulled away and shook his head miserably. He could barely look at Gary.

"I can't," he muttered harshly. "Not now."

Blaze turned and darted off before Gary could say more. Gary stood dejectedly and held his head in his hands, feeling sick inside. He probably just lost one of the best friends he ever had.

There was more motion in the hallway. Gary turned his head to see Ned slipping out of the cabinet room, pulling out his cell phone and rapidly dialing. Ned hastened past him going down the hall, but not before Gary caught a few phrases.

"It's me. Something major is going down. We'll need to change our plans immediately . . ."

Gary's head was literally spinning. Martha's action was having an effect alright. So much for a little rebellion! Everyone was going crazy. Donald and Ken were in a state of high anxiety. Who were they rushing out to speak with? And Blaze? Gary had never seen him so angry and unwilling to talk. What did Blaze mean about something being ruined? And Ned! What in the world was he up too? This wasn't the first time Gary had caught Ned discussing some secret business behind the scenes over the phone. It had happened at Taylor's inauguration. Gary took a deep breath. They all sounded guilty. And what made it worse, the one he really wanted to be guilty hadn't said a word or moved a muscle. Myers looked like he had been kicked in the teeth, but he kept his cool, darn it! And he was still in there, dutifully beside Martha, which fact irked Gary the most. And what about McKay? Was he really the true blue general, or was he the cunning mastermind behind a very well planned scheme to control the White House? Was he controlling them all now?

Gary gritted his teeth. He was tired and he was angry.

He couldn't sort it out, but he could not just stand by and do nothing. He had to do something, and he had a debt to pay.

For the second time in not so many days, he marched through the door and down the short carpeted ramp, past old Sam sitting at the green desk, and over to the Press Room. He stood in the open doorway and glanced in. He saw Jack there with a couple of other reporters, playing gin rummy using a large briefcase as a table.

"Look, Parish, it's your friend the pastry chef." The *Washington Post* reporter pointed at Gary and grinned.

There was laughter around the room.

A dark haired CBS reporter quickly grabbed Jack's stale peanut butter sandwich from off a nearby plate and held it up in the air. "Do us a favor, Mr. Craig, and teach our buddy here how to cook."

"Yeah," piped in the ABC reporter merrily. "Start with a lesson on how to boil water."

The reporters in the room snorted and chuckled.

Jack held up his hand defensively.

"Gentlemen, gentlemen, I don't boil water. I microwave Dasani."

There was more merry laughter. Gary faked a smile and beckoned Jack to come out in the hallway. Jack handed his playing cards to his cameramen with strict admonitions not to cheat and followed Gary out of the Press Room.

"What's up, Fred," asked Jack curiously.

"First, hand me your cell phone," ordered Gary firmly.

"What?"

"Just hand me the phone!"

Looking puzzled, Jack obediently pulled out his cell phone and handed it over. Gary took it and then pulled the reporter aside by the sleeve, over to the locked door leading outside to the Rose Garden. He began speaking in a hushed urgent whisper.

"I am going to tell you two things, Jack Parish. One you can publish, one you cannot. Is that clear?"

Jack solemnly nodded. He could tell something very serious was happening.

Gary took a deep breath and started talking. "Now listen up. Madame President and General McKay have good reason to believe that President Taylor and Eric Peters were murdered. Both were assassinated by poison, and we believe a secret international plot exists to kill Madame President as well."

Jack Parish's mouth dropped open.

"Murdered? But they both died of heart attacks."

"Trust me, it's true. It was done with a weaponized high tech poison that leaves no traces in the body and gives the appearance of a heart attack. I'll give you more details on that later. Bad as that news is, it gets worse. We have evidence linking the murders to someone working inside the West Wing."

"Jesus!" Jack was beginning to hyperventilate.

"Yes," said Gary gravely, "and that information is what you can *not* publish, not now anyway. It's strictly on background only for the time being. What you can publish is that Madame President has decided to clean house."

Gary pulled out the business card Jack gave him back on the campaign trail and handed it over.

"I don't understand," said Jack.

"I'm paying back my debt. Madame President has just fired all the members of her cabinet."

Jack gasped.

"All of them?"

"All of them except for Ambassador Porter."

Jack looked incredulous. "What about Secretary Miller?"

"She is keeping him in place a few more weeks until the North Korea talks are wrapped up. The rest are expected to turn in their letters of resignation by 5:00 today. She is in there now in a closed-door session going over transition plans for each department. The meeting will last another hour at least."

Gary handed the cell phone back.

"Which means you have fifty-five minutes to beat everyone to the presses and get the scoop of a lifetime. Run."

Cell phone call four hours later . . .

"What in blue blazes is going on over there? I just turned on the news and all hell is breaking loose. This situation is completely out of control! . . . Of course I blame you, so don't bother with any lame excuses. You should have seen this coming. All this redecorating nonsense was a sign of worse things to come. God, she's just like my mother. She cleaned out the entire attic before divorcing my father. . . . I don't have to tell you how worried we are, which is not happy news for you either! You are to refocus your attention on getting back into the President's good graces and getting our man into the VP slot as soon as possible, before she decides to fire the rest of the West Wing as well. Understood? . . . Fine! Once our guy is in the VP position, we'll decide what happens next. Hopefully, in the meantime, she won't screw up the arrangement we have with the Germans. The new ambassador is right where we want him, smiling face to face with the Americans, but willing to sell out his own country's best interests with his U.N. votes to our powerful allies in the Middle East. I sincerely doubt a mere dinner at the White House will ruin that sweet deal . . ."

Chapter 19

State Dinner Preparations

Tuesday, August 9, and Saturday, August 13

To put it mildly, Washington was going berserk.

So much for Martha's little rebellion. The firing of her entire cabinet was NEWS in all caps. It was a media earthquake, and its ramifications, like rolling aftershocks, were shaking up the body politic.

After the story broke, journalist's demands for White House access doubled, if not tripled. Reporters were camped inside and outside the White House. On air, seasoned experts sat around tables and considered, contemplated, analyzed, criticized, questioned, complained, and prophesied upon the cabinet situation, offering up their own sage opinions. Predictions were flying across the airways at a fever pitch, with wild speculations over whom the new cabinet members would or would not be and when this unpredictable, unconventional president would finally choose her vice president.

Gary's dual status as White House resident and First Family friend did not escape the notice of the zealous press corps and Gary quickly became a target of reporters. Tape recorders, microphones, and pens were poised daily in Gary's direction. Questions were hurled at him like darts, and Gary quickly learned to wave politely, close his mouth, and walk away fast.

Thanks to Gary, however, Jack Parish did get his promised scoop, and Parish broke the story and broadcasted details brilliantly. In the following days, he consistently produced pieces that were fair and factual. It made Gary wonder if Jack's laid-back persona, off-beat humor, and pampered self-centeredness had caused him to grossly underestimate his new friend's professional talents. That was Gary's mistake, one he would not make again. Jack also kept the murder of President Taylor tightly under wraps as promised. Such discretion sealed Gary's faith and respect in the reporter. With the uncertain status of his friendship with Blaze, it was nice to know he had an ally nearby.

While the cabinet turnover had anxieties running high in the West Wing, Gary managed to keep a low profile over in his small, secluded second story East Wing office. The state dinner for the German delegation was coming up fast, and the details for that and the Christmas holidays were pressing hard upon him. Thank heaven for Ryan, who handled the stress seamlessly. Ryan had much experience under his belt, having worked other state dinners and Christmas holidays in the past. Ryan was always gracious and willing to share his expertise with Gary. Gary relied upon him heavily during this crunch and stressful situation.

For the Christmas preparations, good progress was being made. A farm up north was selected to provide the large tree going in the Blue Room, and Morgan flew up to New England to select the tree. Next, three youth choirs were selected from California, Texas, and New York to perform at the lighting of the National Christmas Tree. Finally, the painting to be used for this year's Christmas cards was completed, and cards featuring the print were being made at the printers. Aunt Sophie, Secretary Miller, and Gary's staff were hard at work compiling this year's Christmas card list. Miller had been upstairs to dinner twice in the past week, spending the evenings in the family residence with Martha and the First Family. Aunt Sophie had plied him with lots of cake and coffee as they sat around the dinner table and discussed individuals who should (and who should not) get Christmas cards this year.

Gary enjoyed Miller's presence. Miller played cards with General McKay and wisely let the general win. The secretary of state also joined Josh and Gary in playing several video games, wisely losing to Josh. He flattered Charlotte and Aunt Sophie shamelessly on their cooking, knitting, and good looks. He even got Jane to put her spy novel down once and join a game of gin rummy with him and the general (which she handily won to the general's dismay). It was a pity that Miller was fired with the rest of the cabinet secretaries, but he was a good soldier and was taking it gracefully. Gary was pretty sure that Martha would continue to lean upon this good man's advice, and once the situation with Taylor and Peters was cleared, she would quickly find him another position in her administration.

The German state dinner details were essentially set at this point, although Gary's office and the State Department were still haggling over some last-minute seating arrangements. Of course, Martha had final say on the guest list, but both Secretary Miller and Jim Myers continued to debate who sat where. Until the new State Dining Hall was complete, seats for state dinners were limited to a mere 130 guests, so invitations and seating charts were critical. The German embassy had finally decided where the German chancellor and U.N. ambassador and their wives would be staying. Normally, an invitation to stay at the White House would have been extended. But with so many children and guests already in house (i.e. Gary and Charlotte), and with renovations in the residence still incomplete, there simply wasn't any room at the Presidential Inn.

Nevertheless, the state dinner menu was set, the imported wines had arrived, Chef Roland's desserts were almost complete (and spectacular), and Aunt Sophie had finally chosen a German chocolate cake recipe. With all that in order, Gary could focus his attention on normal matters, such as putting together weekly luncheons in the Green Room for Martha and select members of Congress, where they hashed out spending items for the new Medicare bill and energy bill in private. It was the same old fight. The Democrats wanted to spend more money, the Republicans wanted to spend less. Martha was trying hard to find a middle ground both parties could accept. His role wasn't much, thought Gary, but he took pride in finding and serving the favorites dishes of different senators and congressman, hoping it would help break the ice during these "working lunches." Such were his gourmet contributions towards diplomacy.

It was while planning one of these lunches that Gary learned something quite extraordinary about his assistant.

"I was wondering, sir," asked Ryan tentatively on Tuesday morning, a week and a half before the state dinner. "Since we have most everything arranged for the state dinner, if I might have this coming weekend off. My wife is coming to town, and I'd like to spend some time with her."

"Wife? You're married?" Gary practically fell out of his chair.

Ryan nodded his head sheepishly. "Yes, sir. It will be four years this coming January."

Gary was speechless. "Ryan, this is amazing. You never said you were married! Well, of course you can have the weekend off, you silly goose. You don't have to work every weekend, you know."

Ryan cast Gary a mortified look.

"My mistake. You can work every weekend," said Gary correcting himself. "But, Ryan, you really don't have to, especially if you have a family."

"Oh, we don't have any children, sir. And my wife doesn't mind my long hours and working weekends. We both have very demanding careers."

"Where does she work?" asked Gary inquisitively.

"Abroad. She is an international insurance broker working with major business corporations. Her company has offices in London, Paris, Tokyo, New York, and D.C. She works mostly out of London though. We have a small cottage outside of Windsor."

This revelation totally blew Gary away. "She lives overseas? How do you stand being apart?" Gary paused and anxiously bit his lip. He shouldn't have said that. Perhaps they lived apart because they were having marital problems. Maybe Ryan didn't talk about his marriage for a reason. Gary cautiously asked, "Is everything okay with you two? Are you separated or something?"

Ryan shook his head emphatically. "Oh, no, sir. Everything's just fine, sir. We just prefer our long-distance relationship. We were heavily invested in our careers when we met, and the long distance allows us to continue working in our separate professions. Fortunately we can e-mail each other daily and call each other on weekends. And Galina's work brings her to the states every six weeks or so. So we see each other often enough."

"Galina?" Gary was intrigued. "Russian?"

Ryan nodded. "My wife was born and raised in Moscow, but she went to Cambridge for her undergraduate degree and MBA training, then to the Harvard Business School for her doctorate."

"You met her in Boston?"

A little smile crossed Ryan's face. "Paris, actually."

Gary was quite dazed with this news and looked at his assistant with a bit of envy. So Ryan was a very happily married man! Well, well, will wonders never cease?

"Have the weekend off with my blessing," said Gary sincerely. "I hope I get to meet this wife of yours someday."

Ryan smiled, picked up his clipboard, and pushed the center of his glasses up his nose carefully. "Of course." Ryan stepped back to leave.

"Hey! You stepped on my picture," yelled Abigail loudly. She gave the young man an angry look.

Ryan sighed, looked down, and then bent over to pick up the piece of colored paper to brush it off.

"Sorry, Miss Abigail, I didn't see you there. When did you arrive?"

Abigail ignored him and started busily searching for another crayon in her plastic box. Sheba hissed at Ryan and then madly dashed out of Gary's office. Ryan followed the kitty and left. Abigail stayed.

Like her kitty Sheba, Abigail was increasingly underfoot, shadowing Gary.

Nighttime shadowing was easy. Wherever Gary went in the evenings, Abigail was sure to follow. She was on the sofa playing with her doll while Gary sat and had discussions with Eliza. (Eliza came to Gary often for a male opinion on things.) Abigail was on the floor with her coloring books and crayon box during movie time with Josh (at which times, Gary randomly policed the coloring box for errant tubes of lipstick). Abigail was at the kitchen table looking at storybooks while Gary chatted with Aunt Sophie and Charlotte over tea and cookies.

Daytime shadowing was more difficult, however, given the fact Gary did have to work. However, Abigail managed to cook up some pretty good excuses to visit his East Wing office at least once a day, often with her nanny's apt assistance. Frequently Gary was asked to watch Abigail for an hour or two while Nanny Jane, Aunt Sophie, or Charlotte (or all the above) took an afternoon nap. Insomnia, it seemed, was running rampant around the White House these days. Most adults residing upstairs were affected. Nanny Jane also had a continuing battle with her sinuses. She came to the breakfast table with a handful of tissues some mornings, describing her stuffy voice as "dreadful."

"It's frightfully hard to breathe," moaned Nanny Jane repeatedly. "Honestly, how can one sleep when one's nose is swollen? It doesn't do."

Other medical complaints surfaced upstairs. Aunt Sophie complained of arthritis and was up late unable to fall asleep till after midnight. Charlotte complained of lower back pain, a medical problem that seemed to flare up whenever she lifted something too heavy. With the ongoing renovations, Charlotte was sometimes too enthusiastic and careless, forgetting about her physical limitations and lifting things anyway. Flare-ups with her back occurred every few days or so. Even Martha was having trouble sleeping, often getting up early. With her job, there was a lot to worry about. So, everyone was up and down, pacing the halls at night. Thanks goodness Gary wasn't affected. Except for the night Abigail appeared, he was sleeping like a baby.

So, during naptimes for Nanny Jane, Aunt Sophie, and/or Charlotte, Abigail appeared at Gary's East Wing office, her little backpack full with her coloring books, crayons, and a treat (usually cookies or fruit roll ups and boxed juice). Because of these daily appearances, Ryan took it upon himself to quickly locate a small child's desk and chair from the White House warehouse, which he set up in a corner in Gary's already cramped office. So, while Gary sat at his desk, staring at a computer screen, Abigail sat at her little desk, staring at her coloring book. Only once the past two weeks did lipstick appear in the crayon box, a silver tube of lilac mauve, which Charlotte dutifully informed Gary was the shade worn by her friend Kate Yardley. Unfortunately, lilac mauve drawings of fish (Abigail later identified them as sharks) also appeared on the walls of Ryan's office. Both Gary and Jane apologized lavishly to Ryan and gave Abigail another stern talking about the evils of sneaking about, thievery, and graffiti.

At the end of the week, Gary decided to take a cue from his own assistant and get away. Early Saturday, accompanied by a small Secret Service detail that Martha had assigned to him, Gary slipped away back to his house in northern Virginia, where he spent the morning cleaning up the place, getting ready for Mildred and Harriet's visit. Mildred and Harriet were arriving the next day, Sunday, and would be staying the entire week before attending the state dinner. Gary relished spending time alone in his backyard garden, tenderly weeding and watering his flowering plants. Neighbors had been hired to take on the daily care of his yard while he temporarily lived at the White House, but it was nice to do the work himself. Out in the hot morning sun, Gary felt his muscles begin to relax and his mind slow down as he labored over pots of sage, oregano, mint, and rosemary. It was a time to be quiet, to be still, to leave all the pressures and concerns behind him.

At noon, Gary put down his pruning sheers and gloves and went back into the kitchen, where he opened a can of tuna and made up some tuna fish salad. He was cutting some large homegrown tomatoes when there was a loud knock. It was Jack Parish's face at the door.

"Afternoon, Clyde," said the reporter merrily as he walked into the house carrying a large brown shopping bag. "I come bearing gifts of potato chips and chocolate chip cookies, food of the Gods. Thanks for the invite for lunch by the way. Ever since Madame President turned things upside down at the White House, my diet has severely suffered."

"Your diet has always suffered," said Gary taking the chips and pointing the way to the kitchen. "By the way, you weren't followed, were you?"

Jack cast Gary a narrow look.

"You doubt the driving ability of this native born Washingtonian?"

Gary laughed. "I guess not."

Jack grinned as he opened a bag of cookies and helped himself. "Never fear, no other press is near. Two gumshoe hacks attempted to follow, but I left them in the dust on the 495 Beltway. Poor slobs."

Gary laughed again as he poured them each a soda, then handed Jack a plate with tomato stuffed with tuna salad. They heaped chips and cookies on their plates and went out to the backyard to eat. They enjoyed their lunches, discussing Cubs baseball, Redskins football, Press Room gossip, and harrowing tales of Jack's Aunt Dorothy's latest trip abroad. Jack's crazy rich auntie had taken up scuba diving on a trip to St. Thomas. Gary followed with an account of Mildred's recent escapade in the castle in Scotland.

Their meal finished, the two men finally sat back and sipped their drinks and began talking politics.

"How are things going with the state dinner?" asked Jack still munching on a cookie.

"The East Wing work is pretty much done, as far as food and drink and entertainment goes. But the West Wing is still working the fringe. You know the new German ambassador to the U.N. is coming, a real tough guy I hear."

"Yeah, a real sweetheart," said Jack dryly. "My sources tell me this new chancellor dude is in Ambassador Schneider's hip pocket, totally a front man. Odd, huh? You would think Schneider would want the top spot. The story I am hearing is that Schneider was the power that got the chancellor in office. Then he got himself appointed ambassador so he can play footsies with the boys at the U.N."

"The President and Ambassador Porter are worried about that U.N. situation. Germany is holding up the votes in the U.N. Security Council on Middle East issues. At least, that's what the past ambassador did. Madame President fears the new ambassador won't be much better. They don't know a whole lot about this fellow yet. McKay's people at the Pentagon are looking into his record, and Miller has already made initial contacts, but it sounds pretty dicey."

"Makes you want to be president, doesn't it? No? Me either. Well, we just have to wait and see what happens. By the way, thanks for pulling the strings to get me inside the dinner. Now it's my turn to owe you a favor."

"No problem. You did a great job on the cabinet story, Jack," observed Gary sincerely. "And Ned Baldwin is appreciative. He told me he'd have to take back everything bad he ever said about you."

Jack laughed heartily. "Gee, praise from the press secretary himself. I don't think I can stand it."

Gary grinned and continued. "Milk it for all it's worth. And thanks for keeping the assassination part of the story under wraps."

"My mama didn't raise no fool," replied Jack smartly as he cradled his glass in his hand. "'Never bite the hand that feeds you.' Just let me know if and when we can ever break that story. Until then, you keep supplying the information that's on record, Sam, and I'll keep reporting. Besides, despite evidence to the contrary, some of us poor hacks do have some patriotism left. I actually care about what happens to this country. The Taylor murder is awful and needs solving fast. I understand if I report stuff on that too soon, it could hurt the investigation. So until you say otherwise, my lips are sealed."

"Super," said Gary gratefully. "You know, it's nice to have someone to talk to. It's been pretty hard not being free to say anything. And just thinking about it makes you paranoid."

Jack put his glass down on a small table and leaned back in his chair.

"Well, talk away if it makes you feel better."

Gary tossed him a cookie from off his plate. "Off the record?"

Jack bit into the cookie, and lifted his right hand up in the air.

"The mouth is full, the pen is down. Let her rip."

Gary took a sip of his drink and starting talking.

"We haven't figured out who killed Stan Taylor yet, but according to McKay, it's appearing that Donald Hooper and Ken Friedman are the prime suspects. I think McKay may be close to actually making an arrest."

Jack sputtered cookie crumbs.

"Hooper, the hypochondriac? The guy with pant pockets lined with cough drops, nose spray, and antacids?" Jack laughed hysterically. "No way, Jose! Hooper is nothing more than a stressed-out lawyer with fourteen other stressed-out lawyers working beneath him. He's a bit batty but he's not a crook."

Gary shrugged. "Maybe. But Jack, we intercepted a phone conversation with Ken that is very suspicious. Plus, Ken Friedman and Hooper were observed leaving the White House every day this week at lunchtime and were followed by McKay's men. Ken and Donald acted very secretive. Reports from their private secretaries about luncheon plans don't match up either. Monday McKay's men followed Donald and Ken to a doctor's office, a new French psychiatrist in town."

"And that's scary?" said Jack cynically. "I find it comforting. A man like Donald should never be far from a shrink."

"But Jack, you know how anti-American the French have been lately, and this doctor has a record of being involved in anti-American protests during his college days. That's making McKay nuts. Our guys are taking a close look into the doctor's record now. Other days Donald and Ken were followed to a number of very out-of-the-way restaurants, two Greek, one Japanese, and one Israeli."

Jack shook his head in disbelief. "Eating out is not an act of terrorism, Sam. In fact, eating at ethnic restaurants is a serious religion in this town. It's totally cool to stand in an office doorway and say to a colleague, 'I've discovered this amazing new Thai restaurant on the Hill! You really should try it.' Sorry, but your evidence that Ken and Don are running a conspiracy is mighty slim. They might need to go on a diet, but I highly doubt they are committing espionage."

"Nevertheless General McKay is checking out the restaurant owners. We already know two of them did not have proper visa status. We're trying to determine any possible connection with terrorists overseas."

Jack yawned. "All dead ends. You'll see."

"Well, then there is the matter of drugs."

Jack's eyes quickly popped wide open.

"Drugs?" Jack immediately sat up, his interest perked. "I like the sound of that. Drugs are good."

Gary grimaced and threw Jack another cookie. "Ken has been occupied with pharmacology these days, checking out lots of medical books and journals from the Library of Congress. McKay says Ken was seen leaving the office late one night and going to three different pharmacies, picking up prescriptions for Valium and other sedatives at each."

Jack frowned disappointedly. "Valium? You say drugs, and then you give me Valium? Mack, in this nation's capital, Valium is one of the four basic food groups. It's mother's milk to the overworked and underpaid. Unless someone inside the Oval Office is smoking pot or shooting up crack in the Rose Garden, I'm not interested."

Gary shook his head in disagreement. "But I know Ken. He's is a cool customer. He's not neurotic like Donald at all. Why get the Valium?"

Jack smiled cynically. "Well maybe that's why he is so cool, calm, and collected."

Gary huffed. "Yeah, maybe. But if Ken was just getting sedatives to sooth his nerves, why go to three different places?"

Having finished his meal, Jack took out a pack of cigarettes and pulled one out of the pack.

"Easy. A man in high places needs to lay in a supply. His nerves are fried and he's worried he'll run out, so he shops around and stocks up. They don't hand the stuff out in super-sized bottles you know."

"Okay," said Gary unconvinced. "But suppose he's planning to drug one of the First Family and kidnap them?"

Jack lit his cigarette, took a long drag, and blew the smoke out slowly.

"Are you kidding? I can't smuggle nail clippers into the White House these days, much less smuggle out an adult human being. And as for small human beings, that little shadow of yours, I doubt they could catch her."

Gary smiled.

Jack continued. "Enough with Donald and Ken. They're boring. Let's talk about my favorite suspect, Ned Baldwin."

"Ned?"

"Hmmm. My money is on him. Your little press secretary has become rather shy the last week or haven't you noticed? Normally Ned drops into the Press Room during lunchtime to chat with the boys and girls, to shoot the breeze and deny any rumors we might come up with. But this week, Ned was a no show. He's been hiding out in his corner office, breakfast, lunch, and dinner. Staying rather late, too. Later than usual, that is."

"Okay, Ned has been acting strange, I give you that. He sent me the oddest e-mail the other day, asking for details of the night Taylor died."

Jack's eyes instantly lit up. "Oh, really?"

"Yeah. I can't figure out why."

Jack inhaled deeply, leaned his head back, and confidently blew out smoke. "Maybe he wants to find out exactly what you saw — you know, needs to make sure his tracks are covered. Maybe he's worried you've cottoned on to what the deceased Reverend Palmer did. Have you told anyone else, besides me, about that part of the story?"

Gary shook his head firmly.

"Good," said Jack in a warning voice. "Make sure you don't. That juicy piece of information could just get you killed."

"Thanks so much," said Gary dryly. "You really know how to cheer a guy up."

Jack laughed and put out his cigarette. He reached for another, but Gary stopped him.

"Sorry, Jack. One is your limit."

"Since when?"

"Since now. You save my life. I save yours. Here. Have a Lifesaver." Gary pulled out his pocket stash and handed his reporter friend a wintergreen. Jack accepted it begrudgingly.

"No alcohol and now no cigarettes. You are a thrill a minute, you know that? Okay, back to business. You haven't mentioned your sidekick," observed Jack putting a piece of candy into his mouth.

Gary sighed miserably. "I haven't heard from Blaze all week long. I've called his home phone and cell and left messages every day, but he doesn't answer. The staff in the Press Office told me that he called in Monday and asked for two weeks vacation."

Jack stared at him with concern. "Think your bird has flown the coop?"

"No, he's in town. I was worried that someone might have bumped him off, like they did Palmer. If Blaze is involved, his life could be in danger. But McKay sent someone over to keep tabs on him, and he reported Blaze is holed up in his apartment. And not leaving it either, I understand."

Jack raised a skeptical eyebrow. "The boy who never stops eating?"

"He's ordering in. Pizza is being delivered by the hour."

Jack looked at Gary gravely. "You think he's scared?"

Gary put down his glass and leaned over, his head in his hands in exasperation. "I don't know what I think any more. It can't be Blaze. It just can't."

"Tell you what," said Parish solemnly. "I'll do a little checking out, as only I can do."

"You will?" replied Gary looking up gratefully.

"No problem, Sport."

Gary sat up and breathed a sigh of relief. He was very worried about his friend. "Let me know what you find out."

Jack sat back in his chair and eyed Gary shrewdly. "Sure thing. Speaking of favorite suspects, you've failed to mention yours — that mad man about town, the dashing chief of staff. How is the happy bachelor these days?"

Gary moaned. "I'd rather not say."

"Come on," urged the reporter. "Tell Uncle Jack everything."

"There's nothing to tell," declared Gary hotly, "except for the fact that he doesn't make himself scarce like Blaze. On the contrary, he's everywhere present."

Jack's eyes twinkled. "Do tell."

Gary huffed and helped himself to a Lifesaver. "Oh, he hand delivers the PDB every morning and then helps himself to a free breakfast and Madame President's attention. He's always dressed to the nines. Plus he's showing up at dinnertime. Sometimes he comes with Secretary Miller, thank goodness. I don't think I could bear it if we had to take Myers alone every night."

"And is the family succumbing to Mr. Myers' famous charms?"

At this, Gary smiled. "Jane can't stand him. She accidentally spilled some hot soup on him the other night. She spills things on the general, too. Gets him barking mad. Then Jane drags the general away for clean up using one of her mother's homemade remedies with Aunt Sophie supervising. Poor general. He's always getting injured by the nanny. The other night Jane came into the Oval Sitting Room and asked McKay to help her fix a broken hair dryer. He declined saying she was certain to electrocute him. Sophie had to intervene and scold the general into assisting Jane."

"Did he get zapped?" asked Jack laughing.

"Only once," replied Gary grinning. "Too bad Jane doesn't offer to clean Myers up! That might send him running. Anyway, Aunt Sophie is polite to Myers, and McKay is civil, but they don't exactly turn cartwheels when he shows up. The children are pretty neutral." Gary paused in contemplation. "And then there's Sheba. She doesn't like him either. When Myers came to dinner last night, Sheba came up to him and promptly threw up on his shoe."

Jack threw his head back and roared with laughter.

"Reminds me of a gal I dated in college," he said still holding his sides with glee. "At the end of our torrid affair, her sentiments were exactly the same. Well, I shouldn't worry about Jim Bob. His ego is big enough to take the hit, if not the hint. However, the real question is why is the popular chief of staff haunting the executive mansion late at night? It's not that the poor boy can't get a date. What are his real motives? Could it be he has the hots for Madame P? Maybe kissing, not killing, is what's on his mind."

Gary stared at his friend uneasily. He did not like the implications of either proposition.

"That's not funny."

"It's not meant to be," said Jack flatly. He leaned back in his chair and eyed Gary intently. "As a suspect, Myers certainly is in the best position to do some real damage. He's in the top leadership spot in the West Wing, in control of what comes out of the Oval. If I were an international terrorist, his would be the ideal position to place a mole inside the White House." Jack stopped for a moment and then bit his lip and shook his head. "But it's hard to envision him as a spy. A dandy with an expense account to match, yes, but a criminal, no. No, pal, my guess is Myers is vying for a match with the nation's most famous female. It's about glands and ego. You know that he is going to escort President Johnson to the state dinner next Saturday?"

"Please," objected Gary with displeasure, abruptly getting up and gathering up the lunch plates. "Let's not discuss it any further. Want some coffee?"

"Strike a nerve, did we?" observed Jack suspiciously as he stood and picked up the glasses. He followed Gary into the house.

"I don't know what you are talking about," denied Gary as he walked into the kitchen and put the dishes down into the sink.

"Oh, really?" said Jack. "Then let me put it in plain English. It's time, Fred, that you staked your claim."

"My what?"

Jack shook his head in disgust. He put the glasses down on the counter and spoke his next three sentences very slowly and distinctly. "Stake your claim. Make your move. Go for broke. Listen, chum, I don't know what kind of number the former Mrs. Craig did to you, but it's high time you got yourself over it."

Gary poured Jack a cup of coffee and handed it to him.

"I am over it," Gary said angrily.

Jack wouldn't be swayed. "Oh-ho, I beg to differ. She hurt you, son. She hurt you bad. And you're letting it ruin your life."

Gary grimaced and swallowed his coffee hard.

Jack continued. "Listen, rotten things happen to all of us. We all get our hearts smashed to bits at least once in this crazy life. But you survive. You pick up the pieces, glue them together, and hopefully make better choices the next time around. But you're bitter, kiddo, and it's preventing you from having a next time. I've seen it before. You're afraid to love again. And you do love her, you know."

Gary turned and morosely stared down into the sink, his face away from Jack. Intense feelings both good and bad flooded him, and he fought hard to keep them back, to stay in control. He had to stay in control. But Jack had nailed it on the head, and he could hardly reply.

"I never said I loved her," he said in a hoarse whisper.

In response, the reporter kindly placed a friendly hand upon Gary's shoulder and, in a rare moment, answered back using his actual first name.

"Gary, you didn't have to."

All at once, three phones began to ring in unison. Gary's home phone and cell phone were ringing, and Jack's cell was going off. Gary wanted to keep talking and ignored his phones, but Jack took out his cell and answered it. The phone started barking loudly, and Jack's face suddenly turned ashen white. He looked up at Gary in disbelief, but before he could speak, there was a loud banging at the front door. Something was very wrong. Gary raced to the living room and opened the door.

Agent Lewis stepped briskly inside with a dark look on his face. Gary saw two other agents running up his sidewalk from a black car parked out front of his house. One agent held a gun in his hand.

"There's been a death at the White House, Mr. Craig," said Agent Lewis harshly. "I have orders for you to return to the residence immediately."

A death in the White House? The news shook Gary to the core and instantly he feared the worse. Oh, God, did they get to Martha?

Gary grabbed Lewis fiercely by the arm, dreading the worst.

"Madame President?"

Agent Lewis shook his head.

"No, sir. Donald Hooper was found ten minutes ago in the Oval Office, sitting at Madame President's desk. There was a note. He's killed himself."

Chapter 20

The Oval Office

Saturday, August 13

The news of Donald's suicide was completely devastating. Gary was overcome with feelings of sadness and horror, saddened in the loss of a friend and horrified in the knowledge that Donald was probably guilty of murder. Now Donald had taken his own life rather than be caught and publicly humiliated. It was a terrible conclusion to the whole affair, but at least it was better than a long, drawn out, public investigation and trial. They would at least be spared that.

Gary grabbed his jacket, said goodbye to Jack (who jumped into his own car and sped off), and then got into the limo. During his long ride back to the White House, Gary agonized over the turn of events. He stared out the window blankly and watched the buildings and cars roll endlessly by in a dull blur. He found himself seriously wishing he had never gotten into politics. Had he turned down Ned's offer, he would be home in North Carolina right now, tending his roses and quietly living out his life with his friends, Mildred and Harriet.

The car pulled up to the gated entrance of the White House, and Gary was immediately escorted from the car, being met by Agent Clark waiting outside. The agent took him briskly past the entrance desk and the agent who checked IDs of all persons entering the West Wing. The uniformed officer hurriedly checked their IDs and waved them through, and Gary was ushered inside.

"She wants to see you," said Agent Clark crisply. "She's in the Cabinet Room with the others."

"Where is Donald?" asked Gary solemnly.

"Still in the Oval," replied Clark, adding in a subdued voice. "They haven't moved the body yet."

"I want to see him," said Gary.

Agent Clark shook his head. "I don't know if that's possible, sir. There are lots of people there now — our agents, the FBI crime scene unit, the emergency response team, D.C. police, and the city coroner. It's a bit crowded."

Gary stopped walking and firmly took hold of the Secret Service man's arm.

"I don't care if the whole damn city is in there, Agent Clark. I want to see Donald and I'm going to see him before they remove the body. Understood?"

"Yes, sir. I'll tell them that, sir."

"Thank you," said Gary flatly as they arrived at the Cabinet Room. "Come get me when the coroner is finished."

Agent Clark agreed and promptly left for the Oval Office. Gary turned, took a deep breath, and knocked softly on the door.

A dazed Ned Baldwin immediately opened it.

"Come in, Gary," he said hoarsely, looking at Gary with reddened eyes. He stepped back and allowed Gary to enter the room.

Gary found a crowd gathered at the south side of the room, huddled at the end of the long conference table. Martha, Miller, Jim Myers, and General McKay were standing close to Ken Friedman who was sitting down in a chair. At the north part of the room, Dwight Cook and another White House butler were silently setting up a coffee and hot tea service, putting out cups and saucers, bowls of sliced lemons and oranges, and a plate of cookies, sesame crackers, and sliced cheese. Gary doubted anyone felt like eating, but he was grateful that Morgan and the butlers were on the job, providing domestic comfort during a major in-house crisis.

Ken looked terrible. His face ashen white, he stared blindly down at his hands resting on the tabletop. His hands were shaking. Someone had placed a suit jacket around his shoulders. Clearly Ken was in shock. Nearby was the White House physician, Dr. Edward Goldman, a white haired old gentleman who was administering an injection into Ken's arm. Hopefully it was a strong sedative.

Martha's face was heavy with grief. Miller stood beside her in a protective manner, watching the physician intently. General McKay stood further away in the background next to the window, arms folded, frowning, watching with a grave look on his face. Myers was in the back, pacing nervously. One of Myers' assistants was also in the room, talking in a hushed voice on his cell phone. Agent Lewis and two other Secret Servicemen were present, standing stone still against the wall.

When Gary entered, Martha looked up, her face instantly brightening. She leaned over and whispered something to Miller, then rushed over to embrace Gary. She was trembling. He held her tightly and whispered he was sorry and that everything would be okay. Martha nodded her head and continued to cling to him for strength. A moment passed, then she pulled back and looked at him in complete disbelief.

"I can't believe it," she muttered achingly, looking up and wiping her eyes of tears. "It's just so horrible."

"I know, I know. But it's over now. Did you find him?" asked Gary.

She shook her head fervently. "No. I was upstairs in the residence with the children. Ken found him. He's extremely shaken as you can see. Ken just told us that he has been very concerned about Donald. Now we know why."

Gary hoped Ken would be able to give them more details. Gary took Martha by the arm, and together they walked back to the others.

Dr. Goldman finished giving Ken a shot and closed his black bag.

"That will do. He'll feel the effects almost instantly. Keep him warm and still for another half hour or so. Give him some of that hot tea. I insist someone drive him home and stay with him through the night. I'll call in a prescription for a strong sedative that will need to be picked up and delivered to his home. He can take it tomorrow for certain and the rest of the week as needed. He'll need to see his own doctor this week for follow-up. If there are any changes during the night, don't hesitate to call me."

"Thank you, Dr. Goldman, so much. Our agents will take care of everything, and I'll request a nurse to sit with him as well," answered Martha with assurance and authority. She looked over to Agent Lewis, who nodded and immediately left the room to make the arrangements. Dr. Goldman said goodbye and followed Agent Lewis out the door. Gary sat down at the table and took Ken firmly by the hand.

"Ken, it's Gary. Do you feel like talking? Can you tell us what happened?" asked Gary gently.

Ken looked over at Gary in agony. "It's all my fault," he moaned. "I knew he wasn't well. He was worse than ever in fact. I was trying to help him, you see, taking him to his new doctor after work or during lunch. I took him out to eat, too, to get away from here, away from all the pressure. He was very stressed and was having severe anxiety problems. It got much worse after President Taylor died."

"Was something bothering him specifically about that?" asked Miller intently with alarm in his voice. Dwight Cook stepped over and quietly handed Gary a cup of hot tea and lemon for Ken.

Ken looked up with an uncertain gaze. "I honestly don't know, Mr. Secretary. He didn't say. He just wouldn't say. It seemed like he was falling apart."

Gary sat back, folded his arms and looked up at Martha, who seemed to know what he was thinking. She nodded her approval for Gary to proceed. "Ken, I need to tell you that you were overheard speaking on the phone to someone recently, telling them something was reaching a crisis point and that you may have to directly intervene. Was that about Donald?"

"Yes," said Ken nodding miserably. "I was talking to Donald's psychiatrist, a new fellow that Don was seeing. I've been working with this doctor to help Donald. Donald almost had a nervous breakdown last month, and the doctor wanted to try some new medications, different combinations of anti-depressants and tranquilizers, anything new that Donald hadn't already tried yet. Some medications Donald tried in the past didn't work very well, you see. He experienced some bad side effects when taking them in combination before. God, I've been reading medical journals till I'm blue in the face. Not that I didn't trust Donald's doctor. He's great, but well, you know me. I like to research and I thought I could help. Anyway, the doctor told me if Donald's high anxiety levels didn't subside soon, he might have to intervene and put Donald in the hospital."

"How about today? Did you speak to Donald today?"

Ken shook his head. "No, he was meeting with Jim when I got into the office late this morning."

Surprised, Gary turned around and stared hard at Jim. Myers immediately stopped pacing and stepped forward to explain. "Donald and I did have a meeting this morning to discuss a position statement. Pretty routine stuff. But I noticed that he was pretty upset when he came to my office."

The whole room stared at Jim. He licked his lips nervously, appearing uncertain how to continue. "I hate to say it now, but Donald said that he needed to speak to Martha immediately. He didn't say why. I told him that the President was upstairs and wasn't due back in the office until later this morning. Then I made him take off his coat and loosen his tie, to sit down and relax a bit." Jim shook his head. "God, if I'd only known how upset he really was. Anyway, I made him some coffee, and we worked at my desk, reviewing the statement, and finished our business on schedule. Then Donald got up, took his coat, and said he was going to the Oval to wait for Madame President. That's the last I saw him. After he left, I had to run an errand over at the Old Executive Office. I was there the rest of the morning until I heard the news."

Gary looked over to McKay for confirmation. The general nodded, indicating that Jim's story was supported by White House surveillance video cameras. If anyone had murdered Donald outright, those cameras in the Oval Office and West Wing would have captured it.

McKay stepped forward and took over the inquiry. He turned to the press secretary.

"Did Donald speak to you this morning, Ned?"

"No," said Ned sighing heavily, taking out a handkerchief and rubbing it across his moistened brow. "I'm afraid I was on the phone most of the morning with my publisher."

All eyes turned and stared at Baldwin.

"Guess it's time for me to make a confession," said Ned flatly. "For the past nine months, I've been secretly working on a book deal, writing a biography about President Taylor's life. I was approached by a New York publisher during the campaign and signed a contract. It's all been very hush hush, at their request. They wanted me to work on the book during the election and during the first year of Stan's presidency. Of course, it wasn't going to be published until after Taylor's term in office was over, but after his death, they insisted on moving up the publication date. We've been negotiating a new contract and release date."

"That's why you wanted my observations on the night Taylor died?" asked Gary enlightened.

Ned nodded. "Right. I've asked a number of people to give me their impressions and experiences of that awful night. I wanted to document as many different viewpoints and reactions as possible. And, then, of course, when you fired the entire Taylor cabinet, Madame President, that really got my publishers excited. They wanted to move up the publication date and get the book out immediately. They also want me to include some of the events of your first ninety days in office as Taylor's vice president. Actually, I was going to speak to you about it this week to get your approval." Ned wiped his brow again and shrugged his shoulders. "Now you know."

There was a soft knock at the door and Agent Clark entered the room, holding a plastic bag in his hand. He handed it over to General McKay.

"The coroner has finished his preliminary examination, sir. First impression is that Mr. Hooper died of a massive heart attack, similar to the ones that killed President Taylor and Peters. We found this in Donald's coat pocket along with the note."

"What did the note say?" asked Gary.

"It said he was sorry."

"Sorry?" said Jim with confusion. "Sorry for what?"

McKay held up the clear plastic bag. It contained a small glass vial filled with a clear liquid.

"No one touched this, did they?" asked McKay sharply, ignoring Jim's question. "Opened this up and sampled it or exposed their skin to it in any way?"

"No, sir," replied Agent Clark promptly. "They almost did, but I stopped the FBI guys before they opened the bottle. I told them my suspicions of its contents. We'll get it down to the FBI lab right away, but it's a good bet that it's the same stuff that was used to murder President Taylor."

"Murder?" cried Ned Baldwin. "Taylor was murdered?"

"Yes, murdered," replied McKay quietly. "So was Eric."

Jim Myers face went white.

"Murder?" Miller looked at Martha anxiously. "Madame President, what's this all about?"

Martha spoke solemnly. "Someone killed Stan Taylor and Eric Peters. Their heart attacks were the result of that poison."

"What are you saying?" Ken exclaimed, awakened out of his shocked state. He looked up at McKay in desperation. "Are you implying that Donald poisoned Taylor? That's impossible!"

McKay frowned and put a strong hand on Ken's shoulder. "I'm sorry, Ken. You shouldn't have to hear this now. But it can't be helped. That's exactly what it looks like. We have evidence that both men were killed and suspect they were murdered in a plot designed to get control of the White House. This proves Donald was working for them. Donald killed Eric and Stan with a new weaponized formulation of prussic acid and DSMO, one built with a time delay. Instead of being almost instantaneous, it takes twenty to thirty minutes to take effect. That allows time for the murderer to get away. Pretty wicked stuff! We also have evidence that Bishop Jonathan Palmer was directly involved in Taylor's murder and that the bishop was himself killed to cover up the plot."

Ken put his hands up and covered his face, not wanting to hear any more.

"Oh, my God!" whispered Ned in disbelief.

"Unbelievable," said Jim in wide-eyed amazement. Then Jim turned and looked at Gary severely. "Hey, wait a minute. Was that what you were talking about that day you came to my office? All that stuff about life and death? You weren't talking about my heart problems, were you? You were talking about Taylor and Peters being killed."

Gary nodded gloomily.

Jim looked over at Martha with concern. "I suppose the whole story will come out now?"

General McKay looked at Martha somberly and shook his head. "I think perhaps it should not. The press can be told that Donald was under extreme stress, which is true, and that he committed suicide in the Oval Office, which is also true, but the assassination of Eric Peters and President Taylor and Donald's role in those murders is best left as classified information."

"I agree," said Miller in a firm voice. "No need for the American public and the rest of the world to know of it. It's over, the murderer is caught, and that's that. The less said, the better. And we should go ahead with the German state dinner. Of course, a suicide inside the Oval Office is a big story and will make headlines, but we can ride out that storm. If you don't mind, Madame President, once the story breaks, I think I should contact the German embassy and reassure them in case they have any concerns about security. We will tell them we wish to continue with the state visit as scheduled. The sooner we get back to normal, the better."

Martha silently nodded her head in agreement and looked at the old man appreciatively. He sensed her feelings and went over and put his arm around her.

"Don't worry," he said softly. "The crisis is over."

This was comforting to Gary and Ned, but Jim did not look appeased. He turned to McKay clearly angry. "I want to know something. If you and Madame President knew Stan was murdered, why weren't the rest of us told?"

McKay gave Jim a wilting look. He wasn't about to be intimidated by the chief of staff. "Because, Mr. Myers, we also had information linking their murders to someone working in the West Wing."

At this, Ned's mouth dropped open.

"You knew one of us was involved?"

Martha softly said, "Yes."

Jim then turned to Martha and exclaimed hotly, "And you really suspected one of us?"

Miller interrupted sharply. "Jim, you're only making matters worse. Try to control yourself and calm down. You should see, as now I see, the great stress Madame President and the general have been working under the past few weeks. They didn't know who was behind this plot, but they figured out the plan involved the selection of the vice president. That's probably why they killed Eric, right? To clear the way for their man to be placed inside the White House."

"That's the way we saw it," confirmed McKay gruffly.

Miller looked at Martha compassionately. "And since so many of the cabinet members were nominated by people working in the Oval Office, you didn't know who to trust and couldn't possibly pick a VP. Oh, Martha, I see. How awful."

Miller gave Martha a big hug and held her tight. Martha held on to him tightly and sobbed a little.

"I so wanted to tell you, David. I'm so very sorry."

"Hush, my dear. It's all right," said Miller softly in a comforting fatherly voice. "You're quite safe now."

Martha breathed deeply a sigh of relief. She stepped back and smiled through her moist eyes. "Well, at least the veil of suspicion over the West Wing is finally lifted. And David, if you don't mind, there is no reason now for you to resign. It would please me very much if you stayed on as secretary of state."

Miller handed Martha a well-pressed white handkerchief. "Of course. I'll serve wherever you wish as long as you wish."

Tensions in the room lifted a bit, except for Myers, who clearly was still feeling insulted.

"And I was a suspect in all this?" Jim asked crossly.

Martha looked at Jim with deep regret. "Yes, I'm afraid so. But, like David says, it's over now."

Jim shook his head defensively. "Not if you don't trust me. If I don't have your complete trust, then perhaps it would be best if I did resign."

Martha hurriedly stepped over and stood face to face with Myers.

"No, Jim, don't over react. I'm sorry. I really am. General McKay and I felt we needed to keep this information absolutely secret until we knew. It was a matter of national security, not a matter of personal feelings. I do trust you and need you. So don't leave. I need you now more than ever!"

Jim looked down at her and slowly assented. Martha smiled up at him.

"Friends?" she asked tentatively.

Jim gave her a small smile and then a big hug like Miller had given her.

"You mean a great deal to me, Martha," he whispered sincerely. "More than you know. I promise I won't let anything bad happen to you while I'm around."

"You mean a great deal to me, too, Jim," she said gratefully in return.

Gary could stomach this tender scene no longer. He abruptly turned to Agent Clark and asked, "Can I go see Donald now?"

"In a moment, sir," replied Clark quietly. "The FBI is still taking pictures."

"Fine," said Gary curtly. "I'll go outside and wait."

He promptly left the Cabinet Room and went out into the hall. Gary had been out of the room barely a few moments when Blaze suddenly appeared, bounding up the hallway headed directly at him.

"Ned's secretary called me at home with the news," said Blaze breathlessly. "I came right over as fast as I could. Are you okay? Is Madame President okay? Are the kids okay?"

"Madame President and the family are fine. The rest of us? We're as good as can be expected," said Gary honestly. "Ken is in there really shaken up. He found Donald. The doctor gave Ken a shot to calm his nerves, and Madame President is sending him home with security and nursing care. He'll pull through, I'm sure. As for me, I'm waiting to get in to see Donald before they move him." Gary glanced over at the closed door to the Oval Office, which was blocked with a crush of men in dark suits.

Blaze looked at Gary anxiously. "Can we go somewhere and talk?"

"Sure," said Gary. "Let's go to Ned's office. He's in the Cabinet Room right now. He won't mind."

They quickly walked down the hall to Ned's office and went inside. Blaze closed the door and immediately began a long overdue apology.

"Man, I don't know where to begin, except to say I've been a total jerk. I should have called you long before this, I know, but my head was all screwed up. All I can say is that I'm sorry, really, really, really sorry."

A wave of comfort spread over Gary and he smiled. His old Blaze was back. "Apology accepted," said Gary. And that was that.

Blaze looked at Gary gratefully. "Well, I was a jerk. I guess I was jealous or something over all the attention you've been getting. Really dumb, huh? The stress of this place was getting to me, too. Kind of scary, with what's happened to Donald and all. Anyway, the other part of it is that Kingsley offered me a big position with his staff, as an executive assistant. It was too much to handle, feeling sorry for myself and needing to make a really big decision. I had to get away and think it through. So, I took off and hid out in my apartment."

"Kingsley offered you a job?" exclaimed Gary. "Blaze, that's great!"

Blaze beamed. "Yeah, we started talking about it the night of the July Fourth party. It was pretty exciting, you know. But I've decided to turn it down."

Gary was surprised. "Are you sure? That would be quite a step up."

"Well, I'm not sure I really want to move up," said Blaze frankly. "After thinking it over and after what happened to Donald, my place is here with Ned and you and the President. And besides, who else would you get to try out those delicious dishes that you come up with?"

Gary laughed, grateful for one brief moment of levity. "Blaze, consider yourself the official White House taster!"

They shook hands, friends again, the entire mess behind them. There was a sudden knock on the door and one of the FBI men entered and said that they were getting ready to remove Donald's body. Gary thanked them, took Blaze by the arm, and went to pay his respects to a fallen comrade. They walked out into the hallway and watched the paramedics slowly push out a cold metal stretcher passed them. Gary asked them to stop and pulled back the gray blanket to see Donald's face. In spite of his horrible crimes, Donald looked at peace. Gary stared down at him, feeling confused at Donald's betrayal and despair for a life cut short. Blaze stood steadily close, like the true friend he was.

They covered Donald's face again and rolled him away. Gary turned to Blaze, desiring desperately for many reasons to leave the West Wing.

"Let's get out of here," he said thickly.

"Right," said Blaze.

"Come upstairs with me," suggested Gary. "We can catch up, and you can have some chocolate cake. There's lots of cake."

Chapter 21

Georgetown Bridal Shoppe

Tuesday, August 16

His name was Roosevelt Maximilian Jones.

His austere father, a conservative/self-made millionaire/ Republican, decreed his firstborn son would be named after his favorite president, Teddy Roosevelt. However, upon awaking from her anesthesia, his equally assertive mother, an outspoken feminist/ liberal/Democrat, amended the decision of the Lord of the Jones Manor and insisted her baby boy be named after her favorite Hollywood actor, Maximilian Schell. The resulting appellation was prophetic of their son's future life and work.

Known simply as Max, he was the premier designer residing in the nation's capital. Max specialized in designing bridal gowns, and the richest betrothed women in Washington shopped at his exclusive D.C. boutique, "Maxed Out." The store's name was indicative of his client's credit card balances upon completion of their high-end purchases. The trendy establishment was housed in a charming three-story brownstone in the heart of Georgetown. The first floor was used for customer consultations and private fittings, having a central space decorated in shades of white, black, peach, and muted taupe. Its furnishings included overstuffed leather sofas, cushioned chairs, antique side tables, a large black desk supporting a computer, gigantic oil paintings of exotic birds, and large Oriental vases of fresh-cut flowers.

The shop was open by appointment only. No cash register was in sight. Dress designs were displayed on live models, sketch boards, or computer screen. Fittings were done privately in one of two chintz-draped rooms located in the back. The second floor was the designer's workroom, used for drafting, fabric selection, sewing, alterations, shipping, and storage. The third floor was Max's own private residence. Max managed to keep his private life private, and the Washington social set had a difficult time deciding which side of the street Max leaned in his affections. Which was exactly the way Max wanted it.

Getting an appointment with Max for a wedding gown consultation was a feat in and of itself. Since Max's appearance on *The Oprah Winfrey Show* late last fall, the normal six-month waiting period dramatically expanded to twelve months. However, a phone call from the Oval Office from the leader of free nations got an appointment for Harriet on Tuesday next at 4:00 P.M. Max tactfully informed Martha that he had a fitting booked that day for another important client with congressional connections. This appointment had also been bumped up due to the demands of a senator's bullying secretary. But Max would be most happy to work the President's party in. Martha's daughters would be coming along, so Max and his staff also had to accommodate the Secret Service inspection of the shop prior to the appointment. Agents would be posted upstairs, in the back alley, and on a building's roof across the street. The appointment was set for Tuesday afternoon, because Gary and members of the First Family had to attend a memorial service for Donald Hooper that morning. Per the request of Donald's family, his body was cremated and his ashes would be flown back to Texas.

Following the private funeral, which was very difficult for all emotionally, at the appointed time, a row of black vehicles pulled up at the curbside of Maxed Out, and a Secret Service detail led Gary, Mildred, Harriet, Jane, Eliza, and Abigail quickly into the store. Max was standing inside the doorway ready to greet his important guests.

The designer was a tall, lean man, with strawberry blond hair. He reminded Gary of a younger, more hip version of the actor, Danny Kaye. Max was wearing black leather pants (a bit too tight) and a poet's shirt in pale peach silk (a bit too large). He wore small, square shaped, black-rimmed glasses, and his hair was cut short.

"Welcome, welcome, welcome," gushed Max enthusiastically while ushering in his guests. He motioned toward the furnished area in the center of the floor. "Welcome to Maxed Out. I'm so happy to have you all here this afternoon. Please make yourselves comfortable. Take off your shoes. Relax. Enjoy." Max then turned and addressed the agents in a more somber voice. "People dressed in drab suits and armed with pistols must remain in the front of the store if you please."

Agent Lewis, who was part of the detail, nodded with a straight face, and joined two other agents posted at the doorway. Gary and the rest sat down on the plush sofas.

"Now," said Max broadly beaming, "who is the lucky bride? Is it you?" He had knelt down and looked at Abigail, who was dressed up for the occasion. The child wore a long lilac netted ballerina skirt pinned over her dark blue denim overalls, white gloves, and a toy sequined tiara.

"No," giggled Abigail. "I'm the flower girl."

"But you don't have any flowers! That, princess, will never do. Michael, Michael, bring this little angel a bouquet of silk flowers from the desk upstairs."

One of Max's assistants, a young man with shoulder length dark hair pulled back in a ponytail, appeared from the back of the store, grinned and went dashing up the black iron circular staircase to the second floor work room.

"So, then who is the bride?" asked Max breathlessly, looking about the room.

Harriet smiled and shyly raised her hand. "I am."

"But of course!" said Max dramatically. "You have that glow, dear lady, that happy glow. How could I have missed it? Now, tell Max when is the wedding to take place?"

Harriet bit her lip indecisively. "Well, I'm embarrassed to say we aren't really quite sure. We were thinking about Christmas. I hope that isn't too soon."

"No, no," assured Max confidently, "we'll have plenty of time to make you the perfect dress!"

"It's not perfect!"

The resounding complaint of an unhappy woman came abruptly and loudly from behind one of the back fitting rooms. Another assistant, a slender young woman in her early thirties with short pink-dyed hair, stood by the fitting room door. She had a yellow measuring tape draped around her neck and held a round tomato-red pincushion tightly in her hand. She responded to the client in a perplexed voice.

"But Miss, we've pinned the dress up to tea length as you requested. This is exactly the length you asked for."

"But I say it's still not right!" exclaimed the woman impatiently. "I want it longer."

Max smiled weakly and quickly indicated to his assistant that she go inside and re-pin the dress. The girl rolled her eyes and went into the dressing room.

"Sorry about that," said Max in a hushed voice. "A rather difficult client, you see. But never mind about her. It's you we need to focus on. Tell me, dear lady, what style of dress do you have in mind?"

Harriet blushed. "Well, nothing too fancy. For a lady my age, probably a plain white suit will do."

Max threw his hands up in the air. "Age? We never say that word in my boutique. No, no, no! Talk about age is strictly forbidden. Besides, age means nothing in wedding fashion. All the old rules are broken, the old guidelines smashed, the old boundaries tossed aside. Anything goes. If you want a simple suit, we certainly can do that. *But*, if you dream of a dress that a queen, a gentle southern belle, or a Hollywood starlet would wear, I am here to make those dreams come true."

"Well," said Harriet softly, "I always did admire Grace Kelly."

Max clapped his hands together joyfully. "Grace Kelly! Marvelous! She has such beauty, such style! Wait!" Max closed his eyes and raised his hands in the air. "It's coming. I envision your hair, Miss Simmons, done up in a 1940s style, with the front and the sides rolled back from your face. I see pearls! There will be a single strand of white pearls around your neck. Then, a simple fitted bodice with a dropped waistline in silk. There will be a sheer jacket with a hint of lace to cover the arms and chest. And yards and yards and yards of white chiffon! And lastly, a dash of color! We will weave a pale coral blush chiffon sash. I'm sure you'll be most pleased . . ."

"I am not pleased!" screeched the voice in the fitting room. "Get me Max this instant!"

Max look mortified. He held up one finger in the air.

"Uno momento."

He quickly turned and pranced as fast as his tight leather pants would allow toward the fitting room to placate the irate customer.

"Good heavens," observed Jane aghast, "that one sounds like a nasty sort."

"No kidding," agreed Mildred.

"Something about her sounds familiar," reflected Gary warily. His stomach fluttered nervously.

Harriet stepped over to Gary and grabbed his arm. "Oh, Gary, this is so kind of you, but are you sure you can afford it? I hear Max is very expensive. Maybe we should go to a department store and pick out a plain suit instead."

"Nonsense," said Gary giving his friend a hug. "I have a little nest egg saved up for just such an occasion. You took me in when my life fell apart, Harriet. You took good care of me, and you nursed me mentally and emotionally back to health. Now it's my turn to do something nice for you."

"I spoke with Gary earlier," added Mildred gently," and I will be paying half, as my wedding present to you. Think of it as gift from both Harrison and I."

At this, Harriet broke out in happy tears. Mildred was ready and handed her a tissue.

"Madame President and the First Family would also like to contribute," said Nanny Jane. She reached inside her oversized tapestry handbag and pulled out a white envelope bearing the presidential seal. "She asked me to give you this."

Gary took the envelope and opened it. There was a short handwritten note and a check enclosed.

"Dear Gary,

I hope I am not overstepping my bounds or taking away from your wedding gift to Mrs. Simmons. But you have become a special part of our family, and so have your two dear friends from Greensboro. As you know, my late husband left me with a lot of money, most of which I have no use for whatsoever. Please accept this check as a token of my family's affection for you and your friend.

Sincerely,

Martha."

The check was for $10,000.

Gary read the letter aloud.

Harriet burst out into tears again.

Mildred and Jane reached for tissues and dabbed theirs eyes.

Gary sniffled, his own eyes moistening. Mildred handed him a tissue, too.

Michael reappeared from the upstairs loft, bouncing down the stairs, carrying a bouquet of silk flowers. He was about to hand it to Abigail when someone suddenly burst out of the fitting room door, raced forward, and ripped the flowers out of his hand.

"That's mine! Give it back this instant!"

Gary's stomach had been right. The nasty voice was familiar, all too familiar.

It was Janet.

Gary turned around to see his ex-wife grab the flowers and literally shake them at Max, who was following closely behind in her wake.

"Those are for my wedding!" she shouted at the dress designer. "Why are you giving them to a bratty little kid?"

"Those flowers are still unpaid for, Madame, so technically they are still mine. Consequently I can give them to whomever I please. And that bratty little kid you refer to is Abigail Johnson, the President's daughter," replied Max dryly with a slight smirk on his face.

Janet's unseemly tirade stopped midstream with a gasp of recognition. Emotions turned on a dime, and ugly became sweet in an instant.

"Well, so it is," she said now smiling excessively, her voice purring. "How rude of you, Max, for not telling me who this darling child was. It's totally your fault. Here you go, sweetheart. You may hold the pretty flowers."

Janet handed the flowers to Abigail. Abigail looked down at the flowers, looked up at Janet, and then stuck out her tongue.

"Abigail!" cried Jane disapprovingly, jumping up from the sofa and dashing over to the naughty girl. "That wasn't very nice. Say you're sorry."

"But I'm not sorry," protested Abigail loudly, looking up at her nanny plaintively. "I don't like her. She's mean."

Jane smiled weakly at Janet. "I apologize. She's five and what can you do? Abigail, dearest, let's go look at the wedding veils over there on the wall. And maybe Michael can find you a piece of paper and pencil for you to draw with," said Jane, taking the little girl firmly by the hand and dragging her away towards a display at the back of the store. Michael obediently followed.

"Hello, Janet," said Gary flatly as he got up from the sofa. He stared at her dress. "What a lovely gown. How surprising to see you are wearing white. Or is Max going to dye the dress a darker color to match your disposition?"

Janet wore a white silk gown with a delicate lace overcoat. She turned and looked at Gary disdainfully.

"Hello, my pet. What an unexpected pleasure. What on earth brings you here? Don't tell me that you actually found someone to marry you?"

"One of my friends is getting married," replied Gary evenly, unable to think of a good insult to hurl back at her.

"Oh, yes, I see you've brought your friends from Greensboro." She reached out her hand. "Hello, ladies. Gary, you'll have to introduce us. I'm afraid I've forgotten who's who."

Gary did the introductions. "Janet Benson-Craig, this is Harriet Simmons and Mildred Harrison."

Mildred stiffly shook hands and muttered a strained polite greeting. Harriet ignored Janet and turned towards Gary.

"I think we should leave. I don't want to be under the same roof with that woman!"

"My, my, such temper," said Janet with a wicked smile. Ignoring Harriet's comment, she abruptly turned her attentions to Eliza. " Gary, my precious, you haven't introduced me to this divine creature yet."

Gary sighed. He felt like he was in the middle of a Jane Austen novel, one fraught with endless formal introductions. "Miss Eliza Johnson, Ms. Janet Benson-Craig."

Janet proudly extended her hand. Eliza looked at Janet with a look only a teenager could create.

"Who is she?" asked Eliza frowning.

"My ex-wife," said Gary.

"No *way!*" exclaimed Eliza her eyes widening.

"Eliza, manners!" reminded Nanny Jane from across the room.

Gary smiled weakly. "I would never kid about a thing like that."

The teenager stared at Janet in disbelief.

"But Uncle Gary, why would you ever want to be married to her?"

Mildred immediately stepped forward to intercede. "Come, Eliza. Come Harriet. Let's go look at veils with Jane and Abigail. We might find a nice one for you, Harriet, or perhaps a nice hat." With that, Mildred pushed Harriet and the unwilling teenager out of the verbal fray.

Janet watched them go off with detached amusement. She turned to Gary.

"Well, well, I don't seem to be very welcome around here, do I? But it doesn't matter really. I have better places to go and better people to see. I'll be off then. Oh, by the way, my angel, I wanted you to know I was just a wee bit disappointed in not getting an invitation to the German state dinner this weekend. It was an oversight, I'm quite sure."

No it wasn't. Gary had scratched her boyfriend's name off the list himself.

Gary shrugged his shoulders. "You'll have to take that up with the State Department, Janet. They handled the final invitation list."

"Of course," she replied coolly. "Next time there is a big important dinner, I'll be sure to call Secretary Miller myself. But I wanted you to know, dearest, that I have already had the pleasure of meeting the new German ambassador and his wife. They are such delightful people."

Gary's mouth fell open.

"You've already met them?"

"Hmmm. Yes. My future husband is on the Senate Foreign Relations Committee, and a group of three senators and their significant others flew over to Germany two weeks ago to meet with the German chancellor and the new ambassador and their families. Surely you read about it in the paper? No? Oh, that's right. You only read the comics and the food section. Well, we had a lovely dinner. The new ambassador is not very talkative, a real stick in the mud if you ask me, but his wife Elsa is simply smashing. We got along famously. I'm planning to invite her to my wedding."

"How nice," said Gary lamely, acutely aware he was being upstaged once again.

Seeing she had scored, Janet tossed her head and flipped back her long dark hair across her shoulder with her hand. "Yes, Elsa and I really hit it off. We have so much in common. Like me, she knows all the best people and wears the latest in Paris fashion. I think we'll become good friends."

Janet paused and then said, "But you do have something in common with Elsa and her husband. I hate to admit it, but in one small way, they are your kind of people."

"My kind of people?"

Janet waved her hand impatiently in the air. "You know, flower people."

Gary stared at Janet uncomprehending.

"Flower people? What on earth of you talking about, Janet? Are the German ambassador and his wife hippies?"

"Gary, darling, you are so slow. Flowers! Gardens! Roses! Elsa and her husband thrive on them, just like you. They're simply nuts about the subject. I found it utterly boring but said nothing and pretended to be intrigued. I've had years of practice, thanks to being married to you. Anyway, the ambassador's late sister was something of a rose expert. Rather well known in Europe from the way Elsa talked. Pity. The sister died this past year, and the ambassador is quite torn up about it still. They were very close, you know."

Gary couldn't believe what he was hearing.

"Janet, do you remember the sister's name, the one who died?"

Janet huffed and rolled her eyes impatiently. "God, I don't remember, some German-sounding name. Marta? Gerta? Greta? No, that's not it. Began with a vowel. Adelaide? Inga? No. Wait a minute. Ingrid. That's it. Ingrid something or other."

"Ingrid Kessler?" muttered Gary taken aback.

Janet smiled and snapped her long fingers. "There you are. You have it. Ingrid Kessler. Never heard of her myself, but then I don't run around with florists. So, you see, dearest one, you will have something to talk about when the ambassador arrives. You can discuss mulching while serving dessert . . . Hey, stop that!" cried Janet suddenly. She stomped back towards the dressing rooms. Abigail was sitting on the floor in front of one of them, drawing on Janet's white Dooney and Bourke designer handbag. For a crayon, she was using a tube of bright magenta lipstick.

Janet grabbed the purse away from Abigail furiously.

"You horrid, horrid child!" she screamed. "You've ruined it. That handbag cost me a fortune!"

Abigail looked up at Janet serenely. "It's pretty now," she said.

Jane stepped over and scolded her charge. "Abigail, what a bad girl you are." Nanny Jane's rebuke however didn't sound too severe, and Gary saw the nanny wink down at the little girl.

Ms. Benson-Craig stepped forward in a threatening stance. "How can you allow such behavior?" She then reached for the lipstick Abigail was holding and grabbed it away from the child. "Where did you get this?" asked Janet waving it in the air.

Eliza held out her hand. "Oops. That looks like mine. It must have fallen out of my handbag by accident," she said innocently.

Janet seethed. "This reeks of a conspiracy. Fine. If you two won't do anything to correct this spoiled brat, I most certainly will. I'll teach her a lesson she won't soon forget." Janet raised a hand ready to strike.

Secret Service agents immediately rushed in. A female agent snatched up Abigail, while Agent Lewis came quickly around up and stepped authoritatively between Janet and the child. He took hold of Janet firmly by the arm and held it frozen in mid air.

"I'm sorry, Ms. Craig, but I'm going to have to ask you to leave the store immediately. If you'll follow me." This was not a request. The tone of his voice was deep and threatening.

Janet glared at the agent hatefully and hissed out a warning of her own.

"How dare you! Do you know who I am?" she hissed.

Agent Lewis's face was like stone. "I'm afraid I do, Ma'am."

Her eyes narrowed. "How rude! And do you know who I'm engaged to?"

"Yes, Ma'am. Now, if you will follow me."

Janet seethed. "When I get to the White House, young man, you'll have to answer to me!"

"If you ever get to the White House, I'll put in for a transfer," replied the agent stonily. "Now, you will please exit the building immediately or we will have to use force."

Janet grasped her handbag tightly and stared at Gary.

"Well, darling, it looks like you finally got the family you always wanted," said Janet spitefully. She glanced down at Abigail with disdain. "Frankly, I would never want a child like that!"

Gary looked at Janet now with a surprising new feeling, one of pity. He finally saw what a poor excuse for a human being Janet really was, and in that moment, he realized she meant nothing to him anymore. He was free at last from this woman's awful spell and the hurt she had imposed upon him. He looked at her and laughed.

"Janet, I'm absolutely sure no child would ever want you for a mother either."

Janet cast him a hateful look and then turned to Max.

"And what about my fitting?"

Max stepped forward with Janet's street clothes in hand. He thrust them into her arms. "Madame, here are the rest of your things. I suspect the services of this establishment will not meet with your extremely high standards. I suggest you look elsewhere for a designer. And you may keep the incomplete dress you have on as a parting gift from me."

Janet threw Max a withering look. "Alright. I'll take my business up to New York where I should have gone in the first place. I'm through with you." Clutching her purse and clothes, she stormed arrogantly out of the store, with Agent Lewis following close behind.

Gary began to apologize. "Max, I'm really sorry. Please forgive . . ."

Max held up his hand to stop Gary. "No need for apology, Mr. Craig. I should be thanking you for getting rid of that monstrous woman. Such a headache! You have no idea what I've put up with. On second thought, I think maybe you do. Well, this calls for a celebration. Something to drink and something sweet to eat while we take Ms. Simmons measurements?"

"Good idea," said Mildred. "I would love something chocolate myself.

"Ice cream!" exclaimed Abigail twirling around in her ballerina skirt.

"Root bear floats," suggested Eliza with a broad magenta smile.

"Sounds delightful!" said Nanny Jane.

"Excellent," said Max. The designer called for his frightened female assistant with the pink hair, dug out some money from his own pocket, and shoved it firmly in her hand. "Christina, take this and go to the ice cream shop down the street and buy up as many flavors of chocolate ice cream as you can possibly carry back here. Michael, go upstairs to the kitchen and get bowls and spoons and glasses for everyone. Here's the key to the wet bar. Fruit juices and root beer and sodas for the young ladies! Our best wine for our guests! And for me, I could very well do with a Vodka gimlet. Make it a double."

Happily, the two assistants went scurrying off in different directions, and Max invited Harriet, Jane, Eliza, and Abigail to come over to the computer to watch him sketch the design for Harriet's dress. Gary and Mildred slowly ambled towards the front door where they peered out the window.

"So, Ingrid Kessler was Ambassador Schneider's sister," mused Mildred softly. "Amazing. I didn't know that. Did you know that?"

"No, I had no idea. Our briefings didn't mention it," answered Gary shaking his head while watching Janet being escorted to her car. Agent Lewis seemed to be really enjoying himself. He was almost smiling. Gary would cherish this scene forever. "The State Department only supplied details about the immediate family, his wife and children. I'm surprised Ken and Jim missed it."

"They probably didn't think it was very important," said Mildred in a hushed voice.

"Ingrid Kessler, one of the most important rose experts in all of Europe," said Gary thoughtfully. "She was also a wonderful landscaper. She's designed many formal gardens in France, England, and Spain. And she's judged at top international rose shows. Her work is legendary in my circles."

"She was known in my orchid society as well, especially for display gardens combining various species of old roses and wild orchids. I met her once. She was a lovely woman, quite deserving of recognition."

Gary turned and looked at Mildred wide eyed.

"She was best known, of course, for her love of white roses," he said slowly.

Mildred looked at Gary with a raised eyebrow. "Yes, white roses. She indeed was known for that. You know, when I was traveling back from Scotland recently, I stopped over in England to visit the creator of modern English Roses. You are familiar with him, of course. I visited the greenhouses on this last visit. They have some beautiful new roses in development stages that he showed me, not on the public market yet. One that really caught my eye was a lovely white."

"Did they have a number of specimens of this new variety?"

"They most certainly did. At least twenty or thirty, I think."

"All blooming?" asked Gary hopefully, as a crazy idea began to crystallize in his head.

Mildred nodded her head. "Oh, yes. Most English Roses are constant bloomers during the summer, as you well know. This new one will rival Fair Bianca and Glamis Castle. The new plants that I saw in the greenhouse were covered with very large white blooms, as large as the deep pink Brother Cadfael rose you planted by my greenhouse. It was most impressive. This new white one has a distinctive myrrh fragrance. Delightful!"

"You thinking what I'm thinking?" asked Gary excitedly.

Mildred nodded her head affirmatively. "Do we dare?"

"We dare," said Gary.

Mildred went over to pick up her big black handbag to search for her cell phone. "I'm pretty sure I have his assistant's direct number somewhere in my cell phone directory. It will take me a minute. Should I call now? It will be late there in England, nighttime, but this is important enough to wake him."

"Wake him!" said Gary as he pulled out his own cell phone. "Tell him it's a matter of national security. I'll call Martha and tell her what's up and get her approval. We can have her call William Darby, Mr. Austin's assistant, later on today. And I better call the general as well. He'll need to know. He won't like it one bit, I'm sure. He doesn't like my wild ideas. I can already hear him bluster, but I think we can talk him into it. I'll threaten to have Nanny Jane step on his toes again or hit him with her hair dryer. And I'll put in a call to Jack, too. He might be able to take part. The press just might help us pull this thing off."

Mildred agreed. "Right. I'll get the ball rolling with William. What about State? Should we contact Secretary Miller and let him know our plans?"

Gary thought carefully for a moment then shook his head with determination. "No. We better keep this one under wraps. If it fails, no real harm will be done. It will just look like a social blunder from the East Wing staff. Besides, if there is any flack, Miller can honestly deny everything. But if we succeed, he and Martha can reap all the benefits."

"What will you tell Secretary Miller?"

"The truth," grinned Gary as he started dialing the Oval Office. "We wanted to present the new ambassador and his wife with a bouquet."

Chapter 22

State Dining Room

Saturday, August 20

"You're sitting on my cummerbund."

A small black cat stretched out lazily on top of Gary's white attire that was lying on the edge of the bed. The cat Sheba looked up and blinked contentedly.

"Let me know when you've finished shedding," Gary said dryly. He turned and looked into his chest of drawers mirror and fastened his cuff links and straightened his tie. He needed to hurry up and finish dressing, as the German delegation would be arriving at any moment. Gary assessed his appearance. Not bad. His dark brown hair was coiffed to perfection, and his dark blue eyes looked clear, thanks to a last-minute dose of eye drops. A knock on the door broke his concentration.

"Come in," called Gary.

Blaze entered the room wearing a spanking new black tuxedo. Gary whistled his approval.

"Looking good, Phillips."

"Thanks," said Blaze grinning. "Looking good yourself, man. Well, everyone is here, and everything is ready to go."

Gary raised an eyebrow at his friend.

"No problems getting it inside?"

"Nope. We loaded it into the limo at your house and drove it straight over here without mishap. Mildred held it steady the whole way. Morgan took over at the Oval Office west entrance. Lucky for us most of the press corps are stationed at the east entrance to cover the arriving guests, and the rest are downstairs waiting at the front door for the delegation arrival. Nobody saw us enter, except for the uniformed guard at the door, and he could care less what we brought inside. Glad Mr. Morgan is in on this little adventure. He got it and us into the house tout de suite. Mildred is downstairs with Morgan now in the China Room setting it up."

"Terrific. Where's Harriet?"

"She's with Jane and Charlotte and the kids in the Oval Sitting Room. Madame President and Aunt Sophie are at the front steps waiting for the Germans to arrive. They'll bring the delegation upstairs shortly. Man, you should see the reporters down in the Entrance Hall."

"You see Jack?" asked Gary.

"Yeah. He's front and center."

"He always is."

"Well, he said to tell you that he's all set in the State Dining Room. By the way, Harriet is totally excited about coming. She chattered away non-stop on the way over."

"She's a real sweetheart. I want you to take good care of her tonight."

"Will do," assured Blaze.

"Now, let me go over the seating arrangement with you one more time. By tradition, the visiting head of state and their spouse are to sit at separate tables, as does the president and their spouse. We purposefully split them up. But since we have two leaders bringing spouses, we have four tables set in front by the podium. Now, Madame President will sit at the table to the right of the podium with the German chancellor. Jim Myers will be sitting with them."

"Why am I not surprised," said Blaze sarcastically. "Leave it to Jim to get the best seat in the house."

Gary rolled his eyes in agreement. He continued. "He had the nerve to call Ryan over to his office three times this week to discuss seating charts. You should have seen the look on Ryan's face the last time he met with Myers. He was ready to explode when he came back to the East Wing. He loathes Myers even more than we do, if that's possible. Anyway, the chancellor's wife will be seated at the table left of the podium with Aunt Sophie. The general will be with them. Again on the right, next to Madame President's table, Mildred will sit with the new ambassador and Secretary Miller."

"Sounds good," observed Blaze while leaning over to check his own tie in the mirror. "Mildred can discuss her world travels with them. Maybe she and Miller can soften up the ambassador over dessert. Have you seen this old geezer? He reminds me of a pit bull. His face is all wrinkled and frowning. He doesn't look like a very friendly sort of chap."

"Chap? Blaze, you're either watching too much BBC on cable or you've been hanging around Nanny Jane too long. Okay, where was I? Oh, yes, tables! You'll be sitting with Harriet to the left of Aunt Sophie. The ambassador's wife and Ned and his wife will be seated with you."

"And you? Where will you be sitting?"

"No sitting for me tonight, kid. I'll be lucky to get anything to eat," said Gary matter of factly. "Now, you know the cue?"

"Yep," said Blaze confidently. "I'll keep a close eye on Mildred. She'll give me the signal. She's a cool customer, that one."

"Walking in her husband's footsteps, no doubt," replied Gary finishing with his cufflinks. He looked at his watch and suddenly felt a bit panicked. This was his first state dinner, and weeks of preparation had brought him to this moment.

"I better get down there."

Blaze was staring down at the cat. "Is she supposed to be doing that?"

Gary sighed. "Absolutely. It's part of her job description. Hand me the lint brush there on the table, will you?"

Gary carefully picked up Sheba and placed her at the head of the bed. Her desired location disturbed, the black cat gave him an annoyed look and then plopped herself down on the pillow with her backside to them. She stuck her hind leg up in the air and began grooming.

"We get the message," said Gary to the cat.

Blaze handed the brush to Gary, who sat on the edge of the bed to attend to his befurred cummerbund.

"Let's review the arrival protocol while I get this clean," said Gary crisply. "Madame President and Aunt Sophie meet the delegation at the North Portico with an honor guard in the background. The group will then come upstairs to the Oval Sitting Room for a private reception that will last about thirty minutes. A few select guests will be there, including Secretary Miller and his wife. Charlotte will be there with the children, and then she and Nanny Jane will remain upstairs with them during dinner. After the private reception, the President's party of six — she, Aunt Sophie, the German chancellor and his wife, and the new German ambassador and his wife — will proceed downstairs via the grand stairway. The marine band (set up in the North Entrance) will play 'Hail to the Chief' as the party descends. The party will stop at the bottom of the stairs for photographers. Which reminds me, I should check in with Jack before the President arrives. You and Harriet will come downstairs on the west elevator and Mildred will meet you later in the hallway. After the photo op, Madame President and her party will proceed to the East Room for a receiving line to greet the guests. You will take Mildred and Harriet through the line. Then everyone will go into the State Dining Room for dinner. Toasts are traditionally done before dinner, but tonight, it will be done before dessert."

"Right," confirmed Blaze.

"And remember, there'll be four courses, then dessert. Don't forget."

"I won't," assured Blaze confidently, his stomach rumbling its support.

"And try not to eat too much."

Blaze looked appalled.

Gary stood up, ready.

"Okay, then. Let's do it!"

Gary and Blaze went down to the second level residence where Blaze joined the First Family and friends. Gary proceeded down another flight to the first floor level and entered the large golden East Room. The German embassy had let it be known that the chancellor liked jazz music, so a popular pianist and female vocalist from New York City were performing. As Gary entered the East Room, he saw the musicians and their technical crews doing a final sound check of their equipment. Gary spied Miller and Ryan huddled in a private conservation in the shadows of the northeast corner of the room, Miller with his arms folded and Ryan with his head bent over his clipboard.

They were so engrossed in their conversation that they didn't hear Gary stride up and say hello. Miller literally jumped when Gary greeted them.

"For heavens sake, man! Don't sneak up like that on me again," exclaimed Miller in earnest with his hand over his heart. "You'll give this old man a heart attack!"

"Sorry," said Gary apologetically. "I didn't mean to startle you."

Ryan nervously pushed his glasses up and clutched his clipboard tightly to his chest. "Just reviewing the guest list again with Secretary Miller."

"Wouldn't do if I forgot a name tonight," added Miller with a grin.

Gary reached out and gave his hard working assistant a supportive pat on the back. "Well done. We can always depend on you."

"Thank you, sir." Ryan nervously looked down at his watch. " If you don't mind, I'll check in with the marine band. They should get the signal to start playing soon."

With that, the modest assistant rushed off, leaving Gary alone with the secretary of state.

"Good man," said Miller approvingly as Ryan dashed away.

"Yes, he is," agreed Gary heartily, "and no, you can't have him."

Miller laughed heartily. "Reading my mind? That was my next question."

"I figured. Although I must admit Ryan would do well in the State Department. He is tried and true. Course, the same is commonly said about you, sir."

"That's very kind," said Miller modestly.

"No, really. You are very respected around here."

"Well, I've been around this town a few years," said Miller candidly. "More years than I care to admit."

"I know Madame President truly depends on you after what happened with Donald and the assassination plot," added Gary sincerely.

Miller nodded his head sadly.

"Shocking," was his only reply

Just then, the sound of the marine band in the Entrance Hall began playing. Miller continued.

"I don't know how the President held up in that situation. But she did and she still has us, doesn't she? Ah, the music means the delegation is arriving. I'd better go find Mrs. Miller. The last time I saw her she was wandering off in the direction of the Blue Room. I need to get us upstairs. I just hope she doesn't let that Mrs. Donovan give her any crazy decorating ideas. You coming?"

Gary shook his head.

"No, I need to go to the kitchens and check on dinner. I'll see you later."

Miller and Gary walked out of the East Room together. Miller proceeded ahead into the Entrance Hall crosswalk and Gary took the stairs to the ground floor level. There, in front of the Vermeil Room, Gary ran into Ned Baldwin and his wife. The couple greeted Gary warmly, and then Ned urged his spouse upstairs indicating that he wanted to speak to Gary privately. As soon as Mrs. Baldwin left, Ned took Gary by the arm and pulled him swiftly into the Vermeil Room.

"I thought you might want an update on Ken," said Ned in a hushed voice.

"Of course," said Gary earnestly. "How is he doing?"

"He's okay. Shaken up still, but he'll pull through. I went to see him this morning. His sister from California flew in and is staying with him. I met her today. She's a strong, capable woman. So, he'll be in good hands. With Martha's permission, I ordered Ken to take a few weeks vacation. I also offered my wife's family condo in Miami Beach for a week or two. The sun and rest will do him good. Ken agreed, so he and his sister will fly down early next week."

"That was thoughtful of you, Ned. I'm sure Ken appreciates it. Think he'll come back — to work in the White House, I mean?" asked Gary.

"Yeah, he'll be back," predicted Ned confidently. "Even if we have to drag him back."

"I'll help pull," offered Gary smiling.

Ned laughed, wished Gary good luck on the state dinner, and then excused himself to join his wife. He left Gary alone in the Vermeil Room. Gary knew he should go straight to the kitchen, but instead he paused for a moment and looked around the small room, known in time's past as a ladies sitting room. It was a friendly, warm place, the walls painted a dark yellow with green satin drapes at the windows. There was an elegant Turkish carpet with an intricate pattern of greens, gold, and crimson covering the floor. On the walls were the portraits of three former First Ladies, most notably the Shikler painting of Jacqueline Kennedy Onassis directly in front of him on the south wall.

Gary gazed up at full-length portrait of Mrs. Kennedy. Her striking beauty comforted him.

The crisis was over. Taylor was dead, Donald was dead, the assassination plot uncovered, and Martha was safe and still in place as president. He gazed at Mrs. Kennedy's tranquil face. She had known her share of grief, the terror of assassination, and the stark reality of death. After her husband was killed, she showed the world her true inner strength. Gary guessed Jackie would understand and appreciate what they had just gone through, what they were all feeling.

Thank God it was finally over.

So why couldn't Gary shake this lingering feeling that it wasn't over, that something was amiss, that something still wasn't quite right? Something still felt wrong inside. Gary took a deep breath and exhaled slowly. It probably was nerves over the dinner. Right? He turned and glanced at the larger-than-life portrait of Eleanor Roosevelt that hung on the east wall.

"Okay. What is it?" he asked the formidable former First Lady. "What's bothering me?"

Eleanor stared ahead and said nothing. Thanks a lot! Gary tried to analyze.

Was it his male ego revolting at his unique position as social secretary, a position typically held by a woman? No, that wasn't it. Gary loved his job. Still, he could be subconsciously a bit resentful at not working in the West Wing on more important (and more manly) foreign and domestic matters.

Okay, that aside, was there another reason making Gary uneasy? He faced the Wyeth portrait of Patricia Nixon. Now there was a lady who knew something about betrayal and disappointment. This former First Lady weathered the nasty storms of Watergate and impeachment. She could sympathize with Gary about his issues with betrayed trust. He thought back to the uncomfortable conversation he had with Jack the day Donald died.

Was the problem her?

Not Janet her. Martha her.

Gary closed his eyes tightly. He had to come to grips with his growing attraction for the President of the United States. Why couldn't he just admit it to himself? For Pete's sake, he had admitted it to Jack. Why was it so hard to simply say that he cared for her, that . . . okay, that he loved her? Well, the answer to that was easy enough. The problem was fear, with some good old-fashioned wounded pride mixed in for good measure! Now, there's a combo for you. Fear of being hurt plus the pride of denying you ever really were that hurt. Gary huffed and crossed his arms. Then, to add insult to injury, that rascal, that cad, that bounder Jim Myers was by her side tonight, for the entire world to see. That thought alone was enough to make his stomach churn.

Or was something else bothering him?

"Sir? There you are!"

Startled out of his reverie, Gary turned quickly. Morgan entered the room his hands clasped together.

"We've been looking for you, sir. The private reception for the delegation is drawing to a close, and the Secret Service has just phoned to tell us the party will descend down the stairs in about ten minutes."

"Thank you, Alan. I'm coming. Is the other 'thing' ready?"

Morgan gave him a look of great satisfaction.

"Oh, yes, sir. That is completely taken care of. I think you will be most pleased."

Morgan left. Gary looked around the room once more and silently bid Jackie, Eleanor, and Pat a good evening and pushed his troubled feelings aside.

He would deal with those feelings later.

Gary went directly to the kitchens where there was a mad flurry of activity. The chefs were busy preparing the first course, laying out trays of various appetizers. Gary savored the rich aroma of cooked salmon mixing with the inviting smells of roast beef. White House butlers in formal black attire and white gloves were darting in and out of the kitchen, placing trays of food and bowls of fruited soup on carts. The wonderful scent of hot bread also filled the area. Across the hall, in the Map Room, butlers were opening large cases of imported wines, beer, and champagne, sorting out the beverages for the different courses of dinner.

After making certain all was in order, Gary took the west elevator up to the main floor near the State Dining Room. He glanced in for a final look. Thirteen round tables with ten chairs each filled the large room. In honor of the German flag, the theme colors of red, black, and yellow had been used. Tables were covered with elegant red tablecloths. For dishes, Wilson China, a white Lenox china with a broad black rim and gold edge, had been selected. Ornate yellow gold flatware was set around each plate. Each table had a round centerpiece of red and yellow flowers. A small white table was set up by the fireplace mantle where the massive portrait of Abraham Lincoln hung overhead. On the table was the White House pastry chef's spectacular gingerbread castle. So far, the castle was untouched by the stray little hands of a curious five year old.

Hopefully Nanny Jane would manage to keep it that way for the remainder of the evening.

Gary left the State Dining Room and walked briskly along the red-carpeted area of the Cross Hall towards the large Entrance Hall where the press and guests were gathered. The area was buzzing with excited chatter. The Marine Corps band began playing as Gary approached Blaze and Jack Parish. The music signaled the audience to quiet down and stand at attention as the presidential party appeared.

She moved gracefully down the stairway, eyes bright, chin held high, and her tail straight up in the air.

Gary watched aghast as Martha's cat, Victoria, pranced down the Grand Staircase. Members of the press corps laughed and guests cheered and applauded as the feline reached the bottom of the stairs and struck a regal poise. Cameras flashed.

The Marine Corps band stopped playing, uncertain of protocol for this situation. Hurriedly, Ryan appeared, scooped up the proud cat, and signaled the band to begin playing again.

She moved gracefully down the stairway, eyes bright, chin held high, and her hand on the arm of the tall blond German chancellor.

Martha looked stunning in a sleeveless gown of white silk. The top of the bodice and the bottom of the skirt were bordered in tiny black beads and crystals that formed an intricate floral pattern. Long formal black gloves set off the dress. Martha's blond hair was pulled up in an elaborate French twist. Around her neck, she wore a Harry Winston necklace (borrowed for the evening) of black diamonds and Tahitian pearls.

Aunt Sophie was also looking quite lovely, dressed in a complimentary black and white gown. The flattering bodice and jacket were made of black silk, and the long flowing skirt was made of yards and yards of white taffeta. Aunt Sophie wore two strands of black pearls. The new German ambassador, a short stocky man with dark gray hair and bushy eyebrows, walked down the steps beside Aunt Sophie. The two German wives followed. One of them wore a glittering red gown. The other wore black. Gary noted that the ambassador's face was indeed wrinkled, frowning, and stone-like.

After descending the stairs, the party lined up for pictures. More camera lights flashed. The band continued to play. Gary, Jack, and Blaze stared.

"Wow," whistled Blaze. "Madame President looks awesome!"

"She's beautiful," said Gary.

"She's a knockout," said Jack.

"She is quite amazing," said Jim Myers

Three heads sharply turned left, to find the chief of staff standing right beside them. The rich bachelor smiled broadly while fussing with his expensive white gloves. Jim was dressed to kill.

"Evening, Jim," said Jack smoothly. Gary and Blaze muttered their hellos.

"Evening, gentlemen," replied Jim with a sophisticated air. "Ready for this evening?"

"Certainly," said Jack returning Jim's smile with one of the reporter's own dazzling grins. Jack had no qualms in sparring with the White House chief of staff, not at least in the social arena. Well, if Jack could do it, Gary could too!

"Yes, we are ready . . . on every front," added Gary solemnly, flashing him an exaggerated smile.

Jim looked at Gary with a raised eyebrow.

"Front? You sound like you're about to go to war, Mr. Craig. What, pray tell, will you be using for weapons, bread sticks and herring balls?" said Jim laughing.

"You'd be surprised," responded Gary curtly.

Gary's dark tone gave Jim pause. He regarded Gary narrowly for a moment, then dispassionately looked away again adjusting his gloves.

"My, my, that sounded rather defensive. No need to take that stance with me, Mr. Craig. We're on the same team, remember? I have things well in hand."

That snub was the final straw. Gary had had it.

"Fine," said Gary boldly. "You just keep your hands in the West Wing, and I'll handle the house. And you can leave the First Family to me."

Figuratively, the gloves were coming off. Before Jim could respond, Jack stepped deftly into the middle of the fray, positioning himself between Gary and Jim. Jack quickly changed the subject.

"Jim Bob, my man, it suddenly occurs to me that I should run a solo piece on you, you know, an in-depth interview with Washington's most eligible bachelor. The story would feature facts about your early life and your meteoric rise in politics," "said Jack chattily. "Let's set it up, say next week sometime?"

"Okay," muttered Jim half-heartedly, still eying Gary steadily.

"Fantastic," said Jack brightly. "Oh my stars, look who's over there! Katarina Witt, the Olympic gold medal ice-skater. Doesn't she look stunning? And she's all by herself, poor thing. Perhaps you should go, Jim, and make her feel welcome."

Jim nodded, glanced skeptically over at Gary, and then walked away towards the dark-haired beauty. Once the chief of staff was out of earshot, Jack turned and chastised his friend in a hushed whisper.

"Are you nuts? Jim Myers is the last person we want to tip off. He'd blow his stack and ruin the whole operation for sure. So, close your trap and reel it in, buster."

Gary frowned in resignation. Jack was right. He couldn't lose his cool now.

"Okay! I'm sorry. He just gets to me, that's all."

"Well, don't let him," snapped Jack sharply. "He's a crumb, and he's not worth it. Now, let's get this show on the road."

The three men drew a collective deep breath and parted company. Jack rushed off in the direction of his cameraman, who had just finished filming Martha's arrival. Jack and his team would be relocating in the State Dining Room. Blaze went toward the East Room where he was reunited with Harriet and Mildred, who appeared in the hallway in front the Green Room. They were ready to join the receiving line. Gary headed downstairs for a final check on the meal and the surprise item, which was stashed away securely in a dark corner of the China Room.

With the reception over, the guests were seated in the State Dining Room for dinner. Gary stood sentinel at the doorway to monitor the meal's progression and to observe the guests closely. The room was bristling with excitement. Martha and the chancellor were engaged in lively conversation. He was friendly and relaxed, and his pleasant laugh carried above the din of the crowd. Myers was sitting next to the President, much too close thought Gary bitterly. Martha was sitting straight in her chair, sipping her wine and listening intently to the chancellor.

Mildred appeared to be aptly holding her ground at the next table. She ate slowly and gracefully while chatting with the new ambassador, who listened, said little, and ate a lot. Miller and his wife were diverted in lively conversation with two German bankers from Wall Street sitting beside them. On the other side of the podium, Aunt Sophie sat next to the general, and the two appeared to be deeply engrossed in their own conversation. Both wore thoughtful expressions. The chancellor's wife sat silently beside Aunt Sophie, her head down over her plate, totally absorbed in the food and her own private thoughts. She ate almost in isolation, despite the room full of people surrounding her. At the next table, Blaze was helping himself to the rest of Harriet's beef, which she said she couldn't finish. She wanted to save room for dessert. Harriet, the ambassador's wife, and Ned's wife were busy exchanging recipes.

At last, the moment had come. The final course of dinner had been served, and it was time for dessert and the official toast. Gary looked over at Martha, and with a quick glance, she caught his eye and nodded.

Gary turned and signaled to Mr. Morgan, who was standing far back behind him in front of the Blue Room. Seeing the signal, Morgan disappeared into the Oval Blue Room. Gary stepped into the State Dining Room and instructed several butlers and ushers who were serving to step away from the doorway, clearing a small space. Gary then looked at Mildred, who in turn, leaned over and spoke something softly into the ambassador's ear. He quickly looked up, appearing quite surprised at Mildred's message. With Mildred's prompting, they stood up together and walked over to the podium. The crowd, seeing the movement from one of the head tables, instantly quieted down. The traditional toasts were about to begin.

Blaze got up from his table and made his way toward the door and disappeared. Jack, knowing what was about to happen, gave a signal to his CNN crew and they began filming live, cutting into the CNN broadcast. Martha rose from her place and joined the ambassador and Mildred at the podium.

Everyone was in position. Gary crossed his fingers and prayed for luck.

Martha looked at Gary, smiled, and then spoke clearly into the microphone.

"Good evening! To the chancellor and his wife, to the new ambassador and his wife, to Secretary and Mrs. Miller, and to our distinguished guests, many of you Americans of German descent or German nationals who are now U.S. citizens. I welcome you to the White House and to the first state dinner of the Johnson administration."

Martha paused, and the crowd applauded enthusiastically.

Martha coughed slightly, clearing her throat, then continued. "As you know, it is customary for the president to toast a visiting head of state, in this case, the German chancellor, and this I will do in a moment. But first, I have a very special gift that I would like to present to our other distinguished guest, the new German ambassador. In doing so, Mr. Ambassador, I will ask for the assistance of my daughters, Eliza and Abigail Johnson."

Nanny Jane appeared at the doorway, ushering the two daughters into the dining room. Abigail clung tightly to Eliza with one hand and carried a bouquet of white roses with her other hand. The crowd oohed and aahed at the sight of the first daughters and watch breathlessly as the two walked towards the podium. Eliza let go of Abigail's hand, and Abigail, after a quick glance at Jane for last-minute encouragement, stepped up to the ambassador, curtsied prettily, and handed him the flowers.

"For you," said Abigail.

The crowd applauded and cheered.

The grim-faced ambassador stared down at the roses and at the pretty little girl, then broke out with a rare smile.

"Thank you, dear child," said the ambassador in a deep rattling voice. "The flowers are lovely, just as you are."

"Thank you, Mr. Ambassador," said Abigail with another curtsey. The child had been well rehearsed. Then she looked up at the ambassador and beamed a cherubic smile.

"We have another gift for you," announced Abigail.

"You're supposed to come with us," Eliza said pointing back towards the door. "Our brother Josh is bringing it now,"

The ambassador and guests turned to look. Mr. Morgan and Josh appeared in the doorway, slowly pushing a metal cart that was covered with a black velvet drape. On top of the cart was a rose bush with large fragrant white blooms. Usher Morgan had placed the English Rose bush in a decorative terra cotta pot, with greenery placed around the base of the planter. The roses Abigail had given the ambassador were clearly cut from a similar rose bush. Following the cart, a distinguished gentleman dressed in a dark gray tweed coat appeared in the doorway, standing next to Blaze.

The two girls led the crusty old ambassador over to the cart. The ambassador stood and admired the rosebush, leaned over and closed his eyes as he breathed in deeply the strong scent of roses.

"Magnificent," the ambassador whispered. "Thank you very much."

"It's Ingrid's Rose," said Abigail excitedly.

The ambassador opened his eyes wide and gazed down at the little girl in surprise and bewilderment.

"What did you say?" he demanded.

"My nanny says Ingrid was your sister. I have a sister, too." Abigail smiled up at Eliza.

"Mother will explain," interjected Eliza hurriedly, looking over at her mother anxiously.

It was up to Martha now, and Gary stood in the back, holding his breath. The President spoke. "Mr. Ambassador, in preparing for this meeting, it came to my attention that Ingrid Kessler was your beloved sister. To those in our audience who don't know who Ingrid Kessler was, let me tell you that she was one of the most gifted horticulturists and landscapers in all of Europe. She designed gardens in Germany, France, Spain, and the British Isles. She was known as a lover of roses, especially white roses. They captured her heart, and I am told she planted a white rose in every single garden she ever designed."

The ambassador, his face frozen again with deep emotion, nodded slowly.

"Yes. She did that," he said gruffly.

"Ingrid Kessler unexpectedly passed away recently, and I know this was a deep loss for you and your wife, as well as those of us who loved her gardens."

Again the ambassador nodded, looking over at his wife, who had pulled out a handkerchief and began dabbing her eyes.

"Standing in the doorway," announced Martha with her hand pointing to the back of the room, "is Mr. William Darby of England, assistant to Mr. David Austin, creator of the Modern English Rose. The English Rose is a new breed of rose, a blend of the old heritage roses of the past and the hybrid tea roses of the present. English Roses capture the best of both worlds, with the shapes and scents of old roses with the continuous bloom of today's modern roses. For tonight, Mr. Darby has graciously brought the rose that you see before you, the newest and most beautiful creation of their world famous greenhouses. We have asked, and they have agreed to name this new rose in honor of your sister. Mr. Ambassador, I and the people of the United States proudly present to you the Ingrid Kessler Rose."

The room was completely silent, all eyes focused on the ambassador and the white rose bush.

Jack's cameras rolled on, capturing the scene, with close ups of the white roses and the stunned expression on the ambassador's face.

Gary waited nervously, hardly able to breathe.

Would it work?

Finally, the ambassador lowered his head and a few tears began running down his face. His wife jumped up from her chair and rushed to her husband. With Jane's silent direction, Eliza, Abigail, and Josh stepped away, and the German couple embraced. After a bit, the ambassador regained his composure, kissed his wife, wiped his eyes, and walked back toward the podium to face Martha.

"Your gift it is most wonderful," said the ambassador in a hoarse voice. "My wife and I wish to thank you and Mr. Darby. We accept your gracious gift." He paused and then said softly in amazement. "I did not know that the American president was so good, so kind, so thoughtful. No one told me this. You have greatly honored my sister when many have forgotten her. I will not forget your kindness."

His last words were spoken in a very solemn voice. Martha reached for her champagne glass and lifted it high in the air.

"Then may the first toast of the evening be in memory of your beloved sister and the lovely gardens that she created, places of beauty and places of peace. And may I express to you, Mr. Ambassador, my dearest hope that we may go forward from this night and work together, bringing our two countries more closely together, to make this world a safer and more beautiful place, much like the gardens of Ingrid Kessler."

The ambassador looked at Martha steadily, carefully considering her words and their full meaning. He glanced over to meet the eyes of the chancellor, who was staring back anxiously on the edge of his seat, waiting for the reply and, in actuality, the decision. The ambassador paused, and then turned to Martha and raised his own glass to hers.

"Work together we shall, Madame President, this I promise you. To my sister and to peace."

Cell phone call from the East Wing . . .

"This is absolutely the final straw. Madame President has become a nightmare, my nightmare. And I want it to end! All we wanted her to do was pick our guy for vice president. Was that too much to ask? No, it was not. This has not happened, and now she has won over the heart and soul of foreign dignitaries — people we had control of, mind you — by naming flowers after them? No, we cannot deal with this woman any longer. She has to go!"

"But is taking her out necessary? Thanks to that idiot Craig and his interview with me, we were tipped off that they suspected something. You must admit it was clever of me to give Hooper the drug in his coffee and then slip the vial and the typed note into his coat pocket afterwards. The surveillance cameras never caught it. Now they believe Donald was the mole and the danger is behind us. Now I can persuade Madame President to pick our man for VP as originally planned."

"No. We don't dare leave her in office for the next three and a half years or for another three and a half weeks for that matter. We allowed this lady to ascend to the presidency, thinking we could control her. We were wrong, dead wrong. That was our mistake. She has proven to be independent and incorruptible, and this we can not abide!"

"Okay. She'll be removed if that's what you want. The same method as before?"

"Yes. It will be risky, I admit, given that they know about the DSMO, but we have no choice. You are to do it as soon as possible before I have a nervous breakdown. Any suggestions on how to accomplish it?"

"We could put it in her lipstick. That obnoxious little kid of hers uses lipstick as crayons. The imp has colored all over the place with them. So, Madame President has to replenish her lipstick supply pretty frequently. She just ordered a replacement for a red one that's gone by the coloring book wayside. She placed the order this morning over the phone when we were meeting. I can get you the name and brand, so you can send me a deadly duplicate."

"Excellent. Once she's out of the way, we can use our ties in Congress to get our man into the White House. And I stress man, not woman. I have enough headaches keeping the peace at home with my own wife. How soon can this be done?"

"There is a ballet at Kennedy Center on Saturday. I'm going with her for the Russian company's performance. The new lipstick will be delivered by then. I can make the switch sometime during the evening. I will even suggest that she wear red that night. Don't worry. She'll be dead before the evening is over."

"She better be! I won't call you again till it's done. Good night."

Jim Myers hung up his cell phone and carefully put it back into his pocket. He stood up and straightened his tie, readying himself to take his place by the President's side in the East Room for the evening concert. He glanced down quickly at his watch. He needed to return before he was missed.

Too bad about the orders to kill her. He liked the idea of seducing and marrying the first female president. Not out of love, mind you. He didn't love her. No, he loved the idea of the power and position such a match would bring him. Imagine being America's First Gentleman and the White House chief of staff! In that dual role, the White House would completely be his to run.

Myers paused and frowned unpleasantly. Perhaps the same idea had occurred to his real employers. They would not concede such power to any individual other than themselves. And Myers dared not go against their wishes. They could just as easily and without hesitation kill him. Myers shuddered at the chilling thought. He shook his head a bit to regain his calm persona, turned and departed the East Wing Movie Room.

He did not see the small feet that dangled then disappeared up onto the blue cushioned seat four rows ahead.

Chapter 23

The Kennedy Center and Queen's Bedroom

Saturday Night, August 27

"Oh, bother, I've dropped another stitch."

Nanny Jane stared down at the knitting project in her lap with an unhappy look. She held up her work for review, a long and uneven fluffy pink scarf that she was knitting for Eliza.

"Honestly, this looks quite dreadful."

"Looks good to me," said Eliza cheerfully.

"No. I'm most certainly doing something wrong," said Nanny Jane.

"Let me help you with that, dear," offered Sophie kindly, who put down her own knitting, a navy blue cable sweater for the general, and held out her hand for the scarf. Nanny Jane handed it over promptly with relief.

McKay, who was sitting beside Aunt Sophie on a sofa in the cozy Oval Sitting Room, lowered his newspaper slightly, today's edition of *The Wall Street Journal*, and sourly complained. "She, of all people, shouldn't be armed with sharp objects, Sophie."

Aunt Sophie cast the general a threatening look.

"No one asked you," was her retort.

"No one ever does," was his curt reply. "And I may remind you that, to date, this young lady has crushed my toes, showered me with pink punch, practically electrocuted me with her broken hair dryer, and has committed other acts of trauma upon my person. Trust me, my dear, I'll be skewered before the evening is through." He shut up and hid again behind his newspaper.

"Pay no attention to him, Jane," Sophie advised, as she set to unraveling the crooked portion of Jane's scarf.

The general made an unhappy sound, shook his papers noisily, and turned his back away from the ladies.

Jane laughed.

Charlotte smiled at the friendly banter, glancing up from her own needlework project, an elaborate cross-stitch sampler. Eliza sat next to her, painting her nails. The family (except for Martha) was gathered in the sitting room, spending a final night together. Martha and Jim Myers were out attending the ballet with two top donors of Martha's renovation projects.

With the killer apprehended and the state dinner past, there was no reason for Gary and Charlotte to stay at the White House any longer. Consequently, Gary would be moving back to his Virginia home in the Washington suburbs the next morning, and Charlotte Donovan would return to her own house Monday. So, this evening was special for everyone. Too bad Martha wasn't here, thought Gary bitterly.

The group enjoyed a simple meal that night of Italian pasta and salad, and mini pizzas for the kids. Now they were relaxing before having a dessert, some blueberry cheesecake that Aunt Sophie and Charlotte had cooked up that afternoon. The ladies huddled close and conversed while working on their handiwork projects while the general checked on his portfolio stocks. Gary invited Blaze as his guest, and his skinny friend was sprawled out on the floor engrossed in a basketball video game with Josh. Josh's team was way ahead. As for Gary, he was sitting on the floor next to Abigail, who was being very quiet. She was coloring while Gary held Sheba in his lap and gave the cat an ear rub.

"I'm so glad you joined us, Mr. Phillips," said Aunt Sophie as she worked to unravel Jane's knitting.

"Me, too!" exclaimed Josh as he successfully hit a foul shot on his video game.

"My pleasure," replied Blaze honestly. "Oops. Time for me to take over the ball! Get your defense ready, Josh."

Aunt Sophie watched the two play their video game with a satisfied smile. Then she turned her head to one side thoughtfully.

"We should do this more often, especially now that you two are moving out. You know, the White House can be so isolating. I should like to invite that nice young man sometime, the one who works for you, Mr. Craig."

"Adams," replied Gary as he rubbed Sheba's ears. The cat leaned her head back and blinked in ecstasy. "Too bad he couldn't come tonight. He's out of town visiting his wife. They went up to New York for the weekend."

"Wife? That boring man with the thick glasses has a wife?" said Eliza shocked, looking up momentarily from painting her right big toe.

"Eliza, watch your colorful adjectives, dearest," cautioned Nanny Jane severely. "Mr. Adams is a decent sort."

"Well, I think he's boring," said Eliza defensively. "He never says anything, and he's always hanging around and writing stuff on his clipboard! And Abigail doesn't like him much."

"That's because she's gotten in trouble for coloring all over his office, dearest. I find sometimes the quiet ones are the most interesting, once you get to know them," cautioned Nanny Jane wisely. "And speaking of quiet, I've hardly heard a word out of you all day, Missy." She leaned over and patted Abigail on top of her head.

"Be grateful," came the sarcastic word from behind the newspaper.

Nanny Jane ignored the caustic remark and put her hand across Abigail's forehead.

"You're not getting sick, are you, Abby?"

"No," replied Abigail crossly pulling away. She reached for a blue crayon from her coloring box and commenced coloring vigorously a picture of an apple tree. The apples were being colored a bright shade of turquoise.

Jane looked at Gary and shrugged her shoulders.

"She's been like that all day, absolutely beastly. I could hardly get her out of the West Wing for lunch. She insisted on staying with her mother all morning and most of the afternoon as well. When I tried to pull her away for a nap around two, she pitched a complete fit. It was most embarrassing. Good thing it was a Saturday and Madame President didn't have any meetings scheduled."

Gary frowned. There it was again. Why did he keep having this nagging feeling that something was wrong? He picked up Sheba and put her down on the rug. The cat yawned and arched upwards in a contented stretch. "Well, we shouldn't blame Abigail for being clingy. Madame President has been pretty busy this week. Abigail probably just misses her mom." Gary looked down at the blue apple tree that Abigail was creating. It was really an obnoxiously bright shade of blue, and it hurt his eyes just to look at it. "Here, Abigail, let me get you a red crayon," Gary offered helpfully. "Apples are supposed to be red."

Gary reached for the plastic crayon box and started sifting through the layers of crayons when he discovered something metallic and round. He knew exactly what it was before looking, a tube of lipstick buried at the bottom of the box. He groaned. The lipstick thief had struck again. He pulled it out and held it up for all to see.

"Good Lord," moaned Nanny Jane fretfully, "not again. Honestly, Abigail, you can be most trying at times. Let me see that, Mr. Craig. It might be mine."

Nanny Jane reached her hand out for the lipstick.

Abigail suddenly jumped up from the floor and angrily knocked the lipstick out of Gary's hand. It fell to the floor with a loud crash.

"No, it's bad!" cried the little girl.

Abigail stood with her hands on her hips, looking defiantly at Gary. The child was clearly distraught.

"Abigail!" shouted Aunt Sophie loudly with disapproval. "What's this about? How dare you speak to Mr. Craig that way?"

Gary held up his hand quickly and stopped Sophie in mid-rebuke. That nagging, bad feeling was growing stronger by the second.

"No, it's okay, Sophie. Something else is going on here."

The bad feeling washed over him anew. Abigail wasn't just being headstrong or naughty. As he gazed at Abigail, he saw genuine fear in her eyes.

Abigail was afraid. Very afraid.

Gary pulled her over to him and put his arms securely around her.

"Abigail, honey, what's wrong? Tell Uncle Gary what's bothering you."

Now the little girl clung to him fiercely and started to cry. Gary continued to try to calm her, asking for a tissue. Jane quickly handed him one. By this time, McKay's newspaper had lowered and he stared at them with a puzzled look on his face. Gary took the tissue and began to wipe the tears off Abigail's small face.

"It's okay, sweetheart. We're not angry with you. Now, why did you say the lipstick was bad?" asked Gary reassuringly.

Abigail sniffled loudly and looked up at Gary.

"I took it because he said it was bad."

Gary felt as though someone had pulled the rug out from under him. He stopped dabbing the child's face and looked over at General McKay in alarm. McKay lowered his paper further. Aunt Sophie put down Jane's knitting. Blaze and Josh stopped playing their video game, and the room fell silent. Gary continued to quiz Abigail.

"What else did 'he' say?"

"He said he was going to hurt Mommy!"

McKay's newspaper slipped to the floor, and Aunt Sophie let out a gasp. Gary fought hard to sound calm, to not let the depth of his own fears show in front of the five year old.

"Tell us what happened, sweetheart."

Abigail reached down for her blue crayon and started to explain. "I was hiding in the big movie room. He didn't see me, but I heard him say he would hurt Mommy. So I stayed near Mommy all day and I watched and watched and watched. He was there all right, and when Mommy went away I saw him put that in Mommy's purse." She pointed over at the lipstick lying on the floor.

Gary glanced anxiously up at McKay, who had risen up from the sofa and was now hovering over them. The general wore a stony expression on his face. They were both thinking the same thing. Jim Myers had spent the morning with Martha exclusively. The big general knelt down and addressed the young child in a serious but gentle voice.

"Mr. Myers, Abigail? Jim Myers? The man who took your Mommy to the ballet tonight"

Abigail nodded solemnly at the general.

"Are you sure?" asked the general firmly.

Again her head bobbed up and down.

"He said Mommy would be dead tonight."

"Oh, God," cried Aunt Sophie in alarm.

Gary spoke now more earnestly.

"Abigail, the general and I want to protect your mommy. So you must tell us exactly what the man said? Do you understand?"

Abigail picked up her coloring book, turned the page, and began coloring another apple tree blue. "All right, Uncle Gary." And as she colored she recited verbatim everything she had overheard Jim Myers say in the Movie Room the night of the German state dinner.

When Abigail finished, she reached for a bright orange crayon and began coloring the sky. There was a terrible long pause as everyone else in the room gazed down at the tube of lipstick lying menacingly on the floor.

Jane finally broke the silence. Her voice was markedly changed, more serious sounding than usual, as she addressed her young charge.

"Abigail, dearest, stop coloring for a minute. Are you absolutely sure this is the lipstick you took from Mommy today?"

Abigail put down her orange crayon and nodded quite solemnly.

"And you are certain that you saw Mr. Myers put that lipstick into your mother's handbag?

Again Abigail nodded and leaned forward in a conspiratorial way.

"I watched him from under Mommy's desk," whispered the child.

Visions of Abigail hiding in the Oval Office, undetected, unseen by the chief of staff as he planted his murder weapon, flashed inside Gary's reeling head. Gary felt an icy chill as he realized how much danger Abigail had been in that day. Suppose Myers had discovered her in hiding? What would that cold-blooded murderer have done? Would he have killed Abigail too, right there in the Oval Office? Or kidnap her instead? He shuddered and pressed his hands tightly to his lips as he watched Nanny Jane calmly interrogate the little girl.

"Abigail, did your mommy ever use this lipstick? Did she ever have a chance to put it on?"

The little girl shook her head.

"After the man put in it Mommy's handbag, he left. I got it out and put it in there," she confessed pointing to her crayon box.

"That's right. Martha was looking for it tonight," added Aunt Sophie in a trembling voice. "She wore a red gown this evening and wanted to wear the new lipstick with the outfit. She came to my room as she was getting ready. She assumed correctly that Abigail had swiped it. But she didn't have time to go ask Abigail for it. She borrowed one of my red lipsticks instead."

"Well done," replied the nanny smiling at her charge and giving her a big hug.

Nanny Jane then posed another question to her sticky fingered charge. "Abigail, after you took the lipstick, did you open it? Did you touch it?"

Oh, dear Lord, thought Gary wildly. Abigail had been handling a deadly poison barehanded that day, a poison that had already killed at least two people, two grown male adults.

"No," reported Abigail honestly pointing again to her crayon box. "I put it in there."

Aunt Sophie let out a loud sigh of relief. So did Charlotte and the general.

Jane nodded her head in approval. "Very good, Abigail. You helped save your mum's life. Eliza, you and Josh take Abigail to her room and get her into her pajamas," suggested Jane calmly. "I'll be along shortly to read her a bedtime story and tuck her in. Please stay with her till I come."

The older children readily agreed. Eliza came over looking quite alarmed, and picked up her little sister. Gary gave the teenager and her brother a reassuring smile, and they quickly departed.

Once the children were clear of the room, McKay verbally exploded.

"Holy Mary, Mother of God! You realize what this means? Donald Hooper was not the murderer! He was not the mole, and he did not commit suicide. He was set up, and so were we!" McKay looked angrier than Gary had ever seen him.

"Yes, we were deceived. Poor Mr. Hooper! He was murdered in cold blood, just like the rest," added Jane staring at the general somberly.

"And if Myers is the real mole, then the man he nominated for vice president at Taylor's house that day is one of them too," exclaimed Blaze out loud in amazement. Blaze's statement hit Gary like a ton of bricks. Secretary Miller? But they had trusted him! Martha considered him like a father figure. This nightmare just seemed to get worse and worse.

"Secretary Miller?" gasped Aunt Sophie in a shocked voice. "But it can't be! He's been so kind to us, to Martha, so very helpful."

"Yes, so very helpful," observed Charlotte cynically, putting her cross-stitch carefully down on a side table. "Think about it. He was always around. Always ready to listen. Always ready to give advice. Very helpful indeed."

"What bloody fools we've all been! Somehow they knew our suspicions, and they used it against us," murmured Jane softly.

General McKay shook his head in disbelief. "And now they have decided to remove Martha out of her place since she has refused to put Miller into the VP slot. I was about to suggest to Martha that she consider Miller. I trusted him, the lying jade."

Gary turned and stared out towards the windows of the Truman Balcony and mused aloud.

"It was Myers all along. I should have known. I knew something was wrong. I kept feeling it, but I convinced myself it was just my own jealously wanting me to prove Jim guilty. I never should have let my own feelings for Martha get in the way."

It was said out loud before Gary realized it. A quick intake of breath exposed his verbal slip and he glanced anxiously at his friends. They were all looking at him. He was mortified. Aunt Sophie beamed reassuringly back at him.

"It's all right, Mr. Craig. You mustn't worry. We've known about your true feelings for Martha for quite some time now."

Gary blinked. "You have?"

"Hmmm, yes," replied Aunt Sophie.

"For weeks," ventured Charlotte as she picked up her sewing again.

"For months actually," corrected Jane. "I could tell straight away, the very first day."

Gary stared at them in humiliation. He couldn't have felt worse. Then another more humiliating thought suddenly occurred to him, and he did feel worse.

"Does Martha know?"

"Heavens, no," answered Aunt Sophie promptly picking up Jane's pitiful scarf and unraveling it again. "She's been completely diverted with all her responsibilities. She's still in the dark about you and her own feelings, for that matter. I think she throws herself into work to avoid her feelings. Losing her husband was so painful, you see. But now you're here, Mr. Craig, perfect for her. We all think so. Once this thing is finally over, I would strongly advise you to speak to her . . ."

"Enough!" shouted McKay forcefully, pacing the floor like a caged tiger. "There will be plenty of time in the future to discuss Mr. Craig's love life. Right now, we have to rescue Martha from the clutches of that murderous fraud." The general pulled out his cell phone. "I'm calling the special agent in charge, and they will extract her immediately from the ballet. She'll be brought back to the White House, and we'll send that sorry SOB Jim Myers straight to jail or hell, whichever comes first."

Gary leapt up from the floor and grabbed McKay's hand.

"No, general, wait."

"This is no time for one of your cock-eyed plans," hissed McKay darkly through gritted teeth. He towered in a threatening posture over Gary. "Protocol mandates that we pull the President out of danger immediately. *Now!*"

"But she isn't in any real danger," cried Gary, hearing himself shouting. "She is with her full Secret Service detail. The entire Kennedy Center is surrounded with agents, posted at every door, every entrance. They've searched the facility from top to bottom for two days. It's a secure location. She is protected, and with the Secret Service there, Myers won't be able to escape. What's more important is that the poisoned lipstick is here, and

Myers doesn't know. He's biding his time, waiting for her to collapse in front of him, so he can play the part of aggrieved chief of staff, as she lies dying in his arms. The dog! And once she is dead, he plans to make the switch and replace the poisoned lipstick with the other one. General, he's in the dark, and it's an advantage."

"Listen to him, Charles," begged Aunt Sophie urgently.

"Yes, hear him out," agreed Charlotte.

"I agree," said Jane simply.

"If I want any of your opinions, I'll ask for them," barked McKay sharply.

Gary continued his appeal. "If we pull her out now and arrest Myers, the people he works for — including Secretary Miller — will have time to escape, even if you interrogate Myers and he spills the beans. Myers doesn't matter, General. He's nobody, a well-placed pawn. The people who set this whole thing up do matter. We have to find who they are and eliminate them!"

Clearly outnumbered and out-reasoned, the general exhaled in frustration and folded his cell phone. McKay glared at Gary narrowly.

"I'll give you three minutes, three minutes only, Mr. Craig, to explain this plan of yours. Then I'm making a call to the special agent in charge."

A plan formed quickly in Gary's mind, employing the use of several resources he had readily at hand. He sat down on the sofa and gathered the adults in the room around him into a tight huddle while he spelled out his idea.

"Sheer lunacy," responded the general when Gary had finished talking. "The Secret Service will freak out."

"Well, I think it's bloody brilliant," said Jane flatly in objection.

"No one asked you, Miss Michaels," replied the general curtly. "And you interrupted me. It is sheer lunacy and the Secret Service will freak out *and* it's devilishly clever, to borrow one of your English phrases. And for all the above reasons, it might, it might, just work. All right, Mr. Craig, get on the phone and put this plan of yours into action. I'll call Agent Pullman and then Agent Lewis, who is assigned to Martha tonight, thank heavens, and get them in play. I'll also call Agent Clark, who is off duty tonight. I want him there before we actually do this crazy thing. I'll also call the agents here in residence and get them to up the protection around the house. In the meantime, I want the rest of you to split up. If they got into the White House once, they can do it again. Sophie, you and Charlotte take the older children with you into Sophie's room on the west side of the residence. Mr. Phillips, you stay with them, too. Let no one in. *No one!* Is that clear? Stay in the room. Don't come out for any reason. I'll have Secret Service agents on this and the ground floor alerted to the danger. No one outside the White House will be admitted to the residence this evening. Jane, you will stay with Abigail in the Queen's Bedroom and stand guard in her room."

The general then marched over to Sophie, picked up the knitting and knitting needles, took them over to Jane, and thrust them into her empty hands.

"Here. See to it that nothing happens to that little girl. Gather your shoes, your handbag, your hair dryer, knitting needles, silverware, glassware, and anything else you think appropriate and take any protective measures you deem necessary. Arm yourself, missy."

"Madame President, you have a call."

Agent Lewis stepped forward to the edge of the front row seats on the box tier of the Kennedy Center Opera House and handed Martha a small silver-cased cell phone. Martha glanced up at the expressionless agent with a mild look of surprise. The house lights were up for intermission, and she was right in the middle of a very interesting conversation with Jim and their guests, Mrs. Camilla Dawson, the Washington D.C. philanthropist, and Mr. Kevin McNeil, both wealthy supporters of Martha's White House building projects.

"I'm sorry," apologized Martha to her guests. "I never seem to be able to truly get away from the office."

"Fire them," advised McNeil with a grin.

"Poor thing," Mrs. Dawson laughed gaily. "I don't envy you in the least, my dear, I don't care what the perks of your office are! Go ahead. Take your call. This darling young man will keep Kevin and I company while you save the world." Mrs. Dawson leaned close to Jim and patted him on the face. Myers smiled nervously at the rich patron and then at Martha, staring at her with an odd expression.

Poor Jim. He's been so jumpy this evening, a bit on edge, thought Martha worriedly. I wonder what's making him so restless? He keeps glancing down at his watch and then staring at me in a funny way. Strange. He's normally quite in his element at big events like this. Must be his nerves. Perhaps a vacation is in order.

Martha stood up, walked over to the end of the aisle, took the phone from the agent's hand, and held it up to her ear.

The general's solemn voice instantly came on.

"Martha, be absolutely still and listen to what I have to say. Do not respond. Do not show any emotion. Do not move. Your life may depend upon it."

Obeying the stern orders of her National Security Advisor, Martha stood perfectly still and listened transfixed as General McKay gruffly related to her the revelations of the evening. She cautiously glanced over at Myers. He was watching her closely.

"Everything all right?" asked Jim.

"Oh, fine," said Martha, trying to sound as normal as possible. "Just fine. It's Nanny Jane. Abigail has been creating havoc again."

Jim relaxed, smiled, and turned back his attention to Mr. McNeil and Mrs. Dawson.

Martha gazed at the back of the head of her chief of staff, holding the small phone tightly in her hand. Her knuckles began to turn white. Clutching that phone was all she could do to keep her hand from shaking. Suddenly she felt a firm hand rest upon her shoulder. It was Agent Lewis standing close to her. The large young man stared ahead into the open space of the theatre, but the meaning of his touch was clear. He knew what was happening and he would protect her. He was sworn to protect the President, even if it meant laying down his own life. That was true of the rest of her detail, a group of at least ten dedicated men, all within her immediate vicinity. They know, she kept telling herself. She was not alone.

"Go ahead. I'm listening," said Martha evenly.

The general then quickly outlined the details of Gary's plan.

"Do you think you can go through with this? If not, I can have Agent Lewis and Pullman extract you immediately to safety, which is what we should do. I don't have to tell you what Agent Pullman said when I told him of this plan. The man's livid. So is Agent Lewis. A word from me, and he'll gladly toss Myers over the balcony. They prefer we arrest Myers now and hand him over to the FBI and deal with finding his employers later. But it's your call, Madame President. We await your orders."

Martha licked her lips nervously and took a deep breath.

"I prefer the first plan of action, Jane," answered Martha sounding nonchalantly as possible. "The solution is admittedly unconventional but ingenious. I'll stay here and leave the matter entirely in your capable hands. Good night."

Martha closed the cell phone and handed it back to Agent Lewis.

"Thank you, Agent Lewis. That will be all," said Martha.

"Yes Ma'am," said Agent Lewis in his deep voice. He briefly caught her eye and gave her a quick wink, then stepped back into the shadows.

The overhead lights of the theatre flickered low, and the orchestra began playing. The second half of the Kirov Ballet's performance of *Cinderella* was about to start. Martha took another deep breath, steadied her nerves, and returned to her seat, to spend the remainder of the evening sitting with her distinguished guests and with a murderer.

The drive over to the Kennedy Center seemed endless despite the police escort that quickly led their car down through the ever-congested Washington D.C. traffic. As they proceeded towards the Kennedy Center, McKay was on the car phone, squawking out orders to various law enforcement agencies. Agents were being sent over to Miller's home in Rockcreek Park, Maryland and to Miller's offices in the State Department, which would be sealed until investigators could thoroughly search his files and computers records. Likewise, FBI agents were descending on Jim Myers' office inside the West Wing. Soon the bank records of both these men would be frozen, accounts analyzed, e-mails located, phone records seized. Gary said nothing, just listened to McKay's commanding voice and stared morosely out the window at the capital city at night. The car neared the Kennedy Center, and Gary could see the Lincoln Memorial illuminated in the late summer night. He thought about Stan Taylor and Eric Peters and Donald Hooper and wondered how he would feel facing the man who murdered them all.

As the motorcade finally approached, the Kennedy Center looked like a bright diamond shining beside the mighty Potomac River. The evening was clear, and the moon hung majestically overhead as they got out of their cars along the curb of the entrance plaza. Other cars arrived as they did, and numerous plainclothes agents and D.C. policemen descended upon the Kennedy theatre, taking positions at all entrances and exits. Those entrances to the center were already covered by the Secret Service. Gary reminded himself that whenever a president made a trip to an outside location, the Secret Service would arrive hours ahead of time to "sweep" the facility with bomb-sniffing dogs. Then the facility would be sealed off, and anyone entering the building would be searched and scanned before being allowed in. Now, the security bubble would have additional layers and reinforcements. Overhead two helicopters circled low for aerial surveillance. McKay made doubly sure the Myers would receive no outside help and would have no way of escape.

McKay got out of the car first and walked briskly into the building. Gary followed closely behind the massive National Security Advisor. They were accompanied by their own Secret Service detail of five agents, including agent Clark who was at a nearby restaurant when called back to service. They were met at the door by the SAIC — special agent in charge – Pullman, three Kennedy Center security guards, a high-ranking D.C. cop, and a very worried Kennedy Center administrator. All had been briefed concerning the dangerous situation inside. The administrator, a short balding man named Taggart, nervously made introductions, and then led the way down the long corridor called the Hall of Nations that opened into the Grand Foyer.

Known as one of the world's largest rooms, the Kennedy Center Grand Foyer was 60 feet wide and 630 feet long. With windows on one side facing out towards the Potomac River, the room seemed to stretch out endlessly, its grandeur enhanced with eighteen crystal chandeliers, twenty brass planters, and eight huge Belgium mirrors 58 feet high. In the center of the hallway was an 8-foot bronze statue of President Kennedy, which was situated in front of the steps leading into the Opera House. The group of men walked briskly past the Kennedy statue, and Mr. Taggart led them to the box tier level reserved for the president and other distinguished guests.

Once on the tier level, Mr. Taggart took them to a private reception room called the African Lounge. Objects inside this room were designed to give a Kennedy Center patron the feeling of being deep inside the African village. The carpets were a brown burgundy and the walls were covered with brightly colored African tapestries. In the center of the room was a sculpture from Ghana entitled *Mother Earth, Condolences to You.* This piece was given to the center to represent Africa's grief at the assassination of President Kennedy. How ironic that the capture of one would-be presidential assassin would take place in a room dedicated to an assassinated president. As they entered, Gary saw that his three requests had arrived and were in place. He took a deep breath and readied himself for springing his trap.

Music filtered in from the Opera House, reaching a magnificent crescendo. The Kirov Ballet Company completed their opening night performance with esteemed Mikhail Baryshnikov appearing as a guest principal dancer. Gary listened intently, his own heart pounding loudly, as the bass drums rumbled, cymbals crashed, and the crowd applauded and yelled, "Bravo! Bravo!" Gary impatiently listened, keeping track of the applause. It seemed to go on and on, and Gary's nerves were strained to their limit. Finally the cheering faded, the house lights went up, and the guests seated in the box tier section began to file out of the theatre.

First through the doorway of the African Lounge came Mrs. Dawson and Mr. McNeil, each holding their printed programs tightly in their hands while talking enthusiastically about the performance. They were welcomed immediately by Mr. Taggart and were directed over to several tables set up for the reception. By White House standards, it was a modest fare. There were crackers and imported cheeses, chilled bottles of French champagne and Russian caviar, red seedless grapes and large fresh strawberries dipped in white and dark chocolate. Soon select members of the ballet troop, including Baryshnikov, the choreographer Alexey Ratmansky, the composer Sergei Prokofiev, and the principal ballerina Ekatrina Kazakov, a stunning dark-haired beauty who came wrapped up in a thick, white fur cape, entered the African Lounge. Several other members of the dance troop arrived, breathless and ready to celebrate and shake hands with the American president. Secret Service agents, including Mr. Pullman, Clark, and Lewis, were positioned around the room, but that was normal for such a public event where the President made an appearance.

Finally Jim Myers entered the room, talking casually with a serious-faced Paul Moore, the new American ambassador to Russia. Once Myers arrived, General McKay from a hidden position gave a nod, and a slender young lady with short brown hair, wearing a dark navy blue suit, slipped quietly out of the lounge and into the Opera House tier seats. Simultaneously, two Secret Service agents took position at the entrance to the lounge, sealing it off from any curious patrons. This was done quickly and quietly, and to all appearances, it seemed like normal security procedure. At least Myers didn't take notice.

Jim walked towards the refreshment table and helped himself to some cheese and crackers. He made a joking comment to Ambassador Moore, who laughed and reached for some grapes. Myers was about to help himself to some caviar when the thin silver microphone of Jack Parish magically appeared and inserted itself expertly between Myers and Ambassador Moore. The slick-talking CNN reporter stepped forward, flashing his broadest and brightest smile to the men. Moore looked quite surprised. Myers looked annoyed. But Jack continued his high-powered smile and his CNN cameraman, set up nearby, began filming.

Jack greeted them. "Good evening, gentlemen. Enjoy the show?"

Jim gave Jack the sternest of looks, frowning at the flashy white-haired reporter.

"Evening, Mr. Parish. Who let you in here?"

Jack laughed and responded flippantly. "I crash happening parties anywhere inside the Beltway!"

"And often, I'm told," replied Jim snidely, trying to maneuver around to the caviar and to the side of the beautiful Russian ballerina, now standing nearby holding a fat white ink pen and a copy of the dance program for the President to sign. She looked over at the chief of staff expectantly and cast him a flirtatious look that indicated her interest in his autograph and perhaps his phone number as well. Jim gave the young lady a promising smile. She smiled back nervously and put a strawberry up to her lips, her bejeweled hand, adorned with a large ruby and diamond ring, glittered brightly.

"If you don't mind," said Jim impatiently, "duty calls. I must go over and greet the performers."

Jack, however, would not move out of the way, but instead took Jim firmly by the arm.

"Plenty of time for all that, old chap," said Jack enthusiastically. "How about that interview you promised me?"

"Now? Here?" Jim looked at Jack incredulously.

"Of course here. I want to catch you in the midst of the social high life of Washington." Before Myers could refuse, Jack literally pulled him off to the side. Behind Myers, Agent Pullman came quickly up and dragged Paul Moore backwards, out of the way and out of danger.

Jack's cameraman was set up beside a wall where two ornate panels of scenes from the Dark Continent were hanging. Agent Clark and Agent Lewis were standing nearby. Jim glanced over again at the waiting ballerina, who looked a bit surprised and disappointed at his sudden departure. The strawberry was gone now, and instead she chewed on the end of her pen with a definite pout on her lips. Other guests in the room milled around the table, not paying attention to the reporter nor his camera. The composer and Mr. Baryshnikov stepped over towards the cheese and crackers while Mr. McNeil and Mrs. Dawson headed for the champagne.

"Okay," agreed Myers in frustration. "But make it snappy."

"Great! Just a few questions," said Jack.

Myers paused and looked down at his watch and then around the room, searching. Martha was nowhere in sight.

The lights of Jack's cameraman burned suddenly quite brightly upon Jim and Jack's faces, and Jack took his microphone and began his interview.

"I'm here at the Kennedy Center with Jim Myers, White House chief of staff, who attended tonight's performance of the Kirov Ballet's new worldwide production of *Cinderella* with President Johnson. Madame President's story is also something of a Cinderella story, wouldn't you agree, Mr. Myers?"

"It most certainly is," said Jim smoothly, keeping an eye on the door while he chatted with Jack about Martha and the White House.

Gary and McKay watched from a smaller adjacent room, called the African Lounge West. McKay stood steady like a rock, while Gary struggled to remain composed. His own heart was beating so loudly Gary was having trouble hearing. He listened with his nerves on edge as Jack calmly continued his diversionary interview.

"Originally, you are from New York City, so you must be well-versed in ballet and other Broadway productions. How do you rate tonight's performance?"

"Marvelous! I truly enjoyed it. It was . . ." Jim suddenly stopped speaking as Madame President entered the lounge with the young lady in the dark blue suit. The President smiled and handed the young lady her small black handbag. Then Martha approached the refreshment table, picked up a glass of champagne, and greeted Mrs. Dawson and Mr. McNeil, after which she strode over to Jim and Jack.

"Sorry I'm late, Jim" said Martha apologetically. "I needed to freshen up."

She smiled pleasantly at Jim, who stared transfixed at her deep reddened lips. Martha took a sip of sparkling champagne.

He spoke softly. "It's okay."

"Have I missed anything?" asked Martha brightly, pausing to wipe a bit of lipstick off of her champagne glass with her thumb. Clearly she had put too much on.

"No," said Jim staring straight down at the crimson lipstick stains on the glass. "I was just giving Mr. Parish an interview."

"How nice. Are you about done?"

"Not exactly," interjected Jack turning the microphone and lights on Martha. "We can continue his interview in a few moments. First, a few questions to you, Madame President?"

"Why, I'd be delighted, Mr. Parish. I —"

Martha paused abruptly, looking distressed. Her glass of champagne fell to the floor, shattering to pieces. The President looked up at Jim in alarm, her green eyes widening, as she clutched her hand to her chest. She gasped for breath.

"I . . . I can't breath," she uttered, suddenly leaning forward, her arms reaching for him.

Jim caught Martha before she fell to the floor. Conversation in the room suddenly died, and then there were cries of alarm. Agent Pullman and Agent Lewis rushed to the President's side, while other agents in the room either joined them or hurriedly pushed people back to form a protective barrier around the President. McKay and Gary remained hidden in the adjacent lounge, watching Jim's every move.

Agent Pullman assisted Jim in laying Martha gently down on the floor. Jim awkwardly stood back and watched transfixed as Pullman placed his fingers on the side of her wrist, checking her pulse. She didn't move. She didn't breathe. Agent Clark stood by Jim's side, speaking into his wrist communicator, urgently calling for an ambulance. Agent Lewis moved closer.

Suddenly Martha stirred. Her eyes fluttered open, staring upward into space.

"Jim?" she called out weakly.

"She's come to," barked Pullman turning towards Jim, "and she's asking for you. Get in there"

Jim knelt down and leaned over Martha as she labored hard to breathe.

"I'm here," he said softly, his eyes wide with anxiety.

"Come . . . closer," she whispered haltingly.

Jim leaned over close to her face. Martha slowly reached up and put her right hand around his neck and pulled his face even closer. She held onto his neck tightly.

"Give . . . children . . . my . . . love . . . Give them . . . a . . . kiss!" Martha then pulled his face down to her lips and kissed him full on the mouth, smearing lipstick over his lips and the right side of his face as her eyes closed and her head fell backwards onto the floor.

"She's dead," pronounced Agent Pullman loudly to the people in the room, still holding Martha's wrist in his hand.

At the same moment, Jim suddenly bolted upright.

"*AUGHH!*" he cried in horror, reaching madly for his face. But Agents Clark and Lewis were instantly upon him, each grabbing an arm and twisting it securely backwards as they pulled him back.

"Get it off me! *Get it off me!*" screamed Myers wildly as he wrestled to get away from the firm lock of the two Secret Service agents.

"Get what off you, sir?" asked Agent Lewis.

"The god-damned lipstick!" yelled Myers, wiggling even more. "*Get if off me now!*"

"Why do you want us to do that?" asked Agent Clark.

"IT WILL KILL ME, YOU STUPID FOOL! IT'S POISON!"

You could have heard a pin drop. No one moved. Gary could hardly breathe.

"Poison? Why do you think it is poison, sir?" asked Agent Lewis coolly, painfully twisting Myers arm backwards ever so much more tightly.

Jim looked around like a wild wounded animal caught in a fatal trap. He stared fiercely at the agent, knowing he was a dead man if he answered and a dead man if he stayed silent. His life was over no matter what he did.

Gary watched anxiously. Everything depended on the answer to this question. Gary closed his eyes and waited.

"Because I put it there," hissed Jim in a chilling admission.

It was done.

McKay and Gary bolted into the room, over to Jim and the agents. McKay paused and extended his large sturdy hand down towards Martha.

"I think we've heard enough. You can get up now, Madame President."

Martha's eyes popped open and with the assistance of Agent Pullman, she sat up. There were audible gasps from people across the room. The ballerina looked like she was about to faint. The pen was out of her mouth, as she stood gaping at the scene.

"Thank you, Charles," said the President brushing back the hair from her face.

"You all right?" asked Gary anxiously, offering Martha a hand in getting up off the floor. She stood up and addressed them.

"Yes, I'm fine, thank you," she said speaking with assurance. She turned towards Jack. "Did you get it, Mr. Parish?"

Jack and his cameraman stepped forward. Jack's directional microphone was pointed in their direction, and the red light on the camera was on.

"Yes, Madame President," beamed Jack with pride. "Thanks to satellite transmission, it was broadcasted in its entirety live to the nation."

Myers scowled at Jack and his cameraman.

"Excellent. Your fine reporting will prove quite useful when we go to trial."

She turned and leveled Jim with a hard look.

"And we will be going to trial," she said flatly to Jim. "Mr. Parish, please give the original videotape to my Secret Service detail. I want it impounded into evidence"

"Yes, Ma'am," said Jack, motioning for his cameraman to stop filming and to hand over the video to the woman in the dark navy suit. She took the tape and exited the lounge in company with another agent and two Kennedy Center guards. McKay stood next to Myers, who had collapsed on the floor. Agents Clark and Lewis held the murderer in a vice-like grip. Myers was going nowhere. McKay's facial expression was terrifying, and when he spoke, Gary thought it reminded him of a low rumbling thunderstorm.

"Stand him up," ordered McKay sternly. The agents roughly jerked Myers back up to his feet. McKay stared at Myers narrowly. From his own pocket, McKay pulled out the tube of lipstick found in Abigail's crayon box. It was sealed in a plastic bag. Myers stared at the lipstick hypnotically as beads of sweat began to appear on his forehead.

"I don't have to tell you what this is, do I, Mr. Myers? This was the lipstick into which you placed poison. It will be sent over to the FBI lab, but you could save us all a lot of trouble by revealing exactly what kind of poison you used and where you got it."

Myers, realizing that he had been duped and that the lipstick on Martha's lips and upon his own face was utterly harmless, refused to speak. Instead, he glared at the general with closed lips and a brazen look of defiance.

"What's wrong, Jim?" taunted McKay. "Cat got your tongue? Or have you forgotten? Maybe I can help you remember. Was it the same poison that was found in this?" The general then pulled out of his pocket the vial that had been found in Donald Hooper's coat the day he died. This vial, the lipstick, and Jack and his cameraman, were the three things Gary had arranged for the con. Jim stared at the vial, his eyes popping wide open. It was now Gary's turn to interrogate.

"You poisoned Donald Hooper, didn't you, Jim?" said Gary in a voice that sounded much more calm than he felt. "You killed him and framed him for the other murders you helped commit, the murders of President Stan Taylor and Eric Peters."

The people in the crowded room gasped.

Jim looked at Gary with a sneer.

"You'd like that, wouldn't you!" replied Myers finally in an ugly voice. "I fry and you get the girl."

Gary stared at Jim with a mixed feeling of disgust, rage, and pity.

"My feelings for Martha are none of your god-damned business and are not the topic of the current discussion. We are talking about the murder of three innocent men."

Jim looked at Gary spitefully and actually laughed. "Okay, so you have me on this, but you can't prove the rest."

"Oh, I beg to differ," interjected General McKay in a retort. "I think once we've thoroughly gone through all your files, phone records, and bank accounts, I'm sure we'll be more than able to prove it. Besides, we already have a report of a recent phone conservation of yours wherein you were overheard admitting to Hooper's murder and to framing him for the deaths of Taylor and Peters."

"*That's impossible!*" snapped Jim in a sudden outburst, wrestling in vain against the hold upon him once again. "All calls going out from my office are secure and scrambled. No one could overhear anything."

Martha stared at her former chief of staff in disgust. "You are mistaken, Jim. It is possible. We had the means to intercept your call. How shall I describe the method, gentlemen?"

"Under the radar stealth technology," offered McKay.

"A secret weapon that must be handled very carefully," replied Gary.

"A weapon with excellent mobility and placement," added Martha smiling. "So, Jim, we have your confession on record, but you haven't given us a motive. I suspect the motive was to have Eric Peters removed in order to put someone else on the ticket. And if it hadn't been for Mr. Craig giving Stan Taylor the idea of selecting me, you were in place to nominate Secretary Miller. Tell us, Jim, were you and Secretary Miller working alone or were you working for someone else?"

The mention of Secretary Miller's name sent more gasps and cries of disbelief through the small crowd huddled inside the African Lounge. It was just too awful to believe. Myers continued to say nothing. Gary had had enough.

"McKay has agents surrounding Miller's home, Myers, as we speak," said Gary sharply. "If you won't rat out on him, maybe he'll rat out on you. Think about that while you sit in jail tonight."

"Take him away," snarled McKay gruffly. "I'm sick of looking at him."

"Yes, take him away," said Martha wearily. "At least I can relax knowing my family and the White House are safe at last."

Agent Lewis began to pull Myers aside, but Myers defiantly resisted one last time. He glared at them with a bold mixture of hate and fear.

"Safe? You think the White House is safe?" Jim laughed cynically while shaking his head. "I'm afraid not, Madame President. Sorry to disappoint. If you think I'm dangerous, I regret to inform you there is another lurking underfoot at the White House more deadly than Secretary Miller or I ever were, someone you would never suspect. And once my capture is made public, the Seven . . ."

There was an abrupt popping sound and a funny burnt smell in the air. Jim Myers was unable to complete his sentence, as a bullet pierced his right temple, entered his brain, and shattered soundly against the skull over his left temporal lobe, killing him instantly.

This time the reaction of the Secret Service was for real. Agent Lewis and Pullman leapt in the direction of Martha, forming a human shield against further attack. Jim's body fell backwards violently into Agent Clark's arms, throwing both men hard to the floor. Other agents rushed towards Gary and McKay, protectively encircling them, crushing them hard against the wall. There was yelling and screaming and general all-out pandemonium. Gary felt large hands and arms grabbing at him, literally pulling him and McKay and Martha out of the African Lounge. In his peripheral vision, he saw a crowd of Secret Service and FBI agents piled over against the table where the ballerina had been standing. His glimpse was brief, but he saw her. She was lying on the floor, her arm outstretched, pinned to the ground. Her eyes were opened wide, blank, and unmoving.

It was just a glance, but Gary knew the Russian ballerina was dead.

★ ★ ★

In the chaos that followed, Gary hardly remembered leaving the building. The Secret Service practically carried him feet first out of the Kennedy Center, shoving him inside the large black car with General McKay. Police cars were everywhere, sirens sounding and flashing. Martha was already gone. They had spirited her out of the building first and placed her inside the lead car, which was now speeding away. The door had barely slammed shut when Gary's car screeched off, following the President's car. Law enforcement vehicles surrounded and followed them, as they raced down New Hampshire Avenue towards Washington Circle, then turning right down Pennsylvania Avenue.

Gary was in such a daze that it took a moment for him to realize that Agent Lewis was in the car with him. He was sitting right beside Gary, with his strong arm around him. It was a good thing, too. Gary's heart was racing madly, and he felt a tightness in his chest.

"I . . .can't . . .breathe," Gary gasped.

"You'll be all right, sir," assured Agent Lewis. "It's just your nerves. You're hyperventilating. Just be still and try to relax. I won't leave you. We'll be in the residence shortly. Don't worry about Madame President. She got out safely."

Gary did as he was directed, grateful for the presence of the man sitting next to him. As Gary struggled to calm down, he glanced over at McKay sitting across from him. The general was on the phone swearing loudly, in a voice that sounded like controlled fury.

"It was the damn pen? That pen was a gun? How the hell did that get past security? . . . Plastic? Well, here's a flash bulletin. They make weapons in plastic! . . . Only one round? Guess she was a backup and had to choose between Madame President and Mr. Myers, and she rightly choose Myers who was spilling his guts on national television. I hope to hell her employers are impressed. I sure as hell am. What's the cause of her death? . . . Arsenic on a ruby ring? Damn it! If I hear of any more poison within ten feet of the President tonight, I'm really going to get mad! Do I make myself clear? . . . Good! Now, go with the body to the morgue and be there when they do the autopsy. And try not to mess it up."

McKay slammed the car phone down and swore again under his breath. Gary said nothing, just leaned his head back and concentrated on slowing down his breath. Agent Lewis continued to hold on to him tightly.

Finally the car with its police escort came screeching into the White House entrance. News of the killing was out, and reporters with their cameras flashing blinded them as they made their entrance onto the grounds. Park Police and Secret Service were everywhere. Martha was already inside.

McKay and Gary rushed into the White House. Morgan was on the scene, his face drawn in lines of shock and disbelief. He met them as they entered and walked them to the elevators, taking them up to the residence. There was no talking as they rode up. McKay silently seethed, and Gary kept trying to breathe normally, still feeling light headed.

When the elevator door opened, they came out on the west side of the second floor near Martha and Aunt Sophie's room. Gary stepped out first and was instantly grabbed by an anxious Aunt Sophie. They were on the edge of the West Sitting Hall. Martha was waiting for them, looking tired and weary. Agent Clark and Agent Pullman were also there. Sophie murmured something, but Gary was so drained he didn't hear it. Once Aunt Sophie released Gary, Martha embraced him and held him tightly. Aunt Sophie went to McKay and they embraced. The general said nothing but laid his head against Sophie's in anger and frustration.

Martha pulled back from Gary and turned to Sophie.

"Where are the children?" she asked anxiously. "Do they know?"

Aunt Sophie stepped back from the general, patted him softly on the arm, and then smiled at her niece.

"They're fine, Martha. Yes, they know. We watched it on TV. It was so horrible. They're in my room with Charlotte. She's been wonderful. I gave them strict orders to stay inside with doors locked until you came home."

Martha nodded approvingly.

"Where's Blaze?" asked Gary.

"In the West Wing. After the broadcast, he went downstairs to help manage things from the office. Ned Baldwin called and is on his way in. Blaze wanted to be there when Ned arrived."

"That sounds good," said Gary. "And Abigail?"

He glanced down the hallway. Both the Center Hall and the East Sitting Hall were darkened. That was odd.

"Why are the lights out?" asked Martha sharply, turning to face the Secret Service Agent, a tall, dark-haired man named Douglas posted at the doorway between the West Sitting Room and the Center Hall.

"It was the nanny's request," answered Douglas promptly. "She said the little girl needed to get to sleep, and she didn't want any lights on down that hallway."

Martha relaxed.

"I see," she said comforted.

"And no one's been up here?" asked McKay in follow up.

"No one, sir," replied Douglas firmly.

"Good," said McKay.

"Except, of course, the butler."

All eyes turned sharply towards Agent Douglas.

"What did you say?" asked McKay in a low growl.

The Secret Serviceman paused, looking surprised.

"You know, the butler, Dwight Cook. He came upstairs about ten minutes ago with the big service cart. He said the nanny ordered tea and that the little girl was awake and wanted some of his famous hot chocolate."

"Agent Douglas, my daughter doesn't drink hot chocolate," said Martha.

Perhaps it was Gary's proximity to the east hallway or maybe it was his overwhelming love for the child, but Gary outran Agent Lewis, Agent Clark, Agents Douglas and Pullman, General McKay, Mr. Morgan, and Martha, arriving first to the doorway of the Queen's Bedroom. All the lights were out, and bedroom was pitch black. But the bedroom door was standing wide open, and Gary raced inside and tripped over the body.

He fell flat and hard against the floor inside the dark room.

The body was still warm but did not move. Gary's left hand fell into a wet oozing puddle on the carpet. He could not see, but knew instinctively it was blood. It was coming from the body's head.

Others were rushing into the room as well, and a voice spoke out sharply to them from deep within the dark.

"Leave the overhead lights off," the voice ordered sternly, "and please do be quiet."

Gary rolled over and raised himself up in a sitting position as a small lamp beside the bed was turned on. Transfixed, Gary stared up at a much-changed Nanny Jane. Jane Michaels was sitting in a chair pulled close to the bed. Gone were the bright broomstick skirts, the oversized peasant blouses and sweaters, the clunky Birkenstock sandals, the wild curly hair, and thick glasses. Instead, Jane sat calmly by Abigail's bed, dressed in a sleek black turtleneck top and tightly fit black leather pants. Her hair was pulled straight back and tied in a knot behind her neck. She wore short, spiked, black leather boots, and in her lap, she held a small black handgun with silencer.

Jane looked down lovingly at the sleeping child and continued. "She didn't have a nap today. She was so upset by the things Mr. Myers had said and by what he had done. If she wakes up now, she'll be completely out of sorts in the morning, and I simply won't have it."

By this time, Martha had rushed into the room behind the men and was staring in shock at the figure of the butler Dwight Cook, who had been shot dead, a direct hit in the middle of the forehead. The Secret Service agents began to push her back out of the room, but Martha gave them a look that stopped them cold. She stared briefly down at the dead butler, and then she walked calmly over to the bed.

"Is she okay? Did he touch her or hurt her at all?" asked Martha anxiously.

Jane smiled reassuringly. She answered in a deeper voice, a voice full of authority and assurance.

"No, Madame President. She was absolutely splendid. She slept through it all. Although I must confess the little tyke had some sniffles before going to bed. She's getting a wee cold, I think. So, I hope you'll forgive me, but I took the liberty of giving her some Benadryl, just to help her sleep more soundly."

Martha nodded her head gratefully and murmured a quiet thank you.

The others in the room stood still and in awe. Finally, General McKay stepped forward, over the body of the dead butler and towards the bed. He promptly took over.

"Martha, I suggest that you move Abigail into your room for the night. It's best she leave the room while we attend . . . while we attend to this mess. It's been a long night for all of you. We'll take over from here. You go be with your family. Tell Aunt Sophie and Charlotte what's happened and comfort the children. I'm sure they're very anxious to see you." He looked over at the dead man. "We'll clean this up by morning."

Martha nodded. "Yes, of course, I want Abigail to sleep with me." She slowly pulled back the thick covers and looked over at the one of the agents for help.

Agent Lewis promptly stepped forward.

"Allow me, Madame President." He carefully leaned over and gently lifted the child up into his massive arms and took her out of the room. Martha looked over at Nanny Jane and smiled.

"We can never repay you for what you've done. Thank you again," said the President with glistening eyes, and then left the room.

McKay looked over to Agent Clark and motioned for him to turn on the overhead lights. The room lit up, and Gary looked over at the butler lying beside him. The large cart with hot chocolate and tea stood by the door. A small bright red puddle of blood had formed beside the butler's head. There was blood on Gary's hands as well. In one of the Butler's hands, there was a handgun. Dwight's head was turned to the side, facing Gary, his face frozen. The butler hadn't seen it coming.

General McKay strode over and stood next to Jane. He looked down at the young woman with a strange new expression on his face, one Gary couldn't quite decipher. Normally McKay's response to Jane was one of extreme irritation. Now he was staring at the British nanny fondly and with a look of pride?

McKay authoritatively held out the palm of his hand, and Jane lifted up the black handgun from her lap and gave it to him. McKay took the gun and handed it over to Agent Clark who had walked towards them.

"Take care of this," ordered McKay sharply, "and take the other gun as well. Run the butler's gun through ballistics. I doubt it's traceable, but we can always pray and hope for a miracle. Also notify the FBI and D.C. police, homicide. But have them arrive quietly. No more fanfare and flashing red lights. We've had enough press for one evening, thank you very much. Mr. Morgan, I think we all could use a stiff drink, something hot and numbing."

Agent Clark nodded, took the gun and quickly left taking the other agents in the room with him. Mr. Morgan said he would go down to the kitchens and get liquid refreshments for all concerned, including himself. He departed, leaving Gary alone in the room with the general and the nanny.

"Sorry about the mess," Jane said apologetically. "He entered without knocking and I immediately spotted the gun. I left the lights off in the room and the hallway deliberately so my night vision would be optimal. I could see the barrel of the gun in his hand. I had no choice but to aim and fire."

McKay smiled kindly down at her. "Your aim was perfect, as usual."

Jane looked up at him inquisitively.

"Why did he do it? Could he have actually gotten Abigail out of the house in that?" She pointed to the service cart.

"Possibly. The cart is large enough. In the dark, he could have shot you or knocked you out with the edge of the gun, put the sleeping child inside the cart and taken her down to the kitchens and out through the loading area. That is, if kidnapping was his intention. We'll never really know."

"Is it really over?" asked Jane sounding extremely tired and disgusted.

McKay nodded his head solemnly.

"I think it finally is. Jim Myers confessed to the murders of Peters, President Taylor, and Donald Hooper and he himself is now dead. He was shot by another agent at the ballet, a Russian ballerina. But unfortunately, the dancer swallowed her ring, one heavily laced with poison, and died on the scene. Pity. I would have liked to have interrogated her myself. I'm growing weary of poison. I much prefer manly mechanical devices, guns and grenades and metal objects that explode. Those you can detect. The use of poisoned lipstick and jewelry is not playing fair." The general grimaced. "Fortunately for us, Myers lived long enough to implicate Miller."

"I'm truly sorry about him. I really am," admitted Jane sadly.

McKay nodded grimly. "Our agents surrounded the senator's house in Maryland tonight, but I haven't heard yet what has transpired there. I seriously doubt he'll be alive when they enter."

Jane sighed deeply as she stared up at the general. Sitting there, she looked so vulnerable, so much herself like a little girl.

"I'm so frightfully tired," said Jane.

"I know you are," said McKay tenderly.

Gary watched in amazement as McKay extended his large hand to Jane and raised her gently up from the chair.

They stood very close, standing face to face.

"Would you do something rather silly for me?" asked Jane softly as she gazed at the general with wide entreating eyes.

"Anything," said the general.

"Would you mind terribly tucking me into bed and sitting by me until I fall asleep, like Mother used to do?"

McKay smiled warmly and stepped forward.

"Of course I will, sweetheart." The general enfolded Jane in his powerful arms and held her tight. Jane laid her head upon his strong broad shoulder and closed her eyes in peace.

"I love you, Daddy," whispered Jane Michaels McKay.

"I love you, too," said her father.

Chapter 24

Family Dining Room

Sunday Morning, August 28

"You're a spy???"

Sitting at the breakfast table, Nanny Jane smiled sheepishly at Gary and nodded her head in the affirmative.

Gary picked up his butter knife and waved it warningly at the other guilty adults seated around the breakfast table. "I demand to hear the whole story, *the whole story*, every single sordid detail!"

General McKay put his fist up to his mouth and cleared his throat.

"A-hem. Then I guess it should start with me," he said in an unusual mellow tone of voice. "When President Taylor died, a second death inside our inner circle within six months, I worried that something was quite wrong. If my instincts proved correct, I knew Madame President and her family were in mortal danger. So I decided to secretly place someone inside the White House to keep an eye on them. Couldn't think of anyone better than my own daughter, Jane. So I approached Aunt Sophie and Madame President about the idea on the day they moved into the residence."

"Yes," said Aunt Sophie brightly. "You remember, Mr. Craig. It was right after Martha fired that awful Anderson woman and hired you to be Social Secretary instead. You came upstairs with your friends. Charles and I were talking about hiring a nanny. That afternoon Charles told Martha and me about his concerns and told us about Jane, such a lovely girl and such a good spy, too." Aunt Sophie beamed approvingly at Jane. The nanny blushed at the compliment.

Gary turned and faced the British spy.

"And you are a for real, honest to goodness secret agent?"

Jane tilted her head modestly. "Yes, an agent with the MI5, actually."

Gary almost dropped his half bagel on the floor. "And the wild hair, the broomstick skirts, the thick glasses, and the heavy shoes were a ruse, a disguise?"

"Absolutely," said Jane, who was sitting at the table this morning dressed in a pair of smart black Capri pants and a fitted light blue knit sweater, her hair pulled back straight and neat. The glasses were gone, replaced by contact lenses. Gary had never noticed, but she had lovely blue eyes, the same shade as her father's.

"And what about all the physical abuse you subjected the general to — the stepping on toes, the spilling of drinks, the wreckage of clothing, and injury with household appliances?"

Jane laughed heartily. "Oh, that! Well, we had to have some way to meet privately. So I played the part of the clumsy girl, and he played the part of unwilling victim. Which you do very well, Father. Mother would have been most pleased. When we were alone, Father would give me a security briefing, updating me on the latest intelligence he had from the NSA and CIA. Naturally I would report back anything I had seen out of the ordinary."

"Clever girl," said her father proudly.

"Clever girl," echoed Abigail, eating her Cheerios.

"Thanks, Dad," said Jane. "I hope I didn't hurt you too bad."

McKay beamed. "It was my pleasure, sweetheart. You can step on your old man's toes anytime!"

Another piece of the puzzle fell into place in Gary's mind.

"Let me guess," said Gary, "the sightings of Lincoln's ghost that night. That was you, on patrol?"

Jane nodded with a grin.

"But how did you get around the Secret Service television monitors?"

"Easy," said the general. "I had either Agent Clark or Lewis stationed at the monitors at night. I had Agent Pullman split the shift, at my request. Pullman knew something was up, but he didn't question me too closely. Despite his rough and sometimes blustery exterior, Agent Pullman is a man to be trusted. So when Jane took a night stroll, they all turned a blind eye, shall we say? Security cameras are one thing, but an agent on the floor, in the shadows, is quite another. I wanted my daughter's eyes and ears . . ."

"And gun," added Gary munching on the other half of his bagel.

"And gun in the residence at night. Our agents are very, very good at editing videotapes, by the way. No record exists of Jane's midnight strolls."

Gary's mind was racing in overdrive, enlightened by the facts. The comment caused another puzzle piece to fall into place.

"And the sudden outbreak of insomnia by the adults living upstairs? That was all staged, too?"

Charlotte cleared her throat and spoke up tentatively.

"That was my idea. We couldn't let Jane do all the night patrol, dear girl. Her afternoon naps were helping but she couldn't be expected to be awake all night every night. So, we took turns. Aunt Sophie and I had our 'ailments' to keep us up late, and Martha had her 'worries' to get her up early. Collectively, we kept our eyes on the children, in case someone actually got someone into the White House — which we now know they did. I'm still in shock about Dwight. He seemed like such a nice young man."

"You can't trust appearances," warned McKay sternly, a voice of vast experience. "About the butler's death, the public will get a sanitized account, with the Secret Service credited with the capture and killing of a would-be kidnapper. My daughter's role in this affair will remain strictly classified."

"Strictly classified," echoed Abigail crunching.

Martha smiled weakly. "We'll explain that to you later, Abigail. I agree with you, General, we must protect Jane's cover. Everyone around this table is sworn to secrecy. We certainly have learned not to trust in appearances," said Martha sadly. "I'm devastated at the news about Secretary Miller. Such a loss."

Gary asked, "What about Miller?"

McKay sighed heavily.

"Dead, as I predicted. This time, it was a real suicide. After Jim was shot on national television, our men, who were surrounding Miller's house, busted in, but they were too late. They saw him put the gun to his head. Sad. Very sad indeed."

"And most unfortunately," said Jane in a crisp professional voice, "he died before we could learn anything more about the Seven. Do you know anything about them, Dad? I called this morning and checked with my government contacts, but they had nothing, zilch."

McKay shook his head gravely. "We have nothing on them either. I called the NSA and CIA people, but they came up empty. I've got the NSA folks scanning the airways to intercept any chatter on them. I also put in a call to Ambassador Porter at the U.N. He knows nothing but promises to keep me informed if he hears anything from his internal contacts."

"Find anything in Myers' office?" asked Martha.

"No," replied McKay flatly. "Agents combed through his files, computer, and desk all night long. Went through his home computer as well. We found very little, except an anonymous e-mail account on the internet giving a phone number."

"You found phone records?" asked Jane hopefully.

"Ah, an interesting find there. There were a number of calls on his cell phone throughout the past six months, to various public phone booths inside the city."

"Which city?" asked Gary excitedly.

"This city. He was calling someone in D.C., someone who had brains enough not to be contacted in a place where he or she could later be traced."

"Perhaps Myers made initial contact through the anonymous e-mail account, then the contact e-mailed him the time and location where he could be called," mused Jane aloud.

McKay smiled at his daughter. "That's what I think. We're still connecting the dots. Hopefully we'll come up with something eventually. We need to nail this Seven group and put them out of business fast."

There was a pause, as everyone silently ate their breakfast and considered what the general had said. Gary's mind was still racing, putting together some unrelated facts.

"Has anyone noticed how often the number seven has appeared in this case?" asked Gary.

Everyone in the room looked at Gary blankly. Gary explained.

"We've been surrounded by sevens throughout this entire ordeal. Eric Peters died at 7:00 A.M. Stan Taylor died on April 7. If I remember it correctly, Bishop Palmer was staying in room 477 in Miami, Florida. Jim Myers sent Martha a vase of larkspur, the flower of July, the seventh month, and both Jim Myers and the Russian ballerina were wearing ruby rings. I noticed she wore a ruby ring last night. Ruby is the gemstone for July."

"Well, I'll be double damned," said the general. He looked at Gary with keen admiration. "Son, you'd make a pretty good spy yourself. Whoever this group is, they like to leave sevens behind in their wake."

"You better let the NSA people know about this immediately," ordered Martha. "It may help in intercepting relevant intelligence."

"Will do," agreed McKay.

"Seven," wondered Jane aloud. "But seven what? Seven senators? Seven entrepreneurs? Seven drug lords? Seven Tibetan monks?"

Josh looked over at his mother excitedly. "Hey, Mom, could it be the Secret Seven from UVA?"

"The what?" said Gary.

Martha smiled. "The UVA Seven Society. It's one of the most important and secretive societies on campus. Supposedly third year students are tapped on their shoulder when invited to join for their senior year. Additionally, there is a group of seven alumni of the Seven Society known as the Secret Seven. Rumor has it they are all extremely wealthy, extremely successful people. Only when one of the Seven dies is his or her position on the Seven made known. A wreath of black magnolias in the shape of a seven is placed at the gravesite; and the bell tower at the university chapel chimes at seven-second intervals at seven o'clock for seven minutes on a dissonant seventh chord. And any donations they give to the university are in quantities of seven."

The general looked intrigued. "Martha, this might be something."

The President shook her head and laughed. "Sorry, Charles. The Secret Seven are strictly philanthropic. They hand out scholarships and lots of money for new buildings. I seriously doubt they have branched out into international terrorism."

The general frowned. "In the meantime, I'll get seven ulcers. Well, until our evil Seven is captured, I strongly recommend that we do not speak of the Seven openly to anyone. Madame President, I would go so far to suggest that you not share the information even with members of your cabinet or even your vice president, whoever that might be."

Martha took a sip of her hot morning tea. "Agreed! Aunt Sophie, Charlotte, Gary, children, the need for silence extends to you as well. Don't speak of the Seven to anyone except those at this table. At least it's all over for now," she added gratefully. "We must get on with life as normal, as normal as life can be for us."

Gary finished his bagel. "That's right. But I'm honest enough to say I'm thrilled we have an excellent shot like Jane around in case things get dangerous again."

"I'm afraid not, Mr. Craig," said Jane regretfully. "You see, I'm heading back to England now that the case is closed. I really miss my husband."

Gary sputtered while taking a sip of his orange juice. "You're married!!!"

Jane smiled. "Why, of course, Mr. Craig, quite happily married, in fact."

Gary shook his head in disbelief.

"Doesn't your husband object to your being gone for so long?"

Jane sipped her hot tea slowly. "Oh, heavens no, Trevor doesn't mind at all. He's been working madly on his next novel, you see, and when he's writing, he's such a recluse. Might as well be single when he's in that state. But he should be finished soon, and I like to be around when he resurfaces."

"You mean you're married to Trevor Allyn, the international spy thriller writer?" cried Gary throwing his hands up in the air.

Jane's eyes glimmered with pride. "The one and the same."

Gary gasped. "Is he a spy too?"

Jane laughed gaily. "Absolutely not, Mr. Craig. I'm the only spy in the family. Trevor has trouble finding his own office in the morning. It's a nice arrangement really. I live it and Trevor writes it. Well, writes a watered down and slightly altered version of the cases I work on. The dear boy has been chained to his desk for months now working on last year's adventure. That was rather a fun one, an arms deal for nuclear material. We were involved in a multi-national assignment — the U.S., England, and Canada. We were out for several months all over the globe, chasing the bad guys through England, Egypt, and Australia. It was quite thrilling."

England, Egypt, and Australia.

The final piece of the puzzle fell into place, and now Gary knew everything. It was his turn to laugh. And he did, right out loud.

Jane looked at Gary in alarm. "Mr. Craig, are you quite alright?"

"I'm fine, Jane, just fine. You go back home to England and your husband, knowing you will be greatly missed here. Go with an invitation to return anytime as Jane McKay Allyn or as the toe stomping nanny Jane Michaels. In the meantime, I know exactly where to get a nanny replacement."

There was a bit of a pause, and then Aunt Sophie spoke up.

"Speaking of marriage, Charles and I have a little announcement to make."

She looked over at McKay shyly. The general took Sophie's hand firmly into his own and spoke.

"When I lost my wife Isabelle, I never thought I would marry again. But last night shook me up. I can't live in the past for the rest of my life. Time to get on with it. Sophie has captured my heart and I've asked her to marry me. And the dear woman has agreed to take me on."

There was an eruption in the room, shouts of joy and well wishes.

Martha jumped up and went over to hug her aunt. Jane got up and went over to hug her father. Charlotte took out a tissue, wiped her eyes, and blew her nose.

"How wonderful!" exclaimed Martha happily as she returned to her seat. "We'll have a big wedding in the Rose Garden!"

"Oh no, Martha dear," objected Aunt Sophie firmly. "Charles and I have discussed it, and we feel we're too old for all that nonsense. We don't want any fanfare. We'll do the old fashioned thing and elope to Niagara Falls."

"Are you sure?" asked Martha laughing.

"Quite sure," said Aunt Sophie. "Besides, we thought, well, if there is going to be any big wedding in the Rose Garden . . ."

Aunt Sophie looked expectantly at Martha and then at Gary.

Gary was totally aghast at her remark. Martha turned and looked at her aunt in amazement.

"What ever do you mean?" asked Martha.

Aunt Sophie smiled at her niece with the placid look on her face.

"It's time for you to get on with your own life, too, Martha," she said gently.

Martha looked at Gary with a bit of awkwardness on her face.

"Do you know what my aunt is talking about?"

Gary bit his lip and looked at Aunt Sophie.

"Now?" he asked.

"Now," advised Aunt Sophie smiling at him with assurance.

Martha stared at Gary wide eyed waiting for an explanation.

"A few years ago," began Gary tentatively, "my whole world collapsed around me. I lost everything I thought was important, everything I had worked so hard for and planned so long for. I lost my marriage, I lost my job, and I lost my hope of ever having a family of my own. But now I see that everything had a purpose and everything happened for a reason, and Martha, that reason was you. You are truly the most amazing woman I have ever known — beautiful, loving, smart, and brave. Things turned out better than I could have ever planned, ever dreamed. I found work that fulfills me, I found a family that makes me so happy, and I found a woman that is a dream come true. When I met you, Martha, I literally fell at your feet. And I've been falling hard for you ever since. Martha, dearest Martha, the truth is I love you."

All eyes eagerly turned to Martha. She looked at Gary steadily with her big green eyes. Finally, she calmly reached for her glass and took a sip her orange juice before responding.

"I see. Well, in that case, we need to discuss the matter of your position here," said Martha in a very formal crisp voice. "I'm afraid I am going to ask you for your resignation, effective immediately."

It was a direct hit, his worst nightmare returning, exactly like Janet all over again. The woman he loved was firing him at the breakfast table. Gary suddenly felt very sick.

"Mom, no!" cried Eliza.

"No way!" yelled Josh hotly. "You can't get rid of him. We want Gary to be our new dad."

"Can't get rid of him," echoed Abigail digging furiously down into her cereal bowl.

Aunt Sophie looked like she was about to cry.

"Oh, Martha, are you sure?"

"Children, Sophie, hush!" ordered Martha loudly above the din. She waited for everyone to quiet down. "Please let me finish. I can't let Gary continue to work as social secretary anymore, not if he's going to marry me and become First Gentleman." She turned and looked at Gary expectantly, her green eyes now glistening with tears.

"Can I?" she asked smiling.

Gary stared back in a daze.

"You want me to quit my job and marry you?"

Martha looked at him a bit sheepishly. "Well, yes, that is the general idea. I mean, you are part of this family now. The children love you, Aunt Sophie loves you . . ."

"I love you," said Abigail crunching.

"Hush, dearest," ordered Jane smartly. "Your mother is proposing."

"And I love you," added Martha looking surprised at her own words. "Madly, in fact."

All eyes turned back to Gary. Now it was his turn to respond.

"Well, say something," said Martha nervously.

He stood silently, staring into the eyes of this glorious woman. His dream came back to him, Jefferson playing his violin, the gaping chasm, and his leap of faith. It was time to jump.

"I'm afraid I can't," said Gary.

The faces of the children fell and Martha looked absolutely crestfallen. She gasped. "You mean you won't . . ."

"Now let me finish," interrupted Gary directly, holding up his hand. "I absolutely refuse to quit my job and take on the role of First Lady, or as you phrased it, 'First Gentleman,' a position, may I say, that is being aptly filled by Aunt Sophie."

Aunt Sophie smiled with pleasure, and Martha looked at Gary curiously.

"Okay. So what are you saying? You will marry me?"

"On two conditions," replied Gary.

At this, Martha instantly bristled. Women don't like conditions. She folded her arms and looked at Gary crossly.

"Oh, really? And just what might those two conditions be?"

General McKay rolled his eyes and moaned. "Oh, God, here come the conditions."

"Shhh," ordered Aunt Sophie sternly, slapping him on the arm.

"First of all," said Gary firmly, "I keep my job. I enjoy being social secretary. It suits me well. The best way that I can support and contribute to your presidency is in my service there. After we marry, we can work together, side by side, as a team. You'll run the country while I stay busy keeping house."

Martha kept her crossed-arms stance, but her face softened.

Gary continued. "I mean, who else can cook barbecue, make flower arrangements for a party of two hundred, and color flamingos with stolen coral lipstick?"

"You have a point there," said the President. "All right. You may keep your job. And your second condition?"

At this point, Gary stood up and moved away from the end of the table and began walking towards Martha slowly.

"I will be in charge of planning the wedding. Not that you can't have any input. In this, as in any matter in our relationship, we will be equal partners. But you have way too much to do with the upcoming G8 summit and the appropriation bills stalled in Congress to be bothered with mere wedding details. You need to be focused on the Defense Department budget requests, not ordering flowers and cake. The new Banquet Room in the Ellipse will be completed soon, so we can hold the reception there. I'll work with the State Department on the guest list. Charlotte, if you're game, you can work with me on the wedding. Of course, I want Jack to cover the wedding for the media. And the White House staff needs to start planning for the reception immediately. As far as dates are concerned, I think we should marry right away, perhaps the end of September, before the winter holidays and the G8 summit meeting in Paris at New Years."

"Yes, Paris," said Martha dreamily. "I've always wanted to go to Paris. Paris would be a wonderful place to spend the Christmas holidays."

"And we will take the children," added Gary emphatically.

"Oh, I've always wanted to go to Paris, too," said Eliza chiming in happily. "We can go shopping, and I could buy some real French perfume!"

"Can we go to Normandy?" asked Josh excitedly. "I want to see the beaches and all the World War II stuff!"

"I want to go to Paris," shouted Abigail, not really knowing what Paris was and determined not to be left behind.

By now, Gary was standing close to Martha, face to face.

"And then there's the issue of your dress. You can pick the color, although you would look splendid in white. I was thinking we should call Max since he's already doing Harriet's dress, but then you might have other ideas for a designer . . ."

At this point, General McKay impatiently slammed his large hand down on the table and exclaimed, "Oh, for God sakes, man, shut up and kiss her!"

"Shut up and kiss her," exclaimed Abigail clapping while bouncing up and down in her chair.

"Yes, shut up and kiss her," said the President of the United States.

"Is that an executive order?" asked Gary taking her firmly into his arms.

"It most certainly is," answered the leader of free nations.

"Yes, Madame President," said Gary.

He held her close and kissed her passionately, his heart overflowing with love for this extraordinary woman. Soon he felt himself surrounded and embraced tightly by the arms of three enthusiastically laughing happy children, each holding onto him for dear life.

Gary was home at last.

Chapter 25

The Greenhouse

Friday, September 2

"Anyone for seconds? There's lots of fried chicken left."

Harriet held up her best Blue Willow platter stacked high with brown crispy chicken legs and breasts. The smell was delicious, fattening, and divine.

"I will," said Blaze happily holding out his plate.

"Me, too!" said Gary, pushing his plate out in front of his friend.

"Count me in," said Jack Parish, a bit behind in the count but gaining fast with second helpings of hash brown potatoes, baked tomatoes, and fried apples.

"Harriet, you're spoiling them," warned Mildred critically, wiping her mouth daintily with her napkin. She sat tall in her chair and smiled at the hungry men sitting around their dinner table.

The friends were gathered in the dining room of Harriet's grand Victorian home in Greensboro, North Carolina, enjoying a quiet dinner together. The three exhausted men were down for a weekend getaway, a brief but well-deserved vacation after all they had been through.

"Mildred, hush. These poor boys haven't had a good home-cooked meal in ages. Just look at them! They're wasting away to skin and bones!"

Mildred laughed softly.

"Harriet, if the gentlemen look worn and frazzled, it's because they are worn and frazzled, not because they're starving to death. I'm sure the Navy mess cupboards are very well stocked. Our friends are exhausted because they've been busy capturing killers."

Harriet shuddered at the mere mention of the recent event, a story that had dominated the news.

"I know, poor dears. It gives me the shivers just thinking about it. Which is why they need some spoiling." She dished up seconds for all and then cautioned, "You boys save room for dessert now, you hear?"

Jack's eyes popped wide out, looking around the table with dishes still full of food. There was fried chicken, potatoes, green salad, bread and butter pickle relishes, four hot vegetable dishes, biscuits, fried apples, and gravy. Yet it hardly looked like they had touched anything. Harriet had cooked for an army.

"There's more?"

"Why, yes," said Harriet. "Carrot cake with cream cheese frosting, banana pudding with vanilla wafers, and pecan pie."

"You'll want one of each," Gary whispered to his reporter friend.

"Gotcha. I'm scared to see what happens at breakfast. There a gym nearby?" asked Jack hopefully while digging into his hash browns.

Gary laughed. "We'll go for a walk later in Fisher Park."

It felt good to be back in the old house surrounded by friends old and new, warmed by the aroma and taste of Harriet's old-style cooking, listening to the sounds of light, humorous conversation safe and far away from the manic pace and formality that was the White House. Gary relished the moment, for he knew his own life would be changing dramatically when he returned to Washington D.C. and married Martha. Those changes were already taking place. Already he had his own Secret Service detail assigned permanently. Eight men in three-piece dark suits were outside in front of Harriet's home. No doubt Harriet would soon be feeding them leftovers. He lazily finished his supper and pushed back from the table, feeling content and happy.

"We're so excited about your news," twittered Harriet, switching the topic from murder to matrimony. "I was so happy about my own upcoming marriage, but your engagement to the President made me happier still. Just think, you'll be First Gentleman!"

"In name only," corrected Gary quickly after sipping his sweet iced tea. "Aunt Sophie will continue her duties as First Lady and I'm keeping my job as social secretary. I insisted on that. Speaking of weddings, I did have an ulterior motive for coming down to visit. It has to do with your wedding, Harriet. How strongly do you feel about getting married at Christmas?"

Harriet looked at Gary in surprise, unsure of his meaning. "Well, we are totally committed to getting married, if that's what you are asking. But we aren't particularly set on the Christmas date. Why? Something wrong with Max and the dress?"

Gary's eyes twinkled with delight as he leaned across the supper table and took both of Harriet's hands into his own.

"No, not that. Although once I tell you what I have to say, I'm pretty sure Max will be having a coronary. Harriet, Martha and I have discussed it, and we thought it would be lovely to have a double wedding. We would like to invite you and Bert to be married at the National Cathedral with us."

Harriet's mouth fell open with a shrill of excitement.

"You can't be serious. Really? Me? Married in a double wedding with the President of the United States?"

Mildred gasped in delight.

"Gary, how generous. Are you and Martha quite certain?"

Gary nodded his head vigorously.

"Absolutely. Martha and I know the wedding of a president will be a huge media event . . ."

"Amen," interjected Jack smiling, wiping bread crumbs from his mouth.

" . . . but we thought a double wedding, involving a sweet ordinary citizen, would be even better."

"And amen," sounded Jack finishing his journalist blessing.

"This hasn't been announced to the press (present company excepted). But if you and Bert agree, Ned will announce it during his daily news brief in the Press Room when we return. And we'll fly you and Bert up to D.C. for another press conference with Martha and me. Of course, you realize this means that you'll get married in three weeks, instead of three months, at the end of September."

Harriet jumped up from the table, excited and flustered.

"Well, why not? Yes! Of course! Wait! I need to call Bert! I know he'll say yes (he's such a love!), but I really need to ask him. Oh, my! I can't believe it. Oh, the dishes! I should clear the table first for my company. Where are my manners? And what about dessert?"

"I'll clear the table," offered Jack standing up. "The sooner you call your boyfriend, the sooner I get to call my news producers and break the story."

"And I'll get dessert," added Blaze getting up from the table. "The sooner you call your boyfriend, the sooner I get pecan pie!"

"How magnanimous of you, Blaze," said Gary dryly.

Blaze flashed Gary a big grin and helped Jack gather up the empty plates to take into the kitchen.

"Oh, you two boys are so sweet. I'll go in the living room and call Bert right away. He's home tonight with a bad cold or otherwise he'd be here with us for dinner. This will perk him up for sure. Mildred, you keep Gary company while I'm gone."

"Certainly," replied Mildred glowing with pleasure. "Take your time, dear."

Harriet dashed off into the living room to call Bert and break the news to him. Jack and Blaze walked back into the kitchens, arms full of plates and silverware.

"While you're up, make some coffee," called Gary as they left the room.

"We live to serve," Jack called back loudly as he disappeared through the swinging door.

Gary and Mildred were left alone in the large dining room. Now it was time for Gary to make his other move. He took his white linen napkin, wiped his mouth, and placed the napkin carefully down on the table. He leaned over and spoke to Mildred in a hushed voice.

"Now that we are alone, Mildred, I can tell you the other reason I'm here."

Mildred looked taken aback.

"Other reason?" she replied.

"On the news, you and Harriet heard the official version of what happened at the White House and Kennedy Center. But there is more to the story than what was reported to the press. I have clearance to share it with you concerning the death of the butler."

Mildred nodded. That much she knew.

"The shooting took place in the Queen's Bedroom, Abigail's room. He was shot before he could kidnap or kill her."

Mildred listened intently but showed no emotion.

"Was the child harmed in any way?" she asked.

"No. Not in the least. The would-be assassin was killed instantly by a secret agent working inside the White House, someone I believe you know rather well — Jane Michaels McKay."

Mildred stared at Gary without the slightest hint of surprise. Her controlled silence confirmed all that Gary had deduced and all that he had verified by the general in confidence days earlier. He proceeded with his discussion.

"Our befuddled Nanny Jane turns out to be a top-notch spy working for British intelligence and is the daughter of our National Security Advisor. Her father, the general, put her inside the White House to keep an eye on things. That and the fact that Nanny Jane shot the butler is something the public will never know. Something else is being withheld. Jack turned his camera before Jim Myers was shot, so the public did not hear Myers announce that he and Secretary Miller worked for a group called the Seven."

"The Seven?" murmured Mildred softly, her eyes widening. Her interest in his story increased.

Gary smiled. He knew it would.

"Of the Seven, we know nothing. CIA, FBI, and NSA are scrambling, but so far are coming up empty. So are the British, Japanese, and Russians. We fear the Seven, now technically the Six with Miller gone, will try again. And since they succeeded in getting directly inside the White House, three times mind you with Myers, Miller, and the butler, Martha and I want an agent inside to be around the children."

"Of course," agreed Mildred solemnly.

Gary continued. "Unfortunately, Jane is returning home to England to be with her very famous novelist husband. Therefore, we've decided to recruit another top secret agent to step into her position. And the agent I have recommended would be you."

To her credit, Mildred wasted no effort in feigning shock or surprise. Years of field experience stood her well. Besides, she would know Gary and Martha had been briefed by the general. Instead, Mildred gazed at Gary steadily with her head slightly bent. Then she smiled, placed a finger to her lips, stood, and called out to Harriet.

"Harriet? Gary wants to see the new white orchids just in from Hawaii. We're going out to the greenhouse. We won't be long."

"Take your time, dear," cried a voice from the front of the house. "And check on the boys and the pie on your way out!"

Mildred motioned for Gary to follow her, and Gary rose and obediently followed in her wake, through the kitchen and outside towards the glass greenhouse in the backyard.

Mildred's greenhouse was an architectural marvel. It was about the size of a two-car garage, enhanced with white wood beams, French glass windows, and a high ceiling. The greenhouse had been a renovation of a classical style summerhouse built when Harriet's Victorian home was constructed. A set of French doors opened into the greenhouse. Mildred walked briskly to the doors, unlocked them, and went inside.

Gary quickly followed, and once inside, Mildred closed and securely locked the doors behind them. She again put her fingers to her lips, indicating that he remain silent, and pointed to a high back wicker chair for him to sit in. Gary seated himself and watched in amazement as Mildred took out another key and inserted it into the base of what appeared to be a light switch. After turning that key counterclockwise in one full rotation, she switched on the overhead lights and ceiling fan. Then she took a seat upon the raised barstool she used when working at her potting bench and waved her hand towards the fans.

"There is a scrambling device wired into the overhead lights and ventilation system. It prevents anyone from electronically intercepting verbal or phone conversations. Even your Secret Service detail won't be able to listen in."

"Naturally," replied Gary calmly.

Mildred gazed at Gary. "When did you know?"

"The morning after Myers died. Jane explained to us how she goes on her spy adventures and then her husband writes slightly altered versions later on. She mentioned that she had been on a grand adventure last year — England, Egypt, and Australia. Then I remembered. You were also on an extended trip last year to London, Cairo, and Sydney. It fit, and well, I just knew."

Mildred drew a deep breath and looked around the greenhouse, filled with extraordinary specimens of white, red, and purple orchids from literally all over the world. The bright colors and fragrance were sweet and comforting. She clasped her hands together in her lap and began her story.

"It was my husband's idea, really, after an interesting little experience we had in the former Soviet Union. Harrison and I were stationed in England at the time, and we were invited over to Moscow to attend diplomatic meetings between the U.S. and the Soviets. It just so happened that at the same time, one of our spy planes crashed in Siberia, and the pilot went missing. Of course, everyone was denying everything. We were denying a plane was ever flying over the USSR in the first place, and the Soviets were denying finding the pilot alive. But the plane was down and we were worried. The pilot had signaled that he was alive after the crash, but then all communications had abruptly ceased. The Soviet officials and KGB were hard-lining it, smiling politely but hard as nails to all our requests for information. Anyway, Harrison and our ambassador were getting nowhere. Then something wonderful happened one night when Harrison and I were invited to a formal dinner party at the home of one of the Soviet officials. I was in the bathroom when I overheard the wife of the Soviet official berating a very upset maid. They became aware of my presence, but they continued speaking in Russian. What they didn't know was that I speak Russian fluently. I speak six languages, one of my little quirks. Traveling around the world as an army wife, I found that I had a gift for languages and picked them up rather quickly. I made it my hobby, along with the orchids. Anyway, it turned out the very pilot we were seeking was being held in the Soviet official's home, right there in the basement, and the maid was complaining about having to wait upon this man, who was sick and dirtying his linens. I pretended to be a meek army wife, ignorant of what they were saying, smiled, washed my hands, combed my hair, put on my lipstick, and went back and reported to my husband, in French, the location of the downed pilot. Harrison got word back to the U.S. immediately, and a Black Ops special forces team successfully extracted the man the next night."

"Wow!" exclaimed Gary.

"The experience gave Harrison the brainstorm that I, as a mere woman and army wife, would frequently be overlooked, under appreciated, and generally ignored at official functions and foreign assignments — a perfect set up for intelligence gathering. He passed his idea onto the CIA and soon I was back in the U.S., officially visiting a sick cousin, unofficially training at CIA headquarters."

Gary put up his hand and interjected. "Wait. Let me guess. You weren't the only wife to get involved. Isabelle McKay?"

Mildred solemnly nodded. "You are correct and are surprisingly accurate in your deductions. If you weren't on our side, you might be silenced for knowing that bit of information. I strongly suggest you keep it to yourself."

Gary gulped. "Right."

Mildred continued. "We knew the general and Isabelle (Isabella to her friends!) while living in London. I wished you could have known her. Isabella Michaels McKay was an amazing woman. She had quite a knack for costuming — disguises in spy terms. Oh, you should have seen some of the get ups she would wear. I think Jane has taken up her mother's art. Isabella would be so proud of Jane, I'm quite sure. Anyway, Isabella and I traveled in the same circles and frequently worked together. It was all so simple. We'd go to official gatherings. And then we would wander off, walk around, listen, look around, get lost, gossip and chatter. Amazing what regular household staff, maids, drivers, yardmen, and cooks know and will say in front of two silly middle-aged women."

Mildred then paused, turning her head and staring at a particularly large white, very fragrant orchid, potted in a large blue and white oriental pot. "Isabella died, then Harrison died, and I thought that part of my life was over. But I got a call from another widow, a spry old gal named Madeline. She was going on vacation to Las Vegas and invited me to go along. What she didn't tell me was that she had invited several other old military widows along for the ride. We had a grand time, and it was on that trip that I decided to carry on the work that Harrison began. I contacted the CIA and the Blue Hairs was born."

Gary's eyebrow lifted up.

"Blue Hairs?"

Mildred smiled to herself. "Um, yes. That's what we call ourselves. Something like the Blue Angels, only we stay on the ground armed with digital hearing aids and pain pills. You see, we are all over sixty and have varying shades of white or graying hair. But on trips, to help us quickly locate one another in large crowds, we use a subtle old-fashioned blue rinse on our hair. Hence, the Blue Hairs."

"Awesome!" exclaimed Gary. "Mildred, I'm so impressed. Tell me more about them."

She laughed appreciatively. "Well, this too is classified information, but since you are going to be married to the President, I guess it's okay. There's Madeline or Maddie. She's about four feet eleven inches high and ninety-five pounds soaking wet. She is approaching seventy, drinks beer, wears bizarre eyeglasses, and is perhaps one of the world's finest pick pockets. Don't stand too close to her in a crowd. She excels at lifting things, quite a little daredevil, although she can play the part of crazy old woman when the situation calls for it. But don't be fooled. She's healthy as a horse, swims three to four miles a day, and knows martial arts.

"Then there's Gertrude. She's the mother of the group, very much the detail person on our missions. Gertrude's gift is words and puzzles. She does the *New York Times* crossword puzzles, the hard ones, in twenty minutes flat. Believe me, we've timed her. She also loves Scrabble. Don't ever let her challenge you to a game. You don't stand a chance. And she is one of the nation's finest code breakers. She takes trips to Maryland to visit a 'high-school friend' a couple times a year. She actually goes to the NSA headquarters in Signet City and reviews the latest on code formulations and code breaks.

"Eileen is our computer whiz. Her husband was in the navy, nuclear submariner. He died of a stroke while on patrol in the Baltic. It tore Eileen up. But in her grief, she bought her laptop and discovered the internet, and NSA subsequently discovered her. They regularly give her some advanced training in electronics and computer programming. She just came back from a 'New York Shopping Trip,' actually attending an advanced workshop on wireless technology. Eileen can hack into anything computer run, and she keeps us on our toes.

"Then there's Olivia. She's the baby of the group, just turned sixty-one. But she has the body of a healthy forty year old and can climb up things rather quickly, like staircases, fences, walls, and garden trellises. She has no fear of heights whatsoever. Her husband was a marine, and we think she trained with him all those years. Sort of scary, actually, when you think about it. Anyway, besides her strength and gymnastic ability, Livvy is gifted with languages like me. She speaks about eight languages. She knows some of the old ones, too — Greek, Latin, and Hebrew. She knows Arabic cold, which is quite helpful whenever we take a holiday in the Middle East."

"And that's your cover, vacations?" asked Gary.

"Yes. Officially, we are the War Widows Club. We take vacations together to rather exotic places."

"And to dangerous assignments."

"Exactly. Funny, the enemy looks out for our special forces, the young men and women in the Navy Seals and Army Rangers. Fortunately for us, they don't bother much with a bunch of crazy women with blue hair out sightseeing."

"Brilliant. But, Mildred, you didn't describe your part in the group."

"I'm the team leader. Languages and organization are my specialty. I usually am first on the scene, to scope out the situation and to draw up the play. In the field, I go by the nickname Harrison had for me."

"Which is?"

Mildred exhaled another deep sigh. "Slim."

"Did you have a part in this situation with Myers and Taylor?"

"Yes, we did." said Mildred gravely. "The Blue Hairs is a very top-secret organization, Gary. Only General McKay and a select few in the Pentagon even know we exist. Consequently, we aren't used very often. That would blow our cover. But yes, we were called out. We were sent to Miami to watch and to make contact with Reverend Palmer before he left the country. And we did make contact and discovered his intention to fly to South America. From the information Maddie lifted from the gentleman (she swiped a copy of his airline ticket), we were able to make a preliminary connection in Brazil, a hotel reservation made from someone in Scotland and money wired from Paris."

"Ah, hence your sudden trips to South America and to Scotland, to judge at the 'orchid show' and to help the Scottish lord with his garden," said Gary enlightened.

"Right. And that's where the trail ends for now. At least we know the name of the group. It's either 'The Seven' or 'Seven Something.'"

At that moment, Gary saw Blaze standing at the back door of the house, waving enthusiastically at them.

"I think we are being called in for pie. Well, Mildred (or should I say Slim?), I can't think of anyone better to take over for Jane in the White House till the Seven are unearthed and destroyed. The children need someone like you to protect them. And besides, I would love to have you around in the White House."

"Well, I guess I could," admitted Mildred reluctantly. "Harriet will be okay. She won't be lonely with Bert in the house. But Gary, I would hate leaving the Blue Hairs for so long. Who would take my place?"

Just then, Jack Parish's wide blue eyes and too white teeth appeared at the French doors, waving and knocking to get their attention.

Gary looked at Jack and then at Mildred, and then gave her a quick wink. "Don't worry, Mildred. I know just the person."

Chapter 26

The Rose Garden

Saturday, September 24

It was being hailed as the wedding of the twenty-first century.

Like the royal wedding of Lady Diana Spencer to Prince Charles, the wedding of America's first woman president was a once in a lifetime, worldwide, not to be missed, news-making event. According to Jack Parish, who now had slipped into a dual role of reporter and close family friend, the nation's news media had worked themselves into a complete and utter frenzy. Over lunch one day, Jack complained to the President, on behalf of the nation's press corps, that they were collectively on the brink of a nervous collapse. He reminded the President that in the past eleven months (less than a year, mind you), there had been the murder of a vice presidential candidate, the appointment of the first woman vice president, the assassination of a sitting president, the appointment of the first female American president (on Mother's Day to boot), a murder in Miami of a high ranking American priest, a high profile suicide (which turned out to also be murder) of the White House chief counsel inside the Oval Office, the mysterious death of a White House butler (details a bit sketchy there), the confession of high treason and murder by the White House chief of staff, the subsequent murder of the said chief of staff by a Russian ballerina who turned out to be an international spy, and last but not least, the suicide of the secretary of state. If that was not enough, there followed the announcement of three weddings — the wedding of Harriet Simmons, the wedding of the National Security Advisor to the First Lady, and the wedding of President Johnson to her social secretary!

Having caught his breath, Jack sipped his iced tea and politely asked Martha, once the weddings were over, would she promise to settle down for a few weeks and give them all a rest?

Martha sympathized with the reporter. She understood the great interest the American public had in her upcoming marriage and its political ramifications. Consequently, she agreed with Gary, Morgan, Aunt Sophie, and Ryan to go ahead and play it up for all it was worth. The world wanted a great wedding. Well, they would give them one! However, though her marriage would be a national event, Martha felt the American taxpayers shouldn't be expected to foot the bill. So, Martha decided to make this the moment to publicly reveal that she was a woman of independent means. After Gary returned to Washington from his visit to Greensboro, Ned made the public announcement concerning the Johnson family connection to the Dupont family fortune (so much for presidential promises, winced Jack wearily while writing madly) and that Martha would be donating millions to pay for the wedding. Needless to say, the announcement gave the overworked press corps and the elite Washington social scene something else to talk about.

Gary returned to the White House anxious to see Martha and the kids and ready to begin his new life. Being somewhat old fashioned, he and Martha agreed that he would not move downstairs and they would not consummate their marriage until their wedding night. They would set an example and have a true honeymoon. Besides, there was one aunt, one retired general, two teenagers, ten butlers, four upstairs maids, thirty-five Secret Service agents, five ushers, Charlotte, and one nosy little five-year old watching. So Gary remained upstairs on the third floor and so did Charlotte. Having returned from his overseas mission, Charlotte's husband also came to live at the White House for the next three weeks. Well, why not? The more the merrier, and there was plenty of space. Besides, this arrangement pleased the general greatly. While he and Mr. Donovan sat in the Oval Sitting Room, drinking coffee and debriefing about the Seven and other matters involving intelligence, Charlotte and Aunt Sophie took over the huge task of making the guest list for the engraved invitations.

The wedding would be at the National Cathedral, which could hold plenty of guests. Gary assigned Ryan also to the task, and they, assisted by Charlotte's friends Kate Yardley and Vera Osborne and other ladies from the White House Historical Association, worked feverishly with the White House calligrapher's office and the State Department to get out invitations in time for the late September wedding. One invitation Gary addressed personally and mailed by hand. He sent one to his ex-wife, Janet, and her congressman fiancée. Funny, but Gary didn't feel resentful or bitter. Now that he had found his own happiness, he truly wished Janet well. However, the R.S.V.P was promptly returned, with regrets. Janet and her beau would be out of town.

On the cover of the invitations, Martha had placed a quote from Thomas Jefferson that read:

"Be you the link of love, union, and peace for the whole family."

Meanwhile, down in Georgetown, designer Max Jones was working himself to the bone. Now he had to design not one but three wedding dresses in three short weeks. One of them would be the most important wedding dress of his entire career. Fortunately for him and his staff, the design for Harriet's dress was completed, with materials ordered and shipped. For her, it was only a matter of cutting and sewing. For Aunt Sophie, a new order was begun. Although her wedding would not be public, pictures would be taken and those pictures would be leaked to the media. Her dress would be memorable, so Sophie Johnson had to have a noteworthy gown. She insisted on a simple tea-length dress with traditional lines. A design was made, was approved, measurements taken, and materials ordered.

The issue of Martha's dress was another matter altogether. Who could possibly state the importance of such a dress? It boggled the mind. This dress would be seen worldwide during the live broadcast of the wedding. The President's bridal gown would be enshrined inside the hallowed halls of the Smithsonian Museum. This dress, above anything Max had ever designed before, had to be perfect.

Max spent two long days and two sleepless nights sitting at his desk, drinking endless cups of coffee, pencil in hand, papers scattered across the floor, madly sketching ideas. An interview with Martha had given him the general preferences she had for her gown. Unlike the young starlets walking down the red carpet in Hollywood, Martha made it very clear she did not want a clinging dress nor did she want a sleeveless gown. In fact, she was most insistent upon having sleeves. She had to have sleeves. As far as color was concerned, white or ivory would be fine. Cream was out. She didn't look good in cream. No corsets or slits or shiny sequins either. Pearls were optional.

Max sketched freehand, but nothing quite suited him. He was almost at the point of meltdown when fate finally smiled down upon him. Knowing that Martha and Gary loved Victorian homes and décor, Max's assistant, Christina, brought in a stack of old Victoria magazines from her home for Max to peruse. In a moment of sheer exhaustion, late into the evening, Max turned the page in one of the magazines and found it, the picture of a vintage bridal gown that was the inspiration of what he would create.

The gown was photographed in the famed shop of designer, Basia Zarzycka, on Sloane Square in Chelsea, London. The dress was made of ivory silk taffeta, with a fitted brocade bodice and a traditional belle-shaped skirt. In form, it was very much like the gown Princess Diana had worn. Overtop the elegant puffed sleeves and full skirt were bunches of draped sheer ivory chiffon. What made Max's eyes dilate was the addition of dark colored silk roses, Gary's favorite flower, woven right into the brocade design in the front bodice. Running down the front of the bodice, like a delicate garland, were embroidered antique red and white roses and small delicate green leaves. The addition of such deep and bold colors was surprising, unexpected, and lovely. At the sides of the mid-length sleeves, where the chiffon was gathered tightly in, and at the right side of the skirt one third of the way down, where the chiffon panels were loosely draped together, were small bouquets of actual tiny silk flowers, pink and red rosebuds.

Max was on the phone to London immediately, knowing it was early morning London time. He moved heaven and earth to find the owner of the shop, and by eight o'clock the next morning, Max was on a plane to London to meet and consult with the famous London designer. The original dress in the magazine article had been sold two years previously, but with Basia's help, Max was on the doorstep of the dress's owner by dinnertime that evening. By midnight, he was back on a plane with the original Zarzycka dress, boxed up and on loan, and with Ms. Zarzycka herself for the return trip to Washington. When the plane touched down, a limo and driver were waiting to take the two of them and the dress directly to the White House. Max himself carried the dress into the Oval Office.

Max's instincts proved correct. Martha and Gary immediately loved the dress. It would form the basis of Max's own original creation, made in a rare collaboration with Ms. Zarzycka, with a few alterations of the neckline and with the addition of a very long train. Max took Martha's measurements, bundled up the vintage dress, and headed back to his Georgetown shop where he, Ms. Zarzycka, and Max's staff would create two wedding dresses for Martha.

"Why two?" Martha had asked.

"Two dresses for two reasons," replied Max simply. "First of all, you will need a dress and a spare. If something disastrous should happen, a spill on the dress or a tiny tear, another dress exactly like the first will be there for you to change into. Secondly, one dress is for you to keep and one dress is for the Smithsonian. Trust me. They've already called. I suggest you wear both dresses, one at the wedding and one at the reception. That way both will be legitimate. And if I can push my poor staff any further, there will be a third dress as well."

"Who is that one for?" asked Martha.

"Me," replied Max.

"I'll wear it in the receiving line," said the President graciously.

"Bless you, Madame President," said Max

Max was off, ready to create the dress of a lifetime.

With Charlotte, Aunt Sophie, and Ryan handling the invitations and Max handling the dress, the rest of the wedding plans fell to Gary and Morgan. If the White House press corps were feeling overwhelmed, needless to say the White House staff was being pushed to their utter limits. Normally, at this time of year, the White House is actively preparing for the huge annual Christmas celebration. On any given year, the White House Christmas decorations will include over 41 decorated trees, 250 wreaths, and over 200,000 lights. Now, the staff was given the unbelievable assignment, right in the midst of the vast Christmas plans, to come up with the wedding of the century.

The first issues to be settled were locations. The National Cathedral was contacted and secured as the place for the double ceremony. Given the death of Reverend Palmer, it made Gary feel good to hold the wedding there. It was like a tiny restitution. For the reception, the new Dolly Madison Banquet Hall, constructed under the large Ellipse on the back South Lawn, would accommodate at least five hundred guests. Fortunately, all three outside building projects had been completed, including the Jefferson Arch and the greenhouses. For a receiving line, they would use the East Room. For official photographs, a special white tent would be constructed over the Rose Garden and filled with flowers. Guests would come to the White House, go through the receiving line in the East Room, and then down the pathways and stairs to the underground Banquet Hall for a formal sit-down dinner.

With locations finalized, Agent Pullman and the Secret Service began the long process of getting the National Cathedral and the car route from the church back to the White House enclosed in the security "bubble." The National Cathedral would be closed to tours for the next three weeks, and Secret Service and FBI began the enormous task of putting their security measures into place. Likewise, Mr. Peach of the National Park Service and Leo Patterson of the uniformed division of the Secret Service tackled the job of preparing and securing the White House, Rose Garden, and South Lawn for the reception which included many heads of state and members of royal families across Europe and Japan. They worked with area hotels, which were madly blocking off rooms and suites to accommodate the important clientele coming to Washington for the wedding.

For security reasons, both Mildred and Harriet were moved up to Washington and into the White House residence. However, to everyone's dismay, Nanny Jane made a quiet exit. Obviously, she could not and would not appear on television at the very publicized wedding. Her work done, she hugged and kissed the children and her father in an emotional goodbye, with a firm promise from the general to visit her and her husband soon in London. The general and Aunt Sophie were going to be wed later in November (a small private ceremony on November 22), and they would fly to England for a honeymoon before joining Martha and the children later on in Paris. Jane departed, and Mildred took her place as nanny to the children. She felt a bit overwhelmed in her new assignment, but the children, especially Abigail, took Mildred by the hand and led her about, chatting gaily and pointing things out. The new friendship was solidified when Mildred presented Abigail with a new American

Girl doll. From that moment on, Abigail clung to the doll and Auntie Mildred. Mildred moved into the vacant Lincoln Bedroom while Harriet took a room upstairs, near to where Gary and Charlotte were staying. Harriet's fiancé, Bert, was moved into a secure room down the street at the Hamilton Crowne Hotel. All were given Secret Service protection and according to Bert, no plumber ever had it so good.

Other tasks facing Gary and his staff were the selection of food and flowers. It became apparent that the highly-skilled White House chefs and florists would not have to handle it all by themselves. Not that they couldn't, mind you. They were quite capable, but requests began to pour in with offers from skilled chefs, food companies, florists, and greenhouses from across the country to donate their goods and services. They all wanted to be part of history, too. Of special note, three spectacular chefs (working in five-star hotels in Los Angeles, New York, and Dallas) got leave from their regular employment, literally hopped on planes, and presented themselves downstairs in the White House kitchens for service. These three men, along with several other noted chefs from the D.C., Baltimore, and New York areas, started working with the esteemed White House chefs in planning and preparing foods for the wedding reception. Three hotels in downtown Washington offered their kitchens as extra space for food preparation and storage. A visiting chef was stationed at each and given specific items to plan and prepare.

Then there was the matter of *the cake*. For that, Martha had a definite preference. Martha requested a cake by New York's Sylvia Weinstock, the woman who designed the wedding cakes for the likes of Donald Trump, Mariah Carey, Michael Douglas, and Whitney Houston. Normally a bride would fly up to New York to consult with Ms. Weinstock, but in this rare instance, Ms. Weinstock was flown down to Washington for an Oval Office consultation. Martha selected a six-tier white cake with sugar spun roses cascading down the side in her wedding colors of white, burgundy, royal purple, and hunter green. The extraordinary cake would be made in New York and then flown to D.C. to be reconstructed. White House chief pastry chef Roland would be in charge of that. Roland himself was designing a smaller bachelor's cake to go with the wedding cake. Ms. Weinstock also promised a special little "Flower Girl's Cake," just for Abigail. A group of pastry chefs from all over the United States was invited to come and prepare special trays of small petite dishes for guests to enjoy after dinner.

The American flower industry was not far behind the pastry industry in their contributions. Gary was on the phone for several days with different greenhouses, florists, and nurseries, securing fresh flowers for the Cathedral, Rose Garden, and Banquet Hall. Fortuitously Martha's new greenhouse was complete, the paint barely dry, so it would serve perfectly as additional space for storage and arranging as boxes and boxes of fresh cut flowers began arriving at the White House days before the wedding. Flowers would be everywhere, in the church, in the East Room, the State Dining Room, the Entrance Hall and Grand Staircase, the Rose Garden, the Truman Balcony, and the Madison Dining Hall underground in the South Lawn.

The last item to take care of was music, and Gary and Martha agreed that they wanted to feature regional acoustic music for the reception. They secured the Alison Kraus and Union Station band and John McCutcheon, the folk music artist from Charlottesville, Virginia. For the wedding ceremony at the National Cathedral, bands and choruses of the U.S. military would be providing the music.

After three short weeks of long hours of preparation, the day of America's wedding finally arrived.

With a broad smile on his face, Usher Morgan led Gary and his best man, Blaze, out the White House front entrance and down the steps to the black limo waiting for them. Ryan was also standing there, clipboard in hand.

"Everything is in order, sir," assured Ryan excitedly. "Don't worry about a thing. And may I say, good luck, sir!"

"Thank you so much, Ryan," said Gary sincerely. "I won't worry knowing you're here overseeing things!"

Ryan beamed with modest pleasure, clutching his clipboard happily at Gary's compliment.

"Congratulations, sir," said Mr. Morgan as Gary got ready to get in the car. "We'll all be watching the wedding here on television, and when you return," he said smiling, "we'll have all your things properly moved down to the President's quarters."

"Thank you for everything," said Gary clasping Morgan's hands in a fervent handshake. "See you when I get back."

Morgan and Ryan said goodbye and watched the car slowly pull away. Gary knew that Martha and her group would be leaving in three other limos soon after him. Even though he knew what to expect, he was still taken aback at the crowds of people he saw lined up in front of the White House and those standing along the route as they drove along, cheering and waving at him. Gary felt a flush of feelings — happiness, excitement, fear, and a little bit of embarrassment at being at the center of so much attention. Blaze didn't seen to mind, though. He enthusiastically waved back at the cheering crowds. You'd think he was the one getting married!

They arrived at the church, where they were welcomed by the cheers of even larger crowds and the sound of brass bells peeling loudly overhead from the center cathedral tower. The Secret Service quickly escorted them out of the car and into the cathedral, whereupon the priest performing the wedding ceremony greeted them. Harriet's Bert was waiting there. The best word to describe Bert, Gary thought, was round. This word applied to Bert's head (bald), Bert's nose (bulbous), and Bert's waistline (rotund). Gary liked Bert very much. He was an easy-going man, helpful, generous, and very much in love with Harriet, enough to be willing to go through this very big public display. Bert looked a little nervous, but who wouldn't be with the entire world watching?

The time came at last, and Gary, Blaze, Bert, and Jack Parish (who was standing in for best man for Bert) followed the priest out into the church. The nave was packed full of people with a number of important political guests — the prime minister of Canada, the prime minister of England, the presidents of Russia, France, and Germany, the King and Queen of Spain, the Prince of Wales and his two sons, William and Harry, the King of Sweden and his daughter, the crown princess, members of the Royal family of Monaco, a representative from the Vatican, a delegation from Japan, and members of the royal family of Saudi Arabia. Select members of the U.S. Senate and Congress were present, along with the entire bench of the Supreme Court. One person was purposefully absent, the Speaker of the House, the third in line to the presidency. He had to be in a secure location elsewhere, just in case something happened to the president. Given the events of the last year, no one was going to take any chances.

Gary took his place with the other men at the head of the church. He stared out at the large crowd, in disbelief that this really was happening to him. The organ began playing a melodic prelude, the crowds of people stood and turned, and the wedding procession began. First down the aisle were Eliza and Josh, serving as bridesmaid and usher for both brides. Eliza wore a dark purple gown, and Josh walked beside her, awkwardly dressed in a dark gray tuxedo. They reached the altar, grinned at Gary, and took their places. Then came Mildred as matron of honor to Harriet. And then came Aunt Sophie, matron of honor to Martha. Both women wore crimson gowns and carried large bouquets of red flowers. There was a pause, then Abigail somewhat shyly made her way down the aisle, dressed in the dark purple velvet dress and with red and purple flowers woven into her thick mass of blond curled hair. She carried a white wicker basket of red rose petals, which she carefully took out and tossed one by one upon the floor as she walked. When she got up to the aisle, however, she varied from her rehearsed path. She was supposed to go stand next to Mildred. But caught up in the excitement, when she saw Gary, she put down her basket and rushed over to Gary and reached for him to pick her up.

The crowd gasped, laughed, then cheered, as Gary decided to hell with protocol. He lifted Abigail in his arms and held her close as they watched Martha begin her historic walk down the aisle.

The organ paused and then it began playing the traditional Bridal March. The crowd breathlessly watched as Harriet walked first down the aisle proudly, humbly, happily. She looked simply radiant, and Gary heard Bert gulp, a bit nervous and a bit thrilled. Then all eyes were on the back of the church as Martha appeared on the arm of General McKay. She looked magnificent in her ivory rose brocaded gown. Max and Madame

Zarycka were standing behind Martha, arranging and holding onto her extremely long train. Gary had never seen anyone so beautiful as his future wife, and he fell even more deeply in love with her in that sweet moment than he ever thought possible. Gary and the world watched as the President of the United States slowly walked down the aisle and took her place by his side.

Gary carefully put Abigail down. Smiling at Martha, he took her by the right hand and took Abigail by the left, and the three of them and Harriet and Bert turned and faced the priest. The ceremony was traditional and simple and took less than thirty minutes. The priest then pronounced them husbands and wives. Bert kissed Harriet, and Gary kissed the new Mrs. Craig and Abigail.

The rest of the afternoon was a bit of a blur to Gary — the walk down the aisle, the clapping and cheering of the public, the flash of hundreds of cameras as they stepped outside the church, the carillon bells peeling out as they got into the car, and the slow ride back to the White House through streets lined with hundreds and hundreds of people waving. When they returned the White House, the same people were at the front steps waiting for them — Ryan with his clipboard and Mr. Morgan with his staff.

They had half an hour to rest and change before the guests arrived from the church and the reception began. Martha went upstairs with Abigail to change into dress number two, and Gary went with Ryan to the State Dining Room to check on the preparations for the reception. The long table in the State Dining Room was all set, lined with huge silver trays of cold and hot hors d'oeuvres for guests to munch on as they filed into the White House and waited in the receiving line. Tables with drinks and punch were also set up in the room. Gary momentarily stepped out of role as groom and back into his role as social secretary to review with his assistant what was happening.

There were a few minor mishaps, but most everything was perfect. Soon Gary and Martha and the rest of the wedding party were standing in the reception line in the East Room, formally greeting their guests. They were in line well over two hours. Mr. Morgan personally brought over drinks and small plates of food for them to snack on, keeping their spirits and energies up as an endless parade of guests filed by. Ryan stood close behind Gary, whispering in his ear the names of various diplomats and their spouses as they walked past.

Gary thought the line would never end, but it eventually did. Martha slipped out once again to go upstairs and change into dress number three and freshen up her hair and makeup, and Gary took a much-needed break to the men's room for some refreshing himself. Upon his return, Gary spotted a group of women standing closely around Mildred in the North Entrance Hall in front of the Blue Room, laughing and sipping champagne. These ladies had not come through the receiving line. Gary noticed they all had gray hair, and if he wasn't mistaken, though it might be the light, he was quite certain he spotted a faint tint of blue.

Gary walked up and grabbed Mildred from behind and gave her a hug.

"Introduce me to your friends, Mildred," he demanded happily.

"I'd be delighted," said Mildred. "Gary Craig, these are my friends Gertrude, Eileen, Olivia, and Maddie."

All the women greeted Gary politely, except Maddie. She gave him the once over.

"Up close you're not bad looking, lad," pronounced Maddie decisively. "Got any unmarried uncles?"

"Maddie! Drink your champagne and be quiet," ordered Olivia. "Nice to meet you, Mr. Craig. Slim has told us so much about you."

Gary smiled. "And Slim has told me so much about all of you."

There was a moment of awkward silence as the women and Gary looked at each other. Gary then grinned at them.

"I understand you've gone on some exciting trips together. I feel badly at taking Mildred away from you, but I have someone who might fill her place. And if I'm not mistaken, here she comes with her celebrity nephew now."

They all turned to see Jack Parish arrive, with a white-haired woman with him. She was an attractive lady with a pleasant face and slim build. She was expensively dressed, fairly dripping in diamond jewelry. She seemed relaxed, sure of herself, not in the least bit intimidated by the White House atmosphere.

Jack cheerfully made the introductions.

"Gary, Mildred, I want you to meet my Aunt Dorothy from Dallas, Texas. Aunt Dotty, my friends Gary and Mildred. Afraid I don't know the rest of you gals," he added apologetically.

The Blue Hairs graciously introduced themselves by first name.

"How do!" said Dotty energetically shaking everyone's hand. She smiled and congratulated Gary. "That was some wedding! Many happy returns!"

"Why, thank you," said Gary.

Dotty's eyes twinkled. "So you're the fella that's been keeping my nephew busy the past few months."

"It's a tough job but somebody has to do it," Gary said grinning at his reporter friend and then his aunt.

"Don't I know it? Now, if only he would settle down like you and get married!"

Jack shuddered. "Aunt Dotty, please remember that I'm a very confirmed bachelor."

"I like confirmed bachelors," said Maddie sizing Jack up.

Jack looked over at the old woman in horror.

Gary laughed.

"Dotty, I promise to keep a close eye on Jack. And perhaps in the meantime we could offer you a diversion. What do you think, ladies?"

Jack turned and looked at Gary as if he had lost his mind. Dotty raised a wary eyebrow and bent her head to one side curiously. Mildred and the Blue Hairs nodded in approval.

"Tell me, Dorothy, do you like to travel?"

"Love it," said Dorothy. "My bags are always packed."

"And do you like adventures, my dear?" asked Livvy sweetly.

"Love 'em. The wilder the better."

"Do you speak any foreign languages?" asked Gertrude.

"I speak Spanish and I speak Southern," replied Dotty grinning.

"I see," said Mildred chuckling. "And do you have any unusual gifts or talents?"

At this question, Dotty blushed and fell silent.

Jack piped up. "Come on! Don't be bashful now. Go ahead and tell them, Aunt Dorothy, or shall I?"

"Well, all right. What my nephew is so vulgarly referring to is my little talent at gambling."

"Poker," clarified Jack proudly. "In all its forms and varieties. She can beat the socks off just about anyone. She wanted to enter the World Championship of Poker last year on a trip to Vegas, but I wouldn't let her. Well, I mean, it was on television, for God sakes, and I have my reputation to think of."

"What reputation is that?" asked Gary sarcastically.

"That's not funny. And Dotty, don't forget to tell them about the guns," added Jack wickedly

"Guns?" asked Maddie with her eyes widening.

"Jack, hush," ordered Dotty.

Jack disobeyed. "Aunt Dotty grew up on a West Texas ranch. She was shooting before she could ride a bike. She can take of the wings of a fly with a rifle at fifty paces."

"Sounds like you're our kind of gal," declared Maddie enthusiastically.

"Are you married?" asked Livvy.

"Was," replied Dotty clearly. "But John died about fifteen years ago. I'm a widow."

"A very rich widow," murmured Jack sipping his champagne.

"Tell me," said Gertrude pleasantly. "Was your husband ever in the service?"

Dotty looked at the women with narrowed eyes. "Yes, he was in the air force. Why do you ask?"

"Oh, dear me, Mr. Parish," said Mildred brightly, ignoring Dotty's question and changing the subject. "It seems I've run out of punch. Would you be a peach and go get me another glass? In fact, get another round for all of us. We'll keep your aunt company while you're gone."

"But . . ."

"I'll go with you," added Gary taking his friend by the arm. "I could use a glass of punch myself. Besides, you might want to be one of the first to greet our new vice presidential nominee."

"Your what?" exclaimed Jack loudly, quickly forgetting his aunt, who was now encircled by the women and was walking down the hallway towards the State Dining Room. "What vice presidential nominee?"

"There!" said Gary, pointing towards the Grand Staircase.

Jack gasped.

"Blaze Phillips???"

"No, stupid, although Blaze has a new job, too. Martha is making Baldwin her new chief of staff and Blaze her new press secretary."

"Get out of town!" declared Jack.

"Yes, indeed she has. I was pointing to the man coming down the steps behind Blaze. Secretary Dan Kingsley, formerly the Secretary of Commerce. Remember him?"

Jack huffed in frustration. "Of course I remember him. Madame President fired him, along with all the other cabinet secretaries."

"But now all former cabinet members are cleared of any suspicion. Martha met with Kingsley this morning, and he's accepted the vice presidential offer. Oh, by the way, she's also nominating my good friend, Dr. George Campbell, to be the new secretary of state. He couldn't be here today. His wife is recovering from hip surgery."

"Kingsley is African American," added Jack, his eyes dilating. "The first woman U.S. president picks the first African American vice president. Oh, dear Lord above, what a story! Does anyone else have it yet? Wait. Don't tell me. Doesn't matter. I've *got* to call my producer!"

"Come back before we cut the cake," called Gary as Jack dashed away towards the West Wing Press Room.

"Dad?"

Gary was startled to hear a familiar voice, addressing him by an unfamiliar title. It was Eliza. She was firmly holding Abigail's hand. Abigail was tightly clutching her new dolly, which was wearing a dress that exactly matched her own. Max had made it especially for Abigail. God bless Max.

"You called me Dad. That sounds really great," said Gary. It was the first time he had ever been called Dad.

"Feels great, too," said Eliza happily. "Mom and Mr. Morgan want you to come upstairs. It's time for your official descent down the Grand Staircase as husband and wife. Then you're supposed to lead the guests down the walkway into the new Banquet Hall. Ryan and the Park Police are rounding up the guests to come into the Entrance Hall to greet you. Better hurry."

"I'm on my way."

"Carry me," ordered Abigail.

Gary scooped up his little girl and followed his teenager upstairs. He rushed to the Oval Sitting Room and met Martha, Bert, and Harriet. Having finished the long reception line, they made another grand entrance down the steps, with the marine band playing "Hail to the Chief." Then everyone was herded down to the South Lawn for the grand opening of the new underground Dolly Madison Dining Room, named after the First Lady of two presidents.

The rest of the afternoon passed quickly. A delicious sit-down dinner and dessert were served, expensive wines were poured, auspicious toasts were made, numerous photographs and videos were taken, and wonderful gifts from foreign nations were presented with grand pomp and ceremony. The unreal wedding cake from New York was cut and more photographs were taken of the two brides feeding their new husbands with slices of cake. Finally, Mr. Morgan appeared at the door and motioned for the brides and the grooms to come.

"It's time to take the official wedding pictures," announced Morgan impatiently.

He literally pulled Martha and Gary away from the cake table and hurried them through the new underground hallway, up the circular steps, and out into the Rose Garden. A vast host of television cameramen filled the Rose Garden, ready to witness the official wedding shoot, and a number of guests in the Dining Hall followed them outside to witness the picture taking. There was applause and cheers as Gary and Martha stepped into the Rose Garden area holding hands. They waved and greeted the press and their guests, while Mr. Morgan continued to push them in the direction of the waiting photographer. Eliza, Josh, Aunt Sophie and the general followed and took their places. Martha and Gary briskly walked up and took their positions where the photographer directed them. It was then that they finally noticed a little someone was missing.

"Where's Abigail?" asked Martha.

"I thought she was with you," answered Aunt Sophie, her eyes widening in alarm.

"No, I told her to stay with you," said Martha, turning around and looking directly at Eliza.

"She told me that she was going to find Aunt Sophie," said Eliza.

"Uh-oh," said Josh, looking out over the vast crowd of people outside the White House, milling about the South Lawn. "I bet she's gone hiding and no seeking."

"Abigail! Abigail!" Martha anxiously called out towards the crowd in the Rose Garden.

Nothing. No sign of the naughty little girl.

"Don't worry, Martha," replied Aunt Sophie briskly. "We'll find her. You know she can't have gone too far. She's probably visiting with one of the guests."

"There are over five hundred of those," said Martha skeptically. "We better get some help."

Martha called over Agent Pullman and asked him to call the Secret Service station and get a fix on Abigail. Pullman rapidly repeated the request into his wrist microphone and waited patiently for the reply through his earpiece.

The agent listened and smiled. "They're picking up her signal. It's quite clear . . . down in the new banquet hall, underneath the table where the ice statue and punch bowl are. Looks like she's hiding under the table. They're sending an agent over to check. Wait a minute . . ."

There was an anxious pause then a disappointed frown crossed the face of Agent Pullman as the bad news came in to his earpiece.

"Madame President, I regret to inform you they found her locator device. It was stuck to the leg of her baby doll that was tucked underneath the table." Agent Pullman swallowed hard. "I'm afraid Miss Abigail wasn't there."

"Hell fire and damnation," cried General McKay. "Agent Pullman, in spite of high tech surveillance cameras, the presence of the FBI, the Park Police, the D.C. Police, and the Secret Service, and over five hundred adults, you mean to tell me you have lost a kindergartner?"

"Yes, sir," said Agent Pullman contritely.

"What a time for Abigail to go hiding," muttered Aunt Sophie with visible frustration. "It could take hours to find her in this crowd."

"Find my daughter," ordered Martha pointing her wedding bouquet forcefully at the Secret Service agent. "*Now!*"

"Yes, Ma'am," replied Agent Pullman meekly. "Right away."

"Agent Pullman," said Gary stepping forward and taking the agent aside. "May I suggest you begin your search by looking in the trees. She likes trees."

☆　☆　☆

Cell phone call from inside the White House . . .
"It's me. I've only a moment to talk . . ."
Ryan Adams sat down heavily in the leather seat at Gary's desk and removed his glasses and accompanying fake bland persona. He leaned back in the chair and rubbed his tired eyes.

"Yes, it is disappointing indeed, given years of careful planning and great expense. Senator Miller would have been a good president, and more importantly, our president. His loss to the Seven is great, but at least he did the noble thing and took his own life. Unlike that miserable prig Jim Myers. . . . No, I do not regret his death the least little bit. He was a useful tool, and nothing more. I loathed him from the start. I disliked his oversized ego, his unending pride, and his lust for the spotlight. Not surprisingly, his unbridled urges, greed, and sheer stupidity were his own undoing in the end. The fool utterly failed to comprehend that power, real power, rarely shows itself. It is content to live securely in the shadows, never calling attention to itself, never appearing in the light of day. . . . Thank you! I appreciate the compliment. I've made it my business to blend in, to appear unimportant, to become an invisible permanent fixture inside the White House. No one notices me, but I, of course, notice everything. People would be

quite shocked if they knew this. If they reviewed the last ten months, they would be horrified to realize just how often I was present, how often I was there on the scene when important things were being said and done. They would realize too late my real influence over events. Happily no one knows that I was in charge of the infiltration of the White House and that I personally supervised the activities of Mr. Cook and Mr. Myers, and no one ever will."

Ryan listened for a while and then sighed miserably. "With Miller and Cook gone (another great loss), we're right back to square one. . . . No, I don't know how they found out about the lipstick. That's the one part I'm still unclear about and no one is talking. They are being very tight lipped about that subject, a fact I find most annoying. . . . Tell me about it. I'm surprised that idiot Myers didn't let it slip to General McKay that it was I who gave the lipstick to him and that it was I who gave him the poison that killed Hooper during one of our planning 'conferences' in his office over the state dinner. In the future, we cannot recruit such incompetents, no matter how rich or influential their parents might be. . . . At least our Russian agent made it impossible for Myers to reveal that the Seven is a secret society that consists of a U.S. senator, a French chef, a Vatican priest, a British lord, a world banker, a U.N. ambassador, and you, our master. . . . Well, I better get back to work before I am missed. I just hope I can endure an entire evening with that little kid running around unchecked. I think she's stolen one of my clipboards!"

The cool voice on the other end of the connection laughed and made a sarcastic reply. Ryan put his glasses back on, not noticing a small shiny black patent leather shoe sliding back carefully, disappearing inside the thick curtains hanging next to the window.

"You are quite right. I shouldn't let a mere five-year old upset me so. I mean really, I ask you, how much trouble can one little girl be?"

Acknowledgments

These sayings of Mr. Jefferson (*) are adapted from actual quotes, taken from the work, *Thomas Jefferson in His Own Words* by Maureen Harrison and Steve Gilbert, Editors, Excellent Books, Barnes and Nobles Books, New York, 1993.

My deepest thanks to my publishers at BluewaterPress LLC, Ardis and Joe Clark. Special thanks goes out to: my friends Richard and Karla Giberson for their reading and editing of the manuscript in its early stages; to my mother, Margaret Dameron Tucker, who taught me to love a good mystery; to my Aunt Wanda Dameron Grubbs, who taught me to love politics; to the research staff at Monticello and Poplar Forest for providing information on Mr. Jefferson; to my friends Vicki McCready, Karen Pool, Aline Bowles Jenkins, Myra Rutland, Melissa Livingston, Rita Angleton Sheehan, and Carol Rauch for their constant friendship and support; and finally, to James "Skip" Allen, retired White House usher. Thank you, Skip, for answering my many questions about the inner workings of the White House and for giving me a tour of the President's house I'll never forget.

After enjoying *Keeping House,* may we suggest from our catalog...

Papa's Problem
by Patrick Kendrick

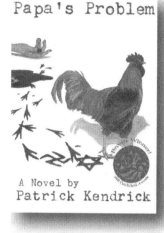

Papa's Problem is a novel set in the history of Key West in the days of Ernest Hemingway.

Emmett McWain is a retired Scotland Yard Inspector who retired to Key West in the days just before the war. He was here earlier in his life, after fighting with Roosevelt and the Rough Riders in Cuba. Following trouble during his first stay in the islands, he went back to England and into law enforcement. After finishing his career at the Yard, he returns to Key West to again find love and trouble.

In this historical mystery, it is up to Emmett to prove Ernest Hemingway innocent of murder. Along the way, he finds more than he or anyone else on the island, bargained for.

You may order online at www.bluewaterpress.com/papa or by mail:

BluewaterPress LLC
52 Tuscan Way Ste 202-309
St. Augustine, FL 32092

Name: _____

Address: _____

City, State, Zip: _____

Phone number: _____

Email Address: _____

(All information kept in the strictest confidence)

Please send me Patrick Kendrick's *Papa's Problem.* Cost is $16.95 per copy. Shipping & handling is $3.95 per book for one copy, $6.95 for up to seven of any titles, and $1.15 per book for any combination of more than seven.

Number of books _____ x $16.95 = _____

Shipping and handling = _____

FL residents, please add sales tax for county of residence = _____

Total remitted = _____

We gladly accept payment of your choice: check, money order, or credit card.

Killing Maria by Hall Taxel

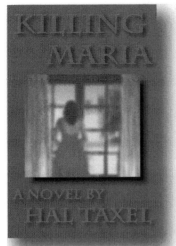

Maria, a very pretty young mother, married to an older man, a poor girl from Puerto Rico. Now she's dead. And the question is – did her husband kill her? Or was it her landlord? Maybe it was the landlord's son, or maybe his younger brother.

They all had reason to kill her.

Or did they? Was it an accident?

Hal Taxel captures the essence of life in New York in his novel, *Killing Maria*. From life on the street, to intricate relationships between old cultures and new within a neighborhood, Taxel expertly tells the story of Maria and all who live around her.

Taxel weaves an intricate tale of love and love lost, youth and old age, dashed hopes and new dreams in this riveting story of relationships and hope set against the backdrop of a multi-cultural neighborhood in the city.

You may order online at www.bluewaterpress.com/maria or by mail:

BluewaterPress LLC
52 Tuscan Way Ste 202-309
St. Augustine, FL 32092

Name: _____

Address: _____

City, State, Zip: _____

Phone number: _____

Email Address: _____

(All information kept in the strictest confidence)

Please send me Hal Taxel's *Killing Maria*. Cost is $16.95 per copy. Shipping & handling is $3.95 per book for one copy, $6.95 for up to seven of any titles, and $1.15 per book for any combination of more than seven.

Number of books _____ x $16.95 = _____

Shipping and handling = _____

FL residents, please add sales tax for county of residence = _____

Total remitted = _____

We gladly accept payment of your choice: check, money order, or credit card.

The Path of Our Destiny
by Calvin Louis Fudge

Growing up is never easy, and Calvin Louis Fudge has written knowingly in The Path of Our Destiny of the pains of twelve-year-old Hunt Hews' living with a mother dying of cancer and an alcoholic father. Set in small town El Dorado, Arkansas beginning in the 1950s, Hunt tells his story of a difficult adolescence, made bearable only with the help of an understanding teacher, Mr. Ash and his wife.

Hunt meets temptations in junior high school as he deals with the problems of coming of age: first love, his first sexual experience, and losing his parents. Through all his troubles, business problems, and frustrations of love, Hunt never forgets his roots in his first real home in El Dorado.

You may order online at www.bluewaterpress.com/destiny or by mail:

BluewaterPress LLC
52 Tuscan Way Ste 202-309
St. Augustine, FL 32092

Name: _____

Address: _____

City, State, Zip: _____

Phone number: _____

Email Address: _____

(All information kept in the strictest confidence)

Please send me Calvin Louis Fudge's *The Path of Our Destiny*. Cost is $16.95 per copy. Shipping & handling is $3.95 per book for one copy, $6.95 for up to seven of any titles, and $1.15 per book for any combination of more than seven.

Number of books _____ x $16.95 = _____

Shipping and handling = _____

FL residents, please add sales tax for county of residence = _____

Total remitted = _____

We gladly accept payment of your choice: check, money order, or credit card.

39475321R00210

Made in the USA
Middletown, DE
21 March 2019